Henry James OM (15 April 1843 – 28 February 1916) was an American-British author regarded as a key transitional figure between literary realism and literary modernism, and is considered by many to be among the greatest novelists in the English language. He was the son of Henry James Sr. and the brother of renowned philosopher and psychologist William James and diarist Alice James.

He is best known for a number of novels dealing with the social and marital interplay between émigré Americans, English people, and continental Europeans. Examples of such novels include The Portrait of a Lady, The Ambassadors, and The Wings of the Dove. His later works were increasingly experimental. In describing the internal states of mind and social dynamics of his characters, James often made use of a style in which ambiguous or contradictory motives and impressions were overlaid or juxtaposed in the discussion of a character's psyche.(Source: Wikipedia)

Literary works:
Watch and Ward (1871)
Roderick Hudson (1875)
The American (1877)
The Europeans (1878)
Confidence (1879)
Washington Square (1880)
The Portrait of a Lady (1881)
The Bostonians (1886)
The Princess Casamassima (1886)
The Reverberator (1888)
The Tragic Muse (1890)
The Other House (1896)
The Spoils of Poynton (1897)
What Maisie Knew (1897)

PRINCE CLASSICS

LADY BARBARINA

HENRY JAMES

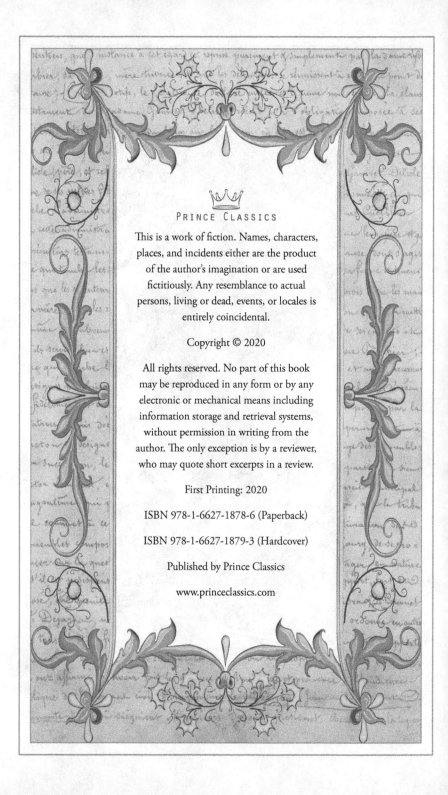

PRINCE CLASSICS

Copyright © 2020

First Printing: 2020

ISBN 978-1-6627-1878-6 (Paperback)

ISBN 978-1-6627-1879-3 (Hardcover)

Published by Prince Classics

www.princeclassics.com

Contents

LADY
BARBARINA

PREFACE

I have gathered into this volume several short fictions of the type I have already found it convenient to refer to as "international"—though I freely recognise, before the array of my productions, of whatever length and whatever brevity, the general applicability of that term. On the interest of *contrasted* things any painter of life and manners inevitably much depends, and contrast, fortunately for him, is easy to seek and to recognise; the only difficulty is in presenting it again with effect, in extracting from it its sense and its lesson. The reader of these volumes will certainly see it offered in no form so frequent or so salient as that of the opposition of aspects from country to country. Their author, I am quite aware, would seem struck with no possibility of contrast in the human lot so great as that encountered as we turn back and forth between the distinctively American and the distinctively European outlook. He might even perhaps on such a showing be represented as scarce aware, before the human scene, of any other sharp antithesis at all. He is far from denying that this one has always been vivid for him; yet there are cases in which, however obvious and however contributive, its office for the particular demonstration has been quite secondary, and in which the work is by no means merely addressed to the illustration of it. These things have had in the latter case their proper subject: as, for instance, the subject of "The Wings of the Dove," or that of "The Golden Bowl," has not been the exhibited behaviour of certain Americans as Americans, of certain English persons as English, of certain Romans as Romans. Americans, Englishmen, Romans are, in the whole matter, agents or victims; but this is in virtue of an association nowadays so developed, so easily to be taken for granted, as to have created a new scale of relations altogether, a state of things from which *emphasised* internationalism has either quite dropped or is well on its way to drop. The dramatic side of human situations subsists of course on contrast; and when we come to the two novels I have just named we shall see, for example, just how they positively provide themselves with that source of interest. We shall see nevertheless at the same time that the subject could in each case have been perfectly expressed had *all* the persons concerned been only American or only English or only Roman or whatever.

If it be asked then, in this light, why they deviate from that natural harmony, why the author resorts to the greater extravagance when the less would serve, the answer is simply that the course taken has been, on reflexion, the course of the greater amusement. That is an explanation adequate, I admit, only when itself a little explained—but I shall have due occasion to explain it. Let me for the moment merely note that the very condition I here glance at—that of the achieved social fusion, say, without the sense and experience of which neither "The Wings of the Dove," nor "The Golden Bowl," nor "The Portrait of a Lady," nor even, after all, I think, "The Ambassadors," would have been written—represents a series of facts of the highest interest and one that, at this time of day, the late-coming observer and painter, the novelist sometimes depressed by all the drawbacks of a literary form overworked and relaxed, can only rejoice to meet in his path and to measure more and more as a portent and an opportunity. In proportion as he intelligently meets it, and more especially in proportion as he may happen to have "assisted" from far back at so many of the odd and fresh phenomena involved, must he see a vast new province, infinitely peopled and infinitely elastic—by which I mean with incalculable power to grow—annexed to the kingdom of the dramatist. On this point, however, much more is to be said than I can touch on by the way—so that I return to my minor contention; which is that in a whole group of tales I here collect the principle of illustration has on the other hand quite definitely been that the idea could *not* have expressed itself without the narrower application of international terms. The contrast in "Lady Barbarina" depends altogether on the immitigable Anglicism of this young woman and that equally marked projection of New York elements and objects which, surrounding and framing her figure, throws it into eminent relief. She has her personal qualities, but the very interest, the very curiosity of the matter is that her imbroglio is able to attest itself with scarce so much as a reference to them. It plays itself out quite consistently on the plane of her general, her instinctive, her exasperatedly conscious ones. The others, the more intimate, the subtler, the finer—so far as there may have been such—virtually become, while the story is enacted, not relevant, though their relevancy might have come up on some other basis.

10

But that this is true, always in its degree, of each of the other contributions to the class before us, we shall sufficiently make out, I think, as we take them in their order. I am only struck, I may indeed parenthesise, with the inveteracy of the general ground (not to say of the extension I give it) over which my present remarks play. It does thus in truth come home to me that, combining and comparing in whatever proportions and by whatever lights, my "America" and its products would doubtless, as a theme, have betrayed gaps and infirmities enough without such a kicking-up of the dramatic dust (mainly in the foreground) as I could set my "Europe" in motion for; just as my Europe would probably have limped across our stage to no great effect of processional state without an ingenuous young America (constantly seen as ingenuous and young) to hold up its legendary train. At the same time I pretend not at all to regret my having had from the very first to see my workable world all and only as an unnatural mixture. No mixture, for that matter, is quite unnatural unless quite sterile, and the particular range of associations that betimes, to my eyes, blocked out everything else, blocked out aspects and combinations more simply conditioned, was at least not open to the reproach of not giving me results. These were but what they could be, of course; but such as they were, at all events, here am I at this time of day quite earnestly grouping, distinguishing, discussing them. The great truth in the whole connexion, however, is, I think, that one never really chooses one's general range of vision—the experience from which ideas and themes and suggestions spring: this proves ever what it has had to be, this is one with the very turn one's life has taken; so that whenever it "gives," whatever it makes us feel and think of, we regard very much as imposed and inevitable. The subject thus pressed upon the artist is the necessity of his case and the fruit of his consciousness; which truth makes and has ever made of any quarrel with his subject, and stupid attempt to go behind *that*, the true stultification of criticism. The author of these remarks has in any case felt it, from far back, quite his least stupid course to meet halfway, as it were, the turn taken and the perceptions engendered by the tenor of his days. Here it is that he has never pretended to "go behind"—which would have been for him a deplorable waste of time. The thing of profit is to have your experience—to recognise and understand it, and for this almost any will do; there being surely no absolute ideal about it beyond getting from it all it has to give. The artist—for it is of this strange brood we speak—has but to have his honest sense of life to find it fed at every pore even as the birds of the air are fed; with more and more to give, in turn, as a consequence, and, quite by the same law that governs the responsive affection of a kindly-used animal, in proportion as more and more is confidently asked.

All of which, however, doubtless wanders a little far from my mild argument—that of my so grateful and above all so well-advised primary acceptance of a *determined* array of appearances. What I was clearly to be treated to by fate—with the early-taken ply I have already elsewhere glanced at—was (should I have the intelligence to embrace it) some considerable occasion to appreciate the mixture of manners. So, as I say, there would be a decent economy in cultivating the intelligence; through the sincerity of which process I have plucked, I hold, every little flower of a "subject" pressed between the leaves of these volumes. I am tempted indeed to make for my original lucidity the claim of something more than bare prudence—almost that of a happy instinctive foresight. This is what I mean by having been "well-advised." It was as if I had, vulgarly speaking, received quite at first the "straight tip"—to back the right horse or buy the right shares. The mixture of manners was to become in other words not a less but a very much more appreciable and interesting subject of study. The mixture of manners was in fine to loom large and constantly larger all round; it was to be a matter, plainly, about which the future would have much to say. Nothing appeals to me more, I confess, as a "critic of life" in any sense worthy of the name, than the finer—if indeed thereby the less easily formulated—group of the conquests of civilisation, the multiplied symptoms among educated people, from wherever drawn, of a common intelligence and a social fusion tending to abridge old rigours of separation. This too, I must admit, in spite of the many-coloured sanctity of such rigours in general, which have hitherto made countries smaller but kept the globe larger, and by which immediate strangeness, immediate beauty, immediate curiosity were so much fostered. Half our instincts work for the maintained differences; without them, for instance, what would have been the point of the history of poor Lady Barbarina? I have but to put that question, I must add, to feel it beautifully large; for there looms before

12

me at its touch the vision of a Lady Barbarina reconciled, domesticated, developed, of possibly greater vividness than the quite other vision expressed in these pages. It is a question, however, of the tendency, perceptive as well as reflective too, of the braver imagination—which faculty, in our future, strikes me as likely to be appealed to much less by the fact, by the pity and the misery and the greater or less grotesqueness, of the courageous, or even of the timid, missing their lives beyond certain stiff barriers, than by the picture of their more and more steadily making out their opportunities and their possible communications. Behind all the small comedies and tragedies of the international, in a word, has exquisitely lurked for me the idea of some eventual sublime consensus of the educated; the exquisite conceivabilities of which, intellectual, moral, emotional, sensual, social, political—all, I mean, in the face of felt difficulty and danger—constitute stuff for such "situations" as may easily make many of those of a more familiar type turn pale. *There*, if one will—in the dauntless fusions to come—is the personal drama of the future.

We are far from it certainly—as I have delayed much too long to remark— in the chronicle of Lady Barb. I have placed this composition (1888) at the top of my list, in the present cluster, despite the earlier date of some of its companions; consistently giving it precedence by reason of its greatest length. The idea at the root of it scarcely brooks indication, so inevitable had it surely become, in all the conditions, that a young Englishwoman in some such predicament should figure as the happy pictorial thought. The whole thing rests, I need scarce point out, on the most primitive logic. The international relation had begun to present itself "socially," after the liveliest fashion, a quarter of a century ago and earlier, as a relation of intermarrying; but nothing was meanwhile so striking as that these manifestations took always the same turn. The European of "position" married the young American woman, or the young American woman married the European of position—one scarce knew how best to express the regularity of it; but the social field was scanned in vain for a different pairing. No American citizen appeared to offer his hand to the "European" girl, or if he did so offered it in vain. The bridal migrations were eastward without exception—as rigidly as if settled by statute. Custom clearly had acquired the force of law; a fact remarkable, significant, interesting and even amusing. And yet, withal, it seemed scarce to demand explanations. So far as they appeared indeed they were confident on the American side. The representatives of that interest had no call in life to go "outside" for their wives—having obviously close at hand the largest and choicest assortment of such conveniences; as was sufficiently proved by the European "run" on the market. What American run on any foreign market had been noted?—save indeed always on the part of the women! It all redounded to the honour and glory of the young woman grown in American conditions—to cast discredit on whose general peerlessness by attested preference for other types could but strike the domestic aspirant as an act of disloyalty or treachery. It was just the observed rarity of the case therefore that prompted one to put it to the imaginative test. Any case so unlikely to happen—taking it for at all conceivable—could only be worth attention when it *should*, once in a blue moon, occur. There was nothing meanwhile, in truth, to "go by"; we had seen the American girl "of position" absorbed again and again into the European social system, but we had only seen young foreign candidates for places as cooks and housemaids absorbed into the American. The more one viewed the possible instance, accordingly, the more it appealed to speculative study; so that, failing all valid testimony, one had studiously, as it were, to forge the very documents.

I have only to add that I found mine, once I had produced them, thoroughly convincing: the most one could do, in the conditions, was to make one's picture appear to hang together, and I should have broken down, no doubt, had my own, after a superficial question or two, not struck me as decently hanging. The essential, at the threshold, I seem to recall, was to get my young man right—I somehow quite took for granted the getting of my young woman. Was this because, for the portrait of Lady Barb, I felt appealed to so little in the name of *shades*? Shades would be decidedly neither of her general world nor of her particular consciousness: the image I had in view was a maiden nature that, after a fashion all its own, should show as fine and complete, show as neither coarse nor poor, show above all as a resultant of many causes, quite without them. I felt in short sure of Lady Barb, and I think there is no question about her, or about the depth of root she might strike in American soil, that I shouldn't have been ready on the spot to answer.

Such is the luck of the conception that imposes itself *en bloc*—or such at least the artist's luck in face of it; such certainly, to begin with and "subjectively" speaking, is the great advantage of a character all of a piece: immediacy of representation, the best omens for felicity, then so honourably await it. It was Jackson Lemon and *his* shades, comparatively, and his comparative sense for shades, that, in the tale, most interested me. The one thing fine-drawn in his wife was that she had been able to care for him as he was: to almost every one and every thing else equally American, to almost every one and everything else so sensibly stamped, toned and warranted, she was to find herself quite otherwise affected. With her husband the law was reversed—he had, much rather, imputed authority and dignity, imputed weight and charm, to the antecedents of which she was so fine and so direct a consequence; his estimate, his appreciation of her being founded thus on a vision of innumerable close correspondences. It is that vision in him that is racked, and at so many fine points, when he finds their experiment come so near failure; all of which—at least as I seem to see it again so late in the day—lights his inward drama as with the never-quenched lamp of a sacred place. His wife's, on the other hand, goes on in comparatively close darkness.

It is indeed late in the day that I thus project the ray of *my* critical lantern, however; for it comes over me even as I write that the general air in which most of these particular flowers of fancy bloom is an air we have pretty well ceased to breathe. "Lady Barbarina" is, as I have said, scarce a quarter of a century old; but so many of the perceived conditions in which it took birth have changed that the account of them embodied in that tale and its associates will already pass for ancient history. "Civilisation" and education move fast, after all, and too many things have happened; too many *sorts* of things, above all, seem more and more likely to happen. This multiplication of kinds of occurrences, I make no doubt, will promote the inspiration of observers and poets to come; but it may meanwhile well make for an effect of superannuation in any record of the leaner years. Jackson Lemon's has become a more frequent adventure, and Lady Barbarina is to-day as much at her ease in New York, in Washington, at Newport, as in London or in Rome. If this is her case, moreover, it is still more that of little Mrs. Headway, of "The Siege of London" (1883), who suffers, I feel, by the sad circumstance that her type

15

of complication, or, more exactly speaking perhaps, that of the gentlemen concerned with her, is no longer eminent, or at least salient. Both she and her friends have had too many companions and successors; so that to reinvest them with historic importance, with individual dignity, I have to think of them rather as brave precursors, as adventurous skirmishers and *éclaireurs*. This doesn't diminish, I recognise, any interest that may reside in the form either of "The Siege" aforesaid or of its congeners "An International Episode," "A Bundle of Letters" and "The Pension Beaurepas." Or rather indeed perhaps I should distinguish among these things and, if presuming to claim for several some hint of the distinction we may see exemplified in any first-class art-museum, the distinction of the archaic subject treated by a "primitive" master of high finish, yet notice duly that others are no more "quaint" than need be. What has really happened, I think, is that the *great* international cases, those that bristle with fifty sorts of social reference and overflow, and, by the same token, with a hundred illustrations of social incoherence, are now equally taken for granted on all sides of the sea, have simply become incidents and examples of the mixture of manners, as I call it, and the thicker fusion: which may mean nothing more, in truth, but that social incoherence (with the sense for its opposite practically extinct among the nations) has at last got itself accepted, right and left, as normal.

So much, as I put it, for the great cases; but a certain freshness, I make out, still hangs strangely enough about the smaller and the more numerous; those to which we owe it that such anecdotes—in my general array—as "Pandora," as "Fordham Castle," as "Flickerbridge," as "Miss Gunton of Poughkeepsie," are by no means false even to present appearances. "The Pension Beaurepas" is not alone, thanks to some of its associations, in glowing for me with the tender grace of a day that is dead; and yet, though the accidents and accessories, in such a picture, may have been marked for change, why shall not the essence of the matter, the situation of Mr. and Mrs. Ruck and their daughter at old Geneva—for there is of course a new, a newer Geneva—freely recur? I am careful to put it as a question, and all for a particular reason—the reason that, to be frank, I find myself, before the vast diluvian occidental presence in Europe, with its remorseless rising tide and its positive expression of almost nothing but quantity and number, deprived, on definite and ample grounds, of the precious faculty of confidence. This confidence was of old all instinctive, in face of the "common run" of appearances, the even then multitudinous, miscellaneous minor international phenomena, those of which the "short story," as contemporaneously practised, could effect a fairly prompt and easy notation; but it is now unmistakable that to come forth, from whatever privacy, to almost any one of the great European highways, and more particularly perhaps to approach the ports of traffic for the lately-developed and so flourishing "southern route" from New York and Boston, is to encounter one of those big general questions that sturdily brush away the multiplication of small answers. "Who are they, what are they, whence and whither and why," the "critic of life," international or other, still, or more and more, asks himself, as he of course always asked, but with the actual difference that the reply that used to come so conveniently straight, "Why, they're just the American vague variety of the dear old Anglo-Saxon race," not only hangs fire and leaves him to wait and wonder, but really affects him as having for this act of deference (as to which he can't choose, I admit) little more than a conscious mocking, baffling, in fact a just all but sinister, grimace. "Don't you wish you knew, or even *could* know?" the inscrutable grin seems to convey; and with resources of cynicism behind it not in the least to be disturbed by any such cheap retort as "Don't you wish that, on your side, *you* could say— or even, for your own convenience, so much as guess?"

For there is no communicating to the diluvian presence, on such a scale, any suspicion that convenience shall anywhere fail it: all its consciousness, on that general head, is that of itself representing and actively *being* the biggest convenience of the world. Little need to insist on the guarantee of subjective ease involved in such an attitude—the immense noted growth of which casts its chill, as I intimate, on the inquirer proceeding from settled premises. He was aware formerly, when it came to an analysis, of all his presumptions; he had but to glance for an immemorial assurance at a dozen of the myriad "registers" disposed in the vestibules of bankers, the reading-rooms of hotels and "exchanges," open on the most conspicuous table of visited palace and castle, to see them bristle with names of a more or less conceivable tradition. Queer enough often, whether in isolation or in association, were these gages of identity: but their queerness, not independent of some more or less traceable weird law, was exactly, after all, their most familiar note. They had their way of not breaking, through it all, the old sweet Anglo-Saxon spell; they had their way of not failing, when all was said, to suggest more communities and comprehensions than conundrums and "stunts." He would be brave, however, who should say that any such ghost of a quiet conformity presides in the fulness of time over the interminable passenger-lists that proclaim the prosperity of the great conveying companies. If little books have their fates, little names—and long ones still more—have their eloquence; the emphasis of nominal reference in the general roll-call falls so strongly upon alien syllables and sounds, representative signs that fit into our "English" legend (as we were mainly conscious up to a few years since of having inherited that boon) scarcely more than if borrowed from the stony slabs of Nineveh. I may not here attempt to weigh the question of what these exotic symbols positively represent—a prodigious question, I cannot but think; I content myself with noting the difference made for fond fancy by the so rapidly established change, by the so considerable drop of old associations. The point is of one's having the heart to assume that the Ninevites, as I may momentarily call them for convenience, are to be constantly taken as feeling in the same way about fifty associational matters as we used, in all satisfaction, to observe our earlier generations feel. One can but speak for one's self, and my imagination, on the great highways, I find, doesn't rise to such people, who are obviously beyond my divination. They strike one, above all, as giving no account of themselves in any terms already consecrated by human use; to this inarticulate state they probably form, collectively, the most unprecedented of monuments; abysmal the mystery of what they think, what they feel, what they want, what they suppose themselves to be saying. There would appear to be to-day no slim scrap even of a Daisy Miller to bridge the chasm; no light-footed Francie Dosson or Pandora Day to dance before one across the wavering plank.

I plead a blank of memory as to the origin of "The Siege of London"; I get no nearer to the birth of the idea than by recalling a certain agitation of the spirit, a lively irritation of the temper, under which, one evening early in the autumn of 1877, that is more than thirty years ago, I walked away from the close of a performance at the Théâtre Français. The play had been "Le Demi-Monde" of the younger Dumas, a masterpiece which I had not heard for the first time, but a particular feature of which on this occasion more than ever yet filled up the measure of my impatience. I could less than ever swallow it, Olivier de Jalin's denunciation of Madame d'Ange; the play, from the beginning, marches toward it—it is the main hinge of the action; but the very perfection with which the part was rendered in those years by Delaunay (just as Croizette was pure perfection as Suzanne) seemed to have made me present at something inhuman and odious. It was the old story—that from the positive, the prodigious *morality* of such a painter of the sophisticated life as Dumas, not from anything else or less edifying, one must pray to be delivered. There are doubtless many possible views of such a dilemma as Olivier's, the conflict of propriety for him between the man he likes and esteems and the woman he has loved but hasn't esteemed and doesn't, and as to whom he sees his friend blind, and, as he thinks, befooled; in consequence of which I am not re-judging his case. But I recover with a pensive pleasure that is almost all a pang the intensity with which I could then feel it; to the extent of wondering whether the general situation of the three persons concerned, or something like it, mightn't be shown as taking quite another turn. Was there not conceivable an Olivier of our race, a different Olivier altogether, moved to ask himself how at such a juncture a "real gentleman," distressed and perplexed, would yet most naturally act? The question would be interesting, it was easy to judge, if only by the light it might throw on some of the other, the antecedent and concomitant, phases of a real gentleman's connexion "at all at all" with such a business and such a world. It remained with me, at all events, and was to prove in time the germ of "The Siege of London"; of the conception of which the state of mind so reflected strikes me as making, I confess, very ancient history.

Far away and unspeakably regretted the days, alas, or, more exactly, the nights, on which one could walk away from the Français under the spell of such fond convictions and such deep and agitating problems. The emphasis of the international proposition has indeed had time, as I say, to place itself elsewhere—if, for that matter, there be any emphasis or any proposition left at all—since the age when that particular pleasure seemed the keenest in life. A few months ago, one evening, I found myself withdrawing from the very temple and the supposedly sacred rites before these latter were a third over: beneath that haunted dome itself they seemed to have become at last so accessible, cynically making their bargain with them, to the profanations long kept at bay. Only, with that evolution of taste possible on the part of the old worshipper in question, what world-convulsions mightn't, in general, well have taken place? Let me continue to speak of the rest of the matter here before us as therefore of almost prehistoric reference. I was to make, in due course, at any rate, my limited application of that glimmering image of a M. de Jalin with whom we might have more fellow-feeling, and I sent "The Siege of London" accordingly to my admirable friend the late Leslie Stephen, then editor of *The Cornhill Magazine*, where it appeared during the first two months of 1883. That is all I remember about it save always the particular London light in which at that period I invoked the muse and drove the pen and with which the compositions resulting strike my fancy to-day as so closely interfused that in reading over those of them I here preserve every aspect and element of my scene of application lives again for me. This scene consisted of small chambers in a small street that opened, at a very near corner, into Piccadilly and a view of the Green Park; I had dropped into them almost instantaneously, under the accepted heavy pressure of the autumnal London of 1876, and was to sit scribbling in them for nearly ten years. The big human rumble of Piccadilly (all human and equine then and long after) was close at hand; I liked to think that Thackeray's Curzon Street, in which Becky Sharp, or rather Mrs. Rawdon Crawley, had lived, was not much further off: I thought of it preponderantly, in my comings and goings, as Becky's and her creator's; just as I was to find fifty other London neighbourhoods speak to me almost only with the voice, the thousand voices, of Dickens.

A "great house," forming the south-west corner of Piccadilly and with its long and practically featureless side, continued by the high wall of its ample court, opposite my open-eyed windows, gloomed, in dusty brick, as the extent of my view, but with a vast convenient neutrality which I found, soon enough, protective and not inquisitive, so that whatever there was of my sedentary life and regular habits took a sort of local wealth of colour from the special greyish-brown tone of the surface always before me. This surface hung there like the most voluminous of curtains—it masked the very stage of the great theatre of the town. To sit for certain hours at one's desk before it was somehow to occupy in the most suitable way in the world the proportionately ample interacts of the mightiest of dramas. When I went out it was as if the curtain rose; so that, to repeat, I think of my tolerably copious artistry of that time as all the fruit of the interacts, with the curtain more or less quietly down and with the tuning of fiddles and only the vague rumble of shifted scenery playing round it and through it. There were absences of course: "A Bundle of Letters," here reproduced, took birth (1879) during certain autumn weeks spent in Paris, where a friend of those years, a young London journalist, the late Theodore Child (of Merton College, Oxford, who was to die, prematurely and lamentedly, during a gallant professional tour of exploration in Persia) was fondly carrying on, under difficulties, an Anglo-American periodical called *The Parisian*. He invited me to contribute to its pages, and, again, a small sharply-resonant street off the Rue de la Paix, where all existence somehow went on as a repercussion from well-brushed asphalt, lives for me as the scene of my response. A snowstorm of a violence rare in Paris raged, I recollect, for many hours, for the greater part of a couple of days; muffling me noiselessly into the small shiny shabby salon of an *hôtel garni* with a droll combinational, almost cosmic sign, and promoting (it comes back to me) a deep concentration, an unusual straightness of labour. "A Bundle of Letters" was written in a single long session and, the temperature apart, at a "heat." Its companion-piece, "The Point of View," marks not less for memory, I find, an excursion associated with diligence. I have no heart to "go into" these mere ingenious and more or less effective pleasantries to any tune beyond this of glancing at the *other*, the extinct, actualities they hold up the glimmering taper to. They are still faintly scented, doubtless, with something of that authenticity, and a living work of art, however limited, pretends always, as for part of its grace, to some good faith of community, however indirect, with its period and place.

To read over "The Point of View" has opened up for me, I confess, no contentious vista whatever, nothing but the faded iridescence of a far-away Washington spring. This, in 1881, had been my first glimpse of that interesting city, where I then spent a few weeks, a visit repeated the following year; and I remember beginning on the first occasion a short imaginary correspondence after the pattern of the then already published "Bundle of Letters." After an absence from America of some five years I inevitably, on the spot again, had impressions; and not less inevitably and promptly, I remember, recognised the truth that if one really was subject to such, and to a good many, and they were at all worth entertaining or imparting, one was likely to bristle with a quite proportionately smaller number of neat and complacent conclusions. Impressions could mutually conflict—which was exactly the interest of them; whereas in ninety-nine connexions out of a hundred, conclusions could but raise the wind for large groups of persons incapable, to all appearance, of intelligently opening their eyes, though much occupied, to make up for it, with opening, and all vociferously, their mouths. "The Point of View," in fine, I fear, was but to commemorate, punctually enough, its author's perverse and incurable disposition to interest himself less in his own (always so quickly stale) experience, under certain sorts of pressure, than in that of conceivable fellow mortals, which might be mysteriously and refreshingly different. The thing indeed may also serve, in its degree, as a punctual small monument to a recognition that was never to fail; that of the nature of the burden bequeathed by such rash multiplications of the candid consciousness. They are splendid for experience, the multiplications, each in its way an intensifier; but expression, liking things above all to be made comfortable and easy for it, views them askance. The case remains, none the less—alas for this faculty!—that no representation of life worth speaking of can go forward without them. All of which will perhaps be judged to have but a strained relevance, however, to the fact that, though the design of the short imaginary correspondence I speak of was interrupted during those first weeks in Washington, a second visit, the following spring, served it better; I had kept the thread (through a return to London and a return again thence) and, if I remember rightly, I brought my small scheme to a climax on the spot. The finished thing appeared in *The Century Magazine* of December 1882. I recently had the chance to "look up," for old sake's sake, that momentary seat of the good-humoured satiric muse—the seats of the muses, even when the merest flutter of one of their robes has been involved, losing no scrap of sanctity for me, I profess, by the accident of my having myself had the honour to offer the visitant the chair. The chair I had anciently been able to push forward in Washington had not, I found, survived the ravage of nearly thirty years; its place knew it no more, infirm and precarious dependence as it had struck me even at the time as being. So, quite exquisitely, as whenever that lapse occurs, the lost presence, the obliterated scene, translated itself for me at last into terms of almost more than earthly beauty and poetry. Fifty intimate figures and objects flushed with life in the other time had passed away since then; a great chapter of history had made itself, tremendous things had happened; the ghosts of old cherished names, of old tragedies, of old comedies, even of old mere mystifications, had marshalled their array. Only the little rounded composition remained; which glowed, ever so strangely, like a swinging playing lantern, with a light that brought out the past. The past had been most concretely that vanished and slightly sordid tenement of the current housing of the muse. I had had "rooms" in it, and I could remember how the rooms, how the whole place, a nest of rickety tables and chairs, lame and disqualified utensils of every sort, and of smiling shuffling procrastinating persons of colour, had exhaled for me, to pungency, the domestic spirit of the "old South." I had nursed the unmistakable scent; I had read history by its aid; I had learned more than I could say of what had anciently been the matter under the reign of the great problem of persons of colour—so badly the matter, by my vision, that a deluge of blood and fire and tears had been needed to correct it. These complacencies of perception swarmed for me again—while yet no brick of the little old temple of the revelation stood on another.

I could scarcely have said where the bricks *had* stood; the other, the superseded Washington of the exquisite springtime, of the earlier initiation, of the hovering plaintive ghosts, reduced itself to a great vague blur of warmth and colour and fragrance. It kept flushing through the present—very much as if I had had my small secret for making it. I could turn on my finger the magic ring—it was strange how slight a thing, a mere handful of pages of light persistent prose, could act as that talisman. So, at all events, I like to date, and essentially to synchronise, these sincere little studies in general. Nothing perhaps can vouch better for their having applied to conditions that superficially at least have changed than the fact that to fond memory—I speak of my own—there hangs about the last item on this list, the picture of "The Pension Beaurepas," the unearthly poetry, as I call it, of the Paquis, and that I should yet have to plunge into gulfs of explanation as to where and what the Paquis may have been. An old-world nook of one's youth was so named, a scrap of the lakeside fringe of ancient Geneva, now practically quite reformed and improved away. The Pension Beaurepas, across the years, looks to me prodigiously archaic and incredibly quaint; I ask myself why, at the time, I so wasted the precious treasure of a sense that absolutely primitive pre-revolutionary "Europe" had never really been swept out of its cupboards, shaken out of its curtains, thumped out of its mattresses. The echoes of the eighteenth century, to go no further back, must have been thick on its rather greasy stone staircase, up down which, unconscious of the character of the fine old wrought-iron *rampe*, as of most other things in the world besides, Mr. and Mrs. and Miss Ruck, to speak only of them, used mournfully to straggle. But I mustn't really so *much* as speak only, as even speak, of them. They would carry me too far back—which possibly outlived verisimilitude in them is what I wish to acknowledge.

HENRY JAMES.

LADY BARBARINA

I

It is well known that there are few sights in the world more brilliant than the main avenues of Hyde Park of a fine afternoon in June. This was quite the opinion of two persons who on a beautiful day at the beginning of that month, four years ago, had established themselves under the great trees in a couple of iron chairs—the big ones with arms, for which, if I mistake not, you pay twopence—and sat there with the slow procession of the Drive behind them while their faces were turned to the more vivid agitation of the Row. Lost in the multitude of observers they belonged, superficially at least, to that class of persons who, wherever they may be, rank rather with the spectators than with the spectacle. They were quiet simple elderly, of aspect somewhat neutral; you would have liked them extremely but would scarcely have noticed them. It is to them, obscure in all that shining host, that we must nevertheless give our attention. On which the reader is begged to have confidence; he is not asked to make vain concessions. It was indicated touchingly in the faces of our friends that they were growing old together and were fond enough of each other's company not to object—since it was a condition—even to that. The reader will have guessed that they were husband and wife; and perhaps while he is about it will further have guessed that they were of that nationality for which Hyde Park at the height of the season is most completely illustrative. They were native aliens, so to speak, and people at once so initiated and so detached could only be Americans. This reflexion indeed you would have made only after some delay; for it must be allowed that they bristled with none of those modern signs that carry out the tradition of the old indigenous war-paint and feathers. They had the American turn of mind, but that was very secret; and to your eye—if your eye had cared about it—they might have been either intimately British or more remotely foreign. It was as if they studied, for convenience, to be superficially colourless; their colour was all in their talk. They were not in the least verdant; they were grey rather, of monotonous hue. If they were interested in the riders, the horses, the walkers, the great exhibition of English wealth and health, beauty, luxury and leisure, it was because all this referred itself to other impressions, because they had the key to almost everything that needed an answer—because, in a word, they were able to compare. They had not arrived, they had only returned; and recognition much more than surprise was expressed in their quiet eyes. Dexter Freer and his wife belonged in fine to that great company of Americans who are constantly "passing through" London. Enjoyers of a fortune of which, from any standpoint, the limits were plainly visible, they were unable to treat themselves to that commonest form of ease, the ease of living at home. They found it much more possible to economise at Dresden or Florence than at Buffalo or Minneapolis. The saving was greater and the strain was less. From Dresden, from Florence, moreover, they constantly made excursions that wouldn't have been possible with an excess of territory; and it is even to be feared they practised some eccentricities of thrift. They came to London to buy their portmanteaus, their toothbrushes, their writing-paper; they occasionally even recrossed the Atlantic westward to assure themselves that westward prices were still the same. They were eminently a social pair; their interests were mainly personal. Their curiosity was so invidiously human that they were supposed to be too addicted to gossip, and they certainly kept up their acquaintance with the affairs of other people. They had friends in every country, in every town; and it was not their fault if people told them their secrets. Dexter Freer was a tall lean man, with an interested eye and a nose that rather drooped than aspired, yet was salient withal. He brushed his hair, which was streaked with white, forward over his ears and into those locks represented in the portraits of clean-shaven gentlemen who flourished fifty years ago and wore an old-fashioned neckcloth and gaiters. His wife, a small plump person, rather polished than naturally fresh, with a white face and hair still evenly black, smiled perpetually, but had never laughed since the death of a son whom she had lost ten years after her marriage. Her husband, on the other hand, who was usually quite grave, indulged on great occasions in resounding mirth. People confided in her less than in him, but that mattered little, as she confided much in herself. Her dress, which was always black or dark grey, was so harmoniously simple that you could see she was fond of it; it was never smart by accident or by fear. She was full of intentions of the most judicious sort and, though perpetually moving about the world, had the air of waiting for every one else to pass. She was celebrated for the promptitude with which she made her sitting-room at an inn, where she might be spending a night or two, appear a real temple of memory. With books, flowers, photographs, draperies, rapidly distributed—she had even a way, for the most part, of not failing of a piano—the place seemed almost hereditary. The pair were just back from America, where they had spent three months, and now were able to face the world with something of the elation of people who have been justified of a stiff conviction. They had found their native land quite ruinous.

"There he is again!" said Mr. Freer, following with his eyes a young man who passed along the Row, riding slowly. "That's a beautiful thoroughbred!"

Mrs. Freer asked idle questions only when she wanted time to think. At present she had simply to look and see who it was her husband meant. "The horse is too big," she remarked in a moment.

"You mean the rider's too small," her husband returned. "He's mounted on his millions."

"Is it really millions?"

"Seven or eight, they tell me."

"How disgusting!" It was so that Mrs. Freer usually spoke of the large fortunes of the day. "I wish he'd see us," she added.

"He does see us, but he doesn't like to look at us. He's too conscious. He isn't easy."

"Too conscious of his big horse?"

"Yes and of his big fortune. He's rather ashamed of that."

"This is an odd place to hang one's head in," said Mrs. Freer.

"I'm not so sure. He'll find people here richer than himself, and other big horses in plenty, and that will cheer him up. Perhaps too he's looking for that girl."

"The one we heard about? He can't be such a fool."

"He isn't a fool," said Dexter Freer. "If he's thinking of her he has some good reason."

"I wonder what Mary Lemon would say," his wife pursued.

"She'd say it was all right if he should do it. She thinks he can do no wrong. He's immensely fond of her."

"I shan't be sure of that," said Mrs. Freer, "if he takes home a wife who'll despise her."

"Why should the girl despise her? She's a delightful woman."

"The girl will never know it—and if she should it would make no difference: she'll despise everything."

"I don't believe it, my dear; she'll like some things very much. Every one will be very nice to her."

"She'll despise them all the more. But we're speaking as if it were all arranged. I don't believe in it at all," said Mrs. Freer.

"Well, something of the sort—in this case or in some other—is sure to happen sooner or later," her husband replied, turning round a little toward the back-water, as it were, formed, near the entrance to the Park, by the confluence of the two great vistas of the Drive and the Row.

Our friends had turned their backs, as I have said, to the solemn revolution of wheels and the densely-packed mass of spectators who had chosen that aspect of the show. These spectators were now agitated by a unanimous impulse: the pushing-back of chairs, the shuffle of feet, the rustle of garments and the deepening murmur of voices sufficiently expressed it. Royalty was approaching—royalty was passing—royalty had passed. Mr. Freer turned his head and his ear a little, but failed to alter his position further, and his wife took no notice of the flurry. They had seen royalty pass, all over Europe, and they knew it passed very quickly. Sometimes it came back; sometimes it didn't; more than once they had seen it pass for the last time.

They were veteran tourists and they knew as perfectly as regular attendants at complicated church-services when to get up and when to remain seated. Mr. Freer went on with his proposition. "Some young fellow's certain to do it, and one of these girls is certain to take the risk. They must take risks over here more and more."

"The girls, I've no doubt, will be glad enough; they have had very little chance as yet. But I don't want Jackson to begin."

"Do you know I rather think I do," said Dexter Freer. "It will be so very amusing."

"For us perhaps, but not for him. He'll repent of it and be wretched. He's too good for that."

"Wretched never! He has no capacity for wretchedness, and that's why he can afford to risk it."

"He'll have to make great concessions," Mrs. Freer persisted.

"He won't make one."

"I should like to see."

"You admit, then, that it will be amusing: all I contend for," her husband replied. "But, as you say, we're talking as if it were settled, whereas there's probably nothing in it after all. The best stories always turn out false. I shall be sorry in this case."

They relapsed into silence while people passed and repassed them— continuous successive mechanical, with strange facial, strange expressional, sequences and contrasts. They watched the procession, but no one heeded them, though every one was there so admittedly to see what was to be seen. It was all striking, all pictorial, and it made a great composition. The wide long area of the Row, its red-brown surface dotted with bounding figures, stretched away into the distance and became suffused and misty in the bright thick air. The deep dark English verdure that bordered and overhung it looked rich and old, revived and refreshed though it was by the breath of June. The mild blue of the sky was spotted with great silvery clouds, and the light drizzled

29

down in heavenly shafts over the quieter spaces of the Park, as one saw them beyond the Row. All this, however, was only a background, for the scene was before everything personal; quite splendidly so, and full of the gloss and lustre, the contrasted tones, of a thousand polished surfaces. Certain things were salient, pervasive—the shining flanks of the perfect horses, the twinkle of bits and spurs, the smoothness of fine cloth adjusted to shoulders and limbs, the sheen of hats and boots, the freshness of complexions, the expression of smiling talking faces, the flash and flutter of rapid gallops. Faces were everywhere, and they were the great effect—above all the fair faces of women on tall horses, flushed a little under their stiff black hats, with figures stiffened, in spite of much definition of curve, by their tight-fitting habits. Their well-secured helmets, their neat compact heads, their straight necks, their firm tailor-made armour, their frequent hardy bloom, all made them look singularly like amazons about to ride a charge. The men, with their eyes before them, with hats of undulating brim, good profiles, high collars, white flowers on their chests, long legs and long feet, had an air more elaboratively decorative, as they jolted beside the ladies, always out of step. These were the younger types; but it was not all youth, for many a saddle sustained a richer rotundity, and ruddy faces with short white whiskers or with matronly chins looked down comfortably from an equilibrium that seemed moral as well as physical. The walkers differed from the riders only in being on foot and in looking at the riders more than these looked at them; for they would have done as well in the saddle and ridden as the others ride. The women had tight little bonnets and still tighter little knots of hair; their round chins rested on a close swathing of lace or in some cases on throttling silver chains and circlets. They had flat backs and small waists, they walked slowly, with their elbows out, carrying vast parasols and turning their heads very little to the right or the left. They were amazons unmounted, quite ready to spring into the saddle. There was a great deal of beauty and a diffused look of happy expansion, all limited and controlled, which came from clear quiet eyes and well-cut lips, rims of stout vessels that didn't overflow and on which syllables were liquid and sentences brief. Some of the young men, as well as the women, had the happiest proportions and oval faces—faces in which line and colour were pure and fresh and the idea of the moment far from intense.

"They're often very good-looking," said Mr. Freer at the end of ten minutes. "They're on the whole the finest whites."

"So long as they remain white they do very well; but when they venture upon colour!" his wife replied. She sat with her eyes at the level of the skirts of the ladies who passed her, and she had been following the progress of a green velvet robe enriched with ornaments of steel and much gathered up in the hands of its wearer, who, herself apparently in her teens, was accompanied by a young lady draped in scant pink muslin, a tissue embroidered esthetically with flowers that simulated the iris.

"All the same, in a crowd, they're wonderfully well turned out," Dexter Freer went on—"lumping men and women and horses and dogs together. Look at that big fellow on the light chestnut: what could be more perfect? By the way, it's Lord Canterville," he added in a moment and as if the fact were of some importance.

Mrs. Freer recognised its importance to the degree of raising her glass to look at Lord Canterville. "How do you know it's he?" she asked with that implement still up.

"I heard him say something the night I went to the House of Lords. It was very few words, but I remember him. A man near me mentioned who he was."

"He's not so handsome as you," said Mrs. Freer, dropping her glass.

"Ah, you're too difficult!" her husband murmured. "What a pity the girl isn't with him," he went on. "We might see something."

It appeared in a moment, however, that the girl was with him. The nobleman designated had ridden slowly forward from the start, then just opposite our friends had pulled up to look back as if waiting for some one. At the same moment a gentleman in the Walk engaged his attention, so that he advanced to the barrier which protects the pedestrians and halted there, bending a little from his saddle and talking with his friend, who leaned against the rail. Lord Canterville was indeed perfect, as his American admirer had said. Upwards of sixty and of great stature and great presence, he was a thoroughly splendid apparition. In capital preservation he had the freshness of middle life—he would have been young indeed to the eye if his large harmonious spread hadn't spoken of the lapse of years. He was clad from head to foot in garments of a radiant grey, and his fine florid countenance was surmounted with a white hat of which the majestic curves were a triumph of good form. Over his mighty chest disposed itself a beard of the richest growth and of a colour, in spite of a few streaks vaguely grizzled, to which the coat of his admirable horse appeared to be a perfect match. It left no opportunity in his uppermost button-hole for the customary orchid; but this was of comparatively little consequence, since the vegetation of the beard itself was tropical. Astride his great steed, with his big fist, gloved in pearl-grey, on his swelling thigh, his face lighted up with good-humoured indifference and all his magnificent surface reflecting the mild sunshine, he was, strikingly, a founded and builded figure, such as could only represent to the public gaze some Institution, some Exhibition or some Industry, in a word some unquenchable Interest. People quite lingered to look up at him as they passed. His halt was brief, however, for he was almost immediately joined by two handsome girls, who were as well turned-out, in Dexter Freer's phrase, as himself. They had been detained a moment at the entrance to the Row and now advanced side by side, their groom close behind them. One was noticeably taller and older than the other, and it was plain at a glance that they were sisters. Between them, with their charming shoulders, their contracted waists and their skirts that hung without a wrinkle, like plates of zinc, they represented in a singularly complete form the pretty English girl in the position in which she is prettiest.

"Of course they're his daughters," said Dexter Freer as these young ladies rode away with Lord Canterville; "and in that case one of them must be Jackson Lemon's sweetheart. Probably the bigger; they said it was the eldest. She's evidently a fine creature."

"She'd hate it over there," Mrs. Freer returned for all answer to this cluster of inductions.

"You know I don't admit that. But granting she should, it would do her good to have to accommodate herself."

"She wouldn't accommodate herself."

"She looks so confoundedly fortunate, perched up on that saddle," he went on without heed of his wife's speech.

"Aren't they supposed to be very poor?"

"Yes, they look it!" And his eyes followed the eminent trio while, with the groom, as eminent in his way as any of them, they started on a canter.

The air was full of sound, was low and economised; and when, near our friends, it became articulate the words were simple and few. "It's as good as the circus, isn't it, Mrs. Freer?" These words correspond to that description, but they pierced the dense medium more effectually than any our friends had lately heard. They were uttered by a young man who had stopped short in the path, absorbed by the sight of his compatriots. He was short and stout, he had a round kind face and short stiff-looking hair, which was reproduced in a small bristling beard. He wore a double-breasted walking-coat, which was not, however, buttoned, and on the summit of his round head was perched a hat of exceeding smallness and of the so-called "pot" category. It evidently fitted him, but a hatter himself wouldn't have known why. His hands were encased in new gloves of a dark-brown colour, and these masquerading members hung consciously, quite ruefully, at his sides. He sported neither umbrella nor stick. He offered one of his stuffed gloves almost with eagerness to Mrs. Freer, blushing a little as he measured his precipitation.

"Oh Doctor Feeder!"—she smiled at him. Then she repeated to her husband, "Doctor Feeder, my dear!" and her husband said, "Oh Doctor, how d'ye do?" I have spoken of the composition of the young man's appearance, but the items were not perceived by these two. They saw but one thing, his delightful face, which was both simple and clever and, as if this weren't enough, showed a really tasteless overheaping of the cardinal virtues. They had lately made the voyage from New York in his company, and he was clearly a person who would shine at sea with an almost intolerable blandness. After he had stood in front of them a moment a chair beside Mrs. Freer became vacant; on which he took possession of it and sat there telling her what he thought of the Park and how he liked London. As she knew every

33

one she had known many of his people at home, and while she listened to him she remembered how large their contribution had been to the moral worth of Cincinnati. Mrs. Freer's social horizon included even that city; she had had occasion to exercise an amused recognition of several families from Ohio and was acquainted with the position of the Feeders there. This family, very numerous, was interwoven into an enormous cousinship. She stood off herself from any Western promiscuity, but she could have told you whom Doctor Feeder's great-grandfather had married. Every one indeed had heard of the good deeds of the descendants of this worthy, who were generally physicians, excellent ones, and whose name expressed not inaptly their numerous acts of charity. Sidney Feeder, who had several cousins of this name established in the same line at Cincinnati, had transferred himself and his ambition to New York, where his practice had at the end of three years begun to grow. He had studied his profession at Vienna and was saturated with German science; had he only worn spectacles he might indeed perfectly, while he watched the performers in Rotten Row as if their proceedings were a successful demonstration, have passed for some famously "materialistic" young German. He had come over to London to attend a medical congress which met this year in the British capital, for his interest in the healing art was by no means limited to the cure of his patients. It embraced every form of experiment, and the expression of his honest eyes would almost have reconciled you to vivisection. This was his first time of looking into the Park; for social experiments he had little leisure. Being aware, however, that it was a very typical and, as might be, symptomatic sight, he had conscientiously reserved an afternoon and dressed himself carefully for the occasion. "It's quite a brilliant show," he said to Mrs. Freer; "it makes me wish I had a mount." Little as he resembled Lord Canterville he rode, as he would have gaily said, first-rate.

"Wait till Jackson Lemon passes again and you can stop him and make him let you take a turn." This was the jocular suggestion of Dexter Freer.

"Why, is he here? I've been looking out for him and should like to see him."

"Doesn't he go to your medical congress?" asked Mrs. Freer.

"Well yes, he attends—but isn't very regular. I guess he goes out a good deal."

"I guess he does," said Mr. Freer; "and if he isn't very regular I guess he has a good reason. A beautiful reason, a charming reason," he went on, bending forward to look down toward the beginning of the Row. "Dear me, what a lovely reason!"

Doctor Feeder followed the direction of his eyes and after a moment understood his allusion. Little Jackson Lemon passed, on his big horse, along the avenue again, riding beside one of the bright creatures who had come that way shortly before under escort of Lord Canterville. His lordship followed in conversation with the other, his younger daughter. As they advanced Jackson Lemon turned his eyes to the multitude under the trees, and it so happened that they rested on the Dexter Freers. He smiled, he raised his hat with all possible friendliness, and his three companions turned to see whom he so frankly greeted. As he settled his hat on his head he espied the young man from Cincinnati, whom he had at first overlooked; whereupon he laughed for the luck of it and waved Sidney Feeder an airy salutation with his hand, reining in a little at the same time just for an instant, as if he half-expected this apparition to come and speak to him. Seeing him with strangers, none the less, Sidney Feeder hung back, staring a little as he rode away.

It is open to us to know that at this moment the young lady by whose side he was riding put him the free question: "Who are those people you bowed to?"

"Some old friends of mine—Americans," said Jackson Lemon.

"Of course they're Americans; there's nothing anywhere but Americans now."

"Oh yes, our turn's coming round!" laughed the young man.

"But that doesn't say who they are," his companion continued. "It's so difficult to say who Americans are," she added before he had time to answer her.

"Dexter Freer and his wife—there's nothing difficult about that. Every one knows them," Jackson explained.

"I never heard of them," said the English girl.

"Ah, that's your fault and your misfortune. I assure you everybody knows them."

"And does everybody know the little man with the fat face to whom you kissed your hand?"

"I didn't kiss my hand, but I would if I had thought of it. He's a great chum of mine—a fellow-student at Vienna."

"And what's *his* name?"

"Doctor Feeder."

Jackson Lemon's companion had a dandling pause. "Are *all* your friends doctors?"

"No—some of them are in other businesses."

"Are they all in some business?"

"Most of them—save two or three like Dexter Freer."

"'Dexter' Freer? I thought you said Doctor Freer."

The young man gave a laugh. "You heard me wrong. You've got doctors on the brain, Lady Barb."

"I'm rather glad," said Lady Barb, giving the rein to her horse, who bounded away.

"Well yes, she's very handsome, the reason," Doctor Feeder remarked as he sat under the trees.

"Is he going to marry her?" Mrs. Freer inquired.

"Marry her? I hope not."

"Why do you hope not?"

"Because I know nothing about her. I want to know something about the woman that man marries."

"I suppose you'd like him to marry in Cincinnati," Mrs. Freer not unadventurously threw out.

"Well, I'm not particular where it is; but I want to know her first." Doctor Feeder was very sturdy.

"We were in hopes you'd know all about it," said his other entertainer.

"No, I haven't kept up with him there."

"We've heard from a dozen people that he has been always with her for the last month—and that kind of thing, in England, is supposed to mean something. Hasn't he spoken of her when you've seen him?"

"No, he has only talked about the new treatment of spinal meningitis. He's very much interested in spinal meningitis."

"I wonder if he talks about it to Lady Barb," said Mrs. Freer.

"Who is she anyway?" the young man wanted to know.

Well, his companions both let him. "Lady Barb Clement."

"And who's Lady Barb Clement?"

"The daughter of Lord Canterville."

"And who's Lord Canterville?"

"Dexter must tell you that," said Mrs. Freer.

And Dexter accordingly told him that the Marquis of Canterville had been in his day a great sporting nobleman and an ornament to English society, and had held more than once a high post in her Majesty's household. Dexter Freer knew all these things—how his lordship had married a daughter of Lord Treherne, a very serious intelligent and beautiful woman who had redeemed him from the extravagance of his youth and presented him in rapid succession with a dozen little tenants for the nurseries at Pasterns—this being, as Mr. Freer also knew, the name of the principal seat of the Cantervilles. The head of that house was a Tory, but not a particular dunce for a Tory, and very popular in society at large; good-natured, good-looking, knowing how to be rather remarkably free and yet remain a *grand seigneur*, clever enough to make an occasional telling speech and much associated with the fine old English pursuits as well as with many of the new improvements—the purification of the Turf, the opening of the museums on Sunday, the propagation of coffee-taverns, the latest ideas on sanitary reform. He disapproved of the extension of the suffrage but had positively drainage on the brain. It had been said of him at least once—and, if this historian is not mistaken, in print—that he was just the man to convey to the popular mind the impression that the British aristocracy is still a living force. He was unfortunately not very rich—for a man who had to exemplify such truths—and of his twelve children no less than seven were daughters. Lady Barb, Jackson Lemon's friend, was the second; the eldest had married Lord Beauchemin. Mr. Freer had caught quite the right pronunciation of this name, which he successfully sounded as Bitumen. Lady Lucretia had done very well, for her husband was rich and she had brought him nothing to speak of; but it was hardly to be expected they would all achieve such flights. Happily the younger girls were still in the schoolroom, and before they had come up, Lady Canterville, who was a woman of bold resource, would have worked off the two that were out. It was Lady Agatha's first season; she wasn't so pretty as her sister, but was thought to be cleverer. Half-a-dozen people had spoken to him of Jackson Lemon's being a great deal at the Cantervilles. He was supposed to be enormously rich.

"Well, so he is," said Sidney Feeder, who had listened to Mr. Freer's report with attention, with eagerness even, but, for all its lucidity, with an air of imperfect apprehension.

"Yes, but not so rich as they probably think."

"Do they want his money? Is that what they're after?"

"You go straight to the point!" Mrs. Freer rang out.

"I haven't the least idea," said her husband. "He's a very good sort in himself."

"Yes, but he's a doctor," Mrs. Freer observed.

"What have they got against that?" asked Sidney Feeder.

"Why, over here, you know, they only call them in to prescribe," said his other friend. "The profession isn't—a—what you'd call aristocratic."

"Well, I don't know it, and I don't know that I want to know it. How do you mean, aristocratic? What profession is? It would be rather a curious one. Professions are meant to do the work of professions; and what work's done without your sleeves rolled up? Many of the gentlemen at the congress there are quite charming."

"I like doctors very much," said Mrs. Freer; "my father was a doctor. But they don't marry the daughters of marquises."

"I don't believe Jackson wants to marry that one," Sidney Feeder calmly argued.

"Very possibly not—people are such asses," said Dexter Freer. "But he'll have to decide. I wish you'd find out, by the way. You can if you will."

"I'll ask him—up at the congress; I can do that. I suppose he has got to marry some one." The young man added in a moment: "And she may be a good thing."

"She's said to be charming."

"Very well then, it won't hurt him. I must say, however, I'm not sure I like all that about her family."

"What I told you? It's all to their honour and glory," said Mr. Freer.

"Are they quite on the square? It's like those people in Thackeray."

"Oh if Thackeray could have done *this*!" And Mrs. Freer yearned over the lost hand.

"You mean all this scene?" asked the young man.

"No; the marriage of a British noblewoman and an American doctor. It would have been a subject for a master of satire."

"You see you do want it, my dear," said her husband quietly.

"I want it as a story, but I don't want it for Doctor Lemon."

"Does he call himself 'Doctor' still?" Mr. Freer asked of young Feeder.

"I suppose he does—I call him so. Of course he doesn't practise. But once a doctor always a doctor."

"That's doctrine for Lady Barb!"

Sidney Feeder wondered. "Hasn't *she* got a title too? What would she expect him to be? President of the United States? He's a man of real ability—he might have stood at the head of his profession. When I think of that I want to swear. What did his father want to go and make all that money for?"

"It must certainly be odd to them to see a 'medical man' with six or eight millions," Mr. Freer conceded.

"They use much the same term as the Choctaws," said his wife.

"Why, some of their own physicians make immense fortunes," Sidney Feeder remarked.

"Couldn't he," she went on, "be made a baronet by the Queen?"

"Yes, then he'd be aristocratic," said the young man. "But I don't see why he should want to marry over here; it seems to me to be going out of his way. However, if he's happy I don't care. I like him very much; he has 'A1' ability. If it hadn't been for his father he'd have made a splendid doctor. But, as I say, he takes a great interest in medical science and I guess he means to promote it all he can—with his big fortune. He'll be sure to keep up his interest in research. He thinks we *do* know something and is bound we shall know more. I hope she won't lower him, the young marchioness—is that her rank? And I hope they're really good people. He ought to be very useful. I should want to know a good deal about the foreign family I was going to marry into."

"He looked to me, riding there, as if he knew a good deal about the Clements," Dexter Freer said, getting to his feet as his wife suggested they ought to be going; "and he looked to me pleased with the knowledge. There they come down the other side. Will you walk away with us or will you stay?"

"Stop him and ask him, and then come and tell us—in Jermyn Street." This was Mrs. Freer's parting injunction to Sidney Feeder.

"He ought to come himself—tell him that," her husband added.

"Well, I guess I'll stay," said the young man as his companions merged themselves in the crowd that now was tending toward the gates. He went and stood by the barrier and saw Doctor Lemon and his friends pull up at the entrance to the Row, where they apparently prepared to separate. The separation took some time and Jackson's colleague became interested. Lord Canterville and his younger daughter lingered to talk with two gentlemen, also mounted, who looked a good deal at the legs of Lady Agatha's horse. Doctor Lemon and Lady Barb were face to face, very near each other, and she, leaning forward a little, stroked the overlapping neck of his glossy bay. At a distance he appeared to be talking and she to be listening without response. "Oh yes, he's making love to her," thought Sidney Feeder. Suddenly her father and sister turned away to leave the Park, and she joined them and disappeared while Jackson came up on the left again as for a final gallop. He hadn't gone far before he perceived his comrade, who awaited him at the rail; and he repeated the gesture Lady Barb had described as a kiss of the hand, though it had not to his friend's eyes that full grace. When he came within hail he pulled up.

"If I had known you were coming here I'd have given you a mount," he immediately and bountifully cried. There was not in his person that irradiation of wealth and distinction which made Lord Canterville glow like a picture; but as he sat there with his neat little legs stuck out he looked very bright and sharp and happy, wearing in his degree the aspect of one of Fortune's favourites. He had a thin keen delicate face, a nose very carefully finished, a quick eye, a trifle hard in expression, and a fine dark moustache, a good deal cultivated. He was not striking, but he had his intensity, and it was easy to see that he had his purposes.

"How many horses have you got—about forty?" his compatriot inquired in response to his greeting.

"About five hundred," said Jackson Lemon.

"Did you mount your friends—the three you were riding with?"

"Mount them? They've got the best horses in England."

"Did they sell you this one?" Sidney Feeder continued in the same humorous strain.

"What do you think of him?" said his friend without heed of this question.

"Well, he's an awful old screw. I wonder he can carry you."

"Where did you get your hat?" Jackson asked both as a retort and as a relevant criticism.

"I got it in New York. What's the matter with it?"

"It's very beautiful. I wish I had brought over one like it."

"The head's the thing—not the hat. I don't mean yours—I mean mine," Sidney Feeder laughed. "There's something very deep in your question. I must think it over."

"Don't—don't," said Jackson Lemon; "you'll never get to the bottom of it. Are you having a good time?"

"A glorious time. Have you been up to-day?"

"Up among the doctors? No—I've had a lot of things to do," Jackson was obliged to plead.

"Well"—and his friend richly recovered it—"we had a very interesting discussion. I made a few remarks."

"You ought to have told me. What were they about?"

"About the intermarriage of races from the point of view—" And Sidney Feeder paused a moment, occupied with the attempt to scratch the nose of the beautiful horse.

42

"From the point of view of the progeny, I suppose?"

"Not at all. From the point of view of the old friends."

"Damn the old friends!" Doctor Lemon exclaimed with jocular crudity.

"Is it true that you're going to marry a young marchioness?"

The face of the speaker in the saddle became just a trifle rigid, and his firm eyes penetrated the other. "Who has played that on you?"

"Mr. and Mrs. Freer, whom I met just now."

"Mr. and Mrs. Freer be hanged too. And who told *them*?"

"Ever so many fashionable people. I don't know who."

"Gad, how things are tattled!" cried Jackson Lemon with asperity.

"I can see it's true by the way you say that," his friend ingenuously stated.

"Do Freer and his wife believe it?" Jackson went on impatiently.

"They want you to go and see them. You can judge for yourself."

"I'll go and see them and tell them to mind their business."

"In Jermyn Street; but I forget the number. I'm sorry the marchioness isn't one of ours," Doctor Feeder continued.

"If I should marry her she *would* be quick enough. But I don't see what difference it can make to you," said Jackson.

"Why, she'll look down on the profession, and I don't like that from your wife."

"That will touch me more than you."

"Then it *is* true?" Doctor Feeder cried with a finer appeal.

"She won't look down. I'll answer for that."

"You won't care. You're out of it all now."

"No, I'm not. I mean to do no end of work."

"I'll believe that when I see it," said Sidney Feeder, who was by no means perfectly incredulous, but who thought it salutary to take that tone. "I'm not sure you've any right to work—you oughtn't to have everything; you ought to leave the field to us, not take the bread out of our mouths and get the *kudos*. You must pay the penalty of being bloated. You'd have been celebrated if you had continued to practise—more celebrated than any one. But you won't be now—you can't be any way you fix it. Some one else is going to be in your place."

Jackson Lemon listened to this, but without meeting the eyes of the prophet; not, however, as if he were avoiding them, but as if the long stretch of the Ride, now less and less obstructed, irresistibly drew him off again and made his companion's talk retarding. Nevertheless he answered deliberately and kindly enough. "I hope it will be you, old boy." And he bowed to a lady who rode past.

"Very likely it will. I hope I make you feel mean. That's what I'm trying to do."

"Oh awfully!" Jackson cried. "All the more that I'm not in the least engaged."

"Well, that's good. Won't you come up to-morrow?" Doctor Feeder went on.

"I'll try, my dear fellow. I can't be sure. By-bye!"

"Oh you're lost anyway!" sighed Sidney Feeder as the other started away.

II

It was Lady Marmaduke, wife of Sir Henry of that clan, who had introduced the amusing young American to Lady Beauchemin; after which Lady Beauchemin had made him acquainted with her mother and sisters. Lady Marmaduke too was of outland strain, remaining for her conjugal baronet the most ponderable consequence of a tour in the United States. At present, by the end of ten years, she knew her London as she had never known her New York, so that it had been easy for her to be, as she called herself, Jackson's social godmother. She had views with regard to his career, and these views fitted into a scheme of high policy which, if our space permitted, I should be glad to lay before the reader in its magnitude. She wished to add an arch or two to the bridge on which she had effected her transit from America; and it was her belief that Doctor Lemon might furnish the materials. This bridge, as yet a somewhat sketchy and rickety structure, she saw—in the future—boldly stretch from one solid pier to another. It could but serve both ways, for reciprocity was the keynote of Lady Marmaduke's plan. It was her belief that an ultimate fusion was inevitable and that those who were the first to understand the situation would enjoy the biggest returns from it. The first time the young man had dined with her he met Lady Beauchemin, who was her intimate friend. Lady Beauchemin was remarkably gracious, asking him to come and see her as if she really meant it. He in fact presented himself and in her drawing-room met her mother, who happened to be calling at the same moment. Lady Canterville, not less friendly than her daughter, invited him down to Pasterns for Eastertide, and before a month had passed it struck him that, though he was not what he would have called intimate at any house in London, the door of the house of Clement opened to him pretty often. This seemed no small good fortune, for it always opened upon a charming picture. The inmates were a blooming and beautiful race, and their interior had an aspect of the ripest comfort. It was not the splendour of New York—as New York had lately begun to appear to the young man—but an appearance and a set of conditions, of factors as he used to say, not to be set in motion in that city by any power of purchase. He himself had a great deal of money, and money was good even when it was new; but old money was somehow *more* to the shilling and the pound. Even after he learned that Lord Canterville's fortune was less present than past it was still the positive golden glow that struck him. It was Lady Beauchemin who had told him her father wasn't rich; having told him furthermore many surprising things—things both surprising in themselves and surprising on her lips. This was to come home to him afresh that evening—the day he met Sidney Feeder in the Park.

He dined out in the company of Lady Beauchemin, and afterwards, as she was alone—her husband had gone down to listen to a debate—she offered to "take him on." She was going to several places, at some of which he must be due. They compared notes, and it was settled they should proceed together to the Trumpingtons', whither, it appeared at eleven o'clock, all the world was proceeding, with the approach to the house choked for half a mile with carriages. It was a close muggy night; Lady Beauchemin's chariot, in its place in the rank, stood still for long periods. In his corner beside her, through the open window, Jackson Lemon, rather hot, rather oppressed, looked out on the moist greasy pavement, over which was flung, a considerable distance up and down, the flare of a public-house. Lady Beauchemin, however, was not impatient, for she had a purpose in her mind, and now she could say what she wished.

"Do you really love her?" That was the first thing she said.

"Well, I guess so," Jackson Lemon answered as if he didn't recognise the obligation to be serious.

She looked at him a moment in silence; he felt her gaze and, turning his eyes, saw her face, partly shadowed, with the aid of a street-lamp. She was not so pretty as Lady Barb; her features had a certain sharpness; her hair, very light in colour and wonderfully frizzled, almost covered her eyes, the expression of which, however, together with that of her pointed nose and the glitter of several diamonds, emerged from the gloom. What she next said seemed somehow to fall in with that. "You don't seem to know. I never saw a man in so vague a state."

"You push me a little too much; I must have time to think of it," the young man returned. "You know in my country they allow us plenty of time." He had several little oddities of expression, of which he was perfectly conscious and which he found convenient, for they guarded him in a society condemning a lonely New Yorker who proceeded by native inspiration to much exposure; they ensured him the profit corresponding with sundry sacrifices. He had no great assortment of vernacular drolleries, conscious or unconscious, to draw upon; but the occasional use of one, discreetly chosen, made him appear simpler than he really was, and reasons determined his desiring this result. He was not simple; he was subtle, circumspect, shrewd—perfectly aware that he might make mistakes. There was a danger of his making one now—a mistake that might gravely count. He was resolved only to succeed. It is true that for a great success he would take a certain risk; but the risk was to be considered, and he gained time while he multiplied his guesses and talked about his country.

"You may take ten years if you like," said Lady Beauchemin. "I'm in no hurry whatever to make you my brother-in-law. Only you must remember that you spoke to me first."

"What did I say?"

"You spoke to me of Barb as the finest girl you had seen in England."

"Oh I'm willing to stand by that." And he had another try, which would have been transparent to a compatriot. "I guess I like her type."

"I should think you might!"

"I like her all round—with all her peculiarities."

"What do you mean by her peculiarities?"

"Well, she has some peculiar ideas," said Jackson Lemon in a tone of the sweetest reasonableness, "and she has a peculiar way of speaking."

"Ah, you can't expect us to speak so well as you!" cried Lady Beauchemin.

"I don't see why not." He was perfectly candid. "You do some things much better."

"We've our own ways at any rate, and we think them the best in the world—as they mostly are!" laughed Lady Beauchemin. "One of them's not to let a gentleman devote himself to a girl for so long a time without some sense of responsibility. If you don't wish to marry my sister you ought to go away."

"I ought never to have come," said Jackson Lemon.

"I can scarcely agree to that," her ladyship good-naturedly replied, "as in that case I should have lost the pleasure of knowing you."

"It would have spared you this duty, which you dislike very much."

"Asking you about your intentions? Oh I don't dislike it at all!" she cried. "It amuses me extremely."

"Should you like your sister to marry me?" asked Jackson with great simplicity.

If he expected to take her by surprise he was disappointed: she was perfectly prepared to commit herself. "I should like it particularly. I think English and American society ought to be but one. I mean the best of each. A great whole."

"Will you allow me to ask whether Lady Marmaduke suggested that to you?" he at once inquired.

"We've often talked of it."

"Oh yes, that's her aim."

"Well, it's my aim too. I think there's a lot to be done."

"And you'd like me to do it?"

"To begin it, precisely. Don't you think we ought to see more of each other? I mean," she took the precaution to explain, "just the best in each country."

Jackson Lemon appeared to weigh it. "I'm afraid I haven't any general ideas. If I should marry an English girl it wouldn't be for the good of the species."

"Well, we want to be mixed a little. That I'm sure of," Lady Beauchemin said.

"You certainly got that from Lady Marmaduke," he commented.

"It's too tiresome, your not consenting to be serious! But my father will make you so," she went on with her pleasant assurance. "I may as well let you

48

know that he intends in a day or two to ask you your intentions. That's all I wished to say to you. I think you ought to be prepared."

"I'm much obliged to you. Lord Canterville will do quite right," the young man allowed.

There was to his companion something really unfathomable in this little American doctor whom she had taken up on grounds of large policy and who, though he was assumed to have sunk the medical character, was neither handsome nor distinguished, but only immensely rich and quite original— since he wasn't strictly insignificant. It was unfathomable to begin with that a medical man should be so rich, or that so rich a man should be medical; it was even, to an eye always gratified by suitability and, for that matter, almost everywhere recognising it, rather irritating. Jackson Lemon himself could have explained the anomaly better than any one else, but this was an explanation one could scarcely ask for. There were other things: his cool acceptance of certain situations; his general indisposition to make comprehension easy, let alone to guess it, with all his guessing, so much hindered; his way of taking refuge in jokes which at times had not even the merit of being American; his way too of appearing to be a suitor without being an aspirant. Lady Beauchemin, however, was, like her puzzling friend himself, prepared to run a certain risk. His reserves made him slippery, but that was only when one pressed. She flattered herself she could handle people lightly. "My father will be sure to act with perfect tact," she said; "though of course if you shouldn't care to be questioned you can go out of town." She had the air of really wishing to act with the most natural delicacy.

"I don't want to go out of town; I'm enjoying it far too much here," Jackson cried. "And wouldn't your father have a right to ask me what I should mean by that?"

Lady Beauchemin thought—she really wondered. But in a moment she exclaimed: "He's incapable of saying anything vulgar!"

She hadn't definitely answered his inquiry, and he was conscious of this; but he was quite ready to say to her a little later, as he guided her steps from the brougham to the strip of carpet which, beneath a rickety border of striped cloth and between a double row of waiting footmen, policemen and dingy amateurs of both sexes, stretched from the curbstone to the portal of the Trumpingtons: "Of course I shan't wait for Lord Canterville to speak to me."

He had been expecting some such announcement as this from Lady Beauchemin and really judged her father would do no more than his duty. He felt he should be prepared with an answer to the high challenge so prefigured, and he wondered at himself for still not having come to the point. Sidney Feeder's question in the Park had made him feel rather pointless; it was the first direct allusion as yet made to his possible marriage by any one but Lady Beauchemin. None of his own people were in London; he was perfectly independent, and even if his mother had been within reach he couldn't quite have consulted her on the subject. He loved her dearly, better than any one; but she wasn't a woman to consult, for she approved of whatever he did: the fact of his doing it settled the case for it. He had been careful not to be too serious when he talked with Lady Barb's relative; but he was very serious indeed as he thought over the matter within himself, which he did even among the diversions of the next half-hour, while he squeezed, obliquely and with tight arrests, through the crush in the Trumpingtons' drawing-room. At the end of the half-hour he came away, and at the door he found Lady Beauchemin, from whom he had separated on entering the house and who, this time with a companion of her own sex, was awaiting her carriage and still "going on." He gave her his arm to the street, and as she entered the vehicle she repeated that she hoped he'd just go out of town.

"Who then would tell me what to do?" he returned, looking at her through the window.

She might tell him what to do, but he felt free all the same; and he was determined this should continue. To prove it to himself he jumped into a hansom and drove back to Brook Street and to his hotel instead of proceeding to a bright-windowed house in Portland Place where he knew he should after midnight find Lady Canterville and her daughters. He recalled a reference to that chance during his ride with Lady Barb, who would probably expect him; but it made him taste his liberty not to go, and he liked to taste his liberty. He was aware that to taste it in perfection he ought to "turn in"; but he didn't turn in, he didn't even take off his hat. He walked up and down his sitting-room with his head surmounted by this ornament, a good deal tipped back, and with his hands in his pockets. There were various cards stuck into the frame of the mirror over his chimney-piece, and every time he passed the place he seemed to see what was written on one of them—the name of the mistress of the house in Portland Place, his own name and in the lower left-hand corner "A small Dance." Of course, now, he must make up his mind; he'd make it up by the next day: that was what he said to himself as he walked up and down; and according to his decision he'd speak to Lord Canterville or would take the night-express to Paris. It was better meanwhile he shouldn't see Lady Barb. It was vivid to him, as he occasionally paused with fevered eyes on the card in the chimney-glass, that he had come pretty far; and he had come so far because he was under the spell—yes, he was under the spell, or whatever it was, of Lady Barb. There was no doubt whatever of this; he had a faculty for diagnosis and he knew perfectly what was the matter with him. He wasted no time in musing on the mystery of his state; in wondering if he mightn't have escaped such a seizure by a little vigilance at first, or if it would abate should he go away. He accepted it frankly for the sake of the pleasure it gave him—the girl was the delight of most of his senses—and confined himself to considering how it would square with his general situation to marry her. The squaring wouldn't at all necessarily follow from the fact that he was in love; too many other things would come in between. The most important of these was the change not only of the geographical but of the social standpoint for his wife, and a certain readjustment that it would involve in his own relation to things. He wasn't inclined to readjustments, and there was no reason why he should be: his own position was in most respects so advantageous. But the girl tempted him almost irresistibly, satisfying his imagination both as a lover and as a student of the human organism; she was so blooming, so complete, of a type so rarely encountered in that degree of perfection. Jackson Lemon was no Anglomaniac, but he took peculiar pleasure in certain physical facts of the English—their complexion, their temperament, their tissue; and Lady Barb had affected him from the first as in flexible virginal form a wonderful compendium of these elements. There was something simple and robust in her beauty; it had the quietness of an old Greek statue, without the vulgarity

51

of the modern simper or of contemporary prettiness. Her head was antique, and though her conversation was quite of the present period Jackson told himself that some primitive sincerity of soul couldn't but match with the cast of her brow, of her bosom, of the back of her neck, and with the high carriage of her head, which was at once so noble and so easy. He saw her as she might be in the future, the beautiful mother of beautiful children in whom the appearance of "race" should be conspicuous. He should like his children to have the appearance of race as well as other signs of good stuff, and wasn't unaware that he must take his precautions accordingly. A great many people in England had these indications, and it was a pleasure to him to see them, especially as no one had them so unmistakably as the second daughter of the Cantervilles. It would be a great luxury to call a creature so constituted one's own; nothing could be more evident than that, because it made no difference that she wasn't strikingly clever. Striking cleverness wasn't one of the signs, nor a mark of the English complexion in general; it was associated with the modern simper, which was a result of modern nerves. If Jackson had wanted a wife all fiddlestrings of course he could have found her at home; but this tall fair girl, whose character, like her figure, appeared mainly to have been formed by riding across country, was differently put together. All the same would it suit his book, as they said in London, to marry her and transport her to New York? He came back to this question; came back to it with a persistency which, had she been admitted to a view of it, would have tried the patience of Lady Beauchemin. She had been irritated more than once at his appearing to attach himself so exclusively to that horn of the dilemma—as if it could possibly fail to be a good thing for a little American doctor to marry the daughter of an English peer. It would have been more becoming in her ladyship's eyes that he should take this for granted a little more and take the consent of her ladyship's—of their ladyships'—family a little less. They looked at the matter so differently! Jackson Lemon was conscious that if he should propose for the young woman who so strongly appealed to him it would be because it suited him, and not because it suited his possible sisters-in-law. He believed himself to act in all things by his own faculty of choice and volition, a feature of his outfit in which he had the highest confidence.

It would have seemed, indeed, that just now this part of his inward machine was not working very regularly, since, though he had come home to go to bed, the stroke of half-past twelve saw him jump not into his sheets but into a hansom which the whistle of the porter had summoned to the door of his hotel and in which he rattled off to Portland Place. Here he found—in a very large house—an assembly of five hundred persons and a band of music concealed in a bower of azaleas. Lady Canterville had not arrived; he wandered through the rooms and assured himself of that. He also discovered a very good conservatory, where there were banks and pyramids of azaleas. He watched the top of the staircase, but it was a long time before he saw what he was looking for, and his impatience grew at last extreme. The reward, however, when it came, was all he could have desired. It consisted of a clear smile from Lady Barb, who stood behind her mother while the latter extended vague finger-tips to the hostess. The entrance of this charming woman and her beautiful daughters—always a noticeable incident—was effected with a certain spread of commotion, and just now it was agreeable to Jackson to feel this produced impression concern him probably more than any one else in the house. Tall, dazzling, indifferent, looking about her as if she saw very little, Lady Barb was certainly a figure round which a young man's fancy might revolve. Very rare, yet very quiet and very simple, she had little manner and little movement; but her detachment was not a vulgar art. She appeared to efface herself, to wait till, in the natural course, she should be attended to; and in this there was evidently no exaggeration, for she was too proud not to have perfect confidence. Her sister, quite another affair, with a little surprised smile which seemed to say that in her extreme innocence she was still prepared for anything, having heard, indirectly, such extraordinary things about society, was much more impatient and more expressive, and had always projected across a threshold the pretty radiance of her eyes and teeth before her mother's name was announced. Lady Canterville was by many persons more admired and more championed than her daughters; she had kept even more beauty than she had given them, and it was a beauty which had been called intellectual. She had extraordinary sweetness, without any definite professions; her manner was mild almost to tenderness; there was even in it a degree of thoughtful pity, of human comprehension. Moreover her features were perfect, and nothing could be more gently gracious than a way she had of speaking, or rather of listening, to people with her head inclined a little to one side. Jackson liked her without trepidation, and she had certainly been "awfully nice" to him. He approached Lady Barb as soon as he could do so without an appearance of rushing up; he remarked to her that he hoped very much she wouldn't dance. He was a master of the art which flourishes in New York above every other, and had guided her through a dozen waltzes with a skill which, as she felt, left absolutely nothing to be desired. But dancing was not his business to-night. She smiled without scorn at the expression of his hope.

"That's what mamma has brought us here for," she said; "she doesn't like it if we don't dance."

"How does she know whether she likes it or not? You always have danced."

"Oh, once there was a place where I didn't," said Lady Barb.

He told her he would at any rate settle it with her mother, and persuaded her to wander with him into the conservatory, where coloured lights were suspended among the plants and a vault of verdure arched above. In comparison with the other rooms this retreat was far and strange. But they were not alone; half a-dozen other couples appeared to have had reasons as good as theirs. The gloom, none the less, was rosy with the slopes of azalea and suffused with mitigated music, which made it possible to talk without consideration of one's neighbours. In spite of this, though it was only in looking back on the scene later that Lady Barb noted the fact, these dispersed couples were talking very softly. She didn't look at them; she seemed to take it that virtually she was alone with the young American. She said something about the flowers, about the fragrance of the air; for all answer to which he asked her, as he stood there before her, a question that might have startled her by its suddenness.

"How do people who marry in England ever know each other before marriage? They have no chance."

"I'm sure I don't know," she returned. "I never was married."

"It's very different in my country. There a man may see much of a girl; he may freely call on her, he may be constantly alone with her. I wish you allowed that over here."

Lady Barb began to examine the less ornamental side of her fan as if it had never invited her before. "It must be so very odd, America," she then concluded.

"Well, I guess in that matter we're right. Over here it's a leap in the dark."

"I'm sure I don't know," she again made answer. She had folded her fan; she stretched out her arm mechanically and plucked a sprig of azalea.

"I guess it doesn't signify after all," Jackson however proceeded. "Don't you know they say that love's blind at the best?" His keen young face was bent upon hers; his thumbs were in the pockets of his trousers; he smiled with a slight strain, showing his fine teeth. She said nothing, only pulling her azalea to pieces. She was usually so quiet that this small movement was striking.

"This is the first time I've seen you in the least without a lot of people," he went on.

"Yes, it's very tiresome."

"I've been sick of it. I didn't want even to come here to-night."

She hadn't met his eyes, though she knew they were seeking her own. But now she looked at him straight. She had never objected to his appearance, and in this respect had no repugnance to surmount. She liked a man to be tall and handsome, and Jackson Lemon was neither; but when she was sixteen, and as tall herself as she was to be at twenty, she had been in love—for three weeks—with one of her cousins, a little fellow in the Hussars, who was shorter even than the American, was of inches markedly fewer than her own. This proved that distinction might be independent of stature—not that she had ever reasoned it out. Doctor Lemon's facial spareness and his bright ocular attention, which had a fine edge and a marked scale, unfolded and applied rule-fashion, affected her as original, and she thought of them as rather formidable to a good many people, which would do very well in a husband of hers. As she made this reflexion it of course never occurred to her that she herself might suffer true measurement, for she was not a sacrificial lamb. She felt sure his features expressed a mind—a mind immensely useful, like a good hack or whatever, and that he knew how to employ. She would never have supposed him a doctor; though indeed when all was said this was very negative and didn't account for the way he imposed himself.

"Why, then, did you come?" she asked in answer to his last speech.

"Because it seems to me after all better to see you this way than not to see you at all. I want to know you better."

"I don't think I ought to stay here," she said as she looked round her.

"Don't go till I've told you I love you," the young man distinctly replied.

She made no exclamation, indulged in no start; he couldn't see even that she changed colour. She took his request with a noble simplicity, her head erect and her eyes lowered. "I don't think you've quite a right to tell me that."

"Why not?" Jackson demanded. "I want to claim the right. I want you to give it to me."

"I can't—I don't know you. You've said that yourself."

"Can't you have a little faith?" he at once asked, speaking as fast as if he were not even a little afraid to urge the pace. "That will help us to know each other better. It's disgusting, the want of opportunity; even at Pasterns I could scarcely get a walk with you. But I've the most absolute trust of you. I *know* I love you, and I couldn't do more than that at the end of six months. I love your beauty, I love your nature, I love you from head to foot. Don't move, please don't move." He lowered his tone now, but it went straight to her ear and we must believe conveyed a certain eloquence. For himself, after he had heard himself say these words, all his being was in a glow. It was a luxury to speak to her of her beauty; it brought him nearer to her than he had ever been. But the colour had come into her face and seemed to remind him that her beauty wasn't all. "Everything about you is true and sweet and grand," he went on; "everything's dear to me. I'm sure you're good. I don't know what you think of me; I asked Lady Beauchemin to tell me, and she told me to judge for myself. Well, then, I judge you like me. Haven't I a right to assume that till the contrary's proved? May I speak to your father? That's what I want to know. I've been waiting, but now what should I wait for longer? I want to be able to tell him you've given me hope. I suppose I ought to speak to him first. I meant to, to-morrow, but meanwhile, to-night, I thought I'd just put this in. In my country it wouldn't matter particularly. You must see all that over there for yourself. If you should tell me not to speak to your father I wouldn't—I'd wait. But I like better to ask your leave to speak to him than ask his to speak to you."

His voice had sunk almost to a whisper, but, though it trembled, the fact of his pleading gave it intensity. He had the same attitude, his thumbs in his trousers, his neat attentive young head, his smile, which was a matter of course; no one would have imagined what he was saying. She had listened without moving and at the end she raised her eyes. They rested on his own a moment, and he remembered for a long time the look, the clear effluence of splendid maidenhood, as deep as a surrender, that passed her lids.

Disconcertingly, however, there was no surrender in what she answered. "You may say anything you please to my father, but I don't wish to hear any more. You've said too much, considering how little idea you've given me before."

"I was watching you," said Jackson Lemon.

She held her head higher, still looking straight at him. Then quite seriously, "I don't like to be watched," she returned.

"You shouldn't be so beautiful then. Won't you give me a word of hope?"

"I've never supposed I should marry a foreigner," said Lady Barb.

"Do you call me a foreigner?"

"I think your ideas are very different and your country different. You've told me so yourself."

"I should like to show it to you. I would make you like it."

"I'm not sure what you'd make me do," she went on very honestly.

"Nothing you don't want."

"I'm sure you'd try," she smiled as for more accommodation.

"Well," said Jackson Lemon, "I'm after all trying now."

To this she returned that she must go to her mother, and he was obliged to lead her out of the place. Lady Canterville was not immediately found, so that he had time to keep it up a little as they went. "Now that I've spoken I'm very happy."

"Perhaps you're happy too soon."

"Ah, don't say that, Lady Barb," he tenderly groaned.

"Of course I must think of it."

"Of course you must!" Jackson abundantly concurred. "I'll speak to your father to-morrow."

"I can't fancy what he'll say."

"How can he dislike me? But I guess he doesn't!" the young man cried in a tone which Lady Beauchemin, had she heard him, would have felt connected with his general retreat upon the quaint. What Lady Beauchemin's sister thought of it is not recorded; but there is perhaps a clue to her opinion in the answer she made him after a moment's silence: "Really, you know, you *are* a foreigner!" With this she turned her back, for she was already in her mother's hands. Jackson Lemon said a few words to Lady Canterville; they were chiefly about its being very hot. She gave him her vague sweet attention, as if he were saying something ingenious but of which she missed the point. He could see she was thinking of the ways of her daughter Agatha, whose attitude toward the contemporary young man was wanting in the perception of differences—a madness too much without method; she was evidently not occupied with Lady Barb, who was more to be depended on. This young woman never met her suitor's eyes again; she let her own rest rather ostentatiously on other objects. At last he was going away without a glance from her. Her mother had asked him to luncheon for the morrow, and he had said he would come if she would promise him he should see his lordship. "I can't pay you another visit till I've had some talk with him."

"I don't see why not, but if I speak to him I daresay he will be at home," she returned.

"It will be worth his while!" At this he almost committed himself; and he left the house reflecting that as he had never proposed to a girl before he couldn't be expected to know how women demean themselves in this emergency. He had heard indeed that Lady Barb had had no end of offers; and though he supposed the number probably overstated, as it always is, he had to infer that her way of appearing suddenly to have dropped him was but the usual behaviour for the occasion.

III

At her mother's the next day she was absent from luncheon, and Lady Canterville mentioned to him—he didn't ask—that she had gone to see a dear old great-aunt who was also her godmother and who lived at Roehampton. Lord Canterville was not present, but Jackson learned from his hostess that he had promised her he would come in exactly at three o'clock. Our young man lunched with her ladyship and the children, who appeared in force at this repast, all the younger girls being present, and two little boys, the juniors of the two sons who were in their teens. Doctor Lemon, who was fond of children and thought these absolutely the finest in the world—magnificent specimens of a magnificent brood, such as it would be so satisfactory in future days to see about his own knee—Doctor Lemon felt himself treated as one of the family, but was not frightened by what he read into the privilege of his admission. Lady Canterville showed no sense whatever of his having mooted the question of becoming her son-in-law, and he believed the absent object of his attentions hadn't told her of their evening's talk. This idea gave him pleasure; he liked to think Lady Barb was judging him for herself. Perhaps indeed she was taking counsel of the old lady at Roehampton: he saw himself the sort of lover of whom a godmother would approve. Godmothers, in his mind, were mainly associated with fairy-tales—he had had no baptismal sponsors of his own; and that point of view would be favourable to a young man with a great deal of gold who had suddenly arrived from a foreign country—an apparition surely in a proper degree elfish. He made up his mind he should like Lady Canterville as a mother-in-law; she would be too well-bred to meddle. Her husband came in at three o'clock, just after they had risen, and observed that it was very good in him to have waited.

"I haven't waited," Jackson replied with his watch in his hand; "you're punctual to the minute."

I know not how Lord Canterville may have judged his young friend, but Jackson Lemon had been told more than once in his life that he would have been all right if he hadn't been so literal. After he had lighted a cigarette in his lordship's "den," a large brown apartment on the ground-floor, which partook at once of the nature of an office and of that of a harness-room—it couldn't have been called in any degree a library or even a study—he went straight to the point in these terms: "Well now, Lord Canterville, I feel I ought to let you know without more delay that I'm in love with Lady Barb and that I should like to make her my wife." So he spoke, puffing his cigarette, with his conscious but unextenuating eyes fixed on his host.

No man, as I have intimated, bore better being looked at than this noble personage; he seemed to bloom in the envious warmth of human contemplation and never appeared so faultless as when most exposed. "My dear fellow, my dear fellow," he murmured almost in disparagement, stroking his ambrosial beard from before the empty fireplace. He lifted his eyebrows, but looked perfectly good-natured.

"Are you surprised, sir?" Jackson asked.

"Why I suppose a fellow's surprised at any one's wanting one of his children. He sometimes feels the weight of that sort of thing so much, you know. He wonders what use on earth another man can make of them." And Lord Canterville laughed pleasantly through the copious fringe of his lips.

"I only want one of them," said his guest, laughing too, but with a lighter organ.

"Polygamy would be rather good for the parents. However, Luke told me the other night she knew you to be looking the way you speak of."

"Yes, I mentioned to Lady Beauchemin that I love Lady Barb, and she seemed to think it natural."

"Oh I suppose there's no want of nature in it! But, my dear fellow, I really don't know what to say," his lordship added.

"Of course you'll have to think of it." In saying which Jackson felt himself make the most liberal concession to the point of view of his interlocutor; being perfectly aware that in his own country it wasn't left much to the parents to think of.

"I shall have to talk it over with my wife."

"Well, Lady Canterville has been very kind to me; I hope she'll continue."

Lord Canterville passed a large fair hand, as for inspiration, over his beard. "My dear fellow, we're excellent friends. No one could appreciate you more than Lady Canterville. Of course we can only consider such a question on the—a—the highest grounds. You'd never want to marry without knowing—as it were—exactly what you're doing. I, on my side, naturally, you know, am bound to do the best I can for my own poor child. At the same time, of course, we don't want to spend our time in—a—walking round the horse. We want to get at the truth about him." It was settled between them after a little that the truth about Lemon's business was that he knew to a certainty the state of his affections and was in a position to pretend to the hand of a young lady who, Lord Canterville might say without undue swagger, had a right to expect to do as well as any girl about the place.

"I should think she had," Doctor Lemon said. "She's a very rare type."

His entertainer had a pleasant blank look. "She's a clever well-grown girl and she takes her fences like a grasshopper. Does she know all this, by the way?"

"Oh yes, I told her last night."

Again Lord Canterville had the air, unusual with him, of sounding, at some expense of precious moments, the expression of face of a visitor so unacquainted with shyness. "I'm not sure you ought to have done that, you know."

"I couldn't have spoken to you first—I couldn't," said Jackson Lemon. "I meant to; but it stuck in my crop."

"They don't in your country, I guess," his lordship amicably laughed.

"Well, not as a general thing. However, I find it very pleasant to have the whole thing out with you now." And in truth it was very pleasant. Nothing could be easier, friendlier, more informal, than Lord Canterville's manner, which implied all sorts of equality, especially that of age and fortune, and made our young man feel at the end of three minutes almost as if he too were a beautifully-preserved and somewhat straitened nobleman of sixty, with the views of a man of the world about his own marriage. Jackson perceived that Lord Canterville waived the point of his having spoken first to the girl herself, and saw in this indulgence a just concession to the ardour of young affection. For his lordship seemed perfectly to appreciate the sentimental side—at least so far as it was embodied in his visitor—when he said without deprecation: "Did she give you any encouragement?"

"Well, she didn't box my ears. She told me she'd think of it, but that I must speak to you. Naturally, however, I shouldn't have said what I did if I hadn't made up my mind during the last fortnight that I'm not disagreeable to her."

"Ah, my dear young man, women are odd fish!" this parent exclaimed rather unexpectedly. "But of course you know all that," he added in an instant; "you take the general risk."

"I'm perfectly willing to take the general risk. The particular risk strikes me as small."

"Well, upon my honour I don't really know my girls. You see a man's time in England is tremendously taken up; but I daresay it's the same in your country. Their mother knows them—I think I had better send for their mother. If you don't mind," Lord Canterville wound up, "I'll just suggest that she join us here."

"I'm rather afraid of you both together, but if it will settle it any quicker—!" Jackson said. His companion rang the bell and, when a servant appeared, despatched him with a message to her ladyship. While they were waiting the young man remembered how easily he could give a more definite account of his pecuniary basis. He had simply stated before that he was abundantly able to marry; he shrank from putting himself forward as a monster of money. With his excellent taste he wished to appeal to Lord Canterville primarily as a gentleman. But now that he had to make a double impression he bethought himself of his millions, for millions were always impressive. "It strikes me as only fair to let you know that my fortune's really considerable."

"Yes, I daresay you're beastly rich," said Lord Canterville with a natural and visible faith.

"Well, I represent, all told, some seven millions."

"Seven millions?"

"I count in dollars. Upwards of a million and a half sterling."

Lord Canterville looked at him from head to foot, exhaling with great promptitude an air of cheerful resignation to a form of grossness threatening to become common. Then he said with a touch of that inconsequence of which he had already given a glimpse: "What the deuce in that case possessed you to turn doctor?"

Jackson Lemon coloured a little and demurred, but bethought himself of his best of reasons. "Why, my having simply the talent for it."

"Of course I don't for a moment doubt your ability. But don't you," his lordship candidly asked, "find it rather a bore?"

"I don't practise much. I'm rather ashamed to say that."

"Ah well, of course in your country it's different. I daresay you've got a door-plate, eh?"

"Oh yes, and a tin sign tied to the balcony!" Jackson laughed.

Here the joke was beyond his friend, who but went on: "What on earth did your father say to it?"

"To my going into medicine? He said he'd be hanged if he'd take any of my doses. He didn't think I should succeed; he wanted me to go into the house."

"Into the House—a—?" Lord Canterville just wondered. "That would be into your Congress?"

"Ah no, not so bad as that. Into the store," Jackson returned with that refinement of the ingenuous which he reserved for extreme cases.

His host stared, not venturing even for the moment to hazard an interpretation; and before a solution had presented itself Lady Canterville was on the scene.

"My dear, I thought we had better see you. Do you know he wants to marry our second girl?" It was in these simple and lucid terms that her husband acquainted her with the question.

She expressed neither surprise nor elation; she simply stood there smiling, her head a little inclined to the side and her beautiful benevolence well to the front. Her charming eyes rested on Doctor Lemon's; and, though they showed a shade of anxiety for a matter of such importance, his own discovered in them none of the coldness of calculation. "Are you talking about dear Barb?" she asked in a moment and as if her thoughts had been far away.

Of course they were talking about dear Barb, and Jackson repeated to her what he had said to her noble spouse. He had thought it all over and his mind was quite made up. Moreover, he had spoken to the young woman.

"Did she tell you that, my dear?" his lordship asked while he lighted another cigar.

64

She gave no heed to this inquiry, which had been vague and accidental on the speaker's part; she simply remarked to their visitor that the thing was very serious and that they had better sit down a moment. In an instant he was near her on the sofa on which she had placed herself and whence she still smiled up at her husband with her air of luxurious patience.

"Barb has told me nothing," she dropped, however, after a little.

"That proves how much she cares for me!" Jackson declared with instant lucidity.

Lady Canterville looked as if she thought this really too ingenious, almost as professional as if their talk were a consultation; but her husband went, all gaily, straighter to the point. "Ah well, if she cares for you I don't object."

This was a little ambiguous; but before the young man had time to look into it his hostess put a bland question. "Should you expect her to live in America?"

"Oh yes. That's my home, you know."

"Shouldn't you be living sometimes in England?"

"Oh yes—we'll come over and see you." He was in love, he wanted to marry, he wanted to be genial and to commend himself to the family; yet it was in his nature not to accept conditions save in so far as they met his taste, not to tie himself or, as they said in New York, give himself away. He preferred in any transaction his own terms to those of any one else, so that the moment Lady Canterville gave signs of wishing to extract a promise he was on his guard.

"She'll find it very different; perhaps she won't like it," her ladyship suggested.

"If she likes me she'll like my country," Jackson Lemon returned with decision.

"He tells me he has a plate on his door," Lord Canterville put in for the right pleasant tone.

"We must talk to her of course; we must understand how she feels"— and his wife looked, though still gracious, more nobly responsible.

"Please don't discourage her, Lady Canterville," Jackson firmly said; "and give me a chance to talk to her a little more myself. You haven't given me much chance, you know."

"We don't offer our daughters to people, however amiable, Mr. Lemon." Her charming grand manner rather quickened.

"She isn't like some women in London, you know," Lord Canterville helpfully explained; "you see we rather stave off the evil day: we like to be together." And Jackson certainly, if the idea had been presented to him, would have said that No, decidedly, Lady Barb hadn't been thrown at him.

"Of course not," he declared in answer to her mother's remark. "But you know you mustn't decline overtures too much either; you mustn't make a poor fellow wait too long. I admire her, I love her, more than I can say; I give you my word of honour for that."

"He seems to think that settles it," said Lord Canterville, shining richly down at the young American from his place before the cold chimney-piece.

"Certainly that's what we desire, Philip," her ladyship returned with an equal grace.

"Lady Barb believes it; I'm sure she does!" Jackson exclaimed with spirit. "Why should I pretend to be in love with her if I'm not?"

Lady Canterville received this appeal in silence, and her husband, with just the least air in the world of repressed impatience, began to walk up and down the room. He was a man of many engagements, and he had been closeted for more than a quarter of an hour with the young American doctor. "Do you imagine you should come often to England?" Lady Canterville asked as if to think of everything.

"I'm afraid I can't tell you that; of course we shall do whatever seems best." He was prepared to suppose they should cross the Atlantic every summer—that prospect was by no means displeasing to him; but he wasn't prepared to tie himself, as he would have said, up to it, nor up to anything in particular. It was in his mind not as an overt pretension but as a tacit implication that he should treat with the parents of his presumed bride on a footing of perfect equality; and there would somehow be nothing equal if he should begin to enter into engagements that didn't belong to the essence of the matter. They were to give their daughter and he was to take her: in this arrangement there would be as much on one side as on the other. But beyond it he had nothing to ask of them; there was nothing he was calling on them to promise, and his own pledges therefore would have no equivalent. Whenever his wife should wish it she should come over and see her people. Her home was to be in New York; but he was tacitly conscious that on the question of absences he should be very liberal, and there was meanwhile something in the very grain of his character that forbade he should be eagerly yielding about times and dates.

Lady Canterville looked at her spouse, but he was now not attentive; he was taking a peep at his watch. In a moment, however, he threw out a remark to the effect that he thought it a capital thing the two countries should become more united, and there was nothing that would bring it about better than a few of the best people on both sides pairing-off together. The English indeed had begun it; a lot of fellows had brought over a lot of pretty girls, and it was quite fair play that the Americans should take their pick. They were all one race, after all; and why shouldn't they make one society—the best of both sides, of course? Jackson Lemon smiled as he recognised Lady Marmaduke's great doctrine, and he was pleased to think Lady Beauchemin had some influence with her father; for he was sure the great old boy, as he mentally designated his host, had got all this from her, though he expressed himself less happily than the cleverest of his daughters. Our hero had no objection to make to it, especially if there were aught in it that would really help his case. But it was not in the least on these high grounds he had sought the hand of Lady Barb. He wanted her not in order that her people and his—the best on both sides!—should make one society; he wanted her simply because he wanted her. Lady Canterville smiled, but she seemed to have another thought.

"I quite appreciate what my husband says, but I don't see why poor Barb should be the one to begin."

"I daresay she'll like it," said his lordship as if he were attempting a short cut. "They say you spoil your women awfully."

"She's not one of their women yet," Lady Canterville remarked in the sweetest tone in the world; and then she added without Jackson Lemon's knowing exactly what she meant: "It seems so strange."

He was slightly irritated, and these vague words perhaps added to the feeling. There had been no positive opposition to his suit, and both his entertainers were most kind; but he felt them hold back a little, and though he hadn't expected them to throw themselves on his neck he was rather disappointed—his pride was touched. Why should they hesitate? He knew himself such a good *parti*. It was not so much his noble host—it was Lady Canterville. As he saw her lord and master look covertly and a second time at his watch he could have believed him glad to settle the matter on the spot. Lady Canterville seemed to wish their aspirant to come forward more, to give certain assurances and pledges. He felt he was ready to say or do anything that was a matter of proper form, but he couldn't take the tone of trying to purchase her ladyship's assent, penetrated as he was with the conviction that such a man as he could be trusted to care for his wife rather more than an impecunious British peer and *his* wife could be supposed—with the lights he had acquired on English society—to care even for the handsomest of a dozen children. It was a mistake on the old lady's part not to recognise that. He humoured this to the extent of saying just a little dryly: "My wife shall certainly have everything she wants."

"He tells me he's disgustingly rich," Lord Canterville added, pausing before their companion with his hands in his pockets.

"I'm glad to hear it; but it isn't so much that," she made answer, sinking back a little on her sofa. If it wasn't that she didn't say what it was, though she had looked for a moment as if she were going to. She only raised her eyes to her husband's face, she asked for inspiration. I know not whether she found it, but in a moment she said to Jackson Lemon, seeming to imply that it was quite another point: "Do you expect to continue your profession?"

He had no such intention, so far as his profession meant getting up at three o'clock in the morning to assuage the ills of humanity; but here, as before, the touch of such a question instantly stiffened him. "Oh, my profession! I rather wince at that grand old name. I've neglected my work so scandalously that I scarce know on what terms with it I shall be—though hoping for the best when once I'm right there again."

Lady Canterville received these remarks in silence, fixing her eyes once more upon her husband's. But his countenance really rather failed her; still with his hands in his pockets, save when he needed to remove his cigar from his lips, he went and looked out of the window. "Of course we know you don't practise, and when you're a married man you'll have less time even than now. But I should really like to know if they call you Doctor over there."

"Oh yes, universally. We're almost as fond of titles as your people."

"I don't call that a title," her ladyship smiled.

"It's not so good as duke or marquis, I admit; but we have to take what we've got."

"Oh bother, what does it signify?" his lordship demanded from his place at the window. "I used to have a horse named Doctor, and a jolly good one too."

"Don't you call bishops Doctors? Well, then, call me Bishop!" Jackson laughed.

Lady Canterville visibly didn't follow. "I don't care for *any* titles," she nevertheless observed. "I don't see why a gentleman shouldn't be called Mr."

It suddenly appeared to her young friend that there was something helpless, confused and even slightly comical in her state. The impression was mollifying, and he too, like Lord Canterville, had begun to long for a short cut. He relaxed a moment and, leaning toward his hostess with a smile and his hands on his little knees, he said softly: "It seems to me a question of no importance. All I desire is that you should call me your son-in-law."

69

She gave him her hand and he pressed it almost affectionately. Then she got up, remarking that before anything was decided she must see her child, must learn from her own lips the state of her feelings. "I don't like at all her not having spoken to me already," she added.

"Where has she gone—to Roehampton? I daresay she has told it all to her godmother," said Lord Canterville.

"She won't have much to tell, poor girl!" Jackson freely commented. "I must really insist on seeing with more freedom the person I wish to marry."

"You shall have all the freedom you want in two or three days," said Lady Canterville. She irradiated all her charity; she appeared to have accepted him and yet still to be making tacit assumptions. "Aren't there certain things to be talked of first?"

"Certain things, dear lady?"

She looked at her husband, and though he was still at his window he felt it this time in her silence and had to come away and speak. "Oh she means settlements and that kind of thing." This was an allusion that came with a much better grace from the father.

Jackson turned from one of his companions to the other; he coloured a little and his self-control was perhaps a trifle strained. "Settlements? We don't make them in my country. You may be sure I shall make a proper provision for my wife."

"My dear fellow, over here—in our class, you know—it's the custom," said Lord Canterville with a truer ease in his face at the thought that the discussion was over.

"I've my own ideas," Jackson returned with even greater confidence.

"It seems to me it's a question for the solicitors to discuss," Lady Canterville suggested.

"They may discuss it as much as they please"—the young man showed amusement. He thought he saw his solicitors discussing it! He had indeed his own ideas. He opened the door for his hostess and the three passed out of the room together, walking into the hall in a silence that expressed a considerable awkwardness. A note had been struck which grated and scratched a little. A pair of shining footmen, at their approach, rose from a bench to a great altitude and stood there like sentinels presenting arms. Jackson stopped, looking for a moment into the interior of his hat, which he had in his hand. Then raising his keen eyes he fixed them a moment on those of Lady Canterville, addressing her instinctively rather than his other critic. "I guess you and Lord Canterville had better leave it to me!"

"We have our traditions, Mr. Lemon," said her ladyship with a firm grace. "I imagine you don't know—!" she gravely breathed.

Lord Canterville laid his hand on their visitor's shoulder. "My dear boy, those fellows will settle it in three minutes."

"Very likely they will!" said Jackson Lemon. Then he asked of Lady Canterville when he might see Lady Barb.

She turned it spaciously over. "I'll write you a note."

One of the tall footmen at the end of the impressive vista had opened wide the portals, as if even he were aware of the dignity to which the small strange gentleman had virtually been raised. But Jackson lingered; he was visibly unsatisfied, though apparently so little conscious he was unsatisfying. "I don't think you understand me."

"Your ideas are certainly different," said Lady Canterville.

His lordship, however, made comparatively light of it. "If the girl understands you that's enough!"

"Mayn't *she* write to me?" Jackson asked of her mother. "I certainly must write to her, you know, if you won't let me see her.".

"Oh yes, you may write to her, Mr. Lemon."

There was a point, for a moment, in the look he returned on this, while he said to himself that if necessary he would transmit his appeal through the old lady at Roehampton. "All right—good-bye. You know what I want at any rate." Then as he was going he turned and added: "You needn't be afraid I won't always bring her over in the hot weather!"

"In the hot weather?" Lady Canterville murmured with vague visions of the torrid zone. Jackson however quitted the house with the sense he had made great concessions.

His host and hostess passed into a small morning-room and—Lord Canterville having taken up his hat and stick to go out again—stood there a moment, face to face. Then his lordship spoke in a summary manner. "It's clear enough he wants her."

"There's something so odd about him," Lady Canterville answered. "Fancy his speaking so about settlements!"

"You had better give him his head. He'll go much quieter."

"He's so obstinate—very obstinate; it's easy to see that. And he seems to think," she went on, "that a girl in your daughter's position can be married from one day to the other—with a ring and a new frock—like a housemaid."

"Well that, of course, over there is the kind of thing. But he seems really to have a most extraordinary fortune, and every one does say they give their women *carte blanche*."

"*Carte blanche* is not what Barb wants; she wants a settlement. She wants a definite income," said Lady Canterville; "she wants to be safe."

He looked at her rather straight. "Has she told you so? I thought you said—" And then he stopped. "I beg your pardon," he added.

She didn't explain her inconsequence; she only remarked that American fortunes were notoriously insecure; one heard of nothing else; they melted away like smoke. It was their own duty to their child to demand that something should be fixed.

Well, he met this in his way. "He has a million and a half sterling. I can't make out what he does with it."

She rose to it without a flutter. "Our child should have, then, something very handsome."

"I agree, my dear; but you must manage it; you must consider it; you must send for Hardman. Only take care you don't put him off; it may be a very good opening, you know. There's a great deal to be done out there; I believe in all that," Lord Canterville went on in the tone of a conscientious parent.

"There's no doubt that he *is* a doctor—in some awful place," his wife brooded.

"He may be a pedlar for all I care."

"If they should go out I think Agatha might go with them," her ladyship continued in the same tone, but a little disconnectedly.

"You may send them all out if you like. Goodbye!"

The pair embraced, but her hand detained him a moment. "Don't you think he's greatly in love?"

"Oh yes, he's very bad—but he's a sharp little beggar."

"She certainly quite likes him," Lady Canterville stated rather formally as they separated.

IV

Jackson Lemon had said to Dr. Feeder in the Park that he would call on Mr. and Mrs. Freer; but three weeks were to elapse before he knocked at their door in Jermyn Street. In the meantime he had met them at dinner and Mrs. Freer had told him how much she hoped he would find time to come and see her. She had not reproached him nor shaken her finger at him, and her clemency, which was calculated and very characteristic of her, touched him so much—for he was in fault, she was one of his mother's oldest and best friends—that he very soon presented himself. It was on a fine Sunday afternoon, rather late, and the region of Jermyn Street looked forsaken and inanimate; the native dulness of the brick scenery reigned undisputed. Mrs. Freer, however, was at home, resting on a lodging-house sofa—an angular couch draped in faded chintz—before she went to dress for dinner. She made the young man very welcome; she told him again how much she had been thinking of him; she had longed so for a chance to talk with him. He immediately guessed what she had in her mind, and he then remembered that Sidney Feeder had named to him what it was this pair took upon themselves to say. This had provoked him at the time, but he had forgotten it afterward; partly because he became aware that same night of his wanting to make the "young marchioness" his own and partly because since then he had suffered much greater annoyance. Yes, the poor young man, so conscious of liberal intentions, of a large way of looking at the future, had had much to irritate and disgust him. He had seen the mistress of his affections but three or four times, and had received a letter from Mr. Hardman, Lord Canterville's solicitor, asking him, in terms the most obsequious it was true, to designate some gentleman of the law with whom the preliminaries of his marriage to Lady Barbarina Clement might be arranged. He had given Mr. Hardman the name of such a functionary, but he had written by the same post to his own solicitor—for whose services in other matters he had had much occasion, Jackson Lemon being distinctly contentious—instructing him that he was at liberty to meet that gentleman, but not at liberty to entertain any proposals as to the odious English idea of a settlement. If marrying Jackson Lemon wasn't settlement enough the house of Canterville had but to alter their point of view. It was quite out of the question he should alter his. It would perhaps be difficult to explain the strong dislike he entertained to the introduction into his prospective union of this harsh diplomatic element; it was as if they mistrusted him and suspected him; as if his hands were to be tied so that he shouldn't be able to handle his own fortune as he thought best. It wasn't the idea of parting with his money that displeased him, for he flattered himself he had plans of expenditure for his wife beyond even the imagination of her distinguished parents. It struck him even that they were fools not to have felt subtly sure they should make a much better thing of it by leaving him perfectly free. This intervention of the solicitor was a nasty little English tradition—totally at variance with the large spirit of American habits—to which he wouldn't submit. It wasn't his way to submit when he disapproved: why should he change his way on this occasion when the matter lay so near him?

These reflexions and a hundred more had flowed freely through his mind for several days before his call in Jermyn Street, and they had engendered a lively indignation and a bitter sense of wrong. They had even introduced, as may be imagined, a certain awkwardness into his relations with the house of Canterville, of which indeed it may be said that these amenities were for the moment virtually suspended. His first interview with Lady Barb after his conference with the old couple, as he called her august elders, had been as frank, had been as sweet, as he could have desired. Lady Canterville had at the end of three days sent him an invitation—five words on a card—asking him to dine with them on the morrow quite *en famille*. This had been the only formal intimation that his engagement to her daughter was recognised; for even at the family banquet, which included half a dozen guests of pleasant address but vague affiliation, there had been no reference on the part either of his host or his hostess to the subject of their converse in Lord Canterville's den. The only allusion was a wandering ray, once or twice, in Lady Barb's own fine eyes. When, however, after dinner, she strolled away with him into the music-room, which was lighted and empty, to play for him something out of "Carmen," of which he had spoken at table, and when the young couple were allowed to enjoy for upwards of an hour, unmolested, the comparative privacy of that elegant refuge, he felt Lady Canterville definitely to count on him. She didn't believe in any serious difficulties. Neither did he then; and that was why it was not to be condoned that there should be a vain appearance of them. The arrangements, he supposed her ladyship would have said, were pending, and indeed they were; for he had already given orders in Bond Street for the setting of an extraordinary number of diamonds. Lady Barb, at any rate, during that hour he spent with her, had had nothing to say about arrangements; and it had been an hour of pure satisfaction. She had seated herself at the piano and had played perpetually, in a soft incoherent manner, while he leaned over the instrument, very close to her, and said everything that came into his head. She was braver and handsomer than ever and looked at him as if she liked him out and out.

This was all he expected of her, for it didn't belong to the cast of her beauty to betray a vulgar infatuation. That beauty was clearly all he had believed it from the first, and with something now thrown in, something ever so touching and stirring, which seemed to stamp her from that moment as his precious possession. He felt more than ever her intimate value and the great social outlay it had taken to produce such a mixture. Simple and girlish as she was, and not particularly quick in the give and take of conversation, she seemed to him to have a part of the history of England in her blood; she was the fine flower of generations of privileged people and of centuries of rich country-life. Between these two of course was no glance at the question which had been put into the hands of Mr. Hardman, and the last thing that occurred to Jackson was that Lady Barb had views as to his settling a fortune upon her before their marriage. It may appear odd, but he hadn't asked himself whether his money operated on her in any degree as a bribe; and this was because, instinctively, he felt such a speculation idle—the point was essentially not to be ascertained—and because he was quite ready to take it for agreeable to her to continue to live in luxury. It was eminently agreeable to him to have means to enable her to do so. He was acquainted with the mingled character of human motives and glad he was rich enough to pretend to the hand of a young woman who, for the best of reasons, would be very expensive. After the good passage in the music-room he had ridden with her twice, but hadn't found her otherwise accessible. She had let him know the second time they rode that Lady Canterville had directed her to make, for the moment, no further appointment with him; and on his presenting himself more than once at the house he had been told that neither the mother nor the daughter was at home: it had been added that Lady Barb was staying at Roehampton. In touching on that restriction she had launched at him just a distinguishable mute reproach—there was always a certain superior dumbness in her eyes—as if he were exposing her to an annoyance she ought to be spared, or taking an eccentric line on a question that all well-bred people treated in the conventional way.

His induction from this was not that she wished to be secure about his money, but that, like a dutiful English daughter, she received her opinions— on points that were indifferent to her—ready-made from a mamma whose fallibility had never been exposed. He knew by this that his solicitor had answered Mr. Hardman's letter and that Lady Canterville's coolness was the fruit of the correspondence. The effect of it was not in the least to make him come round, as he phrased it; he had not the smallest intention of doing that. Lady Canterville had spoken of the traditions of her family; but he had no need to go to his family for his own. They resided within himself; anything he had once undiscussably made up his mind to acquired in three minutes the force, and with that the due dignity of a tradition. Meanwhile he was in the detestable position of not knowing whether or no he were engaged. He wrote to Lady Barb to clear it up, to smooth it down—it being so strange she shouldn't receive him; and she addressed him in return a very pretty little letter, which had to his mind a fine by-gone quality, an old-fashioned, a last-century freshness that might have flowed, a little thinly, from the pen of Clarissa or Sophia. She professed that she didn't in the least understand the situation; that of course she would never give him up; that her mother had said there were the best reasons for their not going too fast; that, thank God, she was yet young and could wait as long as he would; but that she begged he wouldn't write her about money-matters: she had never been able to count even on her fingers. He felt in no danger whatever of making this last mistake; he only noted how Lady Barb thought it natural there should be a discussion; and this made it vivid to him afresh that he had got hold of a daughter of the Crusaders. His ingenious mind could appreciate this hereditary assumption at the very same time that, to light his own footsteps, it remained entirely modern. He believed—or he thought he believed—that in the end he should marry his gorgeous girl on his own terms; but in the interval there was a sensible indignity in being challenged and checked. One effect of it indeed was to make him desire the young woman more intensely. When she wasn't before his eyes in the flesh she hovered before him as an image, and this image had reasons of its own for making him at hours fairly languid with love.

There were moments, however, when he wearied of the mere enshrined memory—it was too impalpable and too thankless. Then it befell that Jackson Lemon for the first time in his life dropped and gave way—gave way, that is, to the sense of sadness. He felt alone in London, and very much out of it, in spite of all the acquaintances he had made and the bills he had paid; he felt the need of a greater intimacy than any he had formed—save of course in the case of Lady Barb. He wanted to vent his disgust, to relieve himself, from the New York point of view. He felt that in engaging in a contest with the great house of Canterville he was after all rather single. That singleness was of course in a great measure an inspiration; but it pinched him hard at moments. Then it would have pleased him could his mother have been near; he used to talk of his affairs a great deal with this delightful parent, who had a delicate way of advising him in the sense he liked best. He had even gone so far as to wish he had never laid eyes on Lady Barb, but had fallen in love instead with some one or other of the rarer home-products. He presently came back of course to the knowledge that in the United States there was—and there could be— nothing nearly so rare as the young lady who had in fact appealed to him so straight, for was it not precisely as a high resultant of the English climate and the British constitution that he valued her? He had relieved himself, from his New York point of view, by speaking his mind to Lady Beauchemin, who confessed that she was infinitely vexed with her parents. She agreed with him that they had made a great mistake; they ought to have left him free; and she expressed her confidence that such freedom could only have been, in him, for her family, like the silence of the sage, golden. He must let them down easily, must remember that what was asked of him had been their custom for centuries. She didn't mention her authority as to the origin of customs, but she promised him she would say three words to her father and mother which would make it all right. Jackson answered that customs were all very well, but that really intelligent people recognised at sight, and then indeed quite enjoyed, the right occasion for departing from them; and with this he awaited the result of Lady Beauchemin's remonstrance. It had not as yet been perceptible, and it must be said that this charming woman was herself not quite at ease.

When on her venturing to hint to her mother that she thought a wrong line had been taken with regard to her sister's *prétendant*, Lady Canterville had replied that Mr. Lemon's unwillingness to settle anything was in itself a proof of what they had feared, the unstable nature of his fortune—since it was useless to talk (this gracious lady could be very decided) as if there could be any serious reason but that one—on meeting this argument, as I say, Jackson's protectress felt considerably baffled. It was perhaps true, as her mother said, that if they didn't insist upon proper pledges Barbarina might be left in a few years with nothing but the stars and stripes—this odd phrase was a quotation from Mr. Lemon—to cover her withal. Lady Beauchemin tried to reason it out with Lady Marmaduke; but these were complications unforeseen by Lady Marmaduke in her project of an Anglo-American society. She was obliged to confess that Mr. Lemon's fortune couldn't have the solidity of long-established things; it was a very new fortune indeed. His father had made the greater part of it all in a lump, a few years before his death, in the extraordinary way in which people made money in America; that of course was why the son had those singular professional attributes. He had begun to study to be a doctor very young, before his expectations were so great. Then he had found he was very clever and very fond of it, and had kept on because after all, in America, where there were no country gentlemen, a young man had to have something to do, don't you know? And Lady Marmaduke, like an enlightened woman, intimated that in such a case she thought it in much better taste not to try to sink anything. "Because in America, don't you see?" she reasoned, "you can't sink it—nothing *will* sink. Everything's floating about—in the newspapers." And she tried to console her friend by remarking that if Mr. Lemon's fortune was precarious it was at all events so big. That was just the trouble for Lady Beauchemin, it was so big and yet they were going to lose it. He was as obstinate as a mule; she was sure he would never come round. Lady Marmaduke declared he really *would* come round; she even offered to bet a dozen pair of *gants de Suède* on it; and she added that this consummation lay quite in the hands of Barbarina. Lady Beauchemin promised herself to contend with her sister, as it was not for nothing she had herself caught the glamour of her friend's international scheme.

Jackson Lemon, to dissipate his chagrin, had returned to the sessions of the medical congress, where, inevitably, he had fallen into the hands of Sidney Feeder, who enjoyed in this disinterested assembly the highest esteem. It was Dr. Feeder's earnest desire that his old friend should share his credit— all the more easily that the medical congress was, as the young physician observed, a perpetual symposium. Jackson entertained the entire body at dinner—entertained it profusely and in a manner befitting one of the patrons of science rather than the humbler votaries; but these dissipations made him forget but for the hour the arrest of his relations with the house of Canterville. It punctually came back to him that he was disconcerted, and Dr. Feeder saw it stamped on his brow. Jackson Lemon, with his acute inclination to open himself, was on the point more than once of taking this sturdy friend into his confidence. His colleague gave him easy occasion—asked him what it was he was thinking of all the time and whether the young marchioness had concluded she couldn't swallow a doctor. These forms of speech were displeasing to our baffled aspirant, whose fastidiousness was nothing new; but he had even deeper reasons for saying to himself that in such complicated cases as his there was no assistance in the Sidney Feeders. To understand his situation one must know the world, and the children of Cincinnati, prohibitively provincial, didn't know the world—at least the world with which this son of New York was now concerned.

"Is there a hitch in your marriage? Just tell me that," Sidney Feeder had said, taking things for granted in a manner that of itself testified to an innocence abysmal. It is true he had added that he supposed he had no business to ask; but he had been anxious about it ever since hearing from Mr. and Mrs. Freer that the British aristocracy was down on the medical profession. "Do they want you to give it up? Is that what the hitch is about? Don't desert your colours, Jackson. The suppression of pain, the mitigation of misery, constitute surely the noblest profession in the world."

"My dear fellow, you don't know what you're talking about," Jackson could only observe in answer to this. "I haven't told any one I was going to be married—still less have I told any one that any one objects to my profession. I should like to see any one do it. I've rather got out of the swim, but I don't regard myself as the sort of person that people object to. And I do expect to do something yet."

"Come home, then, and do it. And don't crush me with grandeur if I say that the facilities for getting married are much greater over there."

"You don't seem to have found them very great," Jackson sniffed.

"I've never had time really to go into them. But wait till my next vacation and you'll see."

"The facilities over there are too great. Nothing's worth while but what's difficult," said Jackson with a sententious ring that quite distressed his mate.

"Well, they've got their backs up, I can see that. I'm glad you like it. Only if they despise your profession what will they say to that of your friends? If they think you're queer what would they think of me?" asked Sidney Feeder, whose spirit was not as a general thing in the least bitter, but who was pushed to this sharpness by a conviction that—in spite of declarations which seemed half an admission and half a denial—his friend was suffering worry, or really perhaps something almost like humiliation, for the sake of a good that might be gathered at home on every bush.

"My dear fellow, all that's 'rot'!" This had been Jackson's retort, which expressed, however, not half his feeling. The other half was inexpressible, or almost, springing as it did from his depth of displeasure at its having struck even so genial a mind as Sidney Feeder's that in proposing to marry a daughter of the highest civilisation he was going out of his way—departing from his natural line. Was he then so ignoble, so pledged to inferior things, that when he saw a girl who—putting aside the fact that she hadn't genius, which was rare, and which, though he prized rarity, he didn't want—seemed to him the most naturally and functionally founded and seated feminine subject he had known, he was to think himself too different, too incongruous, to mate with her? He would mate with whom he "damn pleased"; that was the upshot of Jackson Lemon's passion. Several days elapsed during which everybody—even the pure-minded, like poor Sidney—seemed to him very abject.

All of which is recorded to show how he, in going to see Mrs. Freer, was prepared much less to be angry with people who, like her husband and herself a month before, had given it out that he was engaged to a peer's daughter, than to resent the insinuation that there were obstacles to such a prospect. He sat with the lady of Jermyn Street alone for half an hour in the sabbatical stillness. Her husband had gone for a walk in the Park—he always walked in the Park of a Sunday. All the world might have been there and Jackson and Mrs. Freer in sole possession of the district of Saint James's. This perhaps had something to do with making him at last so confidential; they had such a margin for easy egotism and spreading sympathy. Mrs. Freer was ready for anything—in the critical, the "real" line; she treated him as a person she had known from the age of ten; asked his leave to continue recumbent; talked a great deal about his mother and seemed almost, for a while, to perform the earnest functions of that lady. It had been wise of her from the first not to allude, even indirectly, to his having neglected so long to call; her silence on this point was in the best taste. Jackson had forgotten how it was a habit with her, and indeed a high accomplishment, never to reproach people with these omissions. You might have left her alone for months or years, her greeting was always the same; she never was either too delighted to see you or not delighted enough. After a while, however, he felt her silence to be in some measure an allusion; she appeared to take for granted his devoting all his hours to a certain young lady. It came over him for a moment that his compatriots took a great deal for granted; but when Mrs. Freer, rather abruptly sitting up on her sofa, said to him half-simply, half-solemnly: "And now, my dear Jackson, I want you to tell me something!"—he saw that, after all, she kept within bounds and didn't pretend to know more about his business than he himself did. In the course of a quarter of an hour—so appreciatively she listened—he had given her much information. It was the first time he had said so much to any one, and the process relieved him even more than he would have supposed. There were things it made clear to him by bringing them to a point—above all, the fact that he had been wronged. He made no mention whatever of its being out of the usual way that, as an American doctor, he should sue for the hand of a marquis's daughter; and this reserve was not voluntary, it was quite unconscious. His mind was too full of the sudden rudeness of the Cantervilles and the sordid side of their want of confidence.

He couldn't imagine that while he talked to Mrs. Freer—and it amazed him afterwards that he should have chattered so; he could account for it but by the state of his nerves—she should be thinking only of the strangeness of the situation he sketched for her. She thought Americans as good as other people, but she didn't see where, in American life, the daughter of a marquis

82

would, as she phrased it, work in. To take a simple instance—they coursed through Mrs. Freer's mind with extraordinary speed—wouldn't she always expect to go in to dinner first? As a novelty and for a change, over there, they might like to see her do it—there might be even a pressure for places at the show. But with the increase of every kind of sophistication that was taking place in America the humorous view to which she would owe her immediate ease mightn't continue to be taken; and then where would poor Lady Barb be? This was in truth a scant instance; but Mrs. Freer's vivid imagination—much as she had lived in Europe she knew her native land so well—saw a host of others massing themselves behind it. The consequence of all of which was that after listening to her young friend in the most engaging silence she raised her clasped hands, pressed them against her breast, lowered her voice to a tone of entreaty and, with all the charming cheer of her wisdom, uttered three words: "My dear Jackson, don't—don't—don't."

"Don't what?" He took it at first coldly.

"Don't neglect the chance you have of getting out of it. You see it would never do."

He knew what she meant by his chance of getting out of it; he had in his many meditations of course not overlooked that. The ground the old couple had taken about settlements—and the fact that Lady Beauchemin hadn't come back to him to tell him, as she promised, that she had moved them, proved how firmly they were rooted—would have offered an all-sufficient pretext to a man who should have repented of his advances. Jackson knew this, but knew at the same time that he had not repented. The old couple's want of imagination didn't in the least alter the fact that the girl was, in her perfection, as he had told her father, one of the rarest of types. Therefore he simply said to Mrs. Freer that he didn't in the least wish to get out of it; he was as much in it as ever and intended to remain in it. But what did she mean, he asked in a moment, by her statement that it would never do? Why wouldn't it do? Mrs. Freer replied by another question—should he really like her to tell him? It wouldn't do because Lady Barb wouldn't be satisfied with her place at dinner. She wouldn't be content—in a society of commoners—with any but the best; and the best she couldn't expect (and it was to be supposed he didn't expect her) always grossly to monopolise; as people of her sort, for that matter, did so successfully grab it in England.

"What do you mean by commoners?" Jackson rather grimly demanded.

"I mean you and me and my poor husband and Dr. Feeder," said Mrs. Freer.

"I don't see how there can be commoners where there aren't lords. It's the lord that makes the commoner, and *vice versa*."

"Won't a lady do as well? Our Lady Barb—a single English girl—can make a million inferiors."

"She will be, before anything else, my wife; and she won't on the whole think it any less vulgar to talk about inferiors than I do myself."

"I don't know what she'll talk about, my dear Jackson, but she'll think; and her thoughts won't be pleasant—I mean for others. Do you expect to sink her to your own rank?"

Dr. Lemon's bright little eyes rested more sharply on his hostess. "I don't understand you and don't think you understand yourself." This was not absolutely candid, for he did understand Mrs. Freer to a certain extent; it has been related that before he asked Lady Barb's hand of her parents there had been moments when he himself doubted if a flower only to be described as of the social hothouse, that is of aristocratic air, would flourish in American earth. But an intimation from another person that it was beyond his power to pass off his wife—whether she were the daughter of a peer or of a shoemaker—set all his blood on fire. It quenched on the instant his own perception of difficulties of detail and made him feel only that he was dishonoured—he the heir of all the ages—by such insinuations. It was his belief—though he had never before had occasion to put it forward—that his position, one of the best in the world, had about it the felicity that makes everything possible. He had had the best education the age could offer, for if he had rather wasted his time at Harvard, where he entered very young, he had, as he believed, been tremendously serious at Heidelberg and at Vienna. He had devoted himself to one of the noblest of professions—a profession

84

recognised as such everywhere but in England—and had inherited a fortune far beyond the expectation of his earlier years, the years when he cultivated habits of work which alone (or rather in combination with talents that he neither exaggerated nor undervalued) would have conduced to distinction. He was one of the most fortunate inhabitants of an immense fresh rich country, a country whose future was admitted to be incalculable, and he moved with perfect ease in a society in which he was not overshadowed by others. It seemed to him, therefore, beneath his dignity to wonder whether he could afford, socially speaking, to marry according to his taste. He pretended to general strength, and what was the use of strength if you weren't prepared to undertake things timid people might find difficult? It was his plan to marry the woman he desired and not be afraid of her afterward. The effect of Mrs. Freer's doubt of his success was to represent to him that his own character wouldn't cover his wife's; she couldn't have made him feel worse if she had told him that he was marrying beneath him and would have to ask for indulgence. "I don't believe you know how much I think that any woman who marries me will be doing very well," he promptly added.

"I'm very sure of that; but it isn't so simple—one's being an American," Mrs. Freer rejoined with a small philosophic sigh.

"It's whatever one chooses to make it."

"Well, you'll make it what no one has done yet if you take that young lady to America and make her happy there."

"Do you think our country, then, such a very dreadful place?"

His hostess had a pause. "It's not a question of what I think, but of what she will."

Jackson rose from his chair and took up his hat and stick. He had actually turned a little pale with the force of his emotion; there was a pang of wrath for him in this fact that his marriage to Lady Barbarina might be looked at as too high a flight. He stood a moment leaning against the mantelpiece and very much tempted to say to Mrs. Freer that she was a vulgar-minded old woman. But he said something that was really more to the point. "You forget that she'll have her consolations."

"Don't go away or I shall think I've offended you. You can't console an injured noblewoman."

"How will she be injured? People will be charming to her."

"They'll be charming to her—charming to her!" These words fell from the lips of Dexter Freer, who had opened the door of the room and stood with the knob in his hand, putting himself into relation to his wife's talk with their visitor. This harmony was achieved in an instant. "Of course I know whom you mean," he said while he exchanged greetings with Jackson. "My wife and I—naturally we're great busybodies—have talked of your affair and we differ about it completely. She sees only the dangers, while I see all the advantages."

"By the advantages he means the fun for us," Mrs. Freer explained, settling her sofa-cushions.

Jackson looked with a certain sharp blankness from one of these disinterested judges to the other; even yet they scarce saw how their misdirected freedom wrought on him. It was hardly more agreeable to him to know that the husband wished to see Lady Barb in America than to know that the wife waved away such a vision. There was that in Dexter Freer's face which seemed to forecast the affair as taking place somehow for the benefit of the spectators. "I think you both see too much—a great deal too much—in the whole thing," he rather coldly returned.

"My dear young man, at my age I may take certain liberties," said Dexter Freer. "*Do* what you've planned—I beseech you to do it; it has never been done before." And then as if Jackson's glance had challenged this last assertion he went on: "Never, I assure you, this particular thing. Young female members of the British aristocracy have married coachmen and fishmongers and all that sort of thing; but they've never married you and me."

"They certainly haven't married the 'likes' of either of you!" said Mrs. Freer.

"I'm much obliged to you for your advice." It may be thought that Jackson Lemon took himself rather seriously, and indeed I'm afraid that if he hadn't done so there would have been no occasion even for this summary report of him. But it made him almost sick to hear his engagement spoken of as a curious and ambiguous phenomenon. He might have his own ideas about it—one always had about one's engagement; but the ideas that appeared to have peopled the imagination of his friends ended by kindling a small hot expanse in each of his cheeks. "I'd rather not talk any more about my little plans," he added to his host. "I've been saying all sorts of absurd things to Mrs. Freer."

"They've been most interesting and most infuriating," that lady declared. "You've been very stupidly treated."

"May she tell me when you go?" her husband asked of the young man.

"I'm going now—she may tell you whatever she likes."

"I'm afraid we've displeased you," she went on; "I've said too much what I think. You must pardon me—it's all for your mother."

"It's she whom I want Lady Barb to see!" Jackson exclaimed with the inconsequence of filial affection.

"Deary me!" Mrs. Freer gently wailed.

"We shall go back to America to see how you get on," her husband said; "and if you succeed it will be a great precedent."

"Oh I shall succeed!" And with this he took his departure. He walked away with the quick step of a man labouring under a certain excitement; walked up to Piccadilly and down past Hyde Park Corner. It relieved him to measure these distances, for he was thinking hard, under the influence of irritation, and it was as if his movement phrased his passion. Certain lights flashed on him in the last half-hour turned to fire in him; the more that they had a representative value and were an echo of the common voice. If his prospects wore that face to Mrs. Freer they would probably wear it to others; so he felt a strong sharp need to show such others that they took a mean measure of his position. He walked and walked till he found himself on the highway of Hammersmith. I have represented him as a young man with a stiff back, and I may appear to undermine this plea when I note that he wrote that evening to his solicitor that Mr. Hardman was to be informed he would agree to any proposals for settlements that this worthy should make. Jackson's stiff back was shown in his deciding to marry Lady Barbarina on any terms. It had come over him through the action of this desire to prove he wasn't afraid—so odious was the imputation—that terms of any kind were very superficial things. What was fundamental and of the essence of the matter would be to secure the grand girl and *then* carry everything out.

V

"On Sundays now you might be at home," he said to his wife in the following month of March—more than six months after his marriage.

"Are the people any nicer on Sundays than they are on other days?" Lady Barb asked from the depths of her chair and without looking up from a stiff little book.

He waited ever so briefly before answering. "I don't know whether they are, but I think you might be."

"I'm as nice as I know how to be. You must take me as I am. You knew when you married me that I wasn't American."

Jackson stood before the fire toward which his wife's face was turned and her feet extended; stood there some time with his hands behind him and his eyes dropped a little obliquely on Lady Barb's bent head and richly-draped figure. It may be said without delay that he was sore of soul, and it may be added that he had a double cause. He knew himself on the verge of the first crisis that had occurred between himself and his wife—the reader will note that it had occurred rather promptly—and he was annoyed at his annoyance. A glimpse of his state of mind before his marriage has been given the reader, who will remember that at that period our young man had believed himself lifted above possibilities of irritation. When one was strong one wasn't fidgety, and a union with a species of calm goddess would of course be a source of repose. Lady Barb was a calm, was an even calmer goddess still, and he had a much more intimate view of her divinity than on the day he had led her to the altar; but I'm not sure he felt either as firm or as easy.

"How do you know what people are?" he said in a moment. "You've seen so few; you're perpetually denying yourself. If you should leave New York to-morrow you'd know wonderfully little about it."

"It's all just the same," she pleaded. "The people are all exactly alike. There's only one sort."

"How can you tell? You never see them."

"Didn't I go out every night for the first two months we were here?"

"It was only to about a dozen houses—those, I agree, always the same; people, moreover, you had already met in London. You've got no general impressions."

She raised her beautiful blank face. "That's just what I *have* got; I had them before I came. I see no difference whatever. They've just the same names—just the same manners."

Again for an instant Jackson hung fire; then he said with that practised flat candour of which mention has already been made and which he sometimes used in London during his courtship: "Don't you like it over here?"

Lady Barb had returned to her book, but she looked up again. "Did you expect me to like it?"

"I hoped you would, of course. I think I told you so."

"I don't remember. You said very little about it; you seemed to make a kind of mystery. I knew of course you expected me to live here, but I didn't know you expected me to like it."

"You thought I asked of you the sacrifice, as it were."

"I'm sure I don't know," said Lady Barb. She got up from her chair and tossed her unconsolatory volume into the empty seat. "I recommend you to read that book," she added.

"Is it interesting?"

"It's an American novel."

"I never read novels."

"You had really better look at that one. It will show you the kind of people you want me to know."

"I've no doubt it's very vulgar," Jackson said. "I don't see why you read it."

"What else can I do? I can't always be riding in the Park. I hate the Park," she quite rang out.

"It's just as good as your own," said her husband.

She glanced at him with a certain quickness, her eyebrows slightly lifted. "Do you mean the park at Pasterns?"

"No; I mean the park in London."

"Oh I don't care about London. One was only in London a few weeks." She had a horrible lovely ease.

Yet he but wanted to help her to turn round. "I suppose you miss the country," he suggested. It was his idea of life that he shouldn't be afraid of anything, not be afraid, in any situation, of knowing the worst that was to be known about it; and the demon of a courage with which discretion was not properly commingled prompted him to take soundings that were perhaps not absolutely necessary for safety and yet that revealed unmistakable rocks. It was useless to know about rocks if he couldn't avoid them; the only thing was to trust to the wind.

"I don't know what I miss. I think I miss everything!" This was his wife's answer to his too-curious inquiry. It wasn't peevish, for that wasn't the tone of a calm goddess; but it expressed a good deal—a good deal more than Lady Barb, who was rarely eloquent, had expressed before. Nevertheless, though his question had been precipitate, Jackson said to himself that he might take his time to think over what her fewness of words enclosed; he couldn't help seeing that the future would give him plenty of chance. He was in no hurry to ask himself whether poor Mrs. Freer, in Jermyn Street, mightn't after all have been right in saying that when it came to marrying an English caste-product it wasn't so simple to be an American doctor—it might avail little even in such a case to be the heir of all the ages. The transition was complicated, but in his bright mind it was rapid, from the brush of a momentary contact with such ideas to certain considerations which led him to go on after an instant: "Should you like to go down into Connecticut?"

"Into Connecticut?"

"That's one of our States. It's about as large as Ireland. I'll take you there if you like."

"What does one do there?"

"We can try and get some hunting."

"You and I alone?"

"Perhaps we can get a party to join us."

"The people in the State?"

"Yes—we might propose it to them."

"The tradespeople in the towns?"

"Very true—they'll have to mind their shops," Jackson said. "But we might hunt alone."

"Are there any foxes?"

"No, but there are a few old cows."

Lady Barb had already noted that her husband sought the relief of a laugh at her expense, and she was aware that this present opportunity was neither worse nor better than some others. She didn't mind that trick in him particularly now, though in England it would have disgusted her; she had the consciousness of virtue, an immense comfort, and flattered herself she had learned the lesson of an altered standard of fitness—besides which there were so many more disagreeable things in America than being laughed at by one's husband. But she pretended not to like it because this made him stop, and above all checked discussion, which with Jackson was habitually so facetious and consequently so tiresome. "I only want to be left alone," she said in answer—though indeed it hadn't the style of an answer—to his speech about the cows. With this she wandered away to one of the windows that looked out on the Fifth Avenue. She was very fond of these windows and had taken a great fancy to the Fifth Avenue, which, in the high-pitched winter weather, when everything sparkled, was bright and funny and foreign. It will be seen that she was not wholly unjust to her adoptive country: she found it delightful to look out of the window. This was a pleasure she had enjoyed in London only in the most furtive manner; it wasn't the kind of thing that girls in England did. Besides, in London, in Hill Street, there was nothing particular to see; whereas in the Fifth Avenue everything and every one went by, and observation was made consistent with dignity by the quantities of brocade and lace dressing the embrasure, which somehow wouldn't have been tidy in England and which made an ambush without concealing the brilliant day. Hundreds of women—the queer women of New York, who were unlike any that Lady Barb had hitherto seen—passed the house every hour; and her ladyship was infinitely entertained and mystified by the sight of their clothes. She spent more time than she was aware of in this recreation, and had she been addicted to returning upon herself, to asking herself for an account of her conduct—an inquiry she didn't indeed completely neglect, but made no great form of—she must have had a wan smile for this proof of what she appeared mainly to have come to America for, conscious though she was that her tastes were very simple and that so long as she didn't hunt it didn't much matter what she did.

Her husband turned about to the fire, giving a push with his foot to a log that had fallen out of its place. Then he said—and the connexion with the words she had just uttered was direct enough—"You really must manage to be at home on Sundays, you know. I used to like that so much in London. All the best women here do it. You had better begin to-day. I'm going to see my mother. If I meet any one I'll tell them to come."

"Tell them not to talk so much," said Lady Barb among her lace curtains.

"Ah, my dear," Jackson returned, "it isn't every one who has your concision." And he went and stood behind her in the window, putting his arm round her waist. It was as much of a satisfaction to him as it had been six months before, at the time the solicitors were settling the matter, that this flower of an ancient stem should be worn upon his own breast; he still thought its fragrance a thing quite apart, and it was as clear as day to him that his wife was the handsomest woman in New York. He had begun, after their arrival, by telling her this very often; but the assurance brought no colour to her cheek, no light to her eyes: to be the handsomest woman in New York, now that she was acquainted with that city, plainly failed to strike her as a position in life. The reader may, moreover, be informed that, oddly enough, Lady Barb didn't particularly believe this assertion. There were some very pretty women in New York, and without in the least wishing to be like them—she had seen no woman in America whom she desired to resemble—she envied them some of their peculiar little freshnesses. It's probable that her own finest points were those of which she was most unconscious. But Jackson was intensely aware of all of them; nothing could exceed the minuteness of his appreciation of his wife. It was a sign of this that after he had stood behind her a moment he kissed her very tenderly. "Have you any message for my mother?" he asked.

"Please give her my love. And you might take her that book."

"What book?"

"That nasty one I've been reading."

"Oh bother your books!" he cried with a certain irritation as he went out of the room.

There had been a good many things in her life in New York that cost her an effort, but sending her love to her mother-in-law was not one of these. She liked Mrs. Lemon better than any one she had seen in America; she was the only person who seemed to Lady Barb really simple, as she herself understood that quality. Many people had struck her as homely and rustic and many

93

others as pretentious and vulgar; but in Jackson's mother she had found the golden mean of a discretion, of a native felicity and modesty and decency, which, as she would have said, were really nice. Her sister, Lady Agatha, was even fonder of Mrs. Lemon; but then Lady Agatha had taken the most extraordinary fancy to every one and everything, and talked as if America were the most delightful country in the world. She was having a lovely time—she already spoke the most beautiful American—and had been, during the bright winter just drawing to a close, the most prominent girl in New York. She had gone out at first with her elder; but for some weeks past Lady Barb had let so many occasions pass that Agatha threw herself into the arms of Mrs. Lemon, who found her unsurpassably quaint and amusing and was delighted to take her into society. Mrs. Lemon, as an old woman, had given up such vanities; but she only wanted a motive, and in her good nature she ordered a dozen new caps and sat smiling against the wall while her little English maid, on polished floors, to the sound of music, cultivated the American step as well as the American tone. There was no trouble in New York about going out, and the winter wasn't half over before the little English maid found herself an accomplished diner, finding her way without any chaperon at all to feasts where she could count on a bouquet at her plate. She had had a great deal of correspondence with her own female parent on this point, and Lady Canterville had at last withdrawn her protest, which in the meantime had been perfectly useless. It was ultimately Lady Canterville's feeling that if she had married the handsomest of her daughters to an American doctor she might let another become a professional *raconteuse*—Agatha had written to her that she was expected to talk so much—strange as such a destiny seemed for a girl of nineteen. Mrs. Lemon had even a higher simplicity than Lady Barb imputed to her; for she hadn't noticed that Lady Agatha danced much oftener with Herman Longstraw than with any one else. Jackson himself, though he went little to balls, had discovered this truth, and he looked slightly preoccupied when, after he had sat five minutes with his mother on the Sunday afternoon through which I have invited the reader to trace so much more than—I am afraid—is easily apparent of the progress of this simple story, he learned that his sister-in-law was entertaining Mr. Longstraw in the library. That young man had called half an hour before, and she had taken him into the other room to show him the seal of the Cantervilles, which she had fastened to one of her numerous trinkets—she was adorned with a hundred bangles and chains—and the proper exhibition of which required a taper and a stick of wax. Apparently he was examining it very carefully, for they had been absent a good while. Mrs. Lemon's simplicity was further shown by the fact that she had not measured their absence; it was only when Jackson questioned her that she remembered.

Herman Longstraw was a young Californian who had turned up in New York the winter before and who travelled on his moustache, as they were understood to say in his native State. This moustache and some of its accompanying features were greatly admired; several ladies in New York had been known to declare that they were as beautiful as a dream. Taken in connexion with his tall stature, his familiar good nature and his remarkable Western vocabulary they constituted his only social capital; for of the two great divisions, the rich Californians and the poor Californians, it was well known to which he belonged. Doctor Lemon had viewed him as but a slightly mitigated cowboy, and was somewhat vexed at his own parent, though also aware that she could scarcely figure to herself what an effect such a form of speech as this remarkably straight echo of the prairie would produce in the halls of Canterville. He had no desire whatever to play a trick on the house to which he was allied, and knew perfectly that Lady Agatha hadn't been sent to America to become entangled with a Californian of the wrong denomination. He had been perfectly willing to bring her; he thought, a little vindictively, that this would operate as a hint to her progenitors on what he might have imagined doing if they hadn't been so stupidly bent on Mr. Hardman. Herman Longstraw, according to the legend, had been a trapper, a squatter, a miner, a pioneer—had been everything that one could be in the desperate parts of America, and had accumulated masses of experience before the age of thirty. He had shot bears in the Rockies and buffaloes on the plains; and it was even believed that he had brought down animals of a still more dangerous kind among the haunts of men. There had been a story that he owned a cattle-ranch in Arizona; but a later and apparently more authentic version of it, though representing him as looking after the cattle, didn't depict him as their proprietor.

Many of the stories told about him were false; but there was no doubt his moustache, his native ease and his native accent were the best of their kind. He danced very badly; but Lady Agatha had frankly told several persons that that was nothing new to her, and in short she delighted—this, however, she didn't tell—in Mr. Herman Longstraw. What she enjoyed in America was the revelation of freedom, and there was no such proof of freedom as absolutely unrestricted discourse with a gentleman who dressed in crude skins when not in New York and who, in his usual pursuits, carried his life—as well as that of other persons—in his hand. A gentleman whom she had sat next to at dinner in the early part of her visit had remarked to her that the United States were the paradise of women and of mechanics; and this had seemed to her at the time very abstract, for she wasn't conscious as yet of belonging to either class. In England she had been only a girl, and the principal idea connected with that was simply that for one's misfortune one wasn't a boy. But she presently herself found the odd American world a true sojourn of the youthful blest; and this helped her to know that she must be one of the people mentioned in the axiom of her neighbour—people who could do whatever they wanted, had a voice in everything and made their taste and their ideas felt. She saw what fun it was to be a woman in America, and that this was the best way to enjoy the New York winter—the wonderful brilliant New York winter, the queer long-shaped glittering city, the heterogeneous hours among which you couldn't tell the morning from the afternoon or the night from either of them, the perpetual liberties and walks, the rushings-out and the droppings-in, the intimacies, the endearments, the comicalities, the sleigh-bells, the cutters, the sunsets on the snow, the ice-parties in the frosty clearness, the bright hot velvety houses, the bouquets, the bonbons, the little cakes, the big cakes, the irrepressible inspirations of shopping, the innumerable luncheons and dinners offered to youth and innocence, the quantities of chatter of quantities of girls, the perpetual motion of the "German," the suppers at restaurants after the play, the way in which life was pervaded by Delmonico and Delmonico by the sense that though one's hunting was lost, and this therefore so different, it was very nearly as good. In all, through all, flowed a suffusion of loud unmodulated friendly sound which reminded her of an endless tuning of rather bad fiddles.

Lady Agatha was at present staying for a little change with Mrs. Lemon, and such adventures as that were part of the pleasure of her American season. The house was too close, but physically the girl could bear anything, and it was all she had to complain of; for Mrs. Lemon, as we know, thought her a weird little specimen, and had none of those old-world scruples in regard to spoiling young people to which Lady Agatha herself now knew she must in the past have been unduly sacrificed. In her own way—it was not at all her sister's way—she liked to be of importance; and this was assuredly the case when she saw that Mrs. Lemon had apparently nothing in the world to do, after spending a part of the morning with her servants, but invent little distractions—many of them of the edible sort—for her guest. She appeared to have several friends, but she had no society to speak of, and the people who entered her house came principally to see Lady Agatha. This, as we have noted, was strikingly the case with Herman Longstraw. The whole situation gave the young stranger a great feeling of success—success of a new and unexpected kind. Of course in England she had been born successful, as it might be called, through her so emerging in one of the most beautiful rooms at Pasterns; but her present triumph was achieved more by her own effort—not that she had tried very hard—and by her merit. It wasn't so much what she said—since she could never equal for quantity the girls of New York—as the spirit of enjoyment that played in her fresh young face, with its pointless curves, and shone in her grey English eyes. She enjoyed everything, even the street-cars, of which she made liberal use; and more than everything she enjoyed Mr. Longstraw and his talk about buffaloes and bears. Mrs. Lemon promised to be very careful as soon as her son had begun to warn her; and this time she had a certain understanding of what she promised. She thought people ought to make the matches they liked; she had given proof of this in her late behaviour to Jackson, whose own union was, to her sense, marked with all the arbitrariness of pure love. Nevertheless she could see that Herman Longstraw would probably be thought rough in England; and it wasn't simply that he was so inferior to Jackson, for, after all, certain things were not to be expected. Jackson was not oppressed with his mother-in-law, having taken his precautions against such a danger; but he was certain he should give Lady Canterville a permanent advantage over him if her third daughter should while in America attach herself to a mere moustache.

It was not always, as I have hinted, that Mrs. Lemon entered completely into the views of her son, though in form she never failed to subscribe to them devoutly. She had never yet, for instance, apprehended his reason for marrying poor Lady Barb. This was a great secret, and she was determined, in her gentleness, that no one should ever know it. For herself, she was sure that to the end of time she shouldn't discover Jackson's reason. She might never ask about it, for that of course would betray her. From the first she had told him she was delighted, there being no need of asking for explanations then, as the young lady herself, when she should come to know her, would explain. But the young lady hadn't yet explained and after this evidently never would. She was very tall, very handsome, she answered exactly to Mrs. Lemon's prefigurement of the daughter of a lord, and she wore her clothes, which were peculiar, but to one of her shape remarkably becoming, very well. But she didn't elucidate; we know ourselves that there was very little that was explanatory about Lady Barb. So Mrs. Lemon continued to wonder, to ask herself, "Why that one, more than so many others who'd have been more natural?" The choice struck her, as I have said, as quite arbitrary. She found Lady Barb very different from other girls she had known, and this led her almost immediately to feel sorry for her daughter-in-law. She felt how the girl was to be pitied if she found her husband's people as peculiar as his mother found *her*, since the result of that would be to make her very lonesome. Lady Agatha was different, because she seemed to keep nothing back; you saw all there was of her, and she was evidently not home-sick. Mrs. Lemon could see that Barbarina was ravaged by this last ailment and was also too haughty to show it. She even had a glimpse of the ultimate truth; namely, that Jackson's wife had not the comfort of crying, because that would have amounted to a confession that she had been idiotic enough to believe in advance that, in an American town, in the society of doctors, she should escape such pangs. Mrs. Lemon treated her with studied consideration—all the indulgence that was due to a young woman in the unfortunate position of having been married one couldn't tell why.

The world, to the elder lady's view, contained two great departments, that of people and that of things; and she believed you must take an interest either in one or the other. The true incomprehensible in Lady Barb was that she cared for neither side of the show. Her house apparently inspired her with no curiosity and no enthusiasm, though it had been thought magnificent enough to be described in successive columns of the native newspapers; and she never spoke of her furniture or her domestics, though she had a prodigious show of such possessions. She was the same with regard to her acquaintance, which was immense, inasmuch as every one in the place had called on her. Mrs. Lemon was the least critical woman in the world, but it had occasionally ruffled her just a little that her daughter-in-law should receive every one in New York quite in the same automatic manner. There were differences, Mrs. Lemon knew, and some of them of the highest importance; but poor Lady Barb appeared never to suspect them. She accepted every one and everything and asked no questions. She had no curiosity about her fellow-citizens, and as she never assumed it for a moment she gave Mrs. Lemon no opportunity to enlighten her. Lady Barb was a person with whom you could do nothing unless she left you an opening; and nothing would have been more difficult than to "post" her, as her mother-in-law would have said, against her will. Of course she picked up a little knowledge, but she confounded and transposed American attributes in the most extraordinary way. She had a way of calling every one Doctor; and Mrs. Lemon could scarcely convince her that this distinction was too precious to be so freely bestowed. She had once said to that supporter that in New York there was nothing to know people by, their names were so very monotonous; and Mrs. Lemon had entered into this enough to see that there was something that stood out a good deal in Barbarina's own prefix. It is probable that during her short period of domestication complete justice was not done Lady Barb; she never—as an instance—got credit for repressing her annoyance at the poverty of the nominal signs and styles, a deep desolation. That little speech to her husband's mother was the most reckless sign she gave of it; and there were few things that contributed more to the good conscience she habitually enjoyed than her self-control on this particular point.

Doctor Lemon was engaged in professional researches just now, which took up a great deal of his time; and for the rest he passed his hours unreservedly with his wife. For the last three months, therefore, he had seen his other nearest relative scarcely more than once a week. In spite of researches, in spite of medical societies, where Jackson, to her knowledge, read papers, Lady Barb had more of her husband's company than she had counted on at the time she married. She had never known a married pair to be so much together as she and Jackson; he appeared to expect her to sit with him in the library in the morning. He had none of the occupations of gentlemen and noblemen in England, for the element of politics appeared to be as absent as the element of the chase. There were politics in Washington, she had been told, and even at Albany, and Jackson had proposed to introduce her to these cities; but the proposal, made to her once at dinner, before several people, had excited such cries of horror that it fell dead on the spot. "We don't want you to see anything of that kind," one of the ladies had said, and Jackson had appeared to be discouraged—that is if in regard to Jackson she could really tell.

"Pray what is it you want me to see?" Lady Barb had asked on this occasion.

"Well, New York and Boston (Boston if you want to very much, but not otherwise), and then Niagara. But more than anything Newport."

She was tired of their eternal Newport; she had heard of it a thousand times and felt already as if she had lived there half her life; she was sure, moreover, that she should hate the awful little place. This is perhaps as near as she came to having a lively conviction on any American subject. She asked herself whether she was then to spend her life in the Fifth Avenue with alternations of a city of villas—she detested villas—and wondered if that was all the great American country had to offer her. There were times when she believed she should like the backwoods and that the Far West might be a resource; for she had analysed her feelings just deep enough to discover that when she had—hesitating a good deal—turned over the question of marrying Jackson Lemon it was not in the least of American barbarism she was afraid; her dread had been all of American civilisation. She judged the little lady I have just quoted a goose, but that didn't make New York any more interesting. It would be reckless to say that she suffered from an overdose of Jackson's company, since she quite felt him her most important social resource. She could talk to him about England, about her own England, and he understood more or less what she wished to say—when she wished to say anything, which was not frequent. There were plenty of other people who talked about England; but with them the range of allusion was always the hotels, of which she knew nothing, and the shops and the opera and the photographs: they had the hugest appetite for photographs. There were other people who were always wanting her to tell them about Pasterns and the manner of life there and the parties; but if there was one thing Lady Barb disliked more than another it was describing Pasterns. She had always lived with people who knew of themselves what such a place would be, without demanding these pictorial efforts, proper only, as she vaguely felt, to persons belonging to the classes whose trade was the arts of expression. Lady Barb of course had never gone into it; but she knew that in her own class the business was not to express but to enjoy, not to represent but to be represented— though indeed this latter liability might involve offence; for it may be noted that even for an aristocrat Jackson Lemon's wife was aristocratic.

Lady Agatha and her visitor came back from the library in course of time, and Jackson Lemon felt it his duty to be rather cold to Herman Longstraw. It wasn't clear to him what sort of a husband his sister-in-law would do well to look for in America—if there were to be any question of husbands; but as to that he wasn't bound to be definite provided he should rule out Mr. Longstraw. This gentleman, however, was not given to noticing shades of manner; he had little observation, but very great confidence.

"I think you had better come home with me," Jackson said to Lady Agatha; "I guess you've stayed here long enough."

"Don't let him say that, Mrs. Lemon!" the girl cried. "I like being with you so awfully."

"I try to make it pleasant," said Mrs. Lemon. "I should really miss you now; but perhaps it's your mother's wish." If it was a question of defending her guest from ineligible suitors Mrs. Lemon felt of course that her son was more competent than she; though she had a lurking kindness for Herman Longstraw and a vague idea that he was a gallant genial specimen of unsophisticated young America.

"Oh mamma wouldn't see any difference!" Lady Agatha returned with pleading blue eyes on her brother-in-law. "Mamma wants me to see every one; you know she does. That's what she sent me to America for; she knows—for we've certainly told her enough—that it isn't like England. She wouldn't like it if I didn't sometimes stay with people; she always wanted us to stay at other houses. And she knows all about you, Mrs. Lemon, and she likes you immensely. She sent you a message the other day and I'm afraid I forgot to give it you—to thank you for being so kind to me and taking such a lot of trouble. Really she did, but I forgot it. If she wants me to see as much as possible of America it's much better I should be here than always with Barb—it's much less like one's own country. I mean it's much nicer—for a girl," said Lady Agatha affectionately to Mrs. Lemon, who began also to look at Jackson under the influence of this uttered sweetness which was like some quaint little old air, she thought, played upon a faded spinet with two girlish fingers.

"If you want the genuine thing you ought to come out on the plains," Mr. Longstraw interposed with bright sincerity. "I guess that was your mother's idea. Why don't you all come out?" He had been looking intently at Lady Agatha while the remarks I have just repeated succeeded each other on her lips—looking at her with a fascinated approbation, for all the world as if he had been a slightly slow-witted English gentleman and the girl herself a flower of the West, a flower that knew the celebrated language of flowers. Susceptible even as Mrs. Lemon was he made no secret of the fact that Lady Agatha's voice was music to him, his ear being much more accessible than his own inflexions would have indicated. To Lady Agatha those inflexions were not displeasing, partly because, like Mr. Herman himself in general, she had not a perception of shades; and partly because it never occurred to her to compare them with any other tones. He seemed to her to speak a foreign language altogether—a romantic dialect through which the most comical meanings gleamed here and there.

"I should like it above all things," she said in answer to his last observation.

"The scenery's ahead of anything round here," Mr. Longstraw went on.

Mrs. Lemon, as we have gathered, was the mildest of women; but, as an old New Yorker, she had no patience with some of the new fashions.

Chief among these was the perpetual reference, which had become common only within a few years, to the outlying parts of the country, the States and Territories of which children, in her time, used to learn the names, in their order, at school, but which no one ever thought of going to or talking about. Such places, in her opinion, belonged to the geography-books, or at most to the literature of newspapers, but neither to society nor to conversation; and the change—which, so far as it lay in people's talk, she thought at bottom a mere affectation—threatened to make her native land appear vulgar and vague. For this amiable daughter of Manhattan the normal existence of man, and still more of women, had been "located," as she would have said, between Trinity Church and the beautiful Reservoir at the top of the Fifth Avenue—monuments of which she was personally proud; and if we could look into the deeper parts of her mind I am afraid we should discover there an impression that both the countries of Europe and the remainder of her own continent were equally far from the centre and the light.

"Well, scenery isn't everything," she made soft answer to Mr. Longstraw; "and if Lady Agatha should wish to see anything of that kind all she has got to do is to take the boat up the Hudson." Mrs. Lemon's recognition of this river, I should say, was all it need have been; she held the Hudson existed for the purpose of supplying New Yorkers with poetical feelings, helping them to face comfortably occasions like the present and, in general, meet foreigners with confidence—part of the oddity of foreigners being their conceit about their own places.

"That's a good idea, Lady Agatha; let's take the boat," said Mr. Longstraw. "I've had great times on the boats."

Lady Agatha fixed on her *amoroso* her singular charming eyes, eyes of which it was impossible to say at any moment whether they were the shyest or the frankest in the world; and she was not aware while this contemplation lasted that her brother-in-law was observing her. He was thinking of certain things while he did so, of things he had heard about the English; who still, in spite of his having married into a family of that nation, appeared to him very much through the medium of hearsay. They were more passionate than the Americans, and they did things that would never have been expected; though they seemed steadier and less excitable there was much social evidence to prove them more wildly impulsive.

"It's so very kind of you to propose that," Lady Agatha said in a moment to Mrs. Lemon. "I think I've never been in a ship—except of course coming from England. I'm sure mamma would wish me to see the Hudson. We used to go in immensely for boating in England."

"Did you boat in a ship?" Herman Longstraw asked, showing his teeth hilariously and pulling his moustaches.

"Lots of my mother's people have been in the navy." Lady Agatha perceived vaguely and good-naturedly that she had said something the odd Americans thought odd and that she must justify herself. Something most unnatural was happening to her standard of oddity.

"I really think you had better come back to us," Jackson repeated: "your sister's very lonely without you."

"She's much more lonely *with* me. We're perpetually having differences. Barb's dreadfully vexed because I like America instead of—instead of—" And Lady Agatha paused a moment; for it just occurred to her that this might be treacherous.

"Instead of what?" Jackson inquired.

"Instead of perpetually wanting to go to England, as she does," she went on, only giving her phrase a little softer turn; for she felt the next moment that Barb could have nothing to hide and must of course have the courage of her opinions. "Of course England's best, but I daresay I like to be bad," the girl said artlessly.

"Oh there's no doubt you're awfully bad," Mr. Longstraw broke out, with joyous eagerness. Naturally he couldn't know that what she had principally in mind was an exchange of opinions that had taken place between her sister and herself just before she came to stay with Mrs. Lemon. This incident, of which he himself was the occasion, might indeed have been called a discussion, for it had carried them quite into the cold air of the abstract. Lady Barb had said

104

she didn't see how Agatha could look at such a creature as that—an odious familiar vulgar being who had not about him the rudiments of a gentleman. Lady Agatha had replied that Mr. Longstraw was familiar and rough and that he had a twang and thought it amusing to talk to her as "the Princess"; but that he was a gentleman for all that and was tremendous fun whatever one called him—it didn't seem to matter what one called any one or anything there. Her sister had returned to this that if he was rough and familiar he couldn't be a gentleman, inasmuch as that was just what a gentleman meant—a man who was civil and well-bred and well-born. Lady Agatha had argued that such a point was just where she differed; that a man might perfectly be a gentleman and yet be rough, and even ignorant, so long as he was really nice. The only thing was that he should be really nice, which was the case with Mr. Longstraw, who, moreover, was quite extraordinarily civil—as civil as a man could be. And then Lady Agatha herself made the strongest point she had ever made in her life (she had never been so inspired) in saying that Mr. Longstraw was rough perhaps, but not rude—a distinction altogether wasted on her sister, who declared that she hadn't come to America, of all places, to learn what a gentleman was. The discussion in short had been a trifle grim. I know not whether it was the tonic effect on them too, alien organisms as they were, of the fine winter weather, or that of Lady Barb's being bored and having nothing else to do; but Lord Canterville's daughters went into the question with the moral earnestness of a pair of approved Bostonians. It was part of Lady Agatha's view of her admirer that he after all much resembled other tall people with smiling eyes and tawny moustaches who had ridden a good deal in rough countries and whom she had seen in other places. If he was more familiar he was also more alert; still, the difference was not in himself, but in the way she saw him—the way she saw everybody in America. If she should see the others in the same way no doubt they'd be quite the same; and Lady Agatha sighed a little over the possibilities of life; for this peculiar way, especially regarded in connexion with gentlemen, had become very pleasant to her.

She had betrayed her sister more than she thought, even though Jackson didn't particularly show it in the tone in which he commented: "Of course she knows she's going to see your mother in the summer." His tone was rather that of irritation at so much harping on the very obvious.

"Oh it isn't only mamma," the girl said.

"I know she likes a cool house," Mrs. Lemon contributed.

"When she goes you had better bid her good-bye," Lady Agatha went on.

"Of course I shall bid her good-bye," said Mrs. Lemon, to whom apparently this remark was addressed.

"I'll never bid *you* good-bye, Princess," Herman Longstraw interposed. "You can bet your life on that."

"Oh it doesn't matter about me, for of course I shall come back; but if Barb once gets to England she never will."

"Oh my dear child!" Mrs. Lemon wailed, addressing her young visitor, but looking at her son, who on his side looked at the ceiling, at the floor, looked above all very conscious.

"I hope you don't mind my saying that, Jackson dear," Lady Agatha said to him, for she was very fond of her brother-in-law.

"Ah well then, she shan't go there," he threw off in a moment with a small strange dry laugh that attached his mother's eyes in shy penetration to his face.

"But you promised mamma, you know," said the girl with the confidence of her affection.

Jackson's countenance expressed to her none even of his very moderate hilarity. "Your mother, then, must bring her back."

"Get some of your navy people to supply an ironclad!" cried Mr. Longstraw.

"It would be very pleasant if the Marchioness could come over," said Mrs. Lemon.

"Oh she'd hate it more than poor Barb," Lady Agatha quickly replied. It didn't at all suit her to find a marchioness inserted into her field of vision.

"Doesn't she feel interested from what you've told her?" Lady Agatha's admirer inquired. But Jackson didn't heed his sister-in-law's answer—he was thinking of something else. He said nothing more, however, about the subject of his thought, and before ten minutes were over took his departure, having meanwhile neglected also to revert to the question of Lady Agatha's bringing her visit to his mother to a close. It wasn't to speak to him of this— for, as we know, she wished to keep the girl and somehow couldn't bring herself to be afraid of Herman Longstraw—that when her son took leave she went with him to the door of the house, detaining him a little while she stood on the steps, as people had always done in New York in her time, though it was another of the new fashions she didn't like, the stiffness of not coming out of the parlour. She placed her hand on his arm to keep him on the "stoop" and looked up and down into the lucid afternoon and the beautiful city—its chocolate-coloured houses so extraordinarily smooth—in which it seemed to her that even the most fastidious people ought to be glad to live. It was useless to attempt to conceal it: his marriage had made a difference and a worry, had put a barrier that she was yet under the painful obligation of trying to seem not to notice. It had brought with it a problem much more difficult than his old problem of how to make his mother feel herself still, as she had been in his childhood, the dispenser of his rewards. The old problem had been easily solved, the new was a great tax. Mrs. Lemon was sure her daughter-in-law didn't take her seriously, and that was a part of the barrier. Even if Barbarina liked her better than any one else this was mostly because she liked every one else so little. Mrs. Lemon had in her nature no grain of resentment, and it wasn't to feed a sense of wrong that she permitted herself to criticise her son's wife. She couldn't help feeling that his marriage wasn't altogether fortunate if his wife didn't take his mother seriously. She knew she wasn't otherwise remarkable than as being his mother; but that position, which was no merit of hers—the merit was all Jackson's in being her son—affected her as one which, familiar as Lady Barb appeared to have been in England with positions of various kinds, would naturally strike the girl as very high and to be accepted as freely as a fine morning. If she didn't think of his mother as an indivisible part of him perhaps she didn't think of other things either; and Mrs. Lemon vaguely felt that, remarkable as Jackson was, he was made up of parts, and that it would never do that these should be rated lower one by one, since there was no knowing what that might end in. She feared that things were rather cold for him at home when he had to explain so much to his wife—explain to her, for instance, all the sources of happiness that were to be found in New York. This struck her as a new kind of problem altogether for a husband. She had never thought of matrimony without a community of feeling in regard to religion and country; one took those great conditions for granted just as one assumed that one's food was to be cooked; and if Jackson should have to discuss them with his wife he might, in spite of his great abilities, be carried into regions where he would get entangled and embroiled—from which even possibly he wouldn't come back at all. Mrs. Lemon had a horror of losing him in some way, and this fear was in her eyes as she stood by the doorway of her house and, after she had glanced up and down the street, eyed him a moment in silence. He simply kissed her again and said she would take cold.

"I'm not afraid of that—I've a shawl!" Mrs. Lemon, who was very small and very fair, with pointed features and an elaborate cap, passed her life in a shawl, and owed to this habit her reputation for being an invalid—an idea she scorned, naturally enough, inasmuch as it was precisely her shawl that, as she believed, kept every ill at bay. "Is it true Barbarina won't come back?" she then asked.

"I don't know that we shall ever find out; I don't know that I shall take her to England," Jackson distinctly returned.

She looked more anxious still. "Didn't you promise, dear?"

"I don't know that I promised—not absolutely."

"But you wouldn't keep her here against her will?" quavered Mrs. Lemon.

"I guess she'll get used to it," he returned with a levity that misrepresented the state of his nerves.

Mrs. Lemon looked up and down the street again and gave a little sigh. "What a pity she isn't American!" She didn't mean this as a reproach, a hint of what might have been; it was simply embarrassment resolved into speech.

"She couldn't have been American," said Jackson with decision.

"Couldn't she, dear?" His mother spoke with conscientious respect; she felt there were imperceptible reasons in this.

"It was just as she is that I wanted her," Jackson added.

"Even if she won't come back?" Mrs. Lemon went on with wonder.

"Oh she has got to come back!" Jackson said as he went down the steps.

VI

Lady Barb, after this, didn't decline to see her New York acquaintances on Sunday afternoons, though she refused for the present to enter into a project of her husband's, who thought it would be pleasant she should entertain his friends on the evening of that day. Like all good Americans, Doctor Lemon devoted much consideration to the great question of how, in his native land, society was to be brought into being. It seemed to him it would help on the good cause, for which so many Americans are ready to lay down their lives, if his wife should, as he jocularly called it, open a saloon. He believed, or tried to believe, the *salon* now possible in New York on condition of its being reserved entirely for adults; and in having taken a wife out of a country in which social traditions were rich and ancient he had done something toward qualifying his own house—so splendidly qualified in all strictly material respects—to be the scene of such an effort. A charming woman accustomed only to the best on each side, as Lady Beauchemin said, what mightn't she achieve by being at home—always to adults only—in an easy early inspiring comprehensive way and on the evening of the seven when worldly engagements were least numerous? He laid this philosophy before Lady Barb in pursuance of a theory that if she disliked New York on a short acquaintance she couldn't fail to like it on a long. Jackson believed in the New York mind—not so much indeed in its literary artistic philosophic or political achievements as in its general quickness and nascent adaptability. He clung to this belief, for it was an indispensable neat block in the structure he was attempting to rear. The New York mind would throw its glamour over Lady Barb if she would only give it a chance; for it was thoroughly bright responsive and sympathetic. If she would only set up by the turn of her hand a blest snug social centre, a temple of interesting talk in which this charming organ might expand and where she might inhale its fragrance in the most convenient and luxurious way, without, as it were, getting up from her chair; if she would only just try this graceful good-natured experiment—which would make every one like *her* so much too—he was sure all the wrinkles in the gilded scroll of his fate would be smoothed out. But Lady Barb didn't rise at all to his conception and hadn't the least curiosity about the New York mind. She thought it would be extremely disagreeable to have a lot of people tumbling in on Sunday evening without being invited; and altogether her husband's sketch of the Anglo-American saloon seemed to her to suggest crude familiarity, high vociferation—she had already made a remark to him about "screeching women"—and random extravagant laughter. She didn't tell him—for this somehow it wasn't in her power to express, and, strangely enough, he never completely guessed it—that she was singularly deficient in any natural or indeed acquired understanding of what a saloon might be. She had never seen or dreamed of one—and for the most part was incapable of imagining a thing she hadn't seen. She had seen great dinners and balls and meets and runs and races; she had seen garden-parties and bunches of people, mainly women—who, however, didn't screech—at dull stuffy teas, and distinguished companies collected in splendid castles; but all this gave her no clue to a train of conversation, to any idea of a social agreement that the interest of talk, its continuity, its accumulations from season to season, shouldn't be lost. Conversation, in Lady Barb's experience, had never been continuous; in such a case it would surely have been a bore. It had been occasional and fragmentary, a trifle jerky, with allusions that were never explained; it had a dread of detail—it seldom pursued anything very far or kept hold of it very long.

There was something else she didn't say to her husband in reference to his visions of hospitality, which was that if she should open a saloon—she had taken up the joke as well, for Lady Barb was eminently good-natured—Mrs. Vanderdecken would straightway open another, and Mrs. Vanderdecken's would be the more successful of the two. This lady, for reasons Lady Barb had not yet explored, passed for the great personage of New York; there were legends of her husband's family having behind them a fabulous antiquity. When this was alluded to it was spoken of as something incalculable and lost in the dimness of time. Mrs. Vanderdecken was young, pretty, clever, incredibly pretentious, Lady Barb thought, and had a wonderfully artistic house. Ambition was expressed, further, in every rustle of her garments; and if she was the first lady in America, "bar none"—this had an immense sound—it was plain she intended to retain the character. It was not till after she had been several months in New York that Lady Barb began to perceive this easy mistress of the field, crying out, gracious goodness, before she was hurt, to have flung down the glove; and when the idea presented itself, lighted up by an incident I have no space to report, she simply blushed a little (for Mrs. Vanderdecken) and held her tongue. She hadn't come to America to bandy words about "precedence" with such a woman as that. She had ceased to think of that convenience—of course one was obliged to think in England; though an instinct of self-preservation, old and deep-seated, led her not to expose herself to occasions on which her imputed claim might be tested. This had at bottom much to do with her having, very soon after the first flush of the honours paid her on her arrival and which seemed to her rather grossly overdone, taken the line of scarcely going out. "They can't keep *that* up!" she had said to herself; and in short she would stay, less boringly both for herself and for others, at home. She had a sense that whenever and wherever she might go forth she should meet Mrs. Vanderdecken, who would withhold or deny or contest or even magnanimously concede something—poor Lady Barb could never imagine what. She didn't try to, and gave little thought to all this; for she wasn't prone to confess to herself fears, especially fears from which terror was absent. What in the world *had* Mrs. Vanderdecken that she, Barbarina Lemon (what a name!), could want? But, as I have said, it abode within her as a presentiment that if she should set up a drawing-room in the foreign style (based, that is, on the suppression of prattling chits and hobbledehoys) this sharp skirmisher would be beforehand with her. The continuity of conversation, oh that she would certainly go in for—there was no one so continuous as Mrs. Vanderdecken. Lady Barb, as I have related,

111

didn't give her husband the surprise of confiding to him these thoughts, though she had given him some other surprises. He would have been decidedly astonished, and perhaps after a bit a little encouraged, at finding her liable to any marked form of exasperation.

On the Sunday afternoon she was visible; and at one of these junctures, going into her drawing-room late, he found her entertaining two ladies and a gentleman. The gentleman was Sidney Feeder and one of the ladies none other than Mrs. Vanderdecken, whose ostensible relations with her were indeed of the most cordial nature. Intending utterly to crush her—as two or three persons, not perhaps conspicuous for a narrow accuracy, gave out that she privately declared—Mrs. Vanderdecken yet wished at least to study the weak points of the invader, to penetrate herself with the character of the English girl. Lady Barb verily appeared to have for the representative of the American patriciate a mysterious fascination. Mrs. Vanderdecken couldn't take her eyes off her victim and, whatever might be her estimate of her importance, at least couldn't let her alone. "Why does she come to see me?" poor Lady Barb asked herself. "I'm sure I don't want to see her; she has done enough for civility long ago." Mrs. Vanderdecken had her own reasons, one of which was simply the pleasure of looking at the Doctor's wife, as she habitually called the daughter of the Cantervilles. She wasn't guilty of the rashness of depreciating the appearance of so markedly fine a young woman, but professed a positive unbounded admiration for it, defending it on many occasions against those of the superficial and stupid who pronounced her "left nowhere" by the best of the home-grown specimens. Whatever might have been Lady Barb's weak points, they included neither the curve of her cheek and chin, the setting of her head on her throat, nor the quietness of her deep eyes, which were as beautiful as if they had been blank, like those of antique busts. "The head's enchanting—perfectly enchanting," Mrs. Vanderdecken used to say irrelevantly and as if there were only one head in the place. She always used to ask about the Doctor—which was precisely another reason why she came. She dragged in the Doctor at every turn, asking if he were often called up at night; found it the greatest of luxuries, in a word, to address Lady Barb as the wife of a medical man and as more or less *au courant* of her husband's patients. The other lady, on this Sunday afternoon, was a certain little Mrs. Chew, who

112

had the appearance of a small but very expensive doll and was always asking Lady Barb about England, which Mrs. Vanderdecken never did. The latter discoursed on a purely American basis and with that continuity of which mention has already been made, while Mrs. Chew engaged Sidney Feeder on topics equally local. Lady Barb liked Sidney Feeder; she only hated his name, which was constantly in her ears during the half-hour the ladies sat with her, Mrs. Chew having, like so many persons in New York, the habit, which greatly annoyed her, of re-apostrophising and re-designating every one present.

Lady Barb's relations with Mrs. Vanderdecken consisted mainly in wondering, while she talked, what she wanted of her, and in looking, with her sculptured eyes, at her visitor's clothes, in which there was always much to examine. "Oh Doctor Feeder!" "Now Doctor Feeder!" "Well Doctor Feeder"—these exclamations, on Mrs. Chew's lips, were an undertone in Lady Barb's consciousness. When we say she liked her husband's confrère, as he never failed to describe himself, we understand that she smiled on his appearance and gave him her hand, and asked him if he would have tea. There was nothing nasty, as they so analytically said in London, about Lady Barb, and she would have been incapable of inflicting a deliberate snub on a man who had the air of standing up so squarely to any purpose he might have in hand. But she had nothing of her own at all to say to Sidney Feeder. He apparently had the art of making her shy, more shy than usual—since she was always a little so; she discouraged him, discouraged him completely and reduced him to naught. He wasn't a man who wanted drawing out, there was nothing of that in him, he was remarkably copious; but she seemed unable to follow him in any direction and half the time evidently didn't know what he was saying. He tried to adapt his conversation to her needs; but when he spoke of the world, of what was going on in society, she was more at sea even than when he spoke of hospitals and laboratories and the health of the city and the progress of science. She appeared indeed after her first smile when he came in, which was always charming, scarcely to see him—looking past him and above him and below him, everywhere but at him, till he rose to go again, when she gave him another smile, as expressive of pleasure and of casual acquaintance as that with which she had greeted his entry: it seemed to imply that they had been having delightful communion. He wondered what the deuce Jackson Lemon could find interesting in such a woman, and he believed his perverse, though gifted, colleague not destined to feel her in the long run enrich or illuminate his life. He pitied Jackson, he saw that Lady Barb, in New York, would neither assimilate nor be assimilated; and yet he was afraid, for very compassion, to betray to the poor man how the queer step he had taken—now so dreadfully irrevocable—might be going to strike most others. Sidney Feeder was a man of a strenuous conscience, who did loyal duty overmuch and from the very fear he mightn't do it enough. In order not to appear to he called upon Lady Barb heroically, in spite of pressing engagements and week after week, enjoying his virtue himself as little as he made it fruitful for his hostess, who wondered at last what she had done to deserve this extremity of appreciation.

She spoke of it to her husband, who wondered also what poor Sidney had in his head and yet naturally shrank from damping too brutally his zeal. Between the latter's wish not to let Jackson see his marriage had made a difference and Jackson's hesitation to reveal to him that his standard of friendship was too high, Lady Barb passed a good many of those numerous hours during which she asked herself if they were the "sort of thing" she had come to America for. Very little had ever passed between her and her husband on the subject of the most regular of her bores, a clear instinct warning her that if they were ever to have scenes she must choose the occasion well, and this odd person not being an occasion. Jackson had tacitly admitted that his "confrère" was anything she chose to think him; he was not a man to be guilty in a discussion of the disloyalty of damning a real friend with praise that was faint. If Lady Agatha had been less of an absentee from her sister's fireside, meanwhile, Doctor Feeder would have been better entertained; for the younger of the English pair prided herself, after several months of New York, on understanding everything that was said, on interpreting every sound, no matter from what lips the monstrous mystery fell. But Lady Agatha was never at home; she had learned to describe herself perfectly by the time she wrote her mother that she was always on the go. None of the innumerable victims of old-world tyranny welcomed to the land of freedom had yet offered more lavish incense to that goddess than this emancipated

114

London debutante. She had enrolled herself in an amiable band known by the humorous name of "the Tearers"—a dozen young ladies of agreeable appearance, high spirits and good wind, whose most general characteristic was that, when wanted, they were to be sought anywhere in the world but under the roof supposed to shelter them. They browsed far from the fold; and when Sidney Feeder, as sometimes happened, met Lady Agatha at other houses, she was in the hands of the irrepressible Longstraw. She had come back to her sister, but Mr. Longstraw had followed her to the door. As to passing it, he had received direct discouragement from her brother-in-law; but he could at least hang about and wait for her. It may be confided to the reader at the risk of discounting the effect of the only passage in this very level narrative formed to startle that he never had to wait very long.

When Jackson Lemon came in his wife's visitors were on the point of leaving her; and he didn't even ask his colleague to remain, for he had something particular to say to Lady Barb.

"I haven't put to you half the questions I wanted—I've been talking so much to Doctor Feeder," the dressy Mrs. Chew said, holding the hand of her hostess in one of her own and toying at one of Lady Barb's ribbons with the other.

"I don't think I've anything to tell you; I think I've told people everything," Lady Barb answered rather wearily.

"You haven't told *me* much!" Mrs. Vanderdecken richly radiated.

"What could one tell you? You know everything," Jackson impatiently laughed.

"Ah no—there are some things that are great mysteries for me!" this visitor promptly pronounced. "I hope you're coming to me on the seventeenth," she added to Lady Barb.

"On the seventeenth? I believe we go somewhere."

"Do go to Mrs. Vanderdecken's," said Mrs. Chew; "you'll see the cream of the cream."

115

"Oh gracious!" Mrs. Vanderdecken vaguely cried.

"Well, I don't care; she will, won't she, Doctor Feeder?—the very pick of American society." Mrs. Chew stuck to her point.

"Oh I've no doubt Lady Barb will have a good time," said Sidney Feeder. "I'm afraid you miss the bran," he went on with irrelevant jocosity to Jackson's bride. He always tried the jocose when other elements had failed.

"The bran?" Jackson's bride couldn't think.

"Where you used to ride—in the Park."

"My dear fellow, you speak as if we had met at the circus," her husband interposed. "I haven't married a mountebank!"

"Well, they put some stuff on the road," Sidney Feeder explained, not holding much to his joke.

"You must miss a great many things," said Mrs. Chew tenderly.

"I don't see what," Mrs. Vanderdecken tinkled, "except the fogs and the Queen. New York's getting more and more like London. It's a pity—you ought to have known us thirty years ago."

"*You're* the queen here," said Jackson Lemon, "but I don't know what you know about thirty years ago."

"Do you think she doesn't go back?—she goes back to the last century!" cried Mrs. Chew.

"I daresay I should have liked that," said Lady Barb; "but I can't imagine." And she looked at her husband—a look she often had—as if she vaguely wished him to do something.

He was not called upon, however, to take any violent steps, for Mrs. Chew presently said, "Well, Lady Barb, good-bye"; Mrs. Vanderdecken glared genially and as for excess of meaning at her hostess and addressed a farewell, accompanied very audibly with his title, to her host; and Sidney Feeder made a joke about stepping on the trains of the ladies' dresses as he accompanied them to the door. Mrs. Chew had always a great deal to say at the last; she talked till she was in the street and then she addressed that prospect. But at the end of five minutes Jackson Lemon was alone with his wife, to whom he then announced a piece of news. He prefaced it, however, by an inquiry as he came back from the hall.

"Where's Agatha, my dear?"

"I haven't the least idea. In the streets somewhere, I suppose."

"I think you ought to know a little more."

"How can I know about things here? I've given her up. I can do nothing with her. I don't care what she does."

"She ought to go back to England," Jackson said after a pause.

"She ought never to have come."

"It was not my proposal, God knows!" he sharply returned.

"Mamma could never know what it really is," his wife more quietly noted.

"No, it hasn't been as yet what your mother supposed! The man Longstraw wants to marry her and has made a formal proposal. I met him half an hour ago in Madison Avenue, and he asked me to come with him into the Columbia Club. There, in the billiard-room, which to-day is empty, he opened himself—thinking evidently that in laying the matter before me he was behaving with extraordinary propriety. He tells me he's dying of love and that she's perfectly willing to go and live in Arizona."

"So she is," said Lady Barb. "And what did you tell him?"

"I told him I was convinced it would never do and that at any rate I could have nothing to say to it. I told him explicitly in short what I had told him virtually before. I said we should send Aggie straight back to England, and that if they had the courage they must themselves broach the question over there."

"When shall you send her back?" asked Lady Barb.

"Immediately—by the very first steamer."

"Alone, like an American girl?"

"Don't be rough, Barb," Jackson replied. "I shall easily find some people—lots of them are sailing now."

"I must take her myself," Lady Barb observed in a moment. "I brought her out—so I must restore her to my mother's hands."

He had expected this and believed he was prepared for it, but when it came he found his preparation not complete. He had no answer to make—none at least that seemed to him to go to the point. During these last weeks it had come over him with a quiet irresistible unmerciful force that Mrs. Dexter Freer had been right in saying to him that Sunday afternoon in Jermyn Street, the summer before, that he would find it wasn't so simple to be an American. Such a character was complicated in just the measure that she had foretold by the difficulty of domesticating any wife at all liberally chosen. The difficulty wasn't dissipated by his having taken a high tone about it; it pinched him from morning till night, it hurt him like a misfitting shoe. His high tone had given him courage when he took the great step; but he began to perceive that the highest tone in the world couldn't change the nature of things. His ears tingled as he inwardly noted that if the Dexter Freers, whom he had thought alike abject in their hopes and their fears, had been by ill luck spending the winter in New York, they would have found his predicament as good fun as they could wish. Drop by drop the conviction had entered his mind—the first drop had come in the form of a word from Lady Agatha—that if his wife should return to England she would never again later recross the Atlantic. That word from the competent source had been the touch from the outside at which often a man's fear crystallises. What she would do, how she would resist—this he wasn't yet prepared to tell himself; but he felt every time he looked at her that the beautiful woman he had adored was filled with a dumb insuperable ineradicable purpose. He knew that if she should plant herself firm no power on earth would move her; and her blooming antique beauty and the general loftiness of her breeding came fast to seem to him

118

but the magnificent expression of a dense patient ponderous power to resist. She wasn't light, she wasn't supple, and after six months of marriage he had made up his mind that she wasn't intelligent—in spite of all which she would elude him. She had married him, she had come into his fortune and his consideration—for who was she after all? he was on occasion so angry as to ask himself, remembering that in England Lady Claras and Lady Florences were as thick as blackberries—but she would have nothing to do, if she could help it, with his country. She had gone in to dinner first in every house in the place, but this hadn't satisfied her. It *had* been simple to be an American in the good and easy sense that no one else in New York had made any difficulties; the difficulties had sprung from the very, the consummate, make of her, which were after all what he had married her for, thinking they would be a fine temperamental heritage for his brood. So they would, doubtless, in the coming years and after the brood should have appeared; but meanwhile they interfered with the best heritage of all—the nationality of his possible children. She would do indeed nothing violent; he was tolerably certain of that. She wouldn't return to England without his consent; only when she should return it would be once for all. His one possible line, then, was not to take her back—a position replete with difficulties, since he had in a manner given his word; she herself giving none at all beyond the formal promise murmured at the altar. She had been general, but he had been specific; the settlements he had made were a part of that. His difficulties were such as he couldn't directly face. He must tack in approaching so uncertain a coast. He said to his wife presently that it would be very inconvenient for him to leave New York at that moment: she must remember their plans had been laid for a later move. He couldn't think of letting her make the voyage without him, and on the other hand they must pack her sister off without delay. He would therefore make instant inquiry for a chaperon, and he relieved his irritation by cursing the name and every other attribute of Herman Longstraw.

Lady Barb didn't trouble herself to denounce this gentleman; her manner was that of having for a long time expected the worst. She simply remarked after having listened to her husband for some minutes in silence: "I'd quite as lief she should marry Doctor Feeder!"

The day after this he closeted himself for an hour with his sister-in-law, taking great pains to set forth to her the reasons why she shouldn't marry her Californian. Jackson was kind, he was affectionate; he kissed her and put his arm round her waist, he reminded her that he and she were the best of friends and that she had always been awfully nice to him: therefore he counted on her. She'd break her mother's heart, she'd deserve her father's curse, and she'd get him, Jackson, into a pickle from which no human power might ever disembroil him. Lady Agatha listened and cried, she returned his kiss very affectionately and admitted that her father and mother would never consent to such a marriage; and when he told her that he had made arrangements that she should sail for Liverpool, with some charming people, the next day but one, she embraced him again and assured him she could never thank him enough for all the trouble he had taken about her. He flattered himself he had convinced and in some degree comforted her, and he reflected with complacency that even should his wife take it into her head Barb would never get ready to embark for her native land between a Monday and a Wednesday. The next morning Lady Agatha failed to appear at breakfast, though as she usually rose very late her absence excited no immediate alarm. She hadn't rung her bell and was supposed still to be sleeping. But she had never yet slept later than mid-day; and as this hour approached her sister went to her room. Lady Barb then discovered that she had left the house at seven o'clock in the morning and had gone to meet Mr. Longstraw at a neighbouring corner. A little note on the table explained it very succinctly, and put beyond the power of the Jackson Lemons to doubt that by the time this news reached them their wayward sister had been united to the man of her preference as closely as the laws of the State of New York could bind her. Her little note set forth that as she knew she should never be permitted to marry him she had resolved to marry him without permission, and that directly after the ceremony, which would be of the simplest kind, they were to take a train for the Far West.

Our record is concerned only with the remote consequences of this affair, which made of course a great deal of trouble for poor Jackson. He pursued the fugitives to remote rocky fastnesses and finally overtook them in California; but he hadn't the boldness to propose to them to separate, for he promptly made out that Herman Longstraw was at least as well married

120

as himself. Lady Agatha was already popular in the new States, where the history of her elopement, emblazoned in enormous capitals, was circulated in a thousand newspapers. This question of the newspapers had been for our troubled friend one of the most definite results of his sister-in-law's *coup de tête*. His first thought had been of the public prints and his first exclamation a prayer that they shouldn't get hold of the story. They had, however, got hold of it with a myriad wildly-waved hands and were scattering it broadcast over the world. Lady Barb never caught them in the act—she succeeded perfectly in not seeing what she needn't; but an affectionate friend of the family, travelling at that time in the United States, made a parcel of some of the leading journals, and sent them to Lord Canterville. This missive elicited from her ladyship a letter, addressed to her son-in-law, which shook the young man's position to the base. The phials of a rank vulgarity had been opened on the house of Canterville, and the noble matron demanded that in compensation for the affronts and injuries heaped upon her family, and bereaved and dishonoured as she was, she should at least be allowed to look on the face of her second daughter. "I suppose you'll not, for very pity, be deaf to such a prayer as that," said Lady Barb; and though loth to record a second act of weakness on the part of a man with pretensions to be strong, I may not disguise the fact that poor Jackson, who blushed dreadfully over the newspapers and felt afresh as he read them the force of Mrs. Freer's terrible axiom, poor Jackson paid a visit to the office of the Cunarders. He said to himself later on that it was the newspapers that had done it; he couldn't decently appear to be on their side: they made it so hard to deny that the country was impossible at a time when one was in need of all one's arguments. Lady Barb, before sailing, definitely refused to mention any week or month as the date of their prearranged return to New York. Very many weeks and months have elapsed since then, and she gives no sign of coming back. She will never fix a date. She is much missed by Mrs. Vanderdecken, who still alludes to her—still says the line of the shoulders was superb; putting the statement pensively in the past tense. Lady Beauchemin and Lady Marmaduke are much disconcerted; the international project has not, in their view, received an impetus.

Jackson Lemon has a house in London and he rides in the Park with his wife, who is as beautiful as the day and who a year ago presented him with a little girl exhibiting features that he already scans for the look of race—whether in hope or in fear to-day is more than my muse has revealed. He has occasional scenes with Lady Barb during which the look of race is very clear in her own countenance; but they never terminate in a visit to the Cunarders. He's exceedingly restless and is constantly crossing to the Continent; but he returns with a certain abruptness, for he hates meeting the Dexter Freers, who seem to pervade the more comfortable parts of Europe. He dodges them in every town. Sidney Feeder feels very badly about him; it's months since Jackson has sent him any "results." The excellent fellow goes very often, in a consolatory spirit, to see Mrs. Lemon, but has not yet been able to answer her standing question—"Why that girl more than another?" Lady Agatha Longstraw and her husband arrived a year ago in England, and Mr. Longstraw's personality had immense success during the last London season. It's not exactly known what they live on, though perfectly known that he's looking for something to do. Meanwhile it's as good as known that their really quite responsible brother-in-law supports them.

THE SIEGE OF LONDON

I

That solemn piece of upholstery the curtain of the Comédie Française had fallen upon the first act of the piece, and our two Americans had taken advantage of the interval to pass out of the huge hot theatre in company with the other occupants of the stalls. But they were among the first to return, and they beguiled the rest of the intermission with looking at the house, which had lately been cleansed of its historic cobwebs and ornamented with frescoes illustrative of the classic drama. In the month of September the audience at the Théâtre Français is comparatively thin, and on this occasion the drama—*L'Aventurière* of Emile Augier—had no pretensions to novelty. Many of the boxes were empty, others were occupied by persons of provincial or nomadic appearance. The boxes are far from the stage, near which our spectators were placed; but even at a distance Rupert Waterville was able to appreciate details. He was fond of appreciating details, and when he went to the theatre he looked about him a good deal, making use of a dainty but remarkably powerful glass. He knew that such a course was wanting in true distinction and that it was indelicate to level at a lady an instrument often only less injurious in effect than a double-barrelled pistol; but he was always very curious, and was sure, in any case, that at that moment, at that antiquated play—so he was pleased to qualify the masterpiece of a contemporary—he shouldn't be observed by any one he knew. Standing up therefore with his back to the stage he made the circuit of the boxes while several other persons near him performed the operation with even greater coolness.

"Not a single pretty woman," he remarked at last to his friend; an observation which Littlemore, sitting in his place and staring with a bored expression at the new-looking curtain, received in perfect silence. He rarely indulged in these optical excursions; he had been a great deal in Paris and had ceased to vibrate more than a few times a day; he believed the French capital could have no more surprises for him, though it had had a good many in former days. Waterville was still in the stage of surprise; he suddenly expressed this emotion. "By Jove, I beg your pardon, I beg *her* pardon! There *is* after all a woman who may be called"—he paused a little, inspecting her—"an approach to a beauty!"

"How near an approach?" Littlemore responded.

"An unusual kind—an indescribable kind." Littlemore was not heeding his answer, but presently heard himself appealed to. "I say, I wish very much you'd do me a favour."

"I did you a favour in coming here," said Littlemore. "It's insufferably hot, and the play's like a dinner that has been dressed by the kitchen-maid. The actors are all *doublures*."

"It's simply to answer me this: is *she* respectable now?" Waterville demanded, inattentive to his friend's epigram.

Littlemore gave a groan, without turning his head. "You're always wanting to know if they're respectable. What on earth can it matter?"

"I've made such mistakes—I've lost all confidence," said poor Waterville, to whom European civilisation had not ceased to be a novelty and who during the last six months had found himself confronted with problems for which his training had little prepared him. Whenever he encountered a very nice-looking woman he was sure to discover that she belonged to the class represented by the heroine of M. Augier's drama; and whenever his attention rested upon a person of a florid style of attraction there was the strongest probability that she would turn out a countess. The countesses often looked so unnaturally cheap and the others unnaturally expensive. Littlemore distinguished at a glance; he never made mistakes.

"Simply for looking at them it doesn't matter, I suppose," Waterville ingenuously sighed.

"You stare at them all alike," Littlemore went on, still without moving; "except indeed when I tell you they *aren't* decent—then your eyes, my dear man, grow as large as saucers."

"If your judgement's against this lady I promise never to look at her again. I mean the one in the third box from the passage, in white, with the red flowers," the younger man said as Littlemore slowly rose and stood beside him. "The fellow with her is leaning forward. It's he who makes me doubt. Will you have the glass?"

Littlemore looked about him without concentration. "No, thank you, I can see without staring. The young man's a very good young man," he presently reported.

"Very indeed, but he's several years younger than she. Wait till she turns her head."

She turned it very soon—she apparently had been speaking to the *ouvreuse*, at the door of the box—and presented her face to the public; a fair harmonious face, with smiling eyes, smiling lips, a low brow ornamented with delicate rings of black hair and ears marked by the sparkle of diamonds sufficiently large to be seen across the Théâtre Français. Littlemore looked at her, then started and held out his hand. "The glass, please!"

"Do you know her?" his friend asked as he directed the little instrument.

He made no answer; he only looked in silence; then he gave the glass back. "No, she's not respectable." And he dropped again into his seat. As Waterville remained standing he added: "Please sit down; I think she saw me."

"Don't you want her to see you?" pursued the interrogator, promptly complying.

Littlemore hesitated. "I don't want to spoil her game." By this time the *entr'acte* was at an end and the curtain going up.

It had been Waterville's idea that they should go to the theatre. Littlemore, who was always for not going anywhere, had recommended that, the evening being lovely, they should simply sit and smoke at the door of the Grand Café in comparatively pensive isolation. Nevertheless Waterville enjoyed the second act even less than he had done the first, which he thought heavy. He began to wonder whether his companion would wish to stay to the end; a useless line of speculation, for now that he had got to the theatre Littlemore's aversion to change would certainly keep him from moving. Waterville also wondered what he knew about the lady in the box. Once or twice he glanced at his friend, and then was sure the latter wasn't following the play. He was thinking of something else; he was thinking of that woman. When the curtain fell again he sat in his place, making way for his neighbours, as usual, to edge past him, grinding his knees—his legs were long—with their own protuberances. When the two men were alone in the stalls he spoke. "I think I should like to see her again, after all." He spoke in fact as if Waterville might have known all about her. Waterville was conscious of not doing so, but as there was evidently a good deal to know he recognised he should lose nothing by exerting some art. So for the moment he asked no question; he only said: "Well, here's the glass."

Littlemore gave him a glance of good-natured compassion. "I don't mean I want to keep letting *that* off at her. I mean I should rather like to see her as I used to."

"And how did you use to?" asked Waterville with no art now.

"On the back piazza at San Pablo." And as his comrade, in receipt of this information, only stared he went on: "Come out where we can breathe and I'll tell you more."

They made their way to the low and narrow door, more worthy of a rabbit-hutch than of a great theatre, by which you pass from the stalls of the Comédie to the lobby, and as Littlemore went by first his ingenuous friend behind him could see that he glanced up at the box in the occupants of which they were interested. The more interesting of these had her back to the house; she was apparently just leaving the box, after her companion; but as she hadn't put on her mantle it was evident they weren't quitting the theatre. Littlemore's pursuit of fresh air didn't lead him to the street; he had passed his arm into Waterville's and when they reached the fine frigid staircase that ascends to the public foyer he began silently to mount it. Littlemore was averse to active pleasures, but his friend reflected that now at least he had launched himself—

126

he was going to look for the lady whom, with a monosyllable, he appeared to have classified. The young man resigned himself for the moment to asking no questions, and the two strolled together into the shining saloon where Houdon's admirable statue of Voltaire, reflected in a dozen mirrors, is gaped at by visitors too obviously less acute than the genius expressed in those living features. Waterville knew that Voltaire was witty; he had read *Candide* and had already had several opportunities of appreciating the statue. The foyer was not crowded; only a dozen groups were scattered over the polished floor, several others having passed out to the balcony which overhangs the square of the Palais Royal. The windows were open, the myriad lights of Paris made the dull summer evening look like an anniversary or a revolution; a murmur of voices seemed to come up, and even in the foyer one heard the slow click of the horses and the rumble of the crookedly-driven fiacres on the hard smooth street-surface. A lady and a gentleman, their backs to our friends, stood before the image of the *genius loci*; the lady was dressed in white, including a white bonnet. Littlemore felt in the scene, as so many persons feel it just there, something of the finest essence of France, and he gave a significant laugh.

"It seems comical to see her here! The last time was in New Mexico."

"In New Mexico?"

"At San Pablo."

"Oh on the back piazza," said Waterville, putting things together. He had not been aware of the position of San Pablo, for if on the occasion of his lately being appointed to a subordinate diplomatic post in London he had been paying a good deal of attention to European geography he had rather neglected that of his own country.

They hadn't spoken loud and weren't standing near her, but suddenly, as if she had heard them, the lady in white turned round. Her eye caught Waterville's first, and in that glance he saw that if she was aware of something it wasn't because they had exceeded but because she had extraordinary quickness of ear. There was no prompt recognition in it—none even when it rested lightly on George Littlemore. But recognition flashed out a moment

127

later, accompanied with a delicate increase of colour and a quick extension of her settled smile. She had turned completely round; she stood there in sudden friendliness, with parted lips; with a hand, gloved to the elbow, almost imperiously offered. She was even prettier than at a distance. "Well, I declare!" she cried; so loud that every one in the room appeared to feel personally addressed. Waterville was surprised; he hadn't been prepared, even after the mention of the back piazza, to find her of so unmistakable race. Her companion turned round as she spoke; he was a fresh lean young man in evening dress; he kept his hands in his pockets; Waterville was sure he was of race quite other. He looked very grave—for such a fair festive young man—and gave our two friends, though his height was not superior to theirs, a narrow vertical glance. Then he turned back to the statue of Voltaire as if it had been among his premonitions, after all, that the lady he was attending would recognise people he didn't know and didn't even perhaps care to know. This possibly confirmed slightly Littlemore's assertion that she wasn't respectable. The young man was that at least; consummately so. "Where in the world did you drop from?" the lady inquired.

"I've been here for some time," Littlemore said, going forward rather deliberately to shake hands with her. He took it alertly, yet was more serious than she, keeping his eye on her own as if she had been just a trifle dangerous. Such was the manner in which a duly discreet person would have approached some glossy graceful animal which had an occasional trick of biting.

"Here in Paris, do you mean?"

"No; here and there—in Europe generally."

"Well, it's queer I haven't met you."

"Better late than never!" said Littlemore. His smile was a little fixed.

"Well, you look very natural," the lady went on.

"So do you—or very charming—it's the same thing," he answered, laughing and evidently wishing to be easy. It was as if, face to face and after a considerable lapse of time, he had found her more imposing than he expected when, in the stalls below, he determined to come and meet her. As he spoke the young man who was with her gave up his inspection of Voltaire and faced about listlessly, without looking at his companion's acquaintances.

"I want to introduce you to my friend," she went on. "Sir Arthur Demesne—Mr. Littlemore. Mr. Littlemore—Sir Arthur Demesne. Sir Arthur Demesne's an Englishman—Mr. Littlemore's a countryman of mine, an old friend. I haven't seen him for years. For how long? Don't let's count—I wonder you knew me," she continued, addressing this recovered property. "I'm fearfully changed." All this was said in a clear gay tone which was the more audible as she spoke with an odd sociable slowness. The two men, to do honour to her introduction, silently exchanged a glance; the Englishman perhaps coloured a little. He was very conscious of his companion. "I haven't introduced you to many people yet," she dropped.

"Oh I don't mind," said Sir Arthur Demesne.

"Well, it's queer to see you!" she pursued, with her charming eyes still on Littlemore. "You've changed, too—I can see that."

"Not where you're concerned."

"That's what I want to find out. Why don't you introduce your friend? I see he's dying to know me!" And then when he had proceeded with this ceremony, which he reduced to its simplest elements, merely glancing at Rupert Waterville and murmuring his name, "Ah, you don't tell him who I am!" the lady cried while the young secretary made her a formal salutation. "I hope you haven't forgotten!"

Littlemore showed her a face intended to express more than what he had hitherto permitted himself; if its meaning had been put into words these would have been: "Ah, but by which name?"

She answered the unspoken question, putting out her hand as she had done to Littlemore. "Happy to make your acquaintance, Mr. Waterville. I'm Mrs. Headway—perhaps you've heard of me. If you've ever been in America you must have heard of me. Not so much in New York, but in the Western cities. You *are* an American? Well then we're all compatriots—except Sir Arthur Demesne. Let me introduce you to Sir Arthur. Sir Arthur Demesne,

129

Mr. Waterville—Mr. Waterville, Sir Arthur Demesne. Sir Arthur Demesne's a member of Parliament: don't he look young?" She waited for no judgement on this appeal, but suddenly made another as she moved her bracelets back over long loose gloves. "Well, Mr. Littlemore, what are you thinking of?"

He was thinking that he must indeed have forgotten her name, for the one she had pronounced awakened no association. But he could hardly tell her that. "I'm thinking of San Pablo."

"The back piazza at my sister's? Oh don't; it was too horrid. She has left now. I believe every one has left." The member of Parliament drew out his watch with the air of a man who could take no part in these domestic reminiscences; he appeared to combine a generic self-possession with a degree of individual shyness. He said something about its being time they should go back to their seats, but Mrs. Headway paid no attention to the remark. Waterville wished her to linger and indeed felt almost as free to examine her as he had to walk, in a different spirit, round the statue of the author of *Candide*. Her low-growing hair, with its fine dense undulations, was of a shade of blackness that has now become rare; her complexion had the bloom of a white flower; her profile, when she turned her head, was as pure and fine as the outline of a cameo. "You know this is their first theatre," she continued, as if to rise to the occasion. "And this is Voltaire, the celebrated writer."

"I'm devoted to the Comédie Française"—Waterville rose as well.

"Dreadfully bad house; we didn't hear a word," said Sir Arthur Demesne.

"Ah, yes, the sad far boxes!" murmured Waterville.

"I'm rather disappointed," Mrs. Headway went on. "But I want to see what becomes of that woman."

"Doña Clorinde? Oh I suppose they'll shoot her. They generally shoot the women in French plays," Littlemore said.

"It will remind me of San Pablo!" cried Mrs. Headway.

"Ah, at San Pablo the women did the shooting."

"They don't seem to have killed *you!*" she returned archly.

"No, but I'm riddled with wounds."

"Well, this is very remarkable"—the lady reverted to Houdon's statue. "It's beautifully modelled."

"You're perhaps reading M. de Voltaire," Littlemore suggested.

"No; but I've purchased his works."

"They're not proper reading for ladies," said the young Englishman severely, offering his arm to his charge.

"Ah, you might have told me before I had bought them!" she exclaimed in exaggerated dismay.

"I couldn't imagine you'd buy a hundred and fifty volumes."

"A hundred and fifty? I've only bought two."

"Perhaps two won't hurt you!" Littlemore hopefully contributed.

She darted him a reproachful ray. "I know what you mean—that I'm too bad already! Well, bad as I am you must come and see me." And she threw him the name of her hotel as she walked away with her Englishman. Waterville looked after the latter with a certain interest; he had heard of him in London and had seen his portrait in *Vanity Fair*.

It was not yet time to go down, in spite of this gentleman's saying so, and Littlemore and his friend passed out to the balcony of the foyer. "Headway—Headway? Where the deuce did she get that name?" Littlemore asked as they looked down into the flaring dusk.

"From her husband I suppose," his friend suggested.

"From her husband? From which? The last was named Beck."

"How many has she had?" the younger man inquired, anxious to hear how it was Mrs. Headway wasn't respectable.

"I haven't the least idea. But it wouldn't be difficult to find out, as I believe they're all living. She was Mrs. Beck—Nancy Beck—when I knew her."

"Nancy Beck!" cried Waterville, aghast. He was thinking of her delicate profile, like that of a pretty Roman empress. There was a great deal to be explained.

Littlemore explained it in a few words before they returned to their places, admitting indeed that he wasn't yet able to clear up her present appearance. She was a memory of his Western days; he had seen her last some six years before. He had known her very well and in several places; the circle of her activity was chiefly the South-west. This activity had been during that time of a vague character, except in the sense that it was exclusively social. She was supposed to have a husband, one Philadelphia Beck, the editor of a Democratic newspaper, the *Dakota Sentinel*; but Littlemore had never seen him—the pair were living apart—and it had been the impression at San Pablo that matrimony, for Mr. and Mrs. Beck, was about played out. He remembered now to have heard afterwards that she was getting a divorce. She got divorces very easily, she was so taking in court. She had got one or two before from a man whose name he couldn't remember, and there was a legend that even these were not the first. She had been enormously divorced! When he first met her in California she called herself Mrs. Grenville, which he had been given to understand was not an appellation acquired by matrimony, but her parental name, resumed after the dissolution of an unfortunate union. She had had these episodes—her unions were all unfortunate—and had borne half-a-dozen names. She was a charming woman, especially for New Mexico; but she had been divorced too often—it was a tax on one's credulity: she must have repudiated more husbands than she had married.

At San Pablo she was staying with her sister, whose actual spouse—she too had been divorced—the principal man of the place, kept a bank (with the aid of a six-shooter), and who had never suffered Nancy to want for a home during her unattached periods. Nancy had begun very young; she must be about thirty-seven to-day. That was all he meant by her not being respectable. Her chronology was rather mixed; her sister at least had once told him that there was one winter when she didn't know herself who was Nancy's husband. She had gone in mainly for editors—she esteemed the journalistic profession. They must all have been dreadful ruffians, for her own amiability was manifest. It was well known that whatever she had done she had done in self-defence. In fine she had done things—that was the main point now. She had been as pretty as could still be seen, and as good-natured and as clever as could likewise be yet measured; she had been quite the best company in those parts. She was a genuine product of the wild West—a flower of the Pacific slope; ignorant, absurd, crude, but full of pluck and spirit, of natural intelligence and of a certain intermittent haphazard felicity of impulse. She used to sigh that she only wanted a chance—apparently she had found that now. At one time, without her, he didn't see how he could have put up with the life. He had started a cattle-ranch, to which San Pablo was the nearest town, and he used to ride over to see her. Sometimes he stayed there a week; then he went to see her every evening. It was infernally hot; they used to sit on the back piazza. She was always as attractive and very nearly as well-dressed as they had just beheld her. As far as appearance went she might have been transplanted at an hour's notice from that dusty old settlement to the city by the Seine.

"Some of those barbaric women are wonderful," Littlemore said. "Like her, they only want a chance."

He hadn't been in love with her—there never was anything of that sort between them. There might have been of course, but as happened there wasn't. Headway would have been then the successor of Beck; perhaps there had been others between. She was in no sort of "society"; she only had a local reputation ("the well-known Texan belle," the newspapers called her—the other editors, to whom she wasn't married), though indeed in that spacious civilisation the locality was large. She knew nothing of the East and to the best of his belief at that period had never seen New York. Various things might have happened in those six years, however; no doubt she had "come up." The West was sending us everything (Littlemore spoke as a New Yorker); no doubt it would send us at last our brilliant women. The well-known Texan belle used to look quite over the head of New York; even in those days she

133

thought and talked of Paris, which there was no prospect of her knowing: that was the way she had got on in New Mexico. She had had her ambition, her presentiments; she had known she was meant for better things. Even at San Pablo she had prefigured her member of Parliament; every now and then a wandering Englishman came within her range. They weren't all Sir Arthurs, like her present acquisition, but they were usually a change from the editors. What she was doing with her present acquisition Littlemore was curious to see. She was certainly—if he had any capacity for that state of mind, which was not too apparent—making the gentleman happy. She looked very splendid; Headway had probably made a "pile," an achievement not to be imputed to any of the others. She didn't accept money—he was sure she didn't accept money. With all of which, on their way back to their seats, Littlemore, whose tone had been humorous, but with that strain of the pensive which is inseparable from retrospect, suddenly burst into audible laughter. "The modelling of statues and the works of Voltaire!" he broke out, recurring to two or three things she had said. "It's touching to hear her attempt those flights, for in New Mexico she knew nothing about modelling."

"She didn't strike me as affected," Waterville demurred, feeling a vague impulse to view her in becoming lights.

"Oh no; she's only—as she says—fearfully changed."

They were in their places before the play went on again, and they both gave another glance at Mrs. Headway's box. She now was leaning back behind the slow movements of her fan and evidently watching Littlemore as if she had waited to see him come in. Sir Arthur Demesne sat beside her, rather gloomily resting a round pink chin upon a high stiff collar; neither of them seemed to speak.

"Are you sure she makes him happy?" Waterville asked.

"Yes—that's the way those people show it."

"But does she go about alone with him at that rate? Where's her husband?"

"I suppose she has divorced him."

"And does she want to marry the Baronet?" Waterville went on as if his companion was omniscient.

It amused Littlemore for the moment to appear so. "He wants to marry *her*, I guess."

"And be divorced like the others?"

"Oh no; this time she has got what she wants," said Littlemore as the curtain rose.

He suffered three days to elapse before he called at the Hôtel Meurice, which she had designated, and we may occupy this interval in adding a few words to the story we have taken from his lips. George Littlemore's residence in the Far West had been of the usual tentative sort—he had gone there to replenish a pocket depleted by youthful extravagance. His first attempts had failed; the days had pretty well passed when a fortune was to be picked up even by a young man who might be supposed to have inherited from an honourable father, lately removed, some of those fine abilities, mainly dedicated to the importation of tea, to which the elder Mr. Littlemore was indebted for the power of leaving his son markedly at ease. Littlemore had dissipated his patrimony and was not quick to discover his talents, which, restricted chiefly to an unlimited faculty for smoking and horse-breaking, appeared to lie in the direction of none of the professions called liberal. He had been sent to Harvard to have them cultivated, but here they had taken such a form that repression had been found more necessary than stimulus— repression embodied in an occasional sojourn in one of the lovely villages of the Connecticut Valley. Rustication saved him perhaps in the sense that it detached him; it undermined his ambitions, which had been foolish. At the age of thirty he had mastered none of the useful arts, unless we include in the number the great art of indifference. But he was roused from too consistent an application of it by a stroke of good luck. To oblige a luckless friend, even in more pressing need of cash than himself, he had purchased for a moderate sum—the proceeds of a successful game of poker—a share in a silver-mine which the disposer of it, with unusual candour, admitted to be destitute of metal. Littlemore looked into his mine and recognised the truth of the contention, which, however, was demolished some two years later by a sudden revival of curiosity on the part of one of the other shareholders. This gentleman, convinced that a silver-mine without silver is as rare as an effect without a cause, discovered the sparkle of the precious element deep down in the reasons of things. The discovery was agreeable to Littlemore, and was the beginning of a fortune which, through several dull years and in many rough places, he had repeatedly despaired of, and which a man whose purpose had never been very keen, nor his aim very high, didn't perhaps altogether deserve.

It was before he saw himself successful that he had made the acquaintance of the lady now established at the Hôtel Meurice. To-day he owned the largest share in his mine, which had remained perversely productive and enabled him to buy, among other things, in Montana, a cattle-ranch of higher type than the dry acres near San Pablo. Ranches and mines encourage security, and the consciousness of not having to watch the sources of his income too anxiously—a tax on ideal detachment which spoils the idea—now added itself to his usual coolness. It was not that this same coolness hadn't been considerably tried. To take only one—the principal—instance: he had lost his wife after only a twelvemonth of marriage, some three years before the date at which we meet him. He had been turned thirty-eight when he distinguished and wooed and won an ardent girl of twenty-three, who, like himself, had consulted all the probabilities in expecting a succession of happy years. She had left him a small daughter, now entrusted to the care of his only sister, the wife of an English squire and mistress of a dull park in Hampshire. This lady, Mrs. Dolphin by name, had captivated her landowner during a journey in which Mr. Dolphin had promised himself to examine the institutions of the United States. The institution on which he had reported most favourably was the pretty girls of the larger towns, and he had returned to New York a year or two later to marry Miss Littlemore, who, unlike her brother, had not wasted her patrimony. Her sister-in-law, married several years later and coming to Europe on this occasion, had died in London—where she had flattered herself the doctors were infallible—a week after the birth of her little girl; and poor Littlemore, though relinquishing his child for the moment, had lingered on the scene of his deep disconcertment to be within call of the Hampshire nursery. He was a presence to attract admiring attention, especially since his hair and moustache had turned to so fine a silver. Tall and clean-limbed, with a good figure and a bad carriage, he looked capable but indolent, and was exposed to imputations of credit and renown, those attaching to John Gilpin, of which he was far from being either conscious or desirous. His eye was at once keen and quiet, his smile dim and dilatory, but perfectly sincere. His principal occupation to-day was doing nothing, and he did it with a beautiful consistency. This exercise excited real envy on the part of Rupert Waterville, who was ten years younger and who had too many ambitions and anxieties—none of them very important, but making collectively a considerable incubus—to be able to wait for inspiration. He thought of it as the last social grace, he hoped some day to arrive at it; it made a man so independent—he had his resources within his own breast. Littlemore could sit for a whole evening without utterance or movement, smoking cigars and looking absently at his finger-nails. As every one knew him for a good fellow who had made his fortune this free and even surface offered by him to contact couldn't be attributed to stupidity or moroseness. It seemed to imply a fund of reminiscence, an experience of life that had left him hundreds of things to think about. Waterville felt that if he himself could make a good use of these present years and keep a sharp lookout for experience he too at forty-four might have time to look at his finger-nails. He cultivated the conceit that such contemplations—not of course in their literal but in their symbolic intensity—were a sign of a man of the world. Waterville, reckoning possibly without an ungrateful Department of State, also nursed the fond fancy that he had embraced the diplomatic career. He was the junior of the two secretaries who render the *personnel* of the United States Legation in London exceptionally numerous, and was at present enjoying his annual leave of absence. It became a diplomatist to be inscrutable, and though he had by no means, as a whole, taken Littlemore for his model—there were much better ones in the diplomatic body accredited to the Court of Saint James's— he thought the right effect of fine ease suggested when of an evening, in Paris, after one had been asked what one would like to do, one replied that one would like to do nothing, and simply sat for an interminable time in front of the Grand Café on the Boulevard de la Madeleine (one was very fond of cafés) ordering a succession of *demi-tasses*. It was seldom Littlemore cared even to go to the theatre, and the visit to the Comédie Française, which we have described, had been undertaken at Waterville's instance. He had seen *Le Demi-Monde* a few nights before and had been told that *L'Aventurière* would show him a particular treatment of the same subject—the justice to be meted out to compromised women who attempt to thrust themselves into honourable families. It seemed to him that in both of these cases the ladies had deserved their fate, but he wished it might have been brought about by a little less lying on the part of the representatives of honour. Littlemore and he, without being intimate, were very good friends and spent much of their time together. As it turned out Littlemore was grateful for the chance that had led him to a view of this new incarnation of Nancy Beck.

II

His delay in going to see her was nevertheless calculated; there were more reasons for it than we need at once go into. When he did go, however, Mrs. Headway was at home and he was scarce surprised to find Sir Arthur Demesne in her sitting-room. There was something in the air that spoke of the already ample stretch of this gentleman's visit. Littlemore thought probable that, given the circumstances, he would now bring it to a close; he must have learned from their hostess that this welcomed compatriot was an old and familiar friend. He might of course have definite rights—he had every appearance of it, but the more they were rooted the more gracefully he could afford to waive them. Littlemore made these reflexions while the friend in possession faced him without sign of departure. Mrs. Headway was very gracious—she had ever the manner of having known you a hundred years; she scolded Littlemore extravagantly for not having been to see her sooner, but this was only a form of the gracious. By daylight she looked a little faded, but there was a spirit in her that rivalled the day. She had the best rooms in the hotel and an air of extreme opulence and prosperity; her courier sat outside, in the antechamber, and she evidently knew how to live. She attempted to include Sir Arthur in the conversation, but though the young man remained in his place he failed to grasp the offered perch. He followed

138

but as from the steep bank of the stream, where yet he was evidently not at his ease. The conversation therefore remained superficial—a quality that of old had by no means belonged to Mrs. Headway's interviews with her friends. The Englishman hovered with a distant air which Littlemore at first, with a good deal of private amusement, simply attributed to jealousy.

But after a time Mrs. Headway spoke to the point. "My dear Sir Arthur, I wish very much you'd go."

The member of Parliament got up and took his hat. "I thought I should oblige you by staying."

"To defend me against Mr. Littlemore? I've known him since I was a baby—I know the worst he can do." She fixed her charming smile on her retreating visitor and added with much unexpectedness: "I want to talk to him about my past!"

"That's just what I want to hear," said Sir Arthur, with his hand on the door.

"We're going to talk American; you wouldn't understand us! He speaks in the English style," she explained in her little sufficient way as the Baronet, who announced that at all events he would come back in the evening, let himself out.

"He doesn't know about your past?" Littlemore inquired, trying not to make the question sound impertinent.

"Oh yes; I've told him everything; but he doesn't understand. One has to hold an Englishman by the head, you know, and kind of force it down. He has never heard of a woman being—" But here Mrs. Headway checked herself, while Littlemore filled out the blank. "What are you laughing at? It doesn't matter," she went on; "there are more things in the world than those people have heard of. However, I like them very much; at least I like *him*. He's such a regular gentleman; do you know what I mean? Only, as he stays too long and he ain't amusing, I'm very glad to see you for a change."

"Do you mean I'm not a regular gentleman?" Littlemore asked.

"No indeed; you used to be out there. I think you were the only one—and I hope you are still. That's why I recognised you the other night—I might have cut you, you know."

"You can still, if you like. It's not too late."

"Oh no, that's not what I want. I want you to help me."

"To help you?"

Mrs. Headway fixed her eyes for a moment on the door. "Do you suppose that man is there still?"

"The member of Parliament?"

"No, I mean Max. Max is my courier," said Mrs. Headway with some impressiveness.

"I haven't the least idea. I'll see if you like."

"No—in that case I should have to give him an order, and I don't know what in the world to ask him to do. He sits there for hours; with my simple habits I afford him no employment. I'm afraid I've no grand imagination."

"The burden of grandeur!" said Littlemore.

"Oh yes, I'm very grand for clothes and things. But on the whole I like it. I'm only afraid he'll hear. I talk so very loud. That's another thing I'm trying to get over."

"Why do you want to be different?"

"Well, because everything else is so," Mrs. Headway bravely pleaded. "Did you hear that I had lost my husband?" she went on abruptly.

"Do you mean—a—Mr.—?" and Littlemore paused with an effect that didn't seem to come home to her.

"I mean Mr. Headway," she said with dignity. "I've been through a good deal since you saw me last: marriage and death and trouble and all sorts of things."

140

"You had been through a good deal of marriage before that," her old friend ventured to observe.

She rested her eyes on him with extravagant intensity and without a change of colour. "Not so much, not so much!—"

"Not so much as might have been thought?"

"Not so much as was reported. I forget whether I was married when I saw you last."

"It was one of the reports," said Littlemore. "But I never saw Mr. Beck."

"You didn't lose much; he was too mean to live. I've done certain things in my life that I've never understood; no wonder others can't do much with them. But that's all over! Are you sure Max doesn't hear?" she asked quickly.

"Not at all sure. But if you suspect him of listening at the keyhole I'd send him away."

"I don't think he does that. I'm always rushing to the door."

"Then he doesn't hear. I had no idea you had so many secrets. When I parted with you Mr. Headway was in the future."

"Well, now he's in the past. He was a pleasant man—I can understand my doing that. But he only lived a year. He had neuralgia of the heart; he left me very well off." She mentioned these various facts as if they were quite of the same order.

"I'm glad to hear *that*. You used to have expensive tastes."

"I've plenty of money," said Mrs. Headway. "Mr. Headway had property at Denver, which has increased immensely in value. After his death I tried New York. But I don't take much stock in New York." Littlemore's hostess spoke these last words in a tone that reeked of some strong experience. "I mean to live in Europe. I guess I can do with Europe," she stated; and the manner of it had the touch of prophecy, as the other proposition had had the echo of history.

141

Littlemore was much struck with all this; he was greatly enlivened by Mrs. Headway. "Then you're travelling with that young man?" he pursued, with the coolness of a person who wishes to make his entertainment go as far as possible.

She folded her arms as she leaned back in her chair. "Look here, Mr. Littlemore; I'm about as sweet-tempered as I used to be in America, but I know a great deal more. Of course I ain't travelling with that young man. He's only a good friend."

"He isn't a good lover?" Littlemore ventured.

"Do people travel—publicly—with their lovers? I don't want you to laugh at me—I want you to help me." Her appeal might, in its almost childish frankness, have penetrated; she recognised his wisdom. "As I tell you, I've taken a great fancy to this grand old Europe; I feel as if I should never go back. But I want to see something of the life. I think it would suit me—if I could get started a little. George Littlemore," she added in a moment—"I may as well be *real*, for I ain't at all ashamed. I want to get into society. That's what I'm after!"

He settled himself in his chair with the feeling of a man who, knowing that he will have to pull, seeks to obtain a certain leverage. It was in a tone of light jocosity, almost of encouragement, however, that he repeated: "Into society? It seems to me you're in it already, with the big people over here for your adorers."

"That's just what I want to know—if they *are* big," she promptly said. "Is a Baronet much?"

"So they're apt to think. But I know very little about it."

"Ain't you in society yourself?"

"I? Never in the world! Where did you get that idea? I care no more about society than about Max's buttons."

Mrs. Headway's countenance assumed for a moment a look of extreme disappointment, and Littlemore could see that, having heard of his silver-mine and his cattle-ranch, and knowing that he was living in Europe, she had hoped to find him eminent in the world of fashion. But she speedily took heart. "I don't believe a word of it. You know you're a real gentleman—you can't help yourself."

"I may be a gentleman, but I've none of the habits of one." Littlemore had a pause and then added: "I guess I've sat too much on back piazzas."

She flushed quickly; she instantly understood—understood even more than he had meant to say. But she wished to make use of him, and it was of more importance that she should appear forgiving—especially as she had the happy consciousness of being so—than that she should punish a cruel speech. She would be wise, however, to recognise everything. "That makes no difference—a gentleman's always a gentleman."

"Ah, not the way a lady's always a lady!" he laughed.

"Well, talking of ladies, it's unnatural that, through your sister, you shouldn't know something about European society," said Mrs. Headway.

At the mention of his sister, made with a studied lightness of reference which he caught as it passed, Littlemore was unable to repress a start. "What in the world have you to do with my sister?" he would have liked to say. The introduction of this relative was disagreeable to him; she belonged quite to another order of ideas, and it was out of the question Mrs. Headway should ever make her acquaintance—if this was what, as the latter would have said, she was "after." But he took advantage of a side issue. "What do you mean by European society? One can't talk about that. It's an empty phrase."

"Well, I mean English society; I mean the society your sister lives in; that's what I mean," said his hostess, who was quite prepared to be definite. "I mean the people I saw in London last May—the people I saw at the opera and in the park, the people who go to the Queen's drawing-rooms. When I was in London I stayed at that hotel on the corner of Piccadilly—the one looking straight down Saint James's Street—and I spent hours together at the window there looking at the people in the carriages. I had a carriage of my own, and when I wasn't at my window I was riding all around. I was all alone;

143

I saw every one, but I knew no one—I had no one to tell me. I didn't know Sir Arthur then—I only met him a month ago at Homburg. He followed me to Paris—that's how he came to be my guest." Serenely, prosaically, without a breath of the inflation of vanity, she made this last assertion: it was as if she were used to being followed or as if a gentleman one met at Homburg would inevitably follow. In the same tone she went on: "I attracted a good deal of attention in London—I could easily see that."

"You'll do that wherever you go," Littlemore said—insufficiently enough, as he felt.

"I don't want to attract so much; I think it's vulgar." She spoke as if she liked to use the word. She was evidently open to new sources of pleasure.

"Every one was looking at you the other night at the theatre," Littlemore continued. "How can you hope to escape notice?"

"I don't want to escape notice. People have always looked at me and I guess they always will. But there are different ways of being looked at, and I know the way I want. I mean to have it too!" Mrs. Headway prettily shrilled. Yes, she was full of purpose.

He sat there face to face with her and for some time said nothing. He had a mixture of feelings, and the memory of other places, other hours, was stealing over him. There had been of old a very considerable absence of interposing surfaces between these two—he had known her as one knew people only amid the civilisation of big tornadoes and back piazzas. He had liked her extremely in a place where it would have been ridiculous to be difficult to please. But his sense of this fact was somehow connected with other and such now alien facts; his liking for Nancy Beck was an emotion of which the sole setting was a back piazza. She presented herself here on a new basis—she appeared to want to be classified afresh. Littlemore said to himself that this was too much trouble; he had taken her at the great time in that way—he couldn't begin at this late hour to take her in another way. He asked himself if she were going to be a real bore. It wasn't easy to suppose her bent on ravage, but she might become tiresome if she were too disposed to be different. It made him rather afraid when she began to talk about European society, about his sister, to pronounce things vulgar. Littlemore was naturally merciful and decently just; but there was in his composition an element of the indolent, the sceptical, perhaps even the brutal, which made him decidedly prefer the simplicity of their former terms of intercourse. He had no particular need to see a woman rise again, as the mystic process was called; he didn't believe in women's rising again. He believed in their not going down, thought it perfectly possible and eminently desirable; but held it was much better for society that the divisions, the categories, the differing values, should be kept clear. He didn't believe in bridging the chasms, in muddling the kinds. In general he didn't pretend to say what was good for society—society seemed to him rather in a bad way; but he had a conviction on this particular point. Nancy Beck going in for the great prizes, that spectacle might be entertaining for a simple spectator; but it would be a nuisance, an embarrassment, from the moment anything more than detached "fun" should represent his share. He had no wish to be "mean," but it might be well to show her he wasn't to be humbugged.

"Oh if there's anything you want you'll have it," he said in answer to her last remark. "You've always had what you want."

"Well, I want something new this time. Does your sister reside in London?"

"My dear lady, what do you know about my sister?" Littlemore asked. "She's not a woman you'd care in the least for."

His old friend had a marked pause. "You don't really respect me!" she then abruptly and rather gaily cried. It had one of her "Texan" effects of drollery; so that, yes, evidently, if he wished to preserve the simplicity of their former intercourse she was willing to humour him.

"Ah, my dear Mrs. Beck—!" he vaguely protested, using her former name quite by accident. At San Pablo he—and apparently she—had never thought whether he respected her or not. That never came up.

"That's a proof of it—calling me by that hateful name! Don't you believe I'm married? I haven't been fortunate in my names," she pensively added.

"You make it very awkward when you say such mad things. My sister lives most of the year in the country; she's very simple, rather dull, perhaps a trifle narrow-minded. You're very clever, very lively, and as large and loose and free as all creation. That's why I think you wouldn't like her."

"You ought to be ashamed to run down your sister!" Mrs. Headway made prompt answer. "You told me once—at San Pablo—that she was the nicest woman you knew. I made a note of that, you see. And you told me she was just my age. So that makes it rather inglorious for you if you won't introduce me!" With which she gave a laugh that perhaps a little heralded danger. "I'm not in the least afraid of her being dull. It's all right, it's just refined and nice, to be dull. I'm ever so much too exciting."

"You are indeed, ever so much! But nothing is more easy than to know my sister," said Littlemore, who knew perfectly that what he said was untrue. And then as a diversion from this delicate topic he brought out: "Are you going to marry Sir Arthur?"

"Don't you think I've been married about enough?"

"Possibly; but this is a new line, it would be different. An Englishman—that's a new sensation."

"If I *should* marry it would be a European," she said judiciously.

"Your chance is very good—they're all marrying Americans."

"He would have to be some one fine, the man I should marry now. I have a good deal to make up, you know. That's what I want to learn about Sir Arthur. All this time you haven't told me."

"I've nothing in the world to tell—I've never heard of him. Hasn't he told you himself?"

"Nothing at all; he's very modest. He doesn't brag nor 'blow' nor make himself out anything great. That's what I like him for: I think it's in such good taste. I do love good taste!" said Mrs. Headway. "But all this time," she added, "you haven't told me you'd help me."

"How can I help you? I'm no one here, you know—I've no power."

"You can help me by not preventing me. I want you to promise not to prevent me." She continued to give him her charming conscious eyes, which seemed to look far into his own.

"Good Lord, how could I prevent you?"

"Well, I'm not quite sure of how. But you might try."

"Oh I'm too lazy and too stupid," Littlemore said.

"Yes," she replied, musing as she still looked at him. "I think you're too stupid. But I think you're also too kind," she added more graciously. She was almost irresistible when she said such a thing as that.

They talked for a quarter of an hour longer, and at last—as if she had had scruples—she spoke to him of his own marriage, of the death of his wife, matters to which she alluded more felicitously (as he thought) than to some other points. "If you've a little girl you ought to be very happy; that's what I should like to have. Lord, I should make her a nice woman! Not like me—in another style!" When he rose to leave her she made a great point of his coming again—she was to be some weeks longer in Paris. And he must bring Mr. Waterville.

"Your English friend won't like that—our coming very often," Littlemore reminded her as he stood with his hand on the door.

But she met this without difficulty. "I don't know what he has to do with it."

"Neither do I. Only he must be in love with you."

"That doesn't give him any right. Mercy, if I had had to put myself out for all the men that have been in love with me!"

"Of course you'd have had a terrible life. Even doing as you please you've had rather an agitated one," Littlemore pursued. "But your young Englishman's sentiments appear to give him the right to sit there, after one comes in, looking blighted and bored. That might become very tiresome."

"The moment he becomes tiresome I send him away. You can trust me for that."

"Oh it doesn't matter after all." Our friend was perfectly conscious that nothing would suit him less than to have undisturbed possession of Mrs. Headway.

She came out with him into the antechamber. Mr. Max, the courier, was fortunately not there. She lingered a little; she appeared to have more to say. "On the contrary he likes you to come," she then continued; "he wants to study my friends."

"To study them?"

"He wants to find out about me, and he thinks they may tell him something. Some day he'll ask you right out 'What sort of a woman is she anyway?'"

"Hasn't he found out yet?"

"He doesn't understand me," said Mrs. Headway, surveying the front of her dress. "He has never seen any one like me."

"I should imagine not!"

"So he'll just try to find out from you."

"Well then he *shall* find out," Littlemore returned. "I'll just tell him you're the most charming woman in Europe."

"That ain't a description! Besides, he knows it. He wants to know if I'm respectable."

"Why should he fuss about it?" Littlemore asked—not at once.

She grew a little pale; she seemed to be watching his lips. "Well, mind you tell him all right," she went on, with her wonderful gay glare, the strain of which yet brought none of her colour back.

"Respectable? I'll tell him you're adorable!"

148

She stood a moment longer. "Ah, you're no use!" she rather harshly wailed. And she suddenly turned away and passed back into her sitting-room, with the heavy rustle of her far-trailing skirts.

<h1 style="text-align:center"><u>III</u></h1>

"Elle ne doute de rien!" Littlemore said to himself as he walked away from the hotel; and he repeated the phrase in talking about her to Waterville. "She wants to be right," he added; "but she'll never really succeed. She has begun too late, she'll never get on the true middle of the note. However, she won't know when she's wrong, so it doesn't signify!" And he more or less explained what he meant by this discrimination. She'd remain in certain essentials incurable. She had no delicacy; no discretion; no shading; she was a woman who suddenly said to you, "You don't really respect me!" As if that were a thing for a woman to say!

"It depends upon what she meant by it." Waterville could always imagine alternatives.

"The more she meant by it the less she ought to say it!" Littlemore declared.

But he returned to the Hôtel Meurice and on the next occasion took this companion with him. The secretary of legation, who had not often been in close quarters with pretty women whose respectability, or whose lack of it, was so frankly discussable, was prepared to find the well-known Texan belle a portentous type. He was afraid there might be danger in her, but on the whole he felt armed. The object of his devotion at present was his country, or at least the Department of State; he had no intention of being diverted from that allegiance. Besides, he had his ideal of the attractive woman—a person pitched in a very much lower key than this shining, smiling, rustling, chattering daughter of the Territories. The woman he should care for would have repose, a sense of the private in life, and the implied, even the withheld, in talk; would sometimes let one alone. Mrs. Headway was personal, familiar, intimate, perpetually appealing or accusing, demanding explanations and pledges, saying things one had to answer. All this was accompanied with a hundred smiles and radiations and other natural graces, but the general effect was distinctly fatiguing. She had certainly a great deal of charm, an immense desire to please, and a wonderful collection of dresses and trinkets; but she was eager and clamorous, and it was hard for other people to be put to serve her appetite. If she wanted to get into society there was no reason why those of her visitors who had the luck to be themselves independent, to be themselves placed, and to be themselves by the same token critical, should wish to see her there; for it was this absence of common social encumbrances made her drawing-room attractive. There was no doubt whatever that she was several women in one, and she ought to content herself with that sort of numerical triumph. Littlemore said to Waterville that it was stupid of her to wish to scale the heights; she ought to know how much more she was in her element scouring the plain. She appeared vaguely to irritate him; even her fluttering attempts at self-culture—she had become a great judge of books and pictures and plays, and pronounced off-hand—constituted a vague invocation, an appeal for sympathy onerous to a man who disliked the trouble of revising old decisions consecrated by a certain amount of reminiscence that might be called tender. She exerted, however, effectively enough one of the arts of solicitation—she often startled and surprised. Even Waterville felt a touch of the unexpected, though not indeed an excess of it, to belong to his conception of the woman who should have an ideal repose. Of course there were two kinds of surprises, and only one of them thoroughly pleasant, though Mrs. Headway dealt impartially in both. She had the sudden delights, the odd exclamations, the queer curiosities of a person who has grown up in a country where everything is new and many things ugly, and who, with a natural turn for the arts and amenities of life, makes a tardy acquaintance with some of the finer usages, the higher pleasures. She was provincial; it was easy to see how she embodied that term; it took no great cleverness. But what was Parisian enough—if to be Parisian was the measure of success—was the way she picked up ideas and took a hint from every circumstance. "Only give me time and I guess I'll come out all right," she said to Littlemore, who watched her progress with a mixture of admiration and regret. She delighted to speak of herself as a poor little barbarian grubbing up crumbs of knowledge, and this habit borrowed beautiful relief from her delicate face, her so highly developed dress and the free felicity of her manners.

One of her surprises was, that after that first visit she said no more to Littlemore about Mrs. Dolphin. He did her perhaps the grossest injustice, but he had quite expected her to bring up this lady whenever they met. "If she'll only leave Agnes alone she may do what she will," he said to Waterville, expressing his satisfaction. "My sister would never look at her, and it would be very awkward to have to tell her so." She counted on aid; she made him feel this simply by the way she looked at him; but for the moment she demanded no definite service. She held her tongue but waited, and her patience itself was a deeper admonition. In the way of society, it had to be noted, her privileges were meagre, Sir Arthur Demesne and her two compatriots being, so far as the latter could discover, her only visitors. She might have had other friends, but she held her head very high and liked better to see no one than not to see the best company. She went in, clearly, for producing the effect of being by no means so neglected as fastidious. There were plenty of Americans in Paris, but in this direction she failed to extend her acquaintance; the nice people wouldn't come to her, and nothing would have induced her to receive the others. She had a perfect and inexorable view of those she wished to avoid. Littlemore expected her every day to ask why he didn't bring some of his friends—as to which he had his answer ready. It was rather a poor one, for it consisted but of the "academic" assurance that he wished to keep her for himself. She would be sure to retort that this was "too thin," as indeed it was; yet the days went by without her calling him to account. The little American colony in Paris abounded in amiable women, but there were none to whom Littlemore could make up his mind to say that it would be a favour to him they should call on Mrs. Headway. He shouldn't like them the better for doing so, and he wished to like those of whom he might ask a favour. Except, therefore, that he occasionally spoke of her as a full-blown flower of the West, still very pretty, but of not at all orthodox salon scent, who had formerly been a great chum of his, she remained unknown in the circles of the Avenue Gabriel and the streets that encircle the Arch of Triumph. To ask the men to go see her without asking the ladies would only accentuate the fact that he didn't ask the ladies; so he asked no one at all. Besides, it was true—just a little—that he wished to keep her to himself, and he was fatuous enough to believe she really cared more for him than for any outsider. Of course, however, he would never dream of marrying her, whereas her Englishman apparently was capable of that quaintness. She hated her old past; she often made that point, talking of this "dark backward" as if it were an appendage of the same order as a thieving cook or a noisy bedroom or even an inconvenient protrusion of drapery. Therefore, as Littlemore was part of the very air of the previous it might have been supposed she would hate him too and wish to banish him, with all the images he recalled, from her sight. But she made an exception in his favour, and if she disliked their early relations as a chapter of her own history she seemed still to like them as a chapter of his. He felt how she clung to him, how she believed he could make a great and blest difference for her and in the long run would. It was to the long run that she appeared little by little to have attuned herself.

She succeeded perfectly in maintaining harmony between Sir Arthur Demesne and her American visitors, who spent much less time in her drawing-room. She had easily persuaded him that there were no grounds for jealousy and that they had no wish, as she said, to crowd him out; for it was ridiculous to be jealous of two persons at once, and Rupert Waterville, after he had learned the way to her favour and her fireside, presented himself as often as his original introducer. The two indeed usually came together and they ended by relieving their competitor of a part of the weight of his problem. This amiable and earnest but slightly fatuous young man, who had not yet made up his mind, was sometimes rather oppressed with the magnitude of the undertaking, and when alone with Mrs. Headway occasionally found the tension of his thoughts quite painful. He was very slim and straight and looked taller than his height; he had the prettiest silkiest hair, which waved away from a large white forehead, and he was endowed with a nose of the so-called Roman model. He looked, in spite of these attributes, younger than his years, partly on account of the delicacy of his complexion and the almost child-like candour of his round blue eyes. He was diffident and self-conscious; there were certain letters he couldn't pronounce. At the same time he carried himself as one brought up to fill a considerable place in the world, with whom confidence had become a duty and correctness a habit, and who, though he might occasionally be a little awkward about small things, would be sure to acquit himself honourably in great ones. He was very simple and believed himself very serious; he had the blood of a score of Warwickshire squires in his veins, mingled in the last instance with the somewhat paler fluid still animating the long-necked daughter of a banker who, after promising himself high glories as a father-in-law, had by the turn of events been reduced to looking for them in Sir Baldwin Demesne. The boy who was the only fruit of that gentleman's marriage had come into his title at five years of age; his mother, who was somehow parentally felt to have a second time broken faith with expectation by not having better guarded the neck of her husband, broken in the hunting-field, watched over him with a tenderness that burned as steadily as a candle shaded by a transparent hand. She never admitted even to herself that he was not the cleverest of men; but it took all her own cleverness, which was much greater, to maintain this appearance. Fortunately he wasn't wild, so that he would never marry an actress or a governess, like two or three of the young men who had been at Eton with him. With this ground of nervousness the less Lady Demesne awaited with a proud patience his appointment to some high office. He represented in Parliament the Conservative instincts and vote of a red-roofed market town, and, sending regularly to his bookseller for the new publications on economical subjects, was determined his political development should have a massive statistical basis. He was not conceited; he was only misinformed—misinformed, I mean, about himself. He thought himself essential to the propriety of things—not as an individual, but as an institution. This conviction indeed was too sacred to betray itself by vulgar assumptions. If he was a little man in a big place he never strutted nor talked loud; he merely felt it as a luxury that he had a large social circumference. It was like sleeping in a big bed; practically one didn't toss about the more, but one felt a greater freshness.

He had never seen anything like Mrs. Headway; he hardly knew by what standard to measure her. She was not at all the English lady—not one of those with whom he had been accustomed to converse; yet it was impossible not to make out in her a temper and a tone. He might have been sure she was provincial, but as he was much under her charm he compromised by pronouncing her only foreign. It was of course provincial to be foreign;

but this was after all a peculiarity which she shared with a great many nice people. He wasn't wild, and his mother had flattered herself that in this all-important matter he wouldn't be perverse; yet it was far from regular that he should have taken a fancy to an American widow, five years older than himself, who knew no one and who sometimes didn't appear to understand exactly who he was. Though he believed in no alternative to the dignity of the British consciousness, it was precisely her foreignness that pleased him; she seemed as little as possible of his own race and creed; there wasn't a touch of Warwickshire in her composition. She was like an Hungarian or a Pole, with the difference that he could almost make out her speech. The unfortunate young man was engulfed even while not admitting that he had done more than estimate his distance to the brink. He would love wisely— one might even so love agreeably. He had intelligently arranged his life; he had determined to marry at thirty-two. A long line of ancestors was watching him; he hardly knew what they would think of Mrs. Headway. He hardly knew what he thought himself; the only thing he was absolutely sure of was that she made the time pass as it passed in no other pursuit. That, indeed, rather worried him; he was by no means sure anything so precious should be so little accounted for. There was nothing so to account but the fragments of Mrs. Headway's conversation, the peculiarities of her accent, the sallies of her wit, the audacities of her fancy, the odd echoes of her past. Of course he knew she had had a past; she wasn't a young girl, she was a widow—and widows were essentially the expression of an accomplished fact. He was not jealous of her antecedents, but he would have liked a little to piece them together, and it was here the difficulty occurred. The subject was illumined with fitful flashes, but never placed itself before him as a general picture. He asked her various questions, but her answers were so startling that, like sudden luminous points, they seemed to intensify the darkness round their edges. She had apparently spent her life in a remote province of a barbarous country, but it didn't follow from this that she herself had been low. She had been a lily among thistles, and there was something romantic possibly in the interest taken by a man of his position in a woman of hers. It pleased Sir Arthur to believe he was romantic; that had been the case with several of his ancestors, who supplied a precedent without which he would scarce perhaps

154

have ventured to trust himself. He was the victim of perplexities from which a single spark of direct perception would have saved him. He took everything in the literal sense; a grain of humour or of imagination would have saved him, but such things were never so far from him as when he had begun to stray helplessly in the realm of wonder. He sat there vaguely waiting for something to happen and not committing himself by rash declarations. If he was in love it was in his own way, reflectively, inexpressibly, obstinately. He was waiting for the formula which would justify his conduct and Mrs. Headway's peculiarities. He hardly knew where it would come from; you might have thought from his manner that he would discover it in one of the elaborate *entreés* that were served to the pair when she consented to dine with him at Bignon's or the Café Anglais; or in one of the luxurious band-boxes that arrived from the Rue de la Paix and from which she often lifted the lid in the presence of her admirer. There were moments when he got weary of waiting in vain, and at these moments the arrival of her American friends—he often asked himself why she had so few—seemed to lift the mystery from his shoulders and give him a chance to rest. This apology for a plan she herself might yet scarce contribute to, since she couldn't know how much ground it was expected to cover. She talked about her past because she thought it the best thing to do; she had a shrewd conviction that it was somehow better made use of and confessed to, even in a manner presented or paraded, than caused to stretch behind her as a mere nameless desert. She could at least a little irrigate and plant the waste. She had to have some geography, though the beautiful blank rose-coloured map-spaces of unexplored countries were what she would have preferred. She had no objection to telling fibs, but now that she was taking a new departure wished to indulge only in such as were imperative. She would have been delighted might she have squeezed through with none at all. A few, verily, were indispensable, and we needn't attempt to scan too critically the more or less adventurous excursions into poetry and fable with which she entertained and mystified Sir Arthur. She knew of course that as a product of fashionable circles she was nowhere, but she might have great success as a child of nature.

IV

Rupert Waterville, in the midst of intercourse in which every one perhaps had a good many mental reserves, never forgot that he was in a representative position, that he was official and responsible; and he asked himself more than once how far he was sure it was right, as they said in Boston, to countenance Mrs. Headway's claim to the character even of the American lady thrown to the surface by the late inordinate spread of excavation. In his own way as puzzled as poor Sir Arthur, he indeed flattered himself he was as particular as any Englishman could be. Suppose that after all this free association the well-known Texan belle should come over to London and ask at the Legation to be presented to the Queen? It would be so awkward to refuse her—of course they would have to refuse her—that he was very careful to make no tacit promises. She might construe anything as a tacit promise—he knew how the smallest gestures of diplomatists were studied and interpreted. It was his effort, therefore, to be really diplomatic in his relations with this attractive but dangerous woman. The party of four used often to dine together— Sir Arthur pushed his confidence so far—and on these occasions their fair friend, availing herself of one of the privileges of a *femme du monde* even at the most expensive restaurant, used to wipe her glasses with her napkin. One evening when after polishing a goblet she held it up to the light, giving it, with her head on one side, the least glimmer of a wink, he noted as he watched her that she looked like a highly modern bacchante. He observed at this moment that the Baronet was gazing at her too, and wondered if the same idea had come to him. He often wondered what the Baronet thought; he had devoted first and last a good deal of attention to the psychology of the English "great land-owning" consciousness. Littlemore, alone, at this moment, was characteristically detached; he never appeared to watch Mrs. Headway, though she so often watched him. Waterville asked himself among other things why Sir Arthur hadn't brought his own friends to see her, for Paris during the several weeks that now elapsed abounded in English visitors. He guessed at her having asked him and his having refused; he would have liked particularly to know if she had asked him. He explained his curiosity to

Littlemore, who, however, took very little interest in it. Littlemore expressed nevertheless the conviction that she *would* have asked him; she never would be deterred by false delicacy.

"She has been very delicate with *you*," Waterville returned to this. "She hasn't been at all pressing of late."

"It's only because she has given me up. She thinks I'm a brute."

"I wonder what she thinks of me," Waterville pensively said.

"Oh, she counts upon you to introduce her to the American Minister at the Court of Saint James's," Littlemore opined without mercy. "It's lucky for you our representative here's absent."

"Well, the Minister has settled two or three difficult questions and I suppose can settle this one. I shall do nothing but by the orders of my chief." He was very fond of alluding to his chief.

"She does me injustice," Littlemore added in a moment. "I've spoken to several people about her."

"Oh, but what have you told them?"

"That she lives at the Hôtel Meurice and wants to know nice people."

"They're flattered, I suppose, at your thinking them nice, but they don't go," said Waterville.

"I spoke of her to Mrs. Bagshaw, and Mrs. Bagshaw has promised to go."

"Ah," Waterville murmured; "you don't call Mrs. Bagshaw nice! Mrs. Headway won't take up with Mrs. Bagshaw."

"Well, then, that's exactly what she wants—to be able to cut some one!"

Waterville had a theory that Sir Arthur was keeping Mrs. Headway as a surprise—he meant perhaps to produce her during the next London season. He presently, however, learned as much about the matter as he could have desired to know. He had once offered to accompany his beautiful compatriot to the Museum of the Luxembourg and tell her a little about the modern French school. She had not examined this collection, in spite of her resolve to see everything remarkable—she carried her "Murray" in her lap even when she went to see the great tailor in the Rue de la Paix, to whom, as she said, she had given no end of points—for she usually went to such places with Sir Arthur, who was indifferent to the modern painters of France. "He says there are much better men in England. I must wait for the Royal Academy next year. He seems to think one can wait for anything, but I'm not so good at waiting as he. I can't afford to wait—I've waited long enough." So much as this Mrs. Headway said on the occasion of her arranging with Rupert Waterville that they should some day visit the Luxembourg together. She alluded to the Englishman as if he were her husband or her brother, her natural protector and companion.

"I wonder if she knows how that sounds?" Waterville again throbbingly brooded. "I don't believe she would do it if she knew how it sounds." And he also drew the moral that when one was a well-known Texan belle there was no end to the things one had to learn: so marked was the difference between being well-known and being well-bred. Clever as she was, Mrs. Headway was right in saying she couldn't afford to wait. She must learn, she must live quickly. She wrote to Waterville one day to propose that they should go to the Museum on the morrow; Sir Arthur's mother was in Paris, on her way to Cannes, where she was to spend the winter. She was only passing through, but she would be there three days, and he would naturally give himself up to her. She appeared to have the properest ideas as to what a gentleman would propose to do for his mother. She herself, therefore, should be free, and she named the hour at which she should expect him to call for her. He was punctual to the appointment, and they drove across the river in a large high-hung barouche in which she constantly rolled about Paris. With Mr. Max on the box—the courier sported enormous whiskers—this vehicle had an appearance of great respectability, though Sir Arthur assured her (what she repeated to her other friends) that in London next year they would do the thing much better for her. It struck her other friends, of course, that this backer was prepared to go very far; which on the whole was what Waterville would have expected of him. Littlemore simply remarked that at San Pablo

158

she drove herself about in a ramshackle buggy with muddy wheels and a mule very often in the shafts. Waterville throbbed afresh as he asked himself if the mother of a Tory M.P. would really consent to know her. She must of course be aware that it was a woman who was keeping her son in Paris at a season when English gentlemen were most naturally employed in shooting partridges.

"She's staying at the Hôtel du Rhin, and I've made him feel that he mustn't leave her while she's here," Mrs. Headway said as they drove up the narrow Rue de Seine. "Her name's Lady Demesne, but her full title's the Honourable Lady Demesne, as she's a Baron's daughter. Her father used to be a banker, but he did something or other for the Government—the Tories, you know they call them—and so he was raised to the peerage. So you see one *can* be raised! She has a lady with her as a companion." Waterville's neighbour gave him this information with a seriousness that made him smile; he tried to measure the degree to which it wouldn't have occurred to her that she didn't know how a Baron's daughter was addressed. In that she was truly provincial; she had a way of exaggerating the value of her intellectual acquisitions and of assuming that others had shared her darkness. He noted, too, that she had ended by suppressing poor Sir Arthur's name altogether and designating him only by a sort of conjugal pronoun. She had been so much and so easily married that she was full of these misleading references to gentlemen.

V

They walked through the gallery of the Luxembourg, and, except that Mrs. Headway directed her beautiful gold *face-à-main* to everything at once and to nothing long enough, talked, as usual, rather too loud and bestowed too much attention on the bad copies and strange copyists that formed a circle round several indifferent pictures, she was an agreeable companion and a grateful recipient of "tips." She was quick to understand, and Waterville was sure that before she left the gallery she had made herself mistress of a new subject and was quite prepared to compare the French school critically

159

with the London exhibitions of the following year. As he had remarked more than once with Littlemore, she did alternate in the rummest stripes. Her conversation, her personality, were full of little joints and seams, all of them very visible, where the old and the new had been pieced and white-threaded together. When they had passed through the different rooms of the palace Mrs. Headway proposed that instead of returning directly they should take a stroll in the adjoining gardens, which she wished very much to see and was sure she should like. She had quite seized the difference between the old Paris and the new, and felt the force of the romantic associations of the Latin quarter as perfectly as if she had enjoyed all the benefits of modern culture. The autumn sun was warm in the alleys and terraces of the Luxembourg; the masses of foliage above them, clipped and squared, rusty with ruddy patches, shed a thick lacework over the white sky, which was streaked with the palest blue. The beds of flowers near the palace were of the vividest yellow and red, and the sunlight rested on the smooth grey walls of those parts of its basement that looked south; in front of which, on the long green benches, a row of brown-cheeked nurses, in white caps and white aprons, sat yielding sustenance to as many bundles of white drapery. There were other white caps wandering in the broad paths, attended by little brown French children; the small straw-seated chairs were piled and stacked in some places and disseminated in others. An old lady in black, with white hair fastened over each of her temples by a large black comb, sat on the edge of a stone bench (too high for her delicate length) motionless, staring straight before her and holding a large door-key; under a tree a priest was reading—you could see his lips move at a distance; a young soldier, dwarfish and red-legged, strolled past with his hands in his pockets, which were very much distended. Waterville sat down with Mrs. Headway on the straw-bottomed chairs and she presently said: "I like this—it's even better than the pictures in the gallery. It's more of a picture."

"Everything in France is a picture—even things that are ugly," Waterville replied. "Everything makes a subject."

"Well, I like France!" she summed up with a small incongruous sigh. Then suddenly, from an impulse more conceivably allied to such a sound, she added: "He asked me to go and see her, but I told him I wouldn't. She may come and see me if she likes." This was so abrupt that Waterville was slightly confounded; then he saw she had returned by a short cut to Sir Arthur Demesne and his honourable mother. Waterville liked to know about other people's affairs, yet didn't like this taste to be imputed to him; and therefore, though much desiring to see how the old lady, as he called her, would treat his companion, he was rather displeased with the latter for being so confidential. He had never assumed he was so intimate with her as that. Mrs. Headway, however, had a manner of taking intimacy for granted—a manner Sir Arthur's mother at least wouldn't be sure to like. He showed for a little no certainty of what she was talking about, but she scarcely explained. She only went on through untraceable transitions. "The least she can do is to come. I've been very kind to her son. That's not a reason for my going to her—it's a reason for her coming to me. Besides, if she doesn't like what I've done she can leave me alone. I want to get into European society, but I want to do so in my own way. I don't want to run after people; I want them to run after me. I guess they will, some day!" Waterville listened to this with his eyes on the ground; he felt himself turn very red. There was something in such crudities on the part of the ostensibly refined that shocked and mortified him, and Littlemore had been right in speaking of her lack of the *nuance*. She was terribly distinct; her motives, her impulses, her desires glared like the lighted signs of cafés-concerts. She needed to keep on view, to hand about, like a woman with things to sell on an hotel-terrace, her precious intellectual wares. Vehement thought, with Mrs. Headway, was inevitably speech, though speech was not always thought, and now she had suddenly become vehement. "If she does once come—then, ah then, I shall be too perfect with her; I shan't let her go! But she must take the first step. I confess I hope she'll be nice."

"Perhaps she won't," said Waterville perversely.

"Well, I don't care if she ain't. He has never told me anything about her; never a word about any of his own belongings. If I wished I might believe he's ashamed of them."

"I don't think it's that."

"I know it ain't. I know what it is. It's just regular European refinement. He doesn't want to show off; he's too much of a gentleman. He doesn't want to dazzle me—he wants me to like him for himself. Well, I do like him," she added in a moment. "But I shall like him still better if he brings his mother. They shall know that in America."

"Do you think it will make an impression in America?" Waterville amusedly asked.

"It will show I'm visited by the British aristocracy. They won't love that."

"Surely they grudge you no innocent pleasure," the young man laughed.

"They grudged me common politeness—when I was in New York! Did you ever hear how they treated me when I came on from my own section?"

Waterville stared; this episode was quite new to him. His companion had turned toward him; her pretty head was tossed back like a flower in the wind; there was a flush in her cheek, a more questionable charm in her eye. "Ah, my dear New Yorkers, they're incapable of rudeness!" he cried.

"You're one of them, I see. But I don't speak of the men. The men were well enough—though they did allow it."

"Allow what, Mrs. Headway?" He was quite thrillingly in the dark.

She wouldn't answer at once; her eyes, glittering a little, were fixed on memories still too vivid. "What did you hear about me over there? Don't pretend you heard nothing."

He had heard nothing at all; there had not been a word about Mrs. Headway in New York. He couldn't pretend and he was obliged to tell her this. "But I've been away," he added, "and in America I didn't go out. There's nothing to go out for in New York—only insipid boys and girls."

"There are plenty of spicy old women, who settled I was a bad bold thing. They found out I was in the 'gay' line. They discovered I was known to the authorities. I *am* very well known all out West—I'm known from Chicago to San Francisco; if not personally, at least by reputation. I'm known to all classes. People can tell you out there. In New York they decided I wasn't good enough. Not good enough for New York! What do you say to that?"— it rang out for derision. Whether she had struggled with her pride before making her avowal her confidant of this occasion never knew. The strange want of dignity, as he felt, in her grievance seemed to indicate that she had no pride, and yet there was a sore spot, really a deep wound, in her heart which, touched again, renewed its ache. "I took a house for the winter—one of the handsomest houses in the place—but I sat there all alone. They thought me 'gay,' *me* gay there on Fifty-Eighth Street without so much as a cat!"

Waterville was embarrassed; diplomatist as he was he hardly knew what line to take. He couldn't see the need or the propriety of her overflow; though the incident appeared to have been most curious and he was glad to know the facts on the best authority. It was the first he did know of this remarkable woman's having spent a winter in his native city—which was virtually a proof of her having come and gone in complete obscurity. It was vain for him to pretend he had been a good deal away, for he had been appointed to his post in London only six months before, and Mrs. Headway's social failure ante-dated that event. In the midst of these reflexions he had an inspiration. He attempted neither to question, to explain nor to apologise; he ventured simply to lay his hand for an instant on her own and to exclaim as gallantly as possible: "I wish *I* had known!"

"I had plenty of men—but men don't count. If they're not a positive help they're a hindrance, so that the more you have the worse it looks. The women simply turned their backs."

"They were afraid of you—they were jealous," the young man produced.

"It's very good of you to try and patch it up; all I know is that not one of them crossed my threshold. No, you needn't try and tone it down; I know perfectly how the case stands. In New York, if you please, I didn't go."

"So much the worse for New York!" cried Waterville, who, as he afterwards said to Littlemore, had got quite worked up.

"And now you know why I want to get into society over here?" She jumped up and stood before him; with a dry hard smile she looked down at him. Her smile itself was an answer to her question; it expressed a sharp vindictive passion. There was an abruptness in her movements which left her companion quite behind; but as he still sat there returning her glance he felt he at last in the light of that smile, the flash of that almost fierce demand, understood Mrs. Headway.

She turned away to walk to the gate of the garden, and he went with her, laughing vaguely and uneasily at her tragic tone. Of course she expected him to serve, all obligingly, all effectively, her rancour; but his female relations, his mother and his sisters, his innumerable cousins, had been a party to the slight she had suffered, and he reflected as he walked along that after all they had been right. They had been right in not going to see a woman who could chatter that way about her social wrongs; whether she were respectable or not they had had the true assurance she'd be vulgar. European society might let her in, but European society had its limpness. New York, Waterville said to himself with a glow of civic pride, was quite capable of taking a higher stand in such a matter than London. They went some distance without speaking; at last he said, expressing honestly the thought at that moment uppermost in his mind: "I hate that phrase, 'getting into society.' I don't think one ought to attribute to one's self that sort of ambition. One ought to assume that one's *in* the confounded thing—that one *is* society—and to hold that if one has good manners one has, from the social point of view, achieved the great thing. 'The best company's where I am,' any lady or gentleman should feel. The rest can take care of itself."

For a moment she appeared not to understand, then she broke out: "Well, I suppose I haven't good manners; at any rate I'm not satisfied! Of course I don't talk right—I know that very well. But let me get where I want to first—then I'll look after the details. If I once get there I shall be perfect!" she cried with a tremor of passion. They reached the gate of the garden and stood a moment outside, opposite the low arcade of the Odéon, lined with bookstalls, at which Waterville cast a slightly wistful glance, waiting for Mrs. Headway's carriage, which had drawn up at a short distance. The whiskered

Max had seated himself within and, on the tense elastic cushions, had fallen into a doze. The carriage got into motion without his waking; he came to his senses only as it stopped again. He started up staring and then without confusion proceeded to descend.

"I've learned it in Italy—they call it the *siesta*," he remarked with an agreeable smile, holding the door open to Mrs. Headway.

"Well, I should think you had and they might!" this lady replied, laughing amicably as she got into the vehicle, where Waterville placed himself beside her. It was not a surprise to him that she spoiled her courier; she naturally would spoil her courier. But civilisation begins at home, he brooded; and the incident threw an ironic light on her desire to get into society. It failed, however, to divert her thoughts from the subject she was discussing with her friend, for as Max ascended the box and the carriage went on its way she threw out another note of defiance. "If once I'm all right over here I guess I can make New York do something! You'll see the way those women will squirm."

Waterville was sure his mother and sisters wouldn't squirm; but he felt afresh, as the carriage rolled back to the Hôtel Meurice, that now he understood Mrs. Headway. As they were about to enter the court of the hotel a closed carriage passed before them, and while a few moments later he helped his companion to alight he saw that Sir Arthur Demesne had stepped from the other vehicle. Sir Arthur perceived Mrs. Headway and instantly gave his hand to a lady seated in the coupé. This lady emerged with a certain slow impressiveness, and as she stood before the door of the hotel—a woman still young and fair, with a good deal of height, gentle, tranquil, plainly dressed, yet distinctly imposing—it came over our young friend that the Tory member had brought *his* principal female relative to call on Nancy Beck. Mrs. Headway's triumph had begun; the dowager Lady Demesne had taken the first step. Waterville wondered whether the ladies in New York, notified by some magnetic wave, were beginning to be convulsed. Mrs. Headway, quickly conscious of what had happened, was neither too prompt to appropriate the visit nor too slow to acknowledge it. She just paused, smiling at Sir Arthur.

"I should like to introduce my mother—she wants very much to know you." He approached Mrs. Headway; the lady had taken his arm. She was at once simple and circumspect; she had every resource of the English matron.

Mrs. Headway, without advancing a step, put out a hand as if to draw her quickly closer. "I declare you're too sweet!" Waterville heard her say.

He was turning away, as his own business was over; but the young Englishman, who had surrendered his companion, not to say his victim, to the embrace, as it might now almost be called, of their hostess, just checked him with a friendly gesture. "I daresay I shan't see you again—I'm going away."

"Good-bye then," said Waterville. "You return to England?"

"No—I go to Cannes with my mother."

"You remain at Cannes?"

"Till Christmas very likely."

The ladies, escorted by Mr. Max, had passed into the hotel, and Waterville presently concluded this exchange. He smiled as he walked away, making it analytically out that poor Sir Arthur had obtained a concession, in the domestic sphere, only at the price of a concession.

The next morning he looked up Littlemore, from whom he had a standing invitation to breakfast, and who, as usual, was smoking a cigar and turning over a dozen newspapers. Littlemore had a large apartment and an accomplished cook; he got up late and wandered about his rooms all the morning, stopping from time to time to look out of his windows, which overhung the Place de la Madeleine. They had not been seated many minutes at breakfast when the visitor mentioned that Mrs. Headway was about to be abandoned by her friend, who was going to Cannes.

But once more he was to feel how little he might ever enlighten this comrade. "He came last night to bid me good-bye," Littlemore said.

Again Waterville wondered. "Very civil of him, then, all of a sudden."

"He didn't come from civility—he came from curiosity. Having dined here he had a pretext for calling."

"I hope his curiosity was satisfied," our young man generously dropped.

"Well, I suspect not. He sat here some time, but we talked only about what he didn't want to know."

"And what *did* he want to know?"

"Whether I know anything against Nancy Beck."

Waterville stared. "Did he call her Nancy Beck?"

"We never mentioned her; but I saw what he was after and that he quite yearned to lead up to her. I wouldn't do it."

"Ah, poor man!" Waterville sighed.

"I don't see why you pity him," said Littlemore. "Mrs. Beck's admirers were never pitied."

"Well, of course he wants to marry her."

"Let him do it then. I've nothing to say to it."

"He believes there's something about her, somewhere in time or space, that may make a pretty big mouthful."

"Let him leave it alone then."

"How can he if he's really hit?"—Waterville spoke as from sad experience.

"Ah, my dear fellow, he must settle it himself. He has no right at any rate to put me such a question. There was a moment, just as he was going, when he had it on his tongue's end. He stood there in the doorway, he couldn't leave me—he was going to plump out with it. He looked at me straight, and I looked straight at him; we remained that way for almost a minute. Then he decided not, on the whole, to risk it and took himself off."

Waterville assisted at this passage with intense interest. "And if he had asked you, what would you have said?"

167

"What do you think?"

"Well, I suppose you'd have said that his question wasn't fair."

"That would have been tantamount to admitting the worst."

"Yes," Waterville brooded again, "you couldn't do that. On the other hand if he had put it to you on your honour whether she's a woman to marry it would have been very awkward."

"Awkward enough. Luckily he has no business to put things to me on my honour. Moreover, nothing has passed between us to give him the right to ask me *any* questions about Mrs. Headway. As she's a great friend of mine he can't pretend to expect me to give confidential information."

"You don't think she's a woman to marry, all the same," Waterville returned. "And if a man were to try to corner you on it you might knock him down, but it wouldn't be an answer."

"It would have to serve," said Littlemore. "There are cases where a man must lie nobly," he added.

Waterville looked grave. "What cases?"

"Well, where a woman's honour's at stake."

"I see what you mean. That's of course if he has been himself concerned with her."

"Himself or another. It doesn't matter."

"I think it does matter. I don't like false swearing," said Waterville. "It's a delicate question."

They were interrupted by the arrival of the servant with a second course, and Littlemore gave a laugh as he helped himself. "It would be a lark to see her married to that superior being!"

"It would be a great responsibility."

"Responsibility or not, it would be very amusing."

"Do you mean, then, to give her a leg up?"

"Heaven forbid! But I mean to bet on her."

Waterville gave his companion a serious glance; he thought him strangely superficial. The alternatives looked all formidable, however, and he sighed as he laid down his fork.

VI

The Easter holidays that year were unusually genial; mild watery sunshine assisted the progress of the spring. The high dense hedges, in Warwickshire, were like walls of hawthorn embedded in banks of primrose, and the finest trees in England, springing out of them with a regularity which suggested conservative principles, began more densely and downily to bristle. Rupert Waterville, devoted to his duties and faithful in attendance at the Legation, had had little time to enjoy the rural hospitality that shows the English, as he had promptly learned to say, at their best. Freshly yet not wildly exotic he had repeatedly been invited to grace such scenes, but had had hitherto to practise with reserve the great native art of "staying." He cultivated method and kept the country-houses in reserve; he would take them up in their order, after he should have got a little more used to London. Without hesitation, however, he had accepted the appeal from Longlands; it had come to him in a simple and familiar note from Lady Demesne, with whom he had no acquaintance. He knew of her return from Cannes, where she had spent the whole winter, for he had seen it related in a Sunday newspaper; yet it was with a certain surprise that he heard from her in these informal terms. "Dear Mr. Waterville, my son tells me you will perhaps be able to come down here on the seventeenth to spend two or three days. If you can it will give us much pleasure. We can promise you the society of your charming countrywoman Mrs. Headway."

He had seen Mrs. Headway; she had written him, a fortnight before from an hotel in Cork Street, to say she had arrived in London for the season and should be happy to see him. He had called on her, trembling with the fear that she would break ground about her presentation at Court; but he was agreeably surprised by her overlooking for the hour this topic. She had spent the winter in Rome, travelling directly from that city to England, with just a little stop in Paris to buy a few clothes. She had taken much satisfaction in Rome, where she had made many friends; she assured him she knew half the Roman nobility. "They're charming people; they've only one fault, they stay too long," she said. And in answer to his always slower process, "I mean when they come to see you," she explained. "They used to come every evening and then wanted to stay till the next day. They were all princes and counts. I used to give them cigars and cocktails—nobody else did. I knew as many people as I wanted," she added in a moment, feeling perhaps again in her visitor the intimate intelligence with which six months before he had listened to her account of her discomfiture in New York. "There were lots of English; I knew all the English and I mean to visit them here. The Americans waited to see what the English would do, so as to do the opposite. Thanks to that I was spared some precious specimens. There are, you know, some fearful ones. Besides, in Rome society doesn't matter if you've a feeling for the ruins and the Campagna; I found I had an immense feeling for the Campagna. I was always mooning round in some damp old temple. It reminded me a good deal of the country round San Pablo—if it hadn't been for the temples. I liked to think it all over when I was riding round; I was always brooding over the past." At this moment, nevertheless, Mrs. Headway had dismissed the past; she was prepared to give herself up wholly to the actual. She wished Waterville to advise her as to how she should live—what she should do. Should she stay at an hotel or should she take a house? She guessed she had better take a house if she could find a nice one. Max wanted to look for one, and she didn't know but what she'd let him; he got her such a nice one in Rome. She said nothing about Sir Arthur Demesne, who, it seemed to Waterville, would have been her natural guide and sponsor; he wondered whether her relations with the Tory member had come to an end. Waterville had met him a couple of times since the opening of Parliament, and they had exchanged twenty words, none of which, however, had had reference to Mrs. Headway. Our young man, the previous autumn, had been recalled to London just after the incident of which he found himself witness in the court of the Hôtel Meurice; and all he knew of its consequence was what he had learned from Littlemore, who, proceeding to America, where he had suddenly been advised of reasons for his spending the winter, passed through the British capital. Littlemore had then reported that Mrs. Headway was enchanted with Lady Demesne and had no words to speak of her kindness and sweetness. "She told me she liked to know her son's friends, and I told her I liked to know my friends' mothers," dear Nancy had reported. "I should be willing to be old if I could be like that," she had added, forgetting for the moment that the crown of the maturer charm dangled before her at a diminishing distance. The mother and son, at any rate, had retired to Cannes together, and at this moment Littlemore had received letters from home which caused him to start for Arizona. Mrs. Headway had accordingly been left to her own devices, and he was afraid she had bored herself, though Mrs. Bagshaw had called upon her. In November she had travelled to Italy, not by way of Cannes.

"What do you suppose she's up to in Rome?" Waterville had asked; his imagination failing him here, as he was not yet in possession of that passage.

"I haven't the least idea. And I don't care!" Littlemore had added in a moment. Before leaving London he had further mentioned that Mrs. Headway, on his going to take leave of her in Paris, had made another and rather an unexpected attack. "About the society business—she said I must really do something: she couldn't go on that way. And she appealed to me in the name—I don't think I quite know how to say it."

"I should be ever so glad if you'd try," Waterville had earnestly said, constantly reminding himself that Americans in Europe were after all, in a degree, to a man in his position, as the sheep to the shepherd.

"Well, in the name of the affection we had formerly entertained for each other."

"The affection?"

"So she was good enough to call it. But I deny it all. If one had to have an affection for every woman one used to sit up 'evenings' with—!" And Littlemore had paused, not defining the result of such an obligation.

Waterville had tried to imagine what it would be; while his friend had embarked for New York without telling him how, in the event, he had resisted Mrs. Headway's attack.

At Christmas Waterville knew of Sir Arthur's return to England and believed he also knew that the Baronet hadn't gone down to Rome. He had a theory that Lady Demesne was a very clever woman—clever enough to make her son do what she preferred and yet also make him think it his own choice. She had been politic, accommodating, on the article of the one civility rendered the American lady; but, having seen and judged that heroine, had determined to stop short and to make her son, if possible, stop. She had been sweet and kind, as Mrs. Headway said, because for the moment this was easiest; but she had paid her last visit on the same occasion as her first. She had been sweet and kind, but she had set her face as a stone, and if poor Nancy, camping on this new field, expected to find any vague promises redeemed, she would taste of the bitterness of shattered hopes. He had made up his mind that, shepherd as he was, and Mrs. Headway one of his sheep, it was none of his present duty to run about after her, especially as she could be trusted not to stray too far. He saw her a second time, and she still said nothing about Sir Arthur. Waterville, who always had a theory, made sure she was watching the clock, that this proved admirer was behind the hour. She was also getting into a house; her courier had found her in Chesterfield Street a little gem, which was to cost her only what jewels cost. After all this our young man caught his breath at Lady Demesne's note, and he went down to Longlands with much the same impatience with which, in Paris, he would have gone, had he been able, to the first night of a new comedy. It seemed to him that through a sudden stroke of good fortune he had received a *billet d'auteur*.

It was agreeable to him to arrive at an English country-house at the close of the day. He liked the drive from the station in the twilight, the sight of the fields and copses and cottages, vague and lonely in contrast to his definite lighted goal; the sound of the wheels on the long avenue, which turned and wound repeatedly without bringing him to what he reached however at last— the wide grey front with a glow in its scattered windows and a sweep of

172

still firmer gravel up to the door. The front at Longlands, which was of this sober complexion, had a grand pompous air; it was attributed to the genius of Sir Christopher Wren. There were wings curving forward in a semi-circle, with statues placed at intervals on the cornice; so that in the flattering dusk it suggested a great Italian villa dropped by some monstrous hand in an English park. He had taken a late train, which left him but twenty minutes to dress for dinner. He prided himself considerably on the art of dressing both quickly and well; but this process left him no time to wonder if the apartment to which he had been assigned befitted his diplomatic dignity. On emerging from his room he found there was an ambassador in the house, and this discovery was a check to unrest. He tacitly assumed that he should have had a better room if it hadn't been for the ambassador, who was of course counted first. The large brilliant house gave an impression of the last century and of foreign taste, of light colours, high vaulted ceilings with pale mythological frescoes, gilded doors surmounted by old French panels, faded tapestries and delicate damasks, stores of ancient china among which great jars of pink roses were conspicuous. The company had assembled for dinner in the principal hall, which was animated by a fire of great logs, and the muster was so large that Waterville feared he was last. Lady Demesne gave him a smile and a touch of her hand; she lacked effusiveness and, saying nothing in particular, treated him as if he had been a common guest. He wasn't sure whether he liked or hated that; but these alternatives mattered equally little to his hostess, who looked at her friends as if to verify a catalogue. The master of the house was talking to a lady before the fire; when he caught sight of Waterville across the room he waved "How d'ye do" with an air of being delighted to see him. He had never had that air in Paris, and Waterville had a chance to observe, what he had often heard, to how much greater advantage the English appear in their country-houses. Lady Demesne turned to him again with the sweet vague smile that could somehow present a view without making a point.

"We're waiting for Mrs. Headway."

"Ah, she has arrived?" Waterville had quite forgotten this attraction.

"She came at half-past five. At six she went to dress. She has had two hours."

"Let us hope the results will be proportionate," the young man laughed.

"Oh the results—I don't know!" Lady Demesne murmured without looking at him; and in these simple words he found the confirmation of his theory that she was playing a deep game. He weighed the question of whom he should sit next to at dinner, and hoped, with due deference to Mrs. Headway's charms, that he might abut on a less explored province. The results of a toilet she had protracted through two hours were presently visible. She appeared on the staircase which descended to the hall and which, for three minutes, as she came down rather slowly, facing the people beneath, placed her in considerable relief. Waterville, as he watched her, felt the great importance of the moment for her: it represented her entrance into English society. Well, she entered English society in good shape, as Nancy Beck would have said; with a brave free smile, suggestive of no flutter, on her lips, and with the trophies of the Rue de la Paix trailing behind her. She made a portentous rumour as she moved. People turned their eyes to her; there was soon a perceptible diminution of talk; though talk hadn't been particularly audible. She looked very much alone, and it seemed rather studied of her to come down last, though possibly, before her glass, she had but been unable to please herself. For she evidently felt the importance of the occasion, and Waterville was sure her heart beat fast. She showed immense pluck, however; she smiled more intensely and advanced like a woman acquainted with every social drawback of beauty. She had at any rate the support of these inconveniences; for nothing on this occasion was wanting to her lustre, and the determination to succeed, which might have made her hard, was veiled in the virtuous consciousness that she had neglected nothing. Lady Demesne went forward to meet her; Sir Arthur took no notice of her; and presently Waterville found himself proceeding to dinner with the wife of an ecclesiastic, to whom his hostess had presented him in the desolation of the almost empty hall, when the other couples had flourished away. The rank of this ecclesiastic in the hierarchy he learned early on the morrow; but in the meantime it seemed to him somehow strange that in England ecclesiastics should have wives. English life even at the end of a year was full of those surprises. The lady, however, was very easily accounted for; she was in no sense a violent exception, and there had been no need of the Reformation and the destruction of a hundred abbeys to produce her. Her name was Mrs. April; she was wrapped in a large lace shawl; to eat her dinner she removed but one glove, and the other gave Waterville an odd impression that the whole repast, in spite of its great completeness, was something of the picnic order.

Mrs. Headway was opposite, at a little distance; she had been taken in, as Waterville learned from his neighbour, by a General, a gentleman with a lean aquiline face and a cultivated whisker, and she had on the other side a smart young man of an identity less definite. Poor Sir Arthur sat between two ladies much older than himself, whose names, redolent of history, Waterville had often heard and had associated with figures more romantic. Mrs. Headway gave her countryman no greeting; she evidently hadn't seen him till they were seated at table, when she stared at him with a violence of surprise that was like the interruption of a lively tune. It was a copious and well-ordered banquet, but as he looked up and down the table he sought to appraise the contributed lustre, the collective *scintillae*, that didn't proceed from silver, porcelain, glass or shining damask. Presently renouncing the effort, however, he became conscious he was judging the affair much more from Mrs. Headway's point of view than from his own. He knew no one but Mrs. April, who, displaying an almost motherly desire to give him information, told him the names of many of their companions; in return for which he explained to her that he was not in that set. Mrs. Headway got on in perfection with her warrior; Waterville noticed her more than he showed; he saw how that officer, evidently a cool hand, was drawing her out. Waterville hoped she would be careful. He was capable, in his way, of frolic thought, and as he compared her with the rest of the company said to himself that she was a very plucky little woman and that her present undertaking had a touch of the heroic. She was alone against many, and her opponents were a serried phalanx; those who were there represented a thousand others. Her type so violated every presumption blooming there that to the eye of the imagination she stood very much on her merits. Such people seemed so completely made up, so unconscious of effort, so surrounded with things to rest upon; the men with their clean complexions, their well-hung chins, their cold pleasant eyes, their shoulders set back, their absence of gesture; the women, several very handsome, half-strangled in strings of pearls, with smooth plain tresses, seeming to look at nothing in particular, supporting silence as if it were as becoming as candle-light, yet talking a little sometimes in fresh rich voices. They were all wrapped in a community of ideas, of traditions; they understood each other's accent, even each other's deviations. Mrs. Headway, with all her prettiness, exceeded these licences. She was foreign, exaggerated, she had too much expression; she might have been engaged for the evening. Waterville remarked, moreover, that English society was always clutching at amusement and that the business was transacted on a cash basis. If Mrs. Headway should sufficiently amuse she would succeed, and her fortune—if fortune there was—would be no hindrance.

In the drawing-room, after dinner, he went up to her, but she gave him no greeting. She only faced him with an expression he had never seen before—a strange bold expression of displeasure. It made her fearfully common. "Why have you come down here?" she asked. "Have you come to watch me?"

Waterville coloured to the roots of his hair. He knew it was terribly little like a diplomatist, but he was unable to control his heat. He was justly shocked, he was angry and in addition he was mystified. "I came because I was asked."

"Who asked you?"

"The same person who asked you, I suppose—Lady Demesne."

"She's an old cat!" And Nancy Beck turned away from him.

He turned from her as well. He didn't know what he had done to deserve such treatment. It was a complete surprise; he had never seen her like that before. She was a very vulgar woman; that was the way people dealt with each other, he supposed, on hideous back piazzas. He threw himself almost passionately into contact with the others, who all seemed to him, possibly a little by contrast, extraordinarily genial and friendly. He had not, however, the consolation of seeing Mrs. Headway punished for her rudeness—she wasn't in the least neglected. On the contrary, in the part of the room where she sat the group was denser and repeatedly broke into gusts of unanimous laughter. Yes, if she should amuse them she might doubtless get anywhere and do anything, and evidently she was amusing them.

176

VII

If she was strange, at any rate he hadn't come to the end of her strangeness. The next day was a Sunday and uncommonly fine; he was down before breakfast and took a walk in the park, stopping to gaze at the thin-legged deer on the remoter slopes, who reminded him of small pincushions turned upside down, and wandering along the edge of a large sheet of ornamental water which had a temple in imitation of that of Vesta on an island in the middle. He thought at this time no more of Mrs. Headway; he only reflected that these stately objects had for at least a hundred years furnished a background to a great deal of heavy history. Further reflexion would perhaps have suggested to him that she might yet become a feature in the record that so spread itself. Two or three ladies failed to appear at breakfast; the well-known Texan belle was one of them.

"She tells me she never leaves her room till noon," he heard Lady Demesne say to the General, her companion of the previous evening, who had asked about her. "She takes three hours to dress."

"She's a monstrous clever woman!" the General declared.

"To do it in three hours?"

"No, I mean the way she keeps her wits about her."

"Yes; I think she's very clever," said Lady Demesne on a system in which our young man flattered himself he saw more meaning than the General could. There was something in this tall straight deliberate woman, who seemed at once to yearn and to retire, that Waterville admired. With her delicate surface, her conventional mildness, he made out she was strong; she had set her patience upon a height and carried it like a diadem. She had the young American little visibly on her mind, but every now and then she indulged in some vague demonstration that showed she had not forgotten him. Sir Arthur himself was apparently in excellent spirits, though he too never bustled nor overflowed; he only went about looking very fresh and fair, as if he took a bath every hour or two, and very secure against the unexpected.

Waterville had exchanged even fewer remarks with him than with his mother; but the master of the house had found occasion to say the night before, in the smoking-room, that he was delighted this friend had been able to come, and that if he was fond of real English scenery there were several things about that he should like very much to show him.

"You must give me an hour or two before you go, you know; I really think there are some things you'll care for."

Sir Arthur spoke as if Waterville would be very fastidious; he seemed to wish to do the right thing by him. On the Sunday morning after breakfast he inquired if he should care to go to church; most of the ladies and several of the men were going. "It's just as you please, you know; but there's rather a pretty walk across the fields and a curious little church—they say of King Stephen's time."

Waterville knew what this meant; it was already a treasure. Besides, he liked going to church, above all when he sat in the Squire's pew, which was sometimes as big as a boudoir and all fadedly upholstered to match. So he replied that he should be delighted. Then he added without explaining his reason: "Is Mrs. Headway going?"

"I really don't know," said his host with an abrupt change of tone—as if he inquired into the movements of the housekeeper.

"The English are awfully queer!" Waterville consoled himself with secretly exclaiming; to which wisdom, since his arrival among them, he had had recourse whenever he encountered a gap in the consistency of things. The church was even a rarer treasure than Sir Arthur's description of it, and Waterville felt Mrs. Headway had been a fool not to come. He knew what she was after—she wished to study English life so that she might take possession of it; and to pass in among a hedge of bobbing rustics and sit among the monuments of the old Demesnes would have told her a great deal about English life. If she wished to fortify herself for the struggle she had better come to that old church. When he returned to Longlands—he had walked back across the meadows with the archdeacon's lady, who was a vigorous pedestrian—it wanted half an hour of luncheon and he was unwilling to go indoors. He remembered he had not yet seen the gardens, and wandered away in search of them. They were on a scale that enabled him to find them without difficulty, and they looked as if they had been kept up unremittingly for a century or two. He hadn't advanced very far between their blooming borders when he heard a voice that he recognised, and a moment after, at the turn of an alley, came upon Mrs. Headway, who was attended by the master of the scene. She was bareheaded beneath her parasol, which she flung back, stopping short as she beheld her compatriot.

"Oh it's Mr. Waterville come to spy me out as usual!" It was with this remark she greeted the slightly-embarrassed young man.

"Hallo, you've come home from church?" Sir Arthur said, pulling out his watch.

Waterville was struck with his coolness. He admired it; for, after all, he noted, it must have been disagreeable to him to be interrupted. He felt rather an ass, and wished he had kept hold of Mrs. April, to give him the air of having come for her sake. Mrs. Headway was looking adorably fresh in attire that Waterville, who had his ideas on such matters, felt sure wouldn't be regarded as the proper thing for a Sunday morning in an English country-house: a négligé of white flounces and frills interspersed with yellow ribbons—a garment Madame de Pompadour might have sported to receive Louis XV., but probably wouldn't have worn for a public airing. The sight of this costume gave the finishing touch to his impression that she knew on the whole what she was about. She would take a line of her own; she wouldn't be too accommodating. She wouldn't come down to breakfast; she wouldn't go to church; she would wear on Sunday mornings little elaborately informal dresses and look dreadfully un-British and un-Protestant. Perhaps after all this was best. She began to talk with a certain volubility.

"Isn't this too lovely? I walked all the way from the house. I'm not much at walking, but the grass in this place is like a parlour. The whole thing's driving me wild. Sir Arthur, you ought to go and look after the Ambassador; it's shameful the way I've kept you. You don't trouble about the Ambassador? You said just now you had scarcely spoken to him, and you must make that right up. I never saw such a way of neglecting your guests. Is it the usual style over here? Go and take him out to ride or make him play a game of billiards. Mr. Waterville will take me home; besides, I want to scold him for spying on me."

Our young man sharply resented her charge. "I had no idea whatever you were here."

"We weren't hiding," said Sir Arthur quietly. "Perhaps you'll see Mrs. Headway back to the house. I think I ought to look after old Davidoff. I believe luncheon's at two."

He left them, and Waterville wandered through the gardens with Mrs. Headway. She at once sought again to learn if he had come there to "dog" her; but this inquiry wasn't accompanied, to his surprise, with the acrimony she had displayed the night before. He was determined not to let that pass, however; when people had treated him in that way they shouldn't be allowed to forget it.

"Do you suppose I'm always thinking of you?" he derisively demanded. "You're out of my mind *sometimes*. I came this way to look at the gardens, and if you hadn't spoken to me should have passed on."

Mrs. Headway was perfectly good-natured; she appeared not even to hear his defence. "He has got two other places," she simply rejoined. "That's just what I wanted to know."

He wouldn't nevertheless be turned from his grievance. That mode of reparation to a person whom you had insulted which consisted in forgetting you had done so was doubtless largely in use on back piazzas; but a creature of any spirit required a different form. "What did you mean last night by accusing me of having come down here to watch you? Pardon me if I tell you I think you grossly rude." The sting of the imputation lay in the fact that there was a certain amount of truth in it; yet for a moment Mrs. Headway, looking very blank, failed to recover it. "She's a barbarian, after all," thought Waterville. "She thinks a woman may slap a man's face and run away!"

"Oh," she cried suddenly, "I remember—I was angry with you! I didn't expect to see you. But I didn't really mind about it at all. Every now and then I get mad like that and work it off on any one that's handy. But it's over in three minutes and I never think of it again. I confess I was mad last night; I could have shot the old woman."

"'The old woman'?"

"Sir Arthur's mother. She has no business here anyway. In this country when the husband dies they're expected to clear out. She has a house of her own ten miles from here and another in Portman Square; so she ain't in want of good locations. But she sticks—she sticks to him like a strong plaster. It came over me as I kind of analysed that she didn't invite me here because she liked me, but because she suspects me. She's afraid we'll make a match and she thinks I ain't good enough for her son. She must think I'm in a great hurry to make him mine. I never went after him, he came after me. I should never have thought of anything if it hadn't been for him. He began it last summer at Homburg; he wanted to know why I didn't come to England; he told me I should have great success. He doesn't know much about it anyway; he hasn't got much gumption. But he's a very nice man all the same; it's very pleasant to see him surrounded by his—" And Mrs. Headway paused a moment, her appreciation ranging: "Surrounded by all his old heirlooms. I like the old place," she went on; "it's beautifully mounted; I'm quite satisfied with what I've seen. I thought Lady Demesne well-impressed; she left a card on me in London and very soon after wrote to me to ask me here. But I'm very quick; I sometimes see things in a flash. I saw something yesterday when she came to speak to me at dinner-time. She saw I looked pretty and refined, and it made her blue with rage; she hoped I'd be some sort of a horror. I'd like very much to oblige her, but what can one do? Then I saw she had asked me only because he insisted. He didn't come to see me when I first arrived—he never came near me for ten days. She managed to prevent him; she got him to make some promise. But he changed his mind after a little, and then he had to do something really polite. He called three days in succession, and he made her come. She's one of those women who holds out as long as she can and then seems to give in while she's really fussing more than ever. She hates me as if I knew something about her—when I don't even know what she thinks I've done myself. She's very underhand; she's a regular old cat. When I saw you last night at dinner I thought she had got you here to help her."

"To help her?" Waterville echoed.

"To tell her about me. To give her information she can make use of against me. You may give her all you like!"

Waterville was almost breathless with the attention he had paid this extraordinary burst of confidence, and now he really felt faint. He stopped short; Mrs. Headway went on a few steps and then, stopping too, turned and shone at him in the glow of her egotism. "You're the most unspeakable woman!" he wailed. She seemed to him indeed a barbarian.

She laughed at him—he felt she was laughing at his expression of face—and her laugh rang through the stately gardens. "What sort of a woman's that?"

"You've got no delicacy"—he'd keep it up.

She coloured quickly, though, strange to say, without further irritation. "No delicacy?"

"You ought to keep those things to yourself."

"Oh I know what you mean; I talk about everything. When I'm excited I've got to talk. But I must do things in my own way. I've got plenty of delicacy when people are nice to me. Ask Arthur Demesne if I ain't delicate—ask George Littlemore if I ain't. Don't stand there all day; come on to lunch!" And Mrs. Headway resumed her walk while her companion, having balanced, slowly overtook her. "Wait till I get settled; then I'll be delicate," she pursued. "You can't be delicate when you're trying to save your life. It's very well for *you* to talk, with the whole State Department to back you. Of course I'm excited. I've got right hold of this thing, and I don't mean to let go!" Before they reached the house she let him know why he had been invited to Longlands at the same time as herself. Waterville would have liked to believe his personal attractions sufficiently explained the fact, but she took no account of this supposition. Mrs. Headway preferred to see herself in an element of ingenious machination, where everything that happened referred to her and was aimed at her. Waterville had been asked then because he represented, however modestly, the American Legation, and their host had a friendly desire to make it appear that his pretty American visitor, of whom no one knew anything, was under the protection of that establishment. "It would start me better," the lady in question complacently set forth. "You can't help yourself—you've helped to start me. If he had known the Minister he'd have asked him—or the first secretary. But he don't know them."

They reached the house by the time she had developed her idea, which gave Waterville a pretext more than sufficient for detaining her in the portico. "Do you mean to say Sir Arthur has told you this?" he inquired almost sternly.

"Told me? Of course not! Do you suppose I'd let him take the tone with me that I need any favours? I'd like to hear him tell me I'm in want of assistance!"

"I don't see why he shouldn't—at the pace you go yourself. You say it to every one."

"To every one? I say it to you and to George Littlemore—when I get nervous. I say it to you because I like you, and to him because I'm afraid of him. I'm not in the least afraid of you, by the way. I'm all alone—I haven't got any one. I must have some comfort, mustn't I? Sir Arthur scolded me for putting you off last night—he noticed it; and that was what made me guess his idea."

"I'm much obliged to him," said Waterville rather bewildered.

"So mind you answer for me. Don't you want me to take your arm to go in?"

"You're a most extraordinary combination!" he gave to all the winds as she stood smiling at him.

"Oh come, don't *you* fall in love with me!" she cried with a laugh; and, without taking his arm, she passed in before him.

That evening, before he went to dress for dinner, he wandered into the library, where he felt certain he should find some superior bindings. There was no one in the room and he spent a happy half-hour among treasures of old reading and triumphs of old morocco. He had a great esteem for good literature, he held that it should have handsome covers. The daylight had begun to wane, but whenever, in the rich-looking dimness, he made out the glimmer of a well-gilded back, he took down the volume and carried it to one of the deep-set windows. He had just finished the inspection of a delightfully fragrant folio, and was about to carry it back to its niche, when he found himself face to face with Lady Demesne. He was sharply startled, for her tall slim figure, her preserved fairness, which looked white in the high brown room, and the air of serious intention with which she presented herself, all gave something spectral to her presence. He saw her countenance dimly light, however, and heard her say with the vague despair of her neutrality: "Are you looking at our books? I'm afraid they're rather dull."

"Dull? Why they're as bright as the day they were bound." And he turned on her the glittering panels of his folio.

"I'm afraid I haven't looked at them for a long time," she murmured, going nearer to the window, where she stood looking out. Beyond the clear pane the park stretched away, the menace of night already mantling the great limbs of the oaks. The place appeared cold and empty, and the trees had an air of conscious importance, as if Nature herself had been bribed somehow to take the side of county families. Her ladyship was no easy person for talk; spontaneity had never come to her, and to express herself might have been for her modesty like some act of undressing in public. Her very simplicity was conventional, though it was rather a noble convention. You might have pitied her for the sense of her living tied so tight, with consequent moral cramps, to certain rigid ideals. This made her at times seem tired, like a person who had undertaken too much. She said nothing for a moment, and there was an appearance of design in her silence, as if she wished to let him know she had appealed to him without the trouble of announcing it. She had been accustomed to expect people would suppose things, to save her questions and explanations. Waterville made some haphazard remark about

184

the beauty of the evening—in point of fact the weather had changed for the worse—to which she vouchsafed no reply. But she presently said with her usual gentleness: "I hoped I should find you here—I should like to ask you something."

"Anything I can tell you—I shall be delighted!" the young man declared.

She gave him a pleading look that seemed to say: "Please be very simple—very simple indeed." Then she glanced about her as if there had been other people in the room; she didn't wish to appear closeted with him or to have come on purpose. There she was at any rate, and she proceeded. "When my son told me he should ask you to come down I was very glad. I mean of course we were delighted—" And she paused a moment. But she next went on: "I want to ask you about Mrs. Headway."

"Ah, here it is!" cried Waterville within himself. But he could show no wincing. "Ah yes, I see!"

"Do you mind my asking you? I hope you don't mind. I haven't any one else to ask."

"Your son knows her much better than I do." He said this without intention of malice, simply to escape from the difficulties of the situation, but after he had spoken was almost frightened by his mocking sound.

"I don't think he knows her. She knows *him*—which is very different. When I ask him about her he merely tells me she's fascinating. She *is* fascinating," said her ladyship with inimitable dryness.

"So I think, myself. I like her very much," Waterville returned cheerfully.

"You're in all the better position to speak of her then."

"To speak well of her," the young man smiled.

"Of course—if you can. I should be delighted to hear you do that. That's what I wish—to hear some good of her."

It might have seemed after this that nothing could have remained but for our friend to break out in categoric praise of his fellow guest; but he was no more to be tempted into that danger than into another. "I can only say I like her," he repeated. "She has been very kind to me."

"Every one seems to like her," said Lady Demesne with an unstudied effect of pathos. "She's certainly very amusing."

"She's very good-natured. I think she has no end of good intentions."

"What do you mean by good intentions?" asked Lady Demesne very sweetly.

"Well, it strikes me she wants to be friendly and pleasant."

"Indeed she does! But of course you have to defend her. She's your countrywoman."

"To defend her I must wait till she's attacked," Waterville laughed.

"That's very true. I needn't call your attention to the fact that I'm not attacking her," his hostess observed. "I should never attack a person staying in this house. I only want to know something about her, and if you can't tell me perhaps at least you can mention some one who will."

"She'll tell you herself. Tell you by the hour!"

"What she has told my son? I shouldn't understand it. My son doesn't understand it." She had a full pause, a profusion of patience; then she resumed disappointedly: "It's very strange. I rather hoped you might explain it."

He turned the case over. "I'm afraid I can't explain Mrs. Headway," he concluded.

"I see you admit she's very peculiar."

Even to this, however, he hesitated to commit himself. "It's too great a responsibility to answer you." He allowed he was very disobliging; he knew exactly what Lady Demesne wished him to say. He was unprepared to blight the reputation of Mrs. Headway to accommodate her; and yet, with his cultivated imagination, he could enter perfectly into the feelings of this tender formal serious woman who—it was easy to see—had looked for her own happiness in the observance of duty and in extreme constancy to two or three objects of devotion chosen once for all. She must indeed have had a conception of life in the light of which Nancy Beck would show both for displeasing and for dangerous. But he presently became aware she had taken his last words as a concession in which she might find help.

"You know why I ask you these things then?"

"I think I've an idea," said Waterville, persisting in irrelevant laughter. His laugh sounded foolish in his own ears.

"If you know that, I think you ought to assist me." Her tone changed now; there was a quick tremor in it; he could feel the confession of distress. The distress verily was deep; it had pressed her hard before she made up her mind to speak to him. He was sorry for her and determined to be very serious.

"If I could help you I would. But my position's very difficult."

"It's not so difficult as mine!" She was going all lengths; she was really appealing to him. "I don't imagine you under obligations to Mrs. Headway. You seem to me so different," she added.

He was not insensible to any discrimination that told in his favour; but these words shocked him as if they had been an attempt at bribery. "I'm surprised you don't like her," he ventured to bring out.

She turned her eyes through the window. "I don't think you're really surprised, though possibly you try to be. I don't like her at any rate, and I can't fancy why my son should. She's very pretty and appears very clever; but I don't trust her. I don't know what has taken possession of him; it's not usual in his family to marry people like that. Surely she's of *no* breeding. The person I should propose would be so very different—perhaps you can see what I mean. There's something in her history we don't understand. My son understands it no better than I. If you could throw any light on it, that might be a help. If I treat you with such confidence the first time I see you it's because I don't know where to turn. I'm exceedingly anxious."

It was plain enough she was anxious; her manner had become more vehement; her eyes seemed to shine in the thickening dusk. "Are you very sure there's danger?" Waterville asked. "Has he proposed to her and has she jumped at him?"

"If I wait till they settle it all it will be too late. I've reason to believe that my son's not engaged, but I fear he's terribly entangled. At the same time he's very uneasy, and that may save him yet. He has a great sense of honour. He's not satisfied about her past life; he doesn't know what to think of what we've been told. Even what she admits is so strange. She has been married four or five times. She has been divorced again and again. It seems so extraordinary. She tells him that in America it's different, and I dare say you haven't our ideas; but really there's a limit to everything. There must have been great irregularities—I'm afraid great scandals. It's dreadful to have to accept such things. He hasn't told me all this, but it's not necessary he should tell me. I know him well enough to guess."

"Does he know you're speaking to me?" Waterville asked.

"Not in the least. But I must tell you I shall repeat to him anything you may say against her."

"I had better say nothing then. It's very delicate. Mrs. Headway's quite undefended. One may like her or not, of course. I've seen nothing of her that isn't perfectly correct," our young man wound up.

"And you've heard nothing?"

He remembered Littlemore's view that there were cases in which a man was bound in honour to tell an untruth, and he wondered if this were such a one. Lady Demesne imposed herself, she made him believe in the reality of her grievance, and he saw the gulf that divided her from a pushing little woman who had lived with Western editors. She was right to wish not to be connected with Mrs. Headway. After all, there had been nothing in his relations with that lady to hold him down to lying for her. He hadn't sought her acquaintance, she had sought his; she had sent for him to come and see her. And yet he couldn't give her away—that stuck in his throat. "I'm afraid

I really can't say anything. And it wouldn't matter. Your son won't give her up because I happen not to like her."

"If he were to believe she had done wrong he'd give her up."

"Well, I've no right to say so," said Waterville.

Lady Demesne turned away; he indeed disappointed her and he feared she was going to break out: "Why then do you suppose I asked you here?" She quitted her place near the window and prepared apparently to leave the room. But she stopped short. "You know something against her, but you won't say it."

He hugged his folio and looked awkward. "You attribute things to me. I shall never say anything."

"Of course you're perfectly free. There's some one else who knows, I think—another American—a gentleman who was in Paris when my son was there. I've forgotten his name."

"A friend of Mrs. Headway's? I suppose you mean George Littlemore."

"Yes—Mr. Littlemore. He has a sister whom I've met; I didn't know she was his sister till to-day. Mrs. Headway spoke of her, but I find she doesn't know her. That itself is a proof, I think. Do you think *he* would help me?" Lady Demesne asked very simply.

"I doubt it, but you can try."

"I wish he had come with you. Do you think he'd come?"

"He's in America at this moment, but I believe he soon comes back."

She took this in with interest. "I shall go to his sister; I shall ask her to bring him to see me. She's extremely nice; I think she'll understand. Unfortunately there's very little time."

Waterville bethought himself. "Don't count too much on George Littlemore," he said gravely.

"You men have no pity," she grimly sighed.

189

"Why should we pity you? How can Mrs. Headway hurt such a person as you?" he asked.

Lady Demesne cast about. "It hurts me to hear her voice."

"Her voice is very liquid." He liked his word.

"Possibly. But she's horrible!"

This was too much, it seemed to Waterville; Nancy Beck was open to criticism, and he himself had declared she was a barbarian. Yet she wasn't horrible. "It's for your son to pity you. If he doesn't how can you expect it of others?"

"Oh but he does!" And with a majesty that was more striking even than her logic his hostess moved to the door.

Waterville advanced to open it for her, and as she passed out he said: "There's one thing you can do—try to like her!"

She shot him a woeful glance. "That would be—worst of all!"

VIII

George Littlemore arrived in London on the twentieth of May, and one of the first things he did was to go and see Waterville at the Legation, where he mentioned that he had taken for the rest of the season a house at Queen Anne's Gate, so that his sister and her husband, who, under the pressure of diminished rents, had let their own town residence, might come up and spend a couple of months with him.

"One of the consequences of your having a house will be that you'll have to entertain the Texan belle," our young man said.

Littlemore sat there with his hands crossed on his stick; he looked at his friend with an eye that failed to kindle at the mention of this lady's name. "Has she got into European society?" he rather languidly inquired.

"Very much, I should say. She has a house and a carriage and diamonds and everything handsome. She seems already to know a lot of people; they put her name in the *Morning Post*. She has come up very quickly; she's almost famous. Every one's asking about her—you'll be plied with questions."

Littlemore listened gravely. "How did she get in?"

"She met a large party at Longlands and made them all think her great fun. They must have taken her up; she only wanted a start."

Her old friend rallied after a moment to the interest of this news, marking his full appreciation of it by a burst of laughter. "To think of Nancy Beck! The people here do beat the Dutch! There's no one they won't go after. They wouldn't touch her in New York."

"Oh New York's quite old-fashioned and rococo," said Waterville; and he announced to Littlemore that Lady Demesne was very eager for his arrival and wanted his aid to prevent her son's bringing such a person into the family. Littlemore was apparently not alarmed at her ladyship's projects, and intimated, in the manner of a man who thought them rather impertinent, that he could trust himself to keep out of her way. "It isn't a proper marriage at any rate," the second secretary urged.

"Why not if he loves her?"

"Oh if that's all you want!"—which seemed a degree of cynicism startling to his companion.

"Would you marry her yourself?"

"Certainly if I were in love with her."

"You took care not to be that."

"Yes, I did—and so Demesne had better have done. However, since he's bitten—!" But Littlemore let the rest of his sentence too indifferently drop.

Waterville presently asked him how he would manage, in view of his sister's advent, about asking Mrs. Headway to his house; and he replied that he would manage by simply not asking her. On this Waterville pronounced

191

him highly inconsistent; to which Littlemore rejoined that it was very possible. But he asked whether they couldn't talk about something else than Mrs. Headway. He couldn't enter into the young man's interest in her—they were sure to have enough of her later without such impatience.

Waterville would have been sorry to give a false idea of his interest in the wonderful woman; he knew too well the feeling had definite limits. He had been two or three times to see her, but it was a relief to be able to believe her quite independent of him. There had been no revival of those free retorts which had marked their stay at Longlands. She could dispense with assistance now; she knew herself in the current of success. She pretended to be surprised at her good fortune, especially at its rapidity; but she was really surprised at nothing. She took things as they came and, being essentially a woman of action, wasted almost as little time in elation as she would have done in despondence. She talked a great deal about Lord Edward and Lady Margaret and such others of that "standing" as had shown a desire for her acquaintance; professing to measure perfectly the sources of a growing popularity. "They come to laugh at me," she said; "they come simply to get things to repeat. I can't open my mouth but they burst into fits. It's a settled thing that I'm a grand case of the American funny woman; if I make the least remark they begin to roar. I must express myself somehow; and indeed when I hold my tongue they think me funnier than ever. They repeat what I say to a great person, and a great person told some of them the other night that he wanted to hear me for himself. I'll do for him what I do for the others; no better and no worse. I don't know how I do it; I talk the only way I can. They tell me it isn't so much the things I say as the way I say them. Well, they're very easy to please. They don't really care for me, you know—they don't love me for myself and the way I want to be loved; it's only to be able to repeat Mrs. Headway's 'last.' Every one wants to have it first; it's a regular race." When she found what was expected of her she undertook to supply the article in abundance—the poor little woman worked hard at the vernacular. If the taste of London lay that way she would do her best to gratify it; it was only a pity she hadn't known before: she would have made more extensive preparations. She had thought it a disadvantage of old to live in Arizona, in Dakotah, in the newly-admitted States; but now she saw that, as she phrased it to herself, this was the best thing that ever had happened to her. She tried to recover the weird things she had heard out there, and keenly regretted she hadn't taken them down in writing; she drummed up the echoes of the Rocky Mountains and practised the intonations of the Pacific slope. When she saw her audience in convulsions she argued that this was success: she inferred that had she only come five years sooner she might have married a Duke. That would have been even a greater attraction for the London world than the actual proceedings of Sir Arthur Demesne, who, however, lived sufficiently in the eye of society to justify the rumour that there were bets about town as to the issue of his already protracted courtship. It was food for curiosity to see a young man of his pattern—one of the few "earnest" young men of the Tory side, with an income sufficient for tastes more vivid than those by which he was known—make up to a lady several years older than himself, whose fund of Texan slang was even larger than her stock of dollars. Mrs. Headway had got a good many new ideas since her arrival in London, but she had also not lost her grasp of several old ones. The chief of these—it was now a year old—was that Sir Arthur was the very most eligible and, shrewdly considered, taking one thing with another, most valuable young man in the world. There were of course a good many things he wasn't. He wasn't amusing; he wasn't insinuating; he wasn't of an absolutely irrepressible ardour. She believed he was constant, but he was certainly not eager. With these things, however, she could perfectly dispense; she had in particular quite outlived the need of being amused. She had had a very exciting life, and her vision of happiness at present was to be magnificently bored. The idea of complete and uncriticised respectability filled her soul with satisfaction; her imagination prostrated itself in the presence of this virtue. She was aware she had achieved it but ill in her own person; but she could now at least connect herself with it by sacred ties. She could prove in that way what was her deepest feeling. This was a religious appreciation of Sir Arthur's great quality—his smooth and rounded, his blooming lily-like exemption from social flaws.

She was at home when Littlemore went to see her and surrounded by several visitors to whom she was giving a late cup of tea and to whom she introduced her tall compatriot. He stayed till they dispersed, in spite of the manœuvres of a gentleman who evidently desired to outlinger him, but who, whatever might have been his happy fortune on former visits, received on this occasion no encouragement from their hostess. He looked at Littlemore slowly, beginning with his boots and travelling up as if to discover the reason of so unexpected a preference, and then, with no salutation to him, left the pair face to face.

"I'm curious to see what you'll do for me now you've got your sister with you," Mrs. Headway presently remarked, having heard of this circumstance from Rupert Waterville. "I realise you'll have to do something, you know. I'm sorry for you, but I don't see how you can get off. You might ask me to dine some day when she's dining out. I'd come even then, I think, because I want to keep on the right side of you."

"I call that the wrong side," said Littlemore.

"Yes, I see. It's your sister that's on the right side. You're in rather a bad fix, ain't you? You've got to be 'good' and mean, or you've got to be kind with a little courage. However, you take those things very quietly. There's something in you that exasperates me. What does your sister think of me? Does she hate me?" Nancy persisted.

"She knows nothing about you."

"Have you told her nothing?"

"Never a word."

"Hasn't she asked you? That shows how she hates me. She thinks I ain't creditable to America. I know *that* way of doing it. She wants to show people over here that, however they may be taken in by me, she knows much better. But she'll have to ask you about me; she can't go on for ever. Then what'll you say?"

"That you're the biggest 'draw' in Europe."

"Oh shucks!" she cried, out of her repertory.

"Haven't you got into European society?"

"Maybe I have, maybe I haven't. It's too soon to see. I can't tell this season. Every one says I've got to wait till next, to see if it's the same. Sometimes they take you right up for a few weeks and then just drop you anywhere. You've got to make it a square thing somehow—to drive in a nail."

"You speak as if it were your coffin," said Littlemore.

"Well, it *is* a kind of coffin. I'm burying my past!"

He winced at this—he was tired to death of her past. He changed the subject and turned her on to London, a topic as to which her freshness of view and now unpremeditated art of notation were really interesting, displayed as they were at the expense of most of her new acquaintances and of some of the most venerable features of the great city. He himself looked at England from the outside as much as it was possible to do; but in the midst of her familiar allusions to people and things known to her only since yesterday he was struck with the truth that she would never really be initiated. She buzzed over the surface of things like a fly on a window-pane. This surface immensely pleased her; she was flattered, encouraged, excited; she dropped her confident judgements as if she were scattering flowers, talked about her intentions, her prospects, her discoveries, her designs. But she had really learnt no more about English life than about the molecular theory. The words in which he had described her of old to Waterville came back to him: "*Elle ne doute de rien!*" Suddenly she jumped up; she was going out to dine and it was time to dress. "Before you leave I want you to promise me something," she said off-hand, but with a look he had seen before and that pressed on the point—oh so intensely! "You'll be sure to be questioned about me." And then she paused.

"How do people know I know you?"

"You haven't 'blown' about it? Is that what you mean? You can be a brute when you try. They do know it at any rate. Possibly I may have told them. They'll come to you to ask about me. I mean from Lady Demesne. She's in an awful state. She's so afraid of it—of the way he wants me."

In himself too, after all, she could still press the spring of careless mirth. "*I'm* not afraid, if you haven't yet brought it off."

195

"Well, he can't make up his mind. I appeal to him so, yet he can't quite place me where he'd have to have me." Her lucidity and her detachment were both grotesque and touching.

"He must be a poor creature if he won't take you as you are. I mean for the sweet sake of what you are," Littlemore added.

This wasn't a very gallant form, but she made the best of it. "Well—he wants to be very careful, and so he ought!"

"If he asks too many questions he's not worth marrying," Littlemore rather cheaply opined.

"I beg your pardon—he's worth marrying whatever he does; he's worth marrying for *me*. And I want to marry him—that's what I want to do."

Her old friend had a pause of some blankness. "Is he waiting for me to settle it?"

"He's waiting for I don't know what—for some one to come and tell him that I'm the sweetest of the sweet. Then he'll believe it. Some one who has been out there and knows all about me. Of course you're the man, you're created on purpose. Don't you remember how I told you in Paris he wanted to ask you? He was ashamed and gave it up; he tried to forget me. But now it's all on again—only meanwhile his mother has been at him. She works night and day, like a weasel in a hole, to persuade him that I'm too much beneath him. He's very fond of her and very open to influence; I mean from her—not from any one else. Except me of course. Oh I've influenced him, I've explained everything fifty times over. But some memories, you know, are like those lumpish or pointed things you can't get into your trunk—they won't pack anyway; and he keeps coming back to them. He wants every little speck explained. He won't come to you himself, but his mother will, or she'll send some of her people. I guess she'll send the lawyer—the family solicitor they call him. She wanted to send him out to America to make inquiries, only she didn't know where to send. Of course I couldn't be expected to give the places—they've got to find *them* out the best way they can. She knows all about you and has made up to your sister; a big proof, as she never makes up to any one. So you see how much I know. She's waiting for you; she means to hold you with her glittering eye. She has an idea she *can*—can make you say what'll meet her views. Then she'll lay it before Sir Arthur. So you'll be so good as to have none—not a view."

Littlemore had, however disguisedly, given her every attention; but the conclusion left him all too consciously staring. "You don't mean that anything I can say will make a difference?"

"Don't be affected! You know it will as well as I."

"You make him out not only a laggard in love but almost a dastard in war."

"Never mind what I make him out. I guess if I can understand him you can accept him. And I appeal to you solemnly. You can save me or you can lose me. If you lose me you'll be a coward. And if you say a word against me I'll be lost."

"Go and dress for dinner—that's your salvation," Littlemore returned as he quitted her at the head of the stairs.

IX

It was very well for him to take that tone; but he felt as he walked home that he should scarcely know what to say to people who were determined, as she put it, to hold him with glittering eyes. She had worked a certain spell; she had succeeded in making him feel responsible. The sight of her success, however, rather hardened his heart; he might have pitied her if she had "muffed" it, as they said, but he just sensibly resented her heavy scoring. He dined alone that evening while his sister and her husband, who had engagements every day for a month, partook of their repast at the expense of friends. Mrs. Dolphin, however, came home rather early and immediately sought admittance to the small apartment at the foot of the staircase which was already spoken of as her brother's den. Reggie had gone on to a "squash" somewhere, and she had returned in her eagerness to the third member of their party. She was too impatient even to wait for morning. She looked impatient; she was very unlike George Littlemore. "I want you to tell me about Mrs. Headway," she at once began, while he started slightly at the coincidence of this remark with his own thoughts. He was just making up his mind at last to speak to her. She unfastened her cloak and tossed it over a chair, then pulled off her long tight black gloves, which were not so fine as those Mrs. Headway wore; all this as if she were preparing herself for an important interview. She was a fair neat woman, who had once been pretty, with a small thin voice, a finished manner and a perfect knowledge of what it was proper to do on every occasion in life. She always did it, and her conception of it was so definite that failure would have left her without excuse. She was usually not taken for an American, but she made a point of being one, because she flattered herself that she was of a type which under that banner borrowed distinction from rarity. She was by nature a great conservative and had ended by figuring as a better Tory than her husband; to the effect of being thought by some of her old friends to have changed immensely since her marriage. She knew English society as if she had compiled a red-covered handbook of the subject; had a way of looking prepared for far-reaching social action; had also thin lips and pretty teeth; and was as positive as she was amiable. She told her brother that Mrs. Headway had given out that he was her most intimate friend; whereby she thought it rather odd he had never spoken of her "at home." Littlemore admitted, on this, that he had known her a long time, referred to the conditions in which the acquaintance had sprung up, and added that he had seen her that afternoon. He sat there smoking his cigar and looking up at the cornice while Mrs. Dolphin delivered herself of a series of questions. Was it true that he liked her so much, was it true he thought her a possible woman to marry, was it true that her antecedents had not been most peculiar?

"I may as well tell you I've a letter from Lady Demesne," his visitor went on. "It came to me just before I went out, and I have it in my pocket."

She drew forth the missive, which she evidently wished to read him; but he gave her no invitation to proceed. He knew she had come to him to extract a declaration adverse to Mrs. Headway's projects, and however little

198

edification he might find in this lady's character he hated to be arraigned or prodded. He had a great esteem for Mrs. Dolphin, who, among other Hampshire notions, had picked up that of the major weight of the male members of any family, so that she treated him with a consideration which made his having an English sister rather a luxury. Nevertheless he was not, on the subject of his old Texan friend, very accommodating. He admitted once for all that she hadn't behaved properly—it wasn't worth while to split hairs about that; but he couldn't see that she was much worse than lots of other women about the place—women at once less amusing and less impugned; and he couldn't get up much feeling about her marrying or not marrying. Moreover, it was none of his business, and he intimated that it was none of Mrs. Dolphin's.

"One surely can't resist the claims of common humanity!" his sister replied; and she added that he was very inconsistent. He didn't respect Mrs. Headway, he knew the most dreadful things about her, he didn't think her fit company for his own flesh and blood. And yet he was willing not to save poor Arthur Demesne.

"Perfectly willing!" Littlemore returned. "I've nothing to do with saving others. All I've got to do is not to marry her myself."

"Don't you think then we've any responsibilities, any duties to society?"

"I don't know what you mean. Society can look after itself. If she can bring it off she's welcome. It's a splendid sight in its way."

"How do you mean splendid?"

"Why she has run up the tree as if she were a squirrel!"

"It's very true she has an assurance *à toute épreuve*. But English society has become scandalously easy. I never saw anything like the people who are taken up. Mrs. Headway has had only to appear to succeed. If they can only make out big *enough* spots in you they'll find you attractive. It's like the decadence of the Roman Empire. You can see to look at this person that she's not a lady. She's pretty, very pretty, but she might be a dissipated dressmaker. She wouldn't go down for a minute in New York. I've seen her three times—she apparently goes everywhere. I didn't speak of her—I was wanting to see what you'd do. I judged you meant to do nothing, then this letter decided me. It's written on purpose to be shown you; it's what the poor lady—*such* a nice woman herself—wants you to do. She wrote to me before I came to town, and I went to see her as soon as I arrived. I think it very important. I told her that if she'd draw up a little statement I'd put it before you as soon as we should get settled. She's in real distress. I think you ought to feel for her. You ought to communicate the facts exactly as they stand. A woman has no right to do such things as Mrs. Headway and come and ask to be accepted. She may make it up with her conscience, but she can't make it up with society. Last night at Lady Dovedale's I was afraid she'd know who I was and get somehow at me. I believe she'd really have been capable of it, and I got so frightened I went away. If Sir Arthur wishes to marry her for what she is, of course he's welcome. But at least he ought to know."

Mrs. Dolphin was neither agitated nor voluble; she moved from point to point with the temper and method of a person accustomed to preside at committees and to direct them. She deeply desired, however, that Mrs. Headway's triumphant career should be checked; such a person had sufficiently abused a tolerance already so overstrained. Herself a party to an international marriage, Mrs. Dolphin naturally desired the class to which she belonged to close its ranks and carry its standard high.

"It seems to me she's quite as good as the poor young man himself," said Littlemore, lighting another cigar.

"As good? What do you mean by 'good'? No one has ever breathed a word against him."

"Very likely. But he's a nonentity of the first water, and she at least a positive quantity, not to say a positive force. She's a person, and a very clever one. Besides, she's quite as good as the women lots of them have married. It's new to me that your alliances have been always so august."

"I know nothing about other cases," Mrs. Dolphin said, "I only know about this one. It so happens that I've been brought near it, and that an appeal has been made to me. The English are very romantic—the most romantic people in the world, if that's what you mean. They do the strangest things from the force of passion—even those of whom you would least expect it. They marry their cooks, they marry their coachmen, and their romances always have the most miserable end. I'm sure this one would be wretched. How can you pretend that such a flaming barbarian can be worked into *any* civilisation? What I see is a fine old race—one of the oldest and most honourable in England, people with every tradition of good conduct and high principle—and a dreadful disreputable vulgar little woman, who hasn't an idea of what such things are, trying to force her way into it. I hate to see such things—I want to go to the rescue!"

"Well, I don't," Littlemore returned at his leisure. "I don't care a pin for the fine old race."

"Not from interested motives, of course, any more than I. But surely on artistic grounds, on grounds of decency?"

"Mrs. Headway isn't indecent—you go too far. You must remember that she's an old friend of mine." He had become rather stern; Mrs. Dolphin was forgetting the consideration due, from an English point of view, to brothers.

She forgot it even a little more. "Oh if you're in love with her too!" she quite wailed, turning away.

He made no answer to this, and the words had no sting for him. But at last, to finish the affair, he asked what in the world the old lady wanted him to do. Did she want him to go out into Piccadilly and announce to the passers-by that there had been one winter when even Mrs. Headway's sister didn't know who was her husband?

Mrs. Dolphin's reply was to read out Lady Demesne's letter, which her brother, as she folded it up again, pronounced one of the most extraordinary communications he had ever listened to. "It's very sad—it's a cry of distress," she declared. "The whole meaning of it is that she wishes you'd come and see her. She doesn't say it in so many words, but I can read between the lines. Besides, she told me she'd give anything to see you. Let me assure you it's your duty to go."

"To go and abuse Nancy Beck?"

"Go and rave about her if you like!" This was very clever of Mrs. Dolphin, but her brother was not so easily beguiled. He didn't take that view of his duty, and he declined to cross her ladyship's threshold. "Then she'll come and see you," said his visitor with decision.

"If she does I'll tell her Nancy's an angel."

"If you can say so conscientiously she'll be delighted to hear it." And she gathered up her cloak and gloves.

Meeting Rupert Waterville the next day, as he often did, at the Saint George's Club, which offers a much-appreciated hospitality to secretaries of legation and to the natives of the countries they assist in representing, Littlemore let him know that his prophecy had been fulfilled and that Lady Demesne had been making proposals for an interview. "My sister read me a desperate letter from her."

Our young man was all critical attention again. "'Desperate'?"

"The letter of a woman so scared that she'll do anything. I may be a great brute, but her scare amuses me."

"You're in the position of Olivier de Jalin in *Le Demi-Monde*," Waterville remarked.

"In *Le Demi-Monde*?" Littlemore was not quick at catching literary allusions.

"Don't you remember the play we saw in Paris? Or like Don Fabrice in *L'Aventurière*. A bad woman tries to marry an honourable man, who doesn't know how bad she is, and they who do know step in and push her back."

"Yes, it comes to me. There was a good deal of lying," Littlemore recalled, "all round."

"They prevented the marriage, however—which is the great thing."

"The great thing if your heart's set! One of the active parties was the intimate friend of the man in love, the other was his son. Demesne's nothing at all to me."

"He's a very good fellow," said Waterville.

"Then go and talk to him."

"Play the part of Olivier de Jalin? Oh I can't. I'm not Olivier. But I think I do wish he'd corner me of himself. Mrs. Headway oughtn't really to be allowed to pass."

"I wish to heaven they'd let me alone," Littlemore murmured ruefully and staring a while out of the window.

"Do you still hold to that theory you propounded in Paris? Are you willing to commit perjury?" Waterville asked.

"Assuredly I can refuse to answer questions—even that one."

"As I told you before, that will amount to a condemnation."

Longmore frowningly debated. "It may amount to what it pleases. I guess I'll go back to Paris."

"That will be the same as not answering. But it's quite the best thing you can do. I've really been thinking it out," Waterville continued, "and I don't hold that from the point of view of social good faith she's an article we ought to contribute—!" He looked at the matter clearly now from a great elevation; his tone, the expression of his face, betrayed this lofty flight; the effect of which, as he glanced down at his didactic young friend, Littlemore found peculiarly irritating.

He shifted about. "No, after all, hanged if they shall drive me away!" he exclaimed abruptly; and he walked off while his companion wondered.

X

The morning after this the elder man received a note from Mrs. Headway—a short and simple note, consisting merely of the words: "I shall be at home this afternoon; will you come and see me at five? I've something particular to say to you." He sent no answer to the question, but went to the little house in Chesterfield Street at the hour its mistress had proposed.

"I don't believe you know what sort of a woman I *am*!" she began as soon as he stood before her.

"Oh Lord!" Littlemore groaned as he dropped into a chair. Then he added: "Please don't strike up *that* air!"

"Ah, but it's exactly what I've wanted to say. It's very important. You don't know me—you don't understand me. You think you do—but you don't."

"It isn't for the want of your having told me—many many times!" And Littlemore had a hard critical smile, irritated as he was at so austere a prospect. The last word of all was decidedly that Mrs. Headway was a dreadful bore. It was always the last word about such women, who never really deserved to be spared.

She glared at him a little on this; her face was no longer the hospitable inn-front with the showy sign of the Smile. The sign had come down; she looked sharp and strained, almost old; the change was complete. It made her serious as he had never seen her—having seen her always only either too pleased or too disgusted. "Yes, I know; men are so stupid. They know nothing about women but what women tell them. And women tell them things on purpose to see how stupid they can be. I've told you things like that just for amusement when it was dull. If you believed them it was your own fault. But now I want you really to know."

"I don't want to know. I know enough."

"How do you mean you know enough?" she cried with all her sincerity. "What business have you to know anything?" The poor little woman, in her passionate purpose, was not obliged to be consistent, and the loud laugh with which Littlemore greeted this must have seemed to her unduly harsh. "You shall know what I want you to know, however. You think me a bad woman—you don't respect me; I told you that in Paris. I've done things I don't understand, myself, to-day; that I admit as fully as you please. But I've completely changed, and I want to change everything. You ought to enter into that, you ought to see what I want. I hate everything that has happened

204

to me before this; I loathe it, I despise it. I went on that way trying—trying one thing and another. But now I've got what I want. Do you expect me to go down on my knees to you? I believe I will, I'm so anxious. You can help me—no one else can do a thing; they're only waiting to see if *he'll* do it. I told you in Paris you could help me, and it's just as true now. Say a good word for me for Christ's sake! You haven't lifted your little finger, or I should know it by this time. It will just make the difference. Or if your sister would come and see me I should be all right. Women are pitiless, pitiless, and you're pitiless too. It isn't that Mrs. Dolphin's anything so great, most of my friends are better than that!—but she's the one woman who *knows*, and every one seems to know she knows. *He* knows it, and he knows she doesn't come. So she kills me—she kills me! I understand perfectly what he wants—I'll do everything, be anything, I'll be the most perfect wife. The old woman will adore me when she knows me—it's too stupid of her not to see. Everything in the past's over; it has all fallen away from me; it's the life of another woman. This was what I wanted; I knew I should find it some day. I knew I should be at home in the best—and with the highest. What could I do in those horrible places? I had to take what I could. But now I've got nice surroundings. I want you to do me justice. You've never done me justice. That's what I sent for you for."

Littlemore had suddenly ceased to be bored, but a variety of feelings had taken the place of that one. It was impossible not to be touched; she really meant what she said. People don't change their nature, but they change their desires, their ideal, their effort. This incoherent passionate plea was an assurance that she was literally panting to be respectable. But the poor woman, whatever she did, was condemned, as he had said of old, in Paris, to Waterville, to be only half right. The colour rose to her visitor's face as he listened to her outpouring of anxiety and egotism; she hadn't managed her early life very well, but there was no need of her going down on her knees. "It's very painful to me to hear all this. You're under no obligation to say such things to me. You entirely misconceive my attitude—my influence."

"Oh yes, you shirk it—you only wish to shirk it!" she cried, flinging away fiercely the sofa-cushion on which she had been resting.

"Marry whom you damn please!" Littlemore quite shouted, springing to his feet.

He had hardly spoken when the door was thrown open and the servant announced Sir Arthur Demesne. This shy adventurer entered with a certain briskness, but stopped short on seeing Mrs. Headway engaged with another guest. Recognising Littlemore, however, he gave a light exclamation which might have passed for a greeting. Mrs. Headway, who had risen as he came in, looked with wonderful eyes from one of the men to the other; then, like a person who had a sudden inspiration, she clasped her hands together and cried out: "I'm so glad you've met. If I had arranged it it couldn't be better!"

"If you had arranged it?" said Sir Arthur, crinkling a little his high white forehead, while the conviction rose before Littlemore that she had indeed arranged it.

"I'm going to do something very queer"—and her extravagant manner confirmed her words.

"You're excited, I'm afraid you're ill." Sir Arthur stood there with his hat and his stick; he was evidently much annoyed.

"It's an excellent opportunity; you must forgive me if I take advantage." And she flashed a tender touching ray at the Baronet. "I've wanted this a long time—perhaps you've seen I wanted it. Mr. Littlemore has known me from far back; he's an old old friend. I told you that in Paris, don't you remember? Well he's my only one, and I want him to speak for me." Her eyes had turned now to Littlemore; they rested upon him with a sweetness that only made the whole proceeding more audacious. She had begun to smile again, though she was visibly trembling. "He's my only one," she continued; "it's a great pity, you ought to have known others. But I'm very much alone and must make the best of what I have. I want so much that some one else than myself should speak for me. Women usually can ask that service of a relative or of another woman. I can't; it's a great pity, but it's not my fault, it's my misfortune. None of my people are here—I'm terribly alone in the world. But Mr. Littlemore will tell you; he'll say he has known me for ever so long. He'll tell you if he knows any reason—if there's anything against me. He has been wanting the chance—he thought he couldn't begin himself. You see I treat you as an old friend, dear Mr. Littlemore. I'll leave you with Sir Arthur. You'll both excuse me." The expression of her face, turned towards Littlemore as she delivered herself of this singular proposal, had the intentness of a magician who wishes to work a spell. She darted at Sir Arthur another pleading ray and then swept out of the room.

The two men remained in the extraordinary position she had created for them; neither of them moved even to open the door for her. She closed it behind her, and for a moment there was a deep portentous silence. Sir Arthur Demesne, very pale, stared hard at the carpet.

"I'm placed in an impossible situation," Littlemore said at last, "and I don't imagine you accept it any more than I do." His fellow-visitor kept the same attitude, neither looking up nor answering. Littlemore felt a sudden gush of pity for him. Of course he couldn't accept the situation, but all the same he was half-sick with anxiety to see how this nondescript American, who was both so precious and so superfluous, so easy and so abysmal, would consider Mrs. Headway's challenge. "Have you any question to ask me?" Littlemore went on. At which Sir Arthur looked up. The other had seen the look before; he had described it to Waterville after Mrs. Headway's admirer came to call on him in Paris. There were other things mingled with it now— shame, annoyance, pride; but the great thing, the intense desire to *know*, was paramount. "Good God, how can I tell him?" seemed to hum in Littlemore's ears.

Sir Arthur's hesitation would have been of the briefest; but his companion heard the tick of the clock while it lasted. "Certainly I've no question to ask," the young man said in a voice of cool almost insolent surprise.

"Good-day then, confound you."

"The same to you!"

But Littlemore left him in possession. He expected to find Mrs. Headway at the foot of the staircase; but he quitted the house without interruption.

On the morrow, after luncheon, as he was leaving the vain retreat at Queen Anne's Gate, the postman handed him a letter. Littlemore opened and read it on the steps, an operation which took but a moment.

DEAR MR. LITTLEMORE—It will interest you to know that I'm engaged to be married to Sir Arthur Demesne and that our marriage is to take place as soon as their stupid old Parliament rises. But it's not to come out for some days, and I'm sure I can trust meanwhile to your complete discretion.

Yours very sincerely,
NANCY H.

P.S.—He made me a terrible scene for what I did yesterday, but he came back in the evening and we fixed it all right. That's how the thing comes to be settled. He won't tell me what passed between you—he requested me never to allude to the subject. I don't care—I was bound you should speak!

Littlemore thrust this epistle into his pocket and marched away with it. He had come out on various errands, but he forgot his business for the time and before he knew it had walked into Hyde Park. He left the carriages and riders to one side and followed the Serpentine into Kensington Gardens, of which he made the complete circuit. He felt annoyed, and more disappointed than he understood—than he would have understood if he had tried. Now that Nancy Beck had succeeded her success was an irritation, and he was almost sorry he hadn't said to Sir Arthur: "Oh well, she was pretty bad, you know." However, now they were at one they would perhaps leave him alone. He walked the irritation off and before he went about his original purposes had ceased to think of Mrs. Headway. He went home at six o'clock, and the servant who admitted him informed him in doing so that Mrs. Dolphin had requested he should be told on his return that she wished to see him in the drawing-room. "It's another trap!" he said to himself instinctively; but in spite of this reflexion he went upstairs. On entering his sister's presence he found she had a visitor. This visitor, to all appearance on the point of departing, was a tall elderly woman, and the two ladies stood together in the middle of the room.

"I'm so glad you've come back," said Mrs. Dolphin without meeting her brother's eye. "I want so much to introduce you to Lady Demesne that I hoped you'd come in. Must you really go—won't you stay a little?" she added, turning to her companion; and without waiting for an answer went on hastily: "I must leave you a moment—excuse me. I'll come back!" Before he knew it Littlemore found himself alone with her ladyship and understood that since he hadn't been willing to go and see her she had taken upon herself to make an advance. It had the queerest effect, all the same, to see his sister playing the same tricks as Nancy Beck!

"Ah, she must be in a fidget!" he said to himself as he stood before Lady Demesne. She looked modest and aloof, even timid, as far as a tall serene woman who carried her head very well could look so; and she was such a different type from Mrs. Headway that his present vision of Nancy's triumph gave her by contrast something of the dignity of the vanquished. It made him feel as sorry for her as he had felt for her son. She lost no time; she went straight to the point. She evidently felt that in the situation in which she had placed herself her only advantage could consist in being simple and business-like.

"I'm so fortunate as to catch you. I wish so much to ask you if you can give me any information about a person you know and about whom I have been in correspondence with Mrs. Dolphin. I mean Mrs. Headway."

"Won't you sit down?" asked Littlemore.

"No, thank you. I've only a moment."

"May I ask you why you make this inquiry?"

"Of course I must give you my reason. I'm afraid my son will marry her."

Littlemore was puzzled—then saw she wasn't yet aware of the fact imparted to him in Mrs. Headway's note. "You don't like her?" he asked, exaggerating, in spite of himself, the interrogative inflexion.

"Not at all," said Lady Demesne, smiling and looking at him. Her smile was gentle, without rancour; he thought it almost beautiful.

"What would you like me to say?" he asked.

"Whether you think her respectable."

"What good will that do you? How can it possibly affect the event?"

"It will do me no good, of course, if your opinion's favourable. But if you tell me it's not I shall be able to say to my son that the one person in London who has known her more than six months thinks so and so of her."

This speech, on Lady Demesne's clear lips, evoked no protest from her listener. He had suddenly become conscious of the need to utter the simple truth with which he had answered Rupert Waterville's first question at the Théâtre Français. He brought it out. "I don't think Mrs. Headway respectable."

"I was sure you would say that." She seemed to pant a little.

"I can say nothing more—not a word. That's my opinion. I don't think it will help you."

"I think it will. I wanted to have it from your own lips. That makes all the difference," said Lady Demesne. "I'm exceedingly obliged to you." And she offered him her hand; after which he accompanied her in silence to the door.

He felt no discomfort, no remorse, at what he had said; he only felt relief—presumably because he believed it would make no difference. It made a difference only in what was at the bottom of all things—his own sense of fitness. He only wished he had driven it home that Mrs. Headway would probably be for her son a capital wife. But that at least would make no difference. He requested his sister, who had wondered greatly at the brevity of his interview with her friend, to spare him all questions on the subject; and Mrs. Dolphin went about for some days in the happy faith that there were to be no dreadful Americans in English society compromising her native land.

Her faith, however, was short-lived. Nothing had made any difference; it was perhaps too late. The London world heard in the first days of July, not that Sir Arthur Demesne was to marry Mrs. Headway, but that the pair had been privately and, it was to be hoped as regards Mrs. Headway on this occasion, indissolubly united. His mother gave neither sign nor sound; she only retired to the country.

"I think you might have done differently," said Mrs. Dolphin, very pale, to her brother. "But of course everything will come out now."

"Yes, and make her more the fashion than ever!" Littlemore answered with cynical laughter. After his little interview with the elder Lady Demesne he didn't feel at liberty to call again on the younger; and he never learned—he never even wished to know—whether in the pride of her success she forgave him.

Waterville—it was very strange—was positively scandalised at this success. He held that Mrs. Headway ought never to have been allowed to marry a confiding gentleman, and he used in speaking to Littlemore the same words as Mrs. Dolphin. He thought Littlemore might have done differently. But he spoke with such vehemence that Littlemore looked at him hard—hard enough to make him blush. "Did you want to marry her yourself?" his friend inquired. "My dear fellow, you're in love with her! That's what's the matter with you."

This, however, blushing still more, Waterville indignantly denied. A little later he heard from New York that people were beginning to ask who in the world Lady Demesne "had been."

AN INTERNATIONAL EPISODE

I

Four years ago—in 1874—two young Englishmen had occasion to go to the United States. They crossed the ocean at midsummer and, arriving in New York on the first day of August, were much struck with the high, the torrid temperature. Disembarking upon the wharf they climbed into one of the huge high-hung coaches that convey passengers to the hotels, and with a great deal of bouncing and bumping they took their course through Broadway. The midsummer aspect of New York is doubtless not the most engaging, though nothing perhaps could well more solicit an alarmed attention. Of quite other sense and sound from those of any typical English street was the endless rude channel, rich in incongruities, through which our two travellers advanced—looking out on either side at the rough animation of the sidewalks, at the high-coloured heterogeneous architecture, at the huge white marble façades that, bedizened with gilded lettering, seemed to glare in the strong crude light, at the multifarious awnings, banners and streamers, at the extraordinary number of omnibuses, horse-cars and other democratic vehicles, at the vendors of cooling fluids, the white trousers and big straw hats of the policemen, the tripping gait of the modish young persons on the pavement, the general brightness, newness, juvenility, both of people and things. The young men had exchanged few observations, but in crossing Union Square, in front of the monument to Washington—in the very shadow indeed projected by the image of the *pater patriae*—one of them remarked to the other: "Awfully rum place."

"Ah, very odd, very odd," said the other, who was the clever man of the two.

"Pity it's so beastly hot," resumed the first speaker after a pause.

"You know we're in a low latitude," said the clever man.

"I daresay," remarked his friend.

"I wonder," said the second speaker presently, "if they can give one a bath."

"I daresay not," the other returned.

"Oh I say!" cried his comrade.

This animated discussion dropped on their arrival at the hotel, recommended to them by an American gentleman whose acquaintance they had made—with whom, indeed, they had become very intimate—on the steamer and who had proposed to accompany them to the inn and introduce them in a friendly way to the proprietor. This plan, however, had been defeated by their friend's finding his "partner" in earnest attendance on the wharf, with urgent claims on his immediate presence of mind. But the two Englishmen, with nothing beyond their national prestige and personal graces to recommend them, were very well received at the hotel, which had an air of capacious hospitality. They found a bath not unattainable and were indeed struck with the facilities for prolonged and reiterated immersion with which their apartment was supplied. After bathing a good deal—more indeed than they had ever done before on a single occasion—they made their way to the dining-room of the hotel, which was a spacious restaurant with a fountain in the middle, a great many tall plants in ornamental tubs and an array of French waiters. The first dinner on land, after a sea-voyage, is in any connexion a delightful hour, and there was much that ministered to ease in the general situation of our young men. They were formed for good spirits and addicted and appointed to hilarity; they were more observant than they appeared; they were, in an inarticulate accidentally dissimulative fashion, capable of high appreciation. This was perhaps especially the case with the elder, who was also, as I have said, the man of talent. They sat down at a little table which was a very different affair from the great clattering see-saw in the saloon of the steamer. The wide doors and windows of the restaurant stood open, beneath large awnings, to a wide expanse studded with other plants in tubs and rows of spreading trees—beyond which appeared a large shady square without palings and with marble-paved walks. And above the vivid verdure rose other façades of white marble and of pale chocolate-coloured stone, squaring themselves against the deep blue sky. Here, outside, in the light and the shade and the heat, was a great tinkling of the bells of innumerable street-cars and a constant strolling and shuffling and rustling of many pedestrians, extremely frequent among whom were young women in Pompadour-looking dresses. The place within was cool and vaguely lighted; with the plash of water, the odour of flowers and the flitting of French waiters, as I have said, on soundless carpets.

"It's rather like Paris, you know," said the younger of our two travellers.

"It's like Paris—only more so," his companion returned.

"I suppose it's the French waiters," said the first speaker. "Why don't they have French waiters in London?"

"Ah, but fancy a French waiter at a London club!" said his friend.

The elder man stared as if he couldn't fancy it. "In Paris I'm very apt to dine at a place where there's an English waiter. Don't you know, what's-his-name's, close to the thingumbob? They always set an English waiter at me. I suppose they think I can't speak French."

"No more you can!" And this candid critic unfolded his napkin.

The other paid no heed whatever to his candour. "I say," the latter resumed in a moment, "I suppose we must learn to speak American. I suppose we must take lessons."

"I can't make them out, you know," said the clever man.

"What the deuce is *he* saying?" asked his comrade, appealing from the French waiter.

"He's recommending some soft-shell crabs," said the clever man.

And so, in a desultory view of the mysteries of the new world bristling about them, the young Englishmen proceeded to dine—going in largely, as the phrase is, for cooling draughts and dishes, as to which their attendant submitted to them a hundred alternatives. After dinner they went out and slowly walked about the neighbouring streets. The early dusk of waning summer was at hand, but the heat still very great. The pavements were

214

hot even to the stout boot-soles of the British travellers, and the trees along the kerb-stone emitted strange exotic odours. The young men wandered through the adjoining square—that queer place without palings and with marble walks arranged in black and white lozenges. There were a great many benches crowded with shabby-looking people, and the visitors remarked very justly that it wasn't much like Grosvenor Square. On one side was an enormous hotel, lifting up into the hot darkness an immense array of open and brightly-lighted windows. At the base of this populous structure was an eternal jangle of horse-cars, and all round it, in the upper dusk, a sinister hum of mosquitoes. The ground-floor of the hotel, figuring a huge transparent cage, flung a wide glare of gaslight into the street, of which it formed a public adjunct, absorbing and emitting the passers-by promiscuously. The young Englishmen went in with every one else, from curiosity, and saw a couple of hundred men sitting on divans along a great marble-paved corridor, their legs variously stretched out, together with several dozen more standing in a queue, as at the ticket-office of a railway station, before a vast marble altar of sacrifice, a thing shaped like the counter of a huge shop. These latter persons, who carried portmanteaus in their hands, had a dejected exhausted look; their garments were not fresh, as if telling of some rush, or some fight, for life, and they seemed to render mystic tribute to a magnificent young man with a waxed moustache and a shirt front adorned with diamond buttons, who every now and then dropped a cold glance over their multitudinous patience. They were American citizens doing homage to an hotel-clerk.

"I'm glad he didn't tell us to go there," said one of our Englishmen, alluding to their friend on the steamer, who had told them so many things. They walked up the Fifth Avenue, where he had, for instance, told them all the first families lived. But the first families were out of town, and our friends had but the satisfaction of seeing some of the second—or perhaps even the third—taking the evening air on balconies and high flights of doorsteps in streets at right angles to the main straight channel. They went a little way down one of these side-streets and there saw young ladies in white dresses—charming-looking persons—seated in graceful attitudes on the chocolate-coloured steps. In one or two places these young ladies were conversing across the street with other young ladies seated in similar postures and costumes in

215

front of the opposite houses, and in the warm night air their colloquial tones sounded strangely in the ears of the young Englishmen. One of the latter, nevertheless—the younger—betrayed a disposition to intercept some stray item of this interchange and see what it would lead to; but his companion observed pertinently enough that he had better be careful. They mustn't begin by making mistakes.

"But he told us, you know—he told us," urged the young man, alluding again to the friend on the steamer.

"Never mind what he told us!" answered his elder, who, if he had more years and a more developed wit, was also apparently more of a moralist.

By bedtime—in their impatience to taste of a terrestrial couch again our seafarers went to bed early—it was still insufferably hot, and the buzz of the mosquitoes at the open windows might have passed for an audible crepitation of the temperature. "We can't stand this, you know," the young Englishmen said to each other; and they tossed about all night more boisterously than they had been tossed by Atlantic billows. On the morrow their first thought was that they would re-embark that day for England, but it then occurred to them they might find an asylum nearer at hand. The cave of Æolus became their ideal of comfort, and they wondered where the Americans went when wishing to cool off. They hadn't the least idea, and resolved to apply for information to Mr. J. L. Westgate. This was the name—inscribed in a bold hand on the back of a letter carefully preserved in the pocket-book of our younger gentleman. Beneath the address, in the left-hand corner of the envelope, were the words "Introducing Lord Lambeth and Percy Beaumont Esq." The letter had been given to the two Englishmen by a good friend of theirs in London, who had been in America two years previously and had singled out Mr. J. L. Westgate from the many friends he had left there as the consignee, as it were, of his compatriots. "He's really very decent," the Englishman in London had said, "and he has an awfully pretty wife. He's tremendously hospitable—he'll do everything in the world for you, and as he knows every one over there it's quite needless I should give you any other introduction. He'll make you see every one—trust him for the right kick-off. He has a tremendously pretty wife." It was natural that in the hour of tribulation Lord Lambeth and Mr. Percy Beaumont should have bethought themselves of so possible a benefactor; all the more so that he lived in the Fifth Avenue and that the Fifth Avenue, as they had ascertained the night before, was contiguous to their hotel. "Ten to one he'll be out of town," said Percy Beaumont; "but we can at least find out where he has gone and can at once give chase. He can't possibly have gone to a hotter place, you know."

"Oh there's only one hotter place," said Lord Lambeth, "and I hope he hasn't gone there."

They strolled along the shady side of the street to the number indicated by the precious letter. The house presented an imposing chocolate-coloured expanse, relieved by facings and window-cornices of florid sculpture and by a couple of dusty rose-trees which clambered over the balconies and the portico. This last-mentioned feature was approached by a monumental flight of steps.

"Rather better than a dirty London thing," said Lord Lambeth, looking down from this altitude after they had rung the bell.

"It depends upon what London thing you mean," replied his companion. "You've a tremendous chance to get wet between the house-door and your carriage."

"Well," said Lord Lambeth, glancing at the blaze of the sky, "I 'guess' it doesn't rain so much here!"

The door was opened by a long negro in a white jacket, who grinned familiarly when Lord Lambeth asked for Mr. Westgate. "He ain't at home, sir; he's down town at his office."

"Oh at his office?" said the visitors. "And when will he be at home?"

"Well, when he goes out dis way in de mo'ning he ain't liable to come home all day."

This was discouraging; but the address of Mr. Westgate's office was freely imparted by the intelligent black and was taken down by Percy Beaumont in his pocket-book. The comrades then returned, languidly enough, to their hotel and sent for a hackney-coach; and in this commodious vehicle

217

they rolled comfortably down town. They measured the whole length of Broadway again and found it a path of fire; and then, deflecting to the left, were deposited by their conductor before a fresh light ornamental structure, ten stories high, in a street crowded with keen-faced light-limbed young men who were running about very nimbly and stopping each other eagerly at corners and in doorways. Passing under portals that were as the course of a twofold torrent, they were introduced by one of the keen-faced young men—he was a charming fellow in wonderful cream-coloured garments and a hat with a blue ribbon, who had evidently recognised them as aliens and helpless—to a very snug hydraulic elevator, in which they took their place with many other persons and which, shooting upward in its vertical socket, presently projected them into the seventh heaven, as it were, of the edifice. Here, after brief delay, they found themselves face to face with the friend of their friend in London. His office was composed of several conjoined rooms, and they waited very silently in one of these after they had sent in their letter and their cards. The letter was not one it would take Mr. Westgate very long to read, but he came out to speak to them more instantly than they could have expected; he had evidently jumped up from work. He was a tall lean personage and was dressed all in fresh white linen; he had a thin sharp familiar face, a face suggesting one of the ingenious modern objects with alternative uses, good as a blade or as a hammer, good for the deeps and for the shallows. His forehead was high but expressive, his eyes sharp but amused, and a large brown moustache, which concealed his mouth, made his chin, beneath it, look small. Relaxed though he was at this moment Lord Lambeth judged him on the spot tremendously clever.

"How do you do, Lord Lambeth, how do you do, sir?"—he held the open letter in his hand. "I'm very glad to meet you—I hope you're very well. You had better come in here—I think it's cooler"; and he led the way into another room, where there were law-books and papers and where windows opened wide under striped awnings. Just opposite one of the windows, on a line with his eyes, Lord Lambeth observed the weather-vane of a church-steeple. The uproar of the street sounded infinitely far below, and his lordship felt high indeed in the air. "I say it's cooler," pursued their host, "but everything's relative. How do you stand the heat?"

218

"I can't say we like it," said Lord Lambeth; "but Beaumont likes it better than I."

"Well, I guess it will break," Mr. Westgate cheerfully declared; "there's never anything bad over here but it does break. It was very hot when Captain Littledale was here; he did nothing but drink sherry-cobblers. He expresses some doubt in his letter whether I shall remember him—as if I don't remember once mixing six sherry-cobblers for him in about fifteen minutes. I hope you left him well. I'd be glad to mix him some more."

"Oh yes, he's all right—and without *them*," said Lord Lambeth.

"I'm always very glad to see your countrymen," Mr. Westgate pursued. "I thought it would be time some of you should be coming along. A friend of mine was saying to me only a day or two ago, 'It's time for the water-melons and the Englishmen.'"

"The Englishmen and the water-melons just now are about the same thing," Percy Beaumont observed with a wipe of his dripping forehead.

"Ah well, we'll put you on ice as we do the melons. You must go down to Newport."

"We'll go anywhere!" said Lord Lambeth.

"Yes, you want to go to Newport; that's what you want to do." Mr. Westgate was very positive. "But let's see—when did you get here?"

"Only yesterday," said Percy Beaumont.

"Ah yes, by the *Russia*. Where are you staying?"

"At the Hanover, I think they call it."

"Pretty comfortable?" inquired Mr. Westgate.

"It seems a capital place, but I can't say we like the gnats," said Lord Lambeth.

Mr. Westgate stared and laughed. "Oh no, of course you don't like the gnats. We shall expect you to like a good many things over here, but we shan't insist on your liking the gnats; though certainly you'll admit that, as gnats, they're big things, eh? But you oughtn't to remain in the city."

"So we think," said Lord Lambeth. "If you'd kindly suggest something—"

"Suggest something, my dear sir?"—and Mr. Westgate looked him over with narrowed eyelids. "Open your mouth and shut your eyes! Leave it to me and I'll fix you all right. It's a matter of national pride with me that all Englishmen should have a good time, and as I've been through a good deal with them I've learned to minister to their wants. I find they generally want the true thing. So just please consider yourselves my property; and if any one should try to appropriate you please say, 'Hands off—too late for the market.' But let's see," continued the American with his face of toil, his voice of leisure and his general intention, apparently, of everything; "let's see: are you going to make something of a stay, Lord Lambeth?"

"Oh dear no," said the young Englishman; "my cousin was to make this little visit, so I just came with him, at an hour's notice, for the lark."

"Is it your first time over here?"

"Oh dear yes."

"I was obliged to come on some business," Percy Beaumont explained, "and I brought Lambeth along for company."

"And *you* have been here before, sir?"

"Never, never!"

"I thought from your referring to business—" Mr. Westgate threw off.

"Oh you see I'm just acting for some English shareholders by way of legal advice. Some of my friends—well, if the truth must be told," Mr. Beaumont laughed—"have a grievance against one of your confounded railways, and they've asked me to come and judge, if possible, on the spot, what they can hope."

Mr. Westgate's amused eyes grew almost tender. "What's your railroad?" he asked.

"The Tennessee Central."

The American tilted back his chair and poised it an instant. "Well, I'm sorry you want to attack one of our institutions. But I guess you had better enjoy yourself *first!*"

"I'm certainly rather afraid I can't work in this weather," the young emissary confessed.

"Leave that to the natives," said Mr. Westgate. "Leave the Tennessee Central to me, Mr. Beaumont. I guess I can tell you more about it than most any one. But I didn't know you Englishmen ever did any work—in the upper classes."

"Oh we do a lot of work, don't we, Lambeth?" Percy Beaumont appealed.

"I must certainly be back early for *my* engagements," said his companion irrelevantly but gently.

"For the shooting, eh? or is it the yachting or the hunting or the fishing?" inquired his entertainer.

"Oh I must be in Scotland,"—and Lord Lambeth just amiably blushed.

"Well, then," Mr. Westgate returned, "you had better amuse yourself first also. You must go right down and see Mrs. Westgate."

"We should be so happy—if you'd kindly tell us the train," said Percy Beaumont.

"You don't take any train. You take a boat."

"Oh I see. And what is the name of—a—the—a—town?"

"It's a regular old city—don't you let them hear you call it a village or a hamlet or anything of that kind. They'd half-kill you. Only it's a city of pleasure—of lawns and gardens and verandahs and views and, above all, of good Samaritans," Mr. Westgate developed. "But you'll see what Newport is. It's cool. That's the principal thing. You'll greatly oblige me by going down there and putting yourself in the hands of Mrs. Westgate. It isn't perhaps for me to say it, but you couldn't be in better ones. Also in those of her sister, who's staying with her. She's half-crazy about Englishmen. She thinks there's nothing like them."

"Mrs. Westgate or—a—her sister?" asked Percy Beaumont modestly, yet in the tone of a collector of characteristic facts.

"Oh I mean my wife," said Mr. Westgate. "I don't suppose my sister-in-law knows much about them yet. You'll show her anyhow. She has always led a very quiet life. She has lived in Boston."

Percy Beaumont listened with interest. "That, I believe, is the most intellectual centre."

"Well, yes—Boston knows it's central and feels it's intellectual. I don't go there much—I stay round here," Mr. Westgate more loosely pursued.

"I say, you know, *we* ought to go there," Lord Lambeth broke out to his companion.

"Oh Lord Lambeth, wait till the great heat's over!" Mr. Westgate interposed. "Boston in this weather would be very trying; it's not the temperature for intellectual exertion. At Boston, you know, you have to pass an examination at the city limits, and when you come away they give you a kind of degree."

Lord Lambeth flushed himself, in his charming way, with wonder, though his friend glanced to make sure he wasn't looking too credulous— they had heard so much about American practices. He decided in time, at any rate, to take a safe middle course. "I daresay it's very jolly."

"I daresay it is," Mr. Westgate returned. "Only I must impress on you that at present—to-morrow morning at an early hour—you'll be expected at Newport. We have a house there—many of our most prominent citizens and society leaders go there for the summer. I'm not sure that at this very moment my wife can take you in—she has a lot of people staying with her. I don't know who they all are—only she may have no room. But you can begin with the hotel and meanwhile you can live at my house. In that way—simply sleeping

222

at the hotel—you'll find it tolerable. For the rest you must make yourself at home at my place. You mustn't be shy, you know; if you're only here for a month that will be a great waste of time. Mrs. Westgate won't neglect you, and you had better not undertake to resist her. I know something about that. I guess you'll find some pretty girls on the premises. I shall write to my wife by this afternoon's mail, and to-morrow she and Miss Alden will look out for you. Just walk right in and get into touch. Your steamer leaves from this part of the city, and I'll send right out and get you a cabin. Then at half-past four o'clock just call for me here, and I'll go with you and put you on board. It's a big boat; you might get lost. A few days hence, at the end of the week, I don't know but I'll come down myself and see how you are."

The two young Englishmen inaugurated the policy of not resisting Mrs. Westgate by submitting, with great docility and thankfulness, to her husband. He was evidently a clear thinker, and he made an impression on his visitors; his hospitality seemed to recommend itself consciously—with a friendly wink, as might be, hinting judicially that you couldn't make a better bargain. Lord Lambeth and his cousin left their entertainer to his labours and returned to their hotel, where they spent three or four hours in their respective shower-baths. Percy Beaumont had suggested that they ought to see something of the town, but "Oh damn the town!" his noble kinsman had rejoined. They returned to Mr. Westgate's office in a carriage, with their luggage, very punctually; but it must be reluctantly recorded that this time he so kept them waiting that they felt themselves miss their previous escape and were deterred only by an amiable modesty from dispensing with his attendance and starting on a hasty scramble to embark. But when at last he appeared and the carriage plunged into the purlieus of Broadway they jolted and jostled to such good purpose that they reached the huge white vessel while the bell for departure was still ringing and the absorption of passengers still active. It was indeed, as Mr. Westgate had said, a big boat, and his leadership in the innumerable and interminable corridors and cabins, with which he seemed perfectly acquainted and of which any one and every one appeared to have the *entrée*, was very grateful to the slightly bewildered voyagers. He showed them their state-room—a luxurious retreat embellished with gas-lamps, mirrors *en pied* and florid furniture—and then, long after they had been intimately convinced that the steamer was in motion and launched upon the unknown stream they were about to navigate, he bade them a sociable farewell.

"Well, good-bye, Lord Lambeth," he said. "Goodbye, Mr. Percy Beaumont. I hope you'll have a good time. Just let them do what they want with you. Take it as it's meant. Renounce your own personality. I'll come down by and by and enjoy what's left of you."

II

The young Englishmen emerged from their cabin and amused themselves with wandering about the immense labyrinthine ship, which struck them as a monstrous floating hotel or even as a semi-submerged kindergarten. It was densely crowded with passengers, the larger number of whom appeared to be ladies and very young children; and in the big saloons, ornamented in white and gold, which followed each other in surprising succession, beneath the swinging gas-lights and among the small side-passages where the negro domestics of both sexes assembled with an air of amused criticism, every one was moving to and fro and exchanging loud and familiar observations. Eventually, at the instance of a blackamoor more closely related to the scene than his companions, our friends went and had "supper" in a wonderful place arranged like a theatre, where, from a gilded gallery upon which little boxes appeared to open, a large orchestra played operatic selections and, below, people handed about bills of fare in the manner of programmes. All this was sufficiently curious; but the agreeable thing, later, was to sit out on one of the great white decks in the warm breezy darkness and, the vague starlight aiding, make out the line of low mysterious coast. Our travellers tried American cigars—those of Mr. Westgate—and conversed, as they usually conversed, with many odd silences, lapses of logic and incongruities of transition; like a pair who have grown old together and learned to guess each other's sense; or, more especially, like persons so conscious of a common point of view that missing links and broken lights and loose ends, the unexpressed and the understood, could do the office of talk.

"We really seem to be going out to sea," Percy Beaumont observed. "Upon my honour we're going back to England. He has shipped us off again. I call that 'real mean.'"

"I daresay it's all right," said Lord Lambeth. "I want to see those pretty girls at Newport. You know he told us the place was an island, and aren't all islands in the sea?"

"Well," resumed the elder traveller after a while, "if his house is as good as his cigars I guess we shall muddle through."

"I fancy he's awfully 'prominent,' you know, and I rather liked him," Lord Lambeth pursued as if this appreciation of Mr. Westgate had but just glimmered on him.

His comrade, however, engaged in another thought, didn't so much as appear to catch it. "I say, I guess we had better remain at the inn. I don't think I like the way he spoke of his house. I rather object to turning in with such a tremendous lot of women."

"Oh I don't mind," said Lord Lambeth. And then they smoked a while in silence. "Fancy his thinking we do no work in England!" the young man resumed.

But it didn't rouse his friend, who only replied: "I daresay he didn't really a bit think so."

"Well, I guess they don't know much about England over here!" his lordship humorously sighed. After which there was another long pause. "He *has* got us out of a hole," observed the young nobleman.

Percy Beaumont genially assented. "Nobody certainly could have been more civil."

"Littledale said his wife was great fun," Lord Lambeth then contributed.

"Whose wife—Littledale's?"

"Our benefactor's. Mrs. Westgate. What's his name? J. L. It 'kind of' sounds like a number. But I guess it's a high number," he continued with freshened gaiety.

The same influences appeared, however, with Mr. Beaumont to make rather for anxiety. "What was fun to Littledale," he said at last a little sententiously, "may be death to us."

"What do you mean by that?" his companion asked. "I'm as good a man as Littledale."

"My dear boy, I hope you won't begin to flirt," said the elder man.

His friend smoked acutely. "Well, I daresay I shan't *begin*."

"With a married woman, if she's bent upon it, it's all very well," Mr. Beaumont allowed. "But our friend mentioned a young lady—a sister, a sister-in-law. For God's sake keep free of her."

"How do you mean, 'free'?"

"Depend upon it she'll try to land you."

"Oh rot!" said Lord Lambeth.

"American girls are very 'cute,'" the other urged.

"So much the better," said the young man.

"I fancy they're always up to some wily game," Mr. Beaumont developed.

"They can't be worse than they are in England," said Lord Lambeth judicially.

"Ah, but in England you've got your natural protectors. You've got your mother and sisters."

"My mother and sisters—!" the youth began with a certain energy. But he stopped in time, puffing at his cigar.

"Your mother spoke to me about it with tears in her eyes," said his monitor. "She said she felt very nervous. I promised to keep you out of mischief."

"You had better take care of yourself!" cried Mr. Beaumont's charge.

"Ah," the responsible party returned, "I haven't the expectation of—whatever it is you expect. Not to mention other attractions."

"Well," said Lord Lambeth, "don't cry out before you're hurt!"

It was certainly very much cooler at Newport, where the travellers found themselves assigned to a couple of diminutive bedrooms in a far-away angle of an immense hotel. They had gone ashore in the early summer twilight and had very promptly put themselves to bed; thanks to which circumstance and to their having, during the previous hours, in their commodious cabin, slept the sleep of youth and health, they began to feel, towards eleven o'clock, very alert and inquisitive. They looked out of their windows across a row of small green fields, bordered with low stone dykes of rude construction, and saw a deep blue ocean lying beneath a deep blue sky and flecked now and then with scintillating patches of foam. A strong fresh breeze came in through the curtainless apertures and prompted our young men to observe generously that it didn't seem half a bad climate. They made other observations after they had emerged from their rooms in pursuit of breakfast—a meal of which they partook in a huge bare hall where a hundred negroes in white jackets shuffled about on an uncarpeted floor; where the flies were superabundant and the tables and dishes covered over with a strange voluminous integument of coarse blue gauze; and where several little boys and girls, who had risen late, were seated in fastidious solitude at the morning repast. These young persons had not the morning paper before them, but were engaged in languid perusal of the bill of fare.

This latter document was a great puzzle to our friends, who, on reflecting that its bewildering categories took account of breakfast alone, had the uneasy prevision of an encyclopedic dinner-list. They found copious diversion at their inn, an enormous wooden structure for the erection of which it struck them the virgin forests of the West must have been quite laid waste. It was perforated from end to end with immense bare corridors, through which a strong draught freely blew, bearing along wonderful figures of ladies in white morning-dresses and clouds of Valenciennes lace, who floated down the endless vistas on expanded furbelows very much as angels spread their wings. In front was a gigantic verandah on which an army might have encamped—a vast wooden terrace with a roof as high as the nave of a cathedral. Here our young men enjoyed, as they supposed, a glimpse of American society, which was distributed over the measureless expanse in a variety of sedentary attitudes and appeared to consist largely of pretty young girls, dressed as for a *fête champêtre*, swaying to and fro in rocking-chairs, fanning themselves with large straw fans and enjoying an enviable exemption from social cares. Lord Lambeth had a theory, which it might be interesting to trace to its origin, that it would be not only agreeable, but easily possible, to enter into relations with one of these young ladies; and his companion found occasion to check his social yearning.

"You had better take care—else you'll have an offended father or brother pulling out a bowie-knife."

"I assure you it's all right," Lord Lambeth replied. "You know the Americans come to these big hotels to make acquaintances."

"I know nothing about it, and neither do you," said his comrade, who, like a clever man, had begun to see that the observation of American society demanded a readjustment of their standard.

"Hang it, then, let's find out!" he cried with some impatience. "You know I don't want to miss anything."

"We *will* find out," said Percy Beaumont very reasonably. "We'll go and see Mrs. Westgate and make all the proper inquiries."

And so the inquiring pair, who had this lady's address inscribed in her husband's hand on a card, descended from the verandah of the big hotel and took their way, according to direction, along a large straight road, past a series of fresh-looking villas, embosomed in shrubs and flowers and enclosed in an ingenious variety of wooden palings. The morning shone and fluttered, the villas stood up bravely in their smartness, and the walk of the young travellers turned all to confidence. Everything looked as if it had received a coat of fresh paint the day before—the red roofs, the green shutters, the clean bright browns and buffs of the house-fronts. The flower-beds on the little lawns sparkled in the radiant air and the gravel in the short carriage-sweeps flashed and twinkled. Along the road came a hundred little basket-phaetons in which, almost always, a couple of ladies were sitting—ladies in white dresses and long white gloves, holding the reins and looking at the two Englishmen, whose nationality was not elusive, through fine blue veils, tied tightly about their faces as if to guard their complexions. At last the visitors came within sight of the sea again, and then, having interrogated a gardener over the paling of a villa, turned into an open gate. Here they found themselves face to face with the ocean and with a many-pointed much-balconied structure, resembling a magnified chalet, perched on a green embankment just above it. The house had a verandah of extraordinary width all round, and a great many doors and windows standing open to the verandah. These various apertures had, together, such an accessible hospitable air, such a breezy flutter, within, of light curtains, such expansive thresholds and reassuring interiors, that our friends hardly knew which was the regular entrance and, after hesitating a moment, presented themselves at one of the windows. The room within was indistinct, but in a moment a graceful figure vaguely shaped itself in the rich-looking gloom—a lady came to meet them. Then they saw she had been seated at a table writing, and that, hearing them, she had got up. She stepped out into the light; she wore a frank charming smile, with which she held out her hand to Percy Beaumont.

"Oh you must be Lord Lambeth and Mr. Beaumont. I've heard from my husband that you were coming. I make you warmly welcome." And she shook hands with each of her guests. Her guests were a little shy, but they made a gallant effort; they responded with smiles and exclamations, they apologised for not knowing the front door. The lady returned with vivacity that when she wanted to see people very much she didn't insist on those distinctions, and that Mr. Westgate had written to her of his English friends in terms that made her really anxious. "He says you're so terribly prostrated," she reported.

"Oh you mean by the heat?"—Percy Beaumont rose to it. "We were rather knocked up, but we feel wonderfully better. We had such a jolly—a—voyage down here. It's so very good of you to mind."

"Yes, it's so very kind of you," murmured Lord Lambeth.

Mrs. Westgate stood smiling; Mrs. Westgate was pretty. "Well, I did mind, and I thought of sending for you this morning to the Ocean House. I'm very glad you're better, and I'm charmed you're really with us. You must come round to the other side of the piazza." And she led the way, with a light smooth step, looking back at the young men and smiling.

The other side of the piazza was, as Lord Lambeth presently remarked, a very jolly place. It was of the most liberal proportions and, with its awnings, its fanciful chairs, its cushions and rugs, its view of the ocean close at hand and tumbling along the base of the low cliffs whose level tops intervened in lawnlike smoothness, formed a charming complement to the drawing-room. As such it was in course of employment at the present hour; it was occupied by a social circle. There were several ladies and two or three gentlemen, to whom Mrs. Westgate proceeded to introduce the distinguished strangers. She mentioned a great many names, very freely and distinctly; the young Englishmen, shuffling about and bowing, were rather bewildered. But at last they were provided with chairs—low wicker chairs, gilded and tied with a great many ribbons—and one of the ladies (a very young person with a little snub nose and several dimples) offered Percy Beaumont a fan. The fan was also adorned with pink love-knots, but the more guarded of our couple declined it, though he was very hot. Presently, however, everything turned to ease; the breeze from the sea was delicious and the view charming; the people sitting about looked fresh and fair. Several of the younger ladies were clearly girls, and the gentlemen slim bright youths such as our friends had seen the day before in New York. The ladies were working on bands of tapestry, and one of the young men had an open book in his lap. Percy afterwards learned from a lady that this young man had been reading aloud—that he was from Boston and was very fond of reading aloud. Percy pronounced it a great pity they had interrupted him; he should like so much (from all he had heard) to listen to a Bostonian read. Couldn't the young man be induced to go on?

"Oh no," said this informant very freely; "he wouldn't be able to get the young ladies to attend to him now."

There was something very friendly, Beaumont saw, in the attitude of the company; they looked at their new recruits with an air of animated sympathy and interest; they smiled, brightly and unanimously, at everything that dropped from either. Lord Lambeth and his companion felt they were indeed made cordially welcome. Mrs. Westgate seated herself between them, and while she talked continuously to each they had occasion to observe that she came up to their friend Littledale's promise. She was thirty years old, with the eyes and the smile of a girl of seventeen, and was light and graceful—elegant, exquisite. Mrs. Westgate was, further, what she had occasion to describe some person, among her many winged words, as being, all spontaneity. Frank and demonstrative, she appeared always—while she looked at you delightedly with her beautiful young eyes—to be making sudden confessions and concessions, breaking out after momentary wonders.

"We shall expect to see a great deal of you," she said to Lord Lambeth with her bland intensity. "We're very fond of Englishmen here; that is, there are a great many we've been fond of. After a day or two you must come and stay with us; we hope you'll stay a nice long while. Newport's quite attractive when you come really to know it, when you know plenty of people. Of course you and Mr. Beaumont will have no difficulty about that. Englishmen are very well received here; there are almost always two or three of them about. I think they always like it, and I must say I should think they would. They receive particular attention—I must say I think they sometimes get spoiled; but I'm sure you and Mr. Beaumont are proof against that. My husband tells me you're friends of Captain Littledale's; he was such a charming man. He made himself so agreeable here that I wonder he didn't stay. That would have carried out his system. It couldn't have been pleasanter for him in his own country. Though I suppose it's very pleasant in England too—for English people. I don't know myself; I've been there very little. I've been a great deal abroad, but I always cling to the Continent. I must say I'm extremely fond of Paris; you know we Americans always are; we go there when we die. Did you ever hear that before?—it was said by a great wit. I mean the good Americans; but we're all good—you'll see that for yourself. All I know of England is London, and all I know of London is that place—on that little corner, you know—where you buy jackets, jackets with that coarse braid and those big buttons. They make very good jackets in London, I'll do you the justice to say that. And some people like the hats. But about the hats I was always a heretic; I always got my hats in Paris. You can't wear an English hat—at least, I never could—unless you dress your hair à l'anglaise; and I must say that's a talent I never possessed. In Paris they'll make things to suit your peculiarities; but in England I think you like much more to have—how shall I say it?—one thing for everybody. I mean as regards dress. I don't know about other things; but I've always supposed that in other things everything was different. I mean according to the people—according to the classes and all that. I'm afraid you'll think I don't take a very favourable view; but you know you can't take a very favourable view in Dover Street and the month of November. That has always been my fate. Do you know Jones's Hotel in Dover Street? That's all I know of England. Of course every one admits that the English hotels are your weak point. There was always the most frightful fog—I couldn't see to try my things on. When I got over to America—into the light—I usually found they were twice too big. The next time I mean to go at the right season; I guess I'll go next year. I want very much to take my sister; she has never been to England. I don't know whether you know what I mean by saying that the Englishmen who come here sometimes get spoiled. I mean they take things as a matter of course—things that are done for them. Now naturally anything's a matter of course only when the Englishmen are very nice. But you'll say—oh yes you will, or you would if some of you ever did say much!—they're almost always very nice. You can't expect this to be nearly such an interesting country as England; there are not nearly so many things to see, and we haven't your country life. I've never seen anything of your country life; when I'm in Europe I'm always on the Continent. But I've heard a great deal about it; I know that when you're among yourselves in the country you have the most beautiful time. Of course we've nothing of that sort, we've nothing on that scale. I don't apologise, Lord Lambeth; some Americans are always apologising; you must have noticed that. We've the reputation of always boasting and 'blowing' and waving the American flag; but I must say that what strikes me is that we're perpetually making excuses and trying to smooth things over. The American flag has quite gone out of fashion; it's very carefully folded up, like a tablecloth the worse for wear. Why should we apologise? The English never apologise—do they? No, I must say I never apologise. You must take us as we come—with all our imperfections on our heads. Of course we haven't your country life and your old ruins and your great estates and your leisure-class and all that—though I don't really know anything about them, because when I go over I always cling to the Continent. But if we haven't I should think you might find it a pleasant change—I think any country's pleasant where they have pleasant manners. Captain Littledale told me he had never seen such pleasant manners as at Newport, and he had been a great deal in European society. Hadn't he been in the diplomatic service? He told me the dream of his life was to get appointed to a diplomatic post in Washington. But he doesn't seem to have succeeded. Perhaps that was only a part of his pleasant manners. I suppose at any rate that in England promotion—and all that sort of thing—is fearfully slow. With us, you know, it's a great deal too quick. You see I admit our drawbacks. But I must confess I think Newport an ideal place. I don't know anything like it anywhere. Captain Littledale told me he didn't know anything like it anywhere. It's entirely different from most watering-places; it's a much more refined life. I must say I think that when one goes to a foreign country one ought to enjoy the differences. Of course there are differences; otherwise what did one come abroad for? Look for your pleasure in the differences, Lord Lambeth; that's the way to do it; and then I am sure you'll find American society—at least the Newport phase quite unique. I wish very much Mr. Westgate were here; but he's dreadfully confined to New York. I suppose you think that's very strange—for a gentleman. Only you see we haven't any leisure-class."

Mrs. Westgate's discourse was delivered with a mild merciless monotony, a paucity of intonation, an impartial flatness that suggested a flowery mead scrupulously "done over" by a steam roller that had reduced its texture to that of a drawing-room carpet. Lord Lambeth listened to her with, it must be confessed, a rather ineffectual attention, though he summoned to his aid such a show as he might of discriminating motions and murmurs. He had no great faculty for apprehending generalisations. There were some three or four indeed which, in the play of his own intelligence, he had originated and which had sometimes appeared to meet the case—any case; yet he felt he had never known such a case as Mrs. Westgate or as her presentation of her cases. But at the present time he could hardly have been said to follow this exponent as she darted fish-like through the sea of speculation. Fortunately she asked for no special rejoinder, since she looked about at the rest of the company as well and smiled at Mr. Beaumont on the other side of her as if he too must understand her and agree with her. He was measurably more successful than his companion; for besides being, as we know, cleverer, his attention was not vaguely distracted by close vicinity to a remarkably interesting young person with dark hair and blue eyes. This was the situation of Lord Lambeth, to whom it occurred after a while that the young person with blue eyes and dark hair might be the pretty sister of whom Mrs. Westgate had spoken. She presently turned to him with a remark establishing her identity.

"It's a great pity you couldn't have brought my brother-in-law with you. It's a great shame he should be in New York on such days as these."

"Oh yes—it's very stuffy," said Lord Lambeth.

"It must be dreadful there," said the pretty sister.

"I daresay he's immensely taken up," the young man returned with a sense of conscientiously yearning toward American realities.

"The gentlemen in America work too much," his friend went on.

"Oh do they? Well, I daresay they like it," he hopefully threw out.

"I don't like it. One never sees them."

"Don't you really?" asked Lord Lambeth. "I shouldn't have fancied that."

"Have you come to study American manners?" the blue eyes and dark hair went on.

"Oh I don't know. I just came over for the joke of it. I haven't got long." Then occurred a pause, after which he began again. "But he will turn up here, won't he?"

"I certainly hope he will. He must help to entertain you and Mr. Beaumont."

Lord Lambeth looked at her from handsome eyes that were brown. "Do you suppose he'd have come down with us if we had pressed it?"

The pretty girl treated this as rather an easy conundrum. "I daresay he would," she smiled.

"Really!" said the young Englishman. "Well, he was no end civil."

His young woman seemed much amused; this at least was in her eyes, which freely met Lord Lambeth's. "He would be. He's a perfect husband. But all Americans are that," she confidently continued.

"Really!" Lord Lambeth exclaimed again; and wondered whether all American ladies had such a passion for generalising as these two.

III

He sat there a good while: there was a great deal of talk; it was all pitched in a key of expression and emphasis rather new to him. Every one present, the cool maidens not least, personally addressed him, and seemed to make a particular point of doing so by the friendly repetition of his name. Three or four other persons came in, and there was a shifting of seats, a changing of places; the gentlemen took, individually, an interest in the visitors, putting somehow more imagination and more "high comedy" into this effort than the latter had ever seen displayed save in a play or a story. These well-wishers feared the two Britons mightn't be comfortable at their hotel—it being, as one of them said, "not so private as those dear little English inns of yours." This last gentleman added that as yet perhaps, alas, privacy wasn't quite so easily obtained in America as might be desired; still, he continued, you could generally get it by paying for it; in fact you could get everything in America nowadays by paying for it. The life was really growing more private; it was growing greatly to resemble European—which wasn't to be wondered at when two-thirds of the people leading it were so awfully much at home in Europe. Europe, in the course of this conversation, was indeed, as Lord Lambeth afterwards remarked to his compatriot, rather bewilderingly rubbed into them: did they pretend to be European, and when had they ever been entered under that head? Everything at Newport, at all events, was described to them as thoroughly private; they would probably find themselves, when all was said, a good deal struck with that. It was also represented to the strangers that it mattered very little whether their hotel was agreeable, as every one would want them to "visit round," as somebody called it: they would stay with other people and in any case would be constantly at Mrs. Westgate's. They would find that charming; it was the pleasantest house in Newport. It was only a pity Mr. Westgate was never there—he being a tremendously fine man, one of the finest they had. He worked like a horse and left his wife to play the social part. Well, she played it all right, if that was all he wanted. He liked her to enjoy herself, and she did know how. She was highly cultivated and a splendid converser—the sort of converser people would come miles to hear. But some preferred her sister, who was in a different style altogether. Some even thought her prettier, but decidedly Miss Alden wasn't so smart. She was more in the Boston style—the quiet Boston; she had lived a great deal there and was very highly educated. Boston girls, it was intimated, were more on the English model.

Lord Lambeth had presently a chance to test the truth of this last proposition; for, the company rising in compliance with a suggestion from their hostess that they should walk down to the rocks and look at the sea, the young Englishman again found himself, as they strolled across the grass, in proximity to Mrs. Westgate's sister. Though Miss Alden was but a girl of twenty she appeared conscious of the weight of expectation—unless she quite wantonly took on duties she might have let alone; and this was perhaps the more to be noticed as she seemed by habit rather grave and backward, perhaps even proud, with little of the other's free fraternising. She might have been thought too deadly thin, not to say also too deadly pale; but while she moved over the grass, her arms hanging at her sides, and, seriously or absently, forgot expectations, though again brightly to remember them and to look at the summer sea, as if that was what she really cared for, her companion judged her at least as pretty as Mrs. Westgate and reflected that if this was the Boston style, "the quiet Boston," it would do very well. He could fancy her very clever, highly educated and all the rest of it; but clearly also there were ways in which she could spare a fellow—could ease him; she wouldn't keep him so long on the stretch at once. For all her cleverness, moreover, he felt she had to think a little what to say; she didn't say the first thing that came into her head: he had come from a different part of the world, from a different society, and she was trying to adapt her conversation. The others were scattered about the rocks; Mrs. Westgate had charge of Percy Beaumont.

"Very jolly place for this sort of thing," Lord Lambeth said. "It must do beautifully to sit."

"It does indeed; there are cosy nooks and there are breezy ones, which I often try—as if they had been made on purpose."

"Ah I suppose you've had a lot made," he fell in.

She seemed to wonder. "Oh no, we've had nothing made. It's all pure nature."

"I should think you'd have a few little benches—rustic seats and that sort of thing. It might really be so jolly to 'develop' the place," he suggested.

It made her thoughtful—even a little rueful. "I'm afraid we haven't so many of those things as you."

"Ah well, if you go in for pure nature, as you were saying, there's nothing like that. Nature, over here, must be awfully grand." And Lord Lambeth looked about him.

The little coast-line that contributed to the view melted away, but it too much lacked presence and character—a fact Miss Alden appeared to rise to a perception of. "I'm afraid it seems to you very rough. It's not like the coast-scenery in Kingsley's novels."

He wouldn't let her, however, undervalue it. "Ah, the novels always overdo everything, you know. You mustn't go by the novels."

They wandered a little on the rocks; they stopped to look into a narrow chasm where the rising tide made a curious bellowing sound. It was loud enough to prevent their hearing each other, and they stood for some moments in silence. The girl's eyes took in her companion, observing him attentively but covertly, as those of women even in blinking youth know how to do. Lord Lambeth repaid contemplation; tall straight and strong, he was handsome as certain young Englishmen, and certain young Englishmen almost alone, are handsome; with a perfect finish of feature and a visible repose of mind, an inaccessibility to questions, somehow stamped in by the same strong die and pressure that nature, designing a precious medal, had selected and applied. It was not that he looked stupid; it was only, we assume, that his perceptions didn't show in his face for restless or his imagination for irritable. He was not, as he would himself have said, tremendously clever; but, though there was rather a constant appeal for delay in his waiting, his perfectly patient eye, this registered simplicity had its beauty as well and, whatever it might have appeared to plead for, didn't plead in the name of indifference or inaction. This most searching of his new friends thought him the handsomest young man she had ever seen; and Bessie Alden's imagination, unlike that of her companion, was irritable. He, however, had already made up his mind, quite originally and without aid, that she had a grace exceedingly her own.

"I daresay it's very gay here—that you've lots of balls and parties," he said; since, though not tremendously clever, he rather prided himself on having with women a strict sufficiency of conversation.

"Oh yes, there's a great deal going on. There are not so many balls, but there are a good many other pleasant things," Bessie Alden explained. "You'll see for yourself; we live rather in the midst of it."

"It will be very kind of you to let us see. But I thought you Americans were always dancing."

"I suppose we dance a good deal, though I've never seen much of it. We don't do it much, at any rate in summer. And I'm sure," she said, "that we haven't as many balls as you in England."

He wondered—these so many prompt assumptions about his own country made him gape a little. "Ah, in England it all depends, you know."

"You'll not think much of our gaieties," she said—though she seemed to settle it for him with a quaver of interrogation. The interrogation sounded earnest indeed and the decision arch; the mixture, at any rate, was charming. "Those things with us are much less splendid than in England."

"I fancy you don't really mean that," her companion laughed.

"I assure you I really mean everything I say," she returned. "Certainly from what I've read about English society it is very different."

"Ah well, you know," said Lord Lambeth, who appeared to cling to this general theory, "those things are often described by fellows who know nothing about them. You mustn't mind what you read."

"Ah, what a blasphemous speech—I *must* mind what I read!" our young woman protested. "When I read Thackeray and George Eliot how can I help minding?"

"Oh well, Thackeray and George Eliot"—and her friend pleasantly bethought himself. "I'm afraid I haven't read much of them."

"Don't you suppose they knew about society?" asked Bessie Alden.

"Oh I daresay they knew; they must have got up their subject. Good writers do, don't they? But those fashionable novels are mostly awful rot, you know."

His companion rested on him a moment her dark blue eyes; after which she looked down into the chasm where the water was tumbling about. "Do you mean Catherine Grace Gore, for instance?" she then more aspiringly asked.

But at this he broke down—he coloured, laughed, gave up. "I'm afraid I haven't read that either. I'm afraid you'll think I'm not very intellectual."

"Reading Mrs. Gore is no proof of intellect. But I like reading everything about English life—even poor books. I'm so curious about it," said Bessie Alden.

"Aren't ladies curious about everything?" he asked with continued hilarity.

"I don't think so. I don't think we're enough so—that we care about many things. So it's all the more of a compliment," she added, "that I should want to know so much about England."

The logic here seemed a little close; but Lord Lambeth, advised of a compliment, found his natural modesty close at hand. "I'm sure you know a great deal more than I do."

"I really think I know a great deal—for a person who has never been there."

"Have you really never been there?" cried he. "Fancy!"

"Never—except in imagination. And I *have* been to Paris," she admitted.

"Fancy," he repeated with gaiety—"fancy taking those brutes first! But you *will* come soon?"

"It's the dream of my life!" Bessie Alden brightly professed.

"Your sister at any rate seems to know a tremendous lot about us," Lord Lambeth went on.

She appeared to take her view of this. "My sister and I are two very different persons. She has been a great deal in Europe. She has been in England a little—not intimately. But she has met English people in other countries, and she arrives very quickly at conclusions."

"Ah, I guess she does," he laughed. "But you must have known some too."

"No—I don't think I've ever spoken to one before. You're the first Englishman that—to my knowledge—I've ever talked with."

Bessie Alden made this statement with a certain gravity—almost, as it seemed to the young man, an impressiveness. The impressive always made him feel awkward, and he now began to laugh and swing his stick. "Ah, you'd have been sure to know!" And then he added after an instant: "I'm sorry I'm not a better specimen."

The girl looked away, but taking it more gaily. "You must remember you're only a beginning." Then she retraced her steps, leading the way back to the lawn, where they saw Mrs. Westgate come toward them with Percy Beaumont still at her side. "Perhaps I shall go to England next year," Miss

Alden continued; "I want to immensely. My sister expects to cross about then, and she has asked me to go with her. If I do I shall make her stay as long as possible in London."

"Ah, you must come early in July," said Lord Lambeth. "That's the time when there's most going on."

"I don't think I can wait even till early in July," his friend returned. "By the first of May I shall be very impatient." They had gone further, and Mrs. Westgate and her companion were near. "Kitty," said the younger sister, "I've given out that we go to London next May. So please to conduct yourself accordingly."

Percy Beaumont wore a somewhat animated—even a slightly irritated— air. He was by no means of so handsome an effect as his comrade, though in the latter's absence he might, with his manly stature and his fair dense beard, his fresh clean skin and his quiet outlook, have pleased by a due affirmation of the best British points. Just now Beaumont's clear eyes had a rather troubled light, which, after glancing at Bessie Alden while she spoke, he turned with some intensity on Lord Lambeth. Mrs. Westgate's beautiful radiance of interest and dissent fell meanwhile impartially everywhere.

"You had better wait till the time comes," she said to her sister. "Perhaps next May you won't care so much for London. Mr. Beaumont and I," she went on, smiling at her companion, "have had a tremendous discussion. We don't agree about anything. It's perfectly delightful."

"Oh I say, Percy!" exclaimed Lord Lambeth.

"I disagree," said Beaumont, raising his eyebrows and stroking down his back hair, "even to the point of thinking it *not* delightful."

"Ah, you *must* have been getting it!" cried his friend.

"I don't see anything delightful in my disagreeing with Mrs. Westgate," said Percy Beaumont.

"Well, I do!" Mrs. Westgate declared as she turned again to her sister. "You know you've to go to town. There must be something at the door for you. You had better take Lord Lambeth."

Mr. Beaumont, at this point, looked straight at his comrade, trying to catch his eye. But Lord Lambeth wouldn't look at him; his own eyes were better occupied. "I shall be very happy"—Bessie Alden rose straight to their hostess's suggestion. "I'm only going to some shops. But I'll drive you about and show you the place."

"An American woman who respects herself," said Mrs. Westgate, turning to the elder man with her bright expository air, "must buy something every day of her life. If she can't do it herself she must send out some member of her family for the purpose. So Bessie goes forth to fulfil my mission."

The girl had walked away with Lord Lambeth by her side, to whom she was talking still; and Percy Beaumont watched them as they passed toward the house. "She fulfils her own mission," he presently said; "that of being very attractive."

But even here Mrs. Westgate discriminated. "I don't know that I should precisely say attractive. She's not so much that as she's charming when you really know her. She's very shy."

"Oh indeed?" said Percy Beaumont with evident wonder. And then as if to alternate with a certain grace the note of scepticism: "I guess your shyness, in that case, is different from ours."

"Everything of ours is different from yours," Mrs. Westgate instantly returned. "But my poor sister's given over, I hold, to a fine Boston *gaucherie* that has rubbed off on her by being there so much. She's a dear good girl, however; she's a charming type of girl. She is not in the least a flirt; that isn't at all her line; she doesn't know the alphabet of any such vulgarity. She's very simple, very serious, very *true*. She has lived, however, rather too much in Boston with another sister of mine, the eldest of us, who married a Bostonian. Bessie's very cultivated, not at all like me—I'm not in the least cultivated and am called so only by those who don't know what true culture is. But Bessie does; she has studied Greek; she has read everything; she's what they call in Boston 'thoughtful.'"

"Ah well, it only depends on what one thinks *about*," said Mr. Beaumont, who appeared to find her zeal for distinctions catching.

242

"I really believe," Mrs. Westgate pursued, "that the most charming girl in the world is a Boston superstructure on a New York *fond*, or perhaps a New York superstructure on a Boston *fond*. At any rate it's the mixture," she declared, continuing to supply her guest with information and to do him the honours of the American world with a zeal that left nothing to be desired.

Lord Lambeth got into a light low pony-cart with Bessie Alden, and she drove him down the long Avenue, whose extent he had measured on foot a couple of hours before, into the ancient town, as it was called in that part of the world, of Newport. The ancient town was a curious affair—a collection of fresh-looking little wooden houses, painted white, scattered over a hillside and clustering about a long straight street paved with huge old cobbles. There were plenty of shops, a large allowance of which appeared those of fruit-vendors, with piles of huge water-melons and pumpkins stacked in front of them; while, drawn up before the shops or bumping about on the round stones, were innumerable other like or different carts freighted with ladies of high fashion who greeted each other from vehicle to vehicle and conversed on the edge of the pavement in a manner that struck Lord Lambeth as of the last effusiveness: with a great many "Oh my dears" and little quick sounds and motions—obscure native words, shibboleths and signs. His companion went into seventeen shops—he amused himself with counting them—and accumulated at the bottom of the trap a pile of bundles that hardly left the young Englishman a place for his feet. As she had no other attendant he sat in the phaeton to hold the pony; where, though not a particularly acute observer, he saw much harmlessly to divert him—especially the ladies just mentioned, who wandered up and down with an aimless intentness, as if looking for something to buy, and who, tripping in and out of their vehicles, displayed remarkably pretty feet. It all seemed to Lord Lambeth very odd and bright and gay. And he felt by the time they got back to the villa that he had made a stride in intimacy with Miss Alden.

The young Englishmen spent the whole of that day and the whole of many successive days in the cultivation, right and left, far and near, of this celerity of social progress. They agreed that it was all extremely jolly—that they had never known anything more agreeable. It is not proposed to

243

report the detail of their sojourn on this charming shore; though were it convenient I might present a record of impressions none the less soothing that they were not exhaustively analysed. Many of them still linger in the minds of our travellers, attended by a train of harmonious images—images of early breezy shining hours on lawns and piazzas that overlooked the sea; of innumerable pretty girls saying innumerable quaint and familiar things; of infinite lounging and talking and laughing and flirting and lunching and dining; of a confidence that broke down, of a freedom that pulled up, nowhere; of an idyllic ease that was somehow too ordered for a primitive social consciousness and too innocent for a developed; of occasions on which they so knew every one and everything that they almost ached with reciprocity; of drives and rides in the late afternoon, over gleaming beaches, on long sea-roads, beneath a sky lighted up by marvellous sunsets; of tea-tables, on the return, informal, irregular, agreeable; of evenings at open windows or on the perpetual verandahs, in the summer starlight, above the warm Atlantic and amid irrelevant outbursts of clever minstrelsy. The young Englishmen were introduced to everybody, entertained by everybody, intimate with everybody, and it was all the book of life, of American life, at least; with the chapter of "complications" bodily omitted. At the end of three days they had removed their luggage from the hotel and had gone to stay with Mrs. Westgate—a step as to which Percy Beaumont at first took up an attitude of mistrust apparently founded on some odd and just a little barbaric talk forced on him, he would have been tempted to say, and very soon after their advent, by Miss Alden. He had indeed been aware of her occasional approach or appeal, since she wasn't literally always in conversation with Lord Lambeth. He had meditated on Mrs. Westgate's account of her sister and discovered for himself that the young lady was "sharp" (Percy's critical categories remained few and simple) and appeared to have read a great deal. She seemed perfectly well-bred, though he couldn't make out that, as Mrs. Westgate funnily insisted, she was shy. If she was shy she carried it off with an ease—!

"Mr. Beaumont," she had said, "please tell me something about Lord Lambeth's family. How would you say it in England?—his position."

"His position?" Percy's instinct was to speak as if he had never heard of such a matter.

"His rank—or whatever you call it. Unfortunately we haven't got a 'Peerage,' like the people in Thackeray."

"That's a great pity," Percy pleaded. "You'd find the whole matter in black and white, and upon my honour I know very little about it."

The girl seemed to wonder at this innocence. "You know at least whether he's what they call a great noble."

"Oh yes, he's in that line."

"Is he a 'peer of the realm'?"

"Well, as yet—very nearly."

"And has he any other title than Lord Lambeth?"

"His title's the Marquis of Lambeth." With which the fountain of Bessie's information appeared to run a little dry. She looked at him, however, with such interest that he presently added: "He's the son of the Duke of Bayswater."

"The eldest—?"

"The only one."

"And are his parents living?"

"Naturally—as to his father. If *he* weren't living Lambeth would be a duke."

"So that when 'the old lord' dies"—and the girl smiled with more simplicity than might have been expected in one so "sharp"—"he'll become Duke of Bayswater?"

"Of course," said their common friend. "But his father's in excellent health."

"And his mother?"

Percy seemed amused. "The Duchess is built to last!"

"And has he any sisters?"

"Yes, there are two."

"And what are they called?"

"One of them's married. She's the Countess of Pimlico."

"And the other?"

"The other's unmarried—she's plain Lady Julia."

Bessie entered into it all. "Is she very plain?"

He began to laugh again. "You wouldn't find her so handsome as her brother," he said; and it was after this that he attempted to dissuade the heir of the Duke of Bayswater from accepting Mrs. Westgate's invitation. "Depend upon it," he said, "that girl means to have a go at you."

"It seems to me you're doing your best to make a fool of me," the modest young nobleman answered.

"She has been asking me," his friend imperturbably pursued, "all about your people and your possessions."

"I'm sure it's very good of her!" Lord Lambeth returned.

"Well, then," said Percy, "if you go straight into it, if you hurl yourself bang upon the spears, you do so with your eyes open."

"Damn my eyes!" the young man pronounced. "If one's to be a dozen times a day at the house it's a great deal more convenient to sleep there. I'm sick of travelling up and down this beastly Avenue."

Since he had determined to go Percy would of course have been very sorry to allow him to go alone; he was a man of many scruples—in the direction in which he had any at all—and he remembered his promise to the Duchess. It was obviously the memory of this promise that made Mr. Beaumont say to his companion a couple of days later that he rather wondered he should be so fond of such a girl.

"In the first place how do you know how fond I am?" asked Lord Lambeth. "And in the second why shouldn't I be fond of her?"

"I shouldn't think she'd be in your line."

"What do you call my 'line'? You don't set her down, I suppose, as 'fast'?"

"Exactly so. Mrs. Westgate tells me that there's no such thing as the fast girl in America; that it's an English invention altogether and that the term has no meaning here."

"All the better. It's an animal I detest," said Lord Lambeth.

"You prefer, then, rather a priggish American *précieuse*?"

Lord Lambeth took his time. "Do you call Miss Alden all that?"

"Her sister tells me," said Percy Beaumont, "that she's tremendously literary."

"Well, why shouldn't she be? She's certainly very clever and has every appearance of a well-stored mind."

Percy for an instant watched his young friend, who had turned away. "I should rather have supposed you'd find her stores oppressive."

The young man, after this, faced him again. "Why, do you think me such a dunce?" And then as his friend but vaguely protested: "The girl's all right," he said—and quite as if this judgement covered all the ground. It wasn't that there was no ground—but he knew what he was about.

Percy, for a while further, and a little uncomfortably flushed with the sense of his false position—that of presenting culture in a "mean" light, as they said at Newport—Percy kept his peace; but on August 10th he wrote to the Duchess of Bayswater. His conception of certain special duties and decencies, as I have said, was strong, and this step wholly fell in with it. His companion meanwhile was having much talk with Miss Alden—on the red sea-rocks beyond the lawn; in the course of long island rides, with a slow return in the glowing twilight; on the deep verandah, late in the evening.

Lord Lambeth, who had stayed at many houses, had never stayed at one in which it was possible for a young man to converse so freely and frequently with a young lady. This young lady no longer applied to their other guest for information concerning his lordship. She addressed herself directly to the young nobleman. She asked him a great many questions, some of which did, according to Mr. Beaumont's term, a little oppress him; for he took no pleasure in talking about himself.

"Lord Lambeth"—this had been one of them—"are you an hereditary legislator?"

"Oh I say," he returned, "don't make me call myself such names as that."

"But you're natural members of Parliament."

"I don't like the sound of that either."

"Doesn't your father sit in the House of Lords?" Bessie Alden went on.

"Very seldom," said Lord Lambeth.

"Is it a very august position?" she asked.

"Oh dear no," Lord Lambeth smiled.

"I should think it would be very grand"—she serenely kept it up, as the female American, he judged, would always keep anything up—"to possess simply by an accident of birth the right to make laws for a great nation."

"Ah, but one doesn't make laws. There's a lot of humbug about it."

"I don't believe that," the girl unconfusedly declared. "It must be a great privilege, and I should think that if one thought of it in the right way—from a high point of view—it would be very inspiring."

"The less one thinks of it the better, I guess!" Lord Lambeth after a moment returned.

"I think it's tremendous"—this at least she kept up; and on another occasion she asked him if he had any tenantry. Hereupon it was that, as I have said, he felt a little the burden of her earnestness.

248

But he took it good-humouredly. "Do you want to buy up their leases?"

"Well—have you got any 'livings'?" she demanded as if the word were rich and rare.

"Oh I say!" he cried. "Have *you* got a pet clergyman looking out?" But she made him plead guilty to his having, in prospect, a castle; he confessed to but one. It was the place in which he had been born and brought up, and, as he had an old-time liking for it, he was beguiled into a few pleasant facts about it and into pronouncing it really very jolly. Bessie listened with great interest, declaring she would give the world to see such a place. To which he charmingly made answer: "It would be awfully kind of you to come and stay there, you know." It was not inconvenient to him meanwhile that Percy Beaumont hadn't happened to hear him make this genial remark.

Mr. Westgate, all this time, hadn't, as they said at Newport, "come on." His wife more than once announced that she expected him on the morrow; but on the morrow she wandered about a little, with a telegram in her jewelled fingers, pronouncing it too "fiendish" he should let his business so dreadfully absorb him that he could but platonically hope, as she expressed it, his two Englishmen were having a good time. "I must say," said Mrs. Westgate, "that it's no thanks to him if you are!" And she went on to explain, while she kept up that slow-paced circulation which enabled her well-adjusted skirts to display themselves so advantageously, that unfortunately in America there was no leisure-class and that the universal passionate surrender of the men to business-questions and business-questions only, as if they were the all in all of life, was a tide that would have to be stemmed. It was Lord Lambeth's theory, freely propounded when the young men were together, that Percy was having a very good time with Mrs. Westgate and that under the pretext of meeting for the purpose of animated discussion they were indulging in practices that imparted a shade of hypocrisy to the lady's regret for her husband's absence.

"I assure you we're always discussing and differing," Mr. Beaumont however asseverated. "She's awfully argumentative. American ladies certainly don't mind contradicting you flat. Upon my word I don't think I was ever treated so by a woman before. We have ours ever so much more in hand. She's so devilish positive."

The superlative degree so variously affirmed, however, was evidently a source of attraction in Mrs. Westgate, for the elder man was constantly at his hostess's side. He detached himself one day to the extent of going to New York to talk over the Tennessee Central with her husband; but he was absent only forty-eight hours, during which, with that gentleman's assistance, he completely settled this piece of business. "They know how to put things—and put people—'through' in New York," he subsequently and quite breathlessly observed to his comrade; and he added that Mr. Westgate had seemed markedly to fear his wife might suffer for loss of her guest—he had been in such an awful hurry to send him back to her. "I'm afraid you'll never come up to an American husband—if that's what the wives expect," he said to Lord Lambeth.

Mrs. Westgate, however, was not to enjoy much longer the entertainment with which an indulgent husband had desired to keep her provided. August had still a part of its course to run when his lordship received from his mother the disconcerting news that his father had been taken ill and that he had best at once come home. The young nobleman concealed his chagrin with no great success. "I left the Duke but the other day absolutely all right—so what the deuce does it mean?" he asked of his comrade. "What's a fellow to do?"

Percy Beaumont was scarce less annoyed; he had deemed it his duty, as we know, to report faithfully to the Duchess, but had not expected this distinguished woman to act so promptly on his hint. "It means," he said, "that your father is somehow, and rather suddenly, laid up. I don't suppose it's anything serious, but you've no option. Take the first steamer, but take it without alarm."

This really struck Lord Lambeth as meaning that he essentially needn't take it, since alarm would have been his only good motive; yet he nevertheless, after an hour of intenser irritation than he could quite have explained to himself, made his farewells; in the course of which he exchanged a few last words with Bessie Alden that are the only ones making good their place in our record. "Of course I needn't assure you that if you should come to England next year I expect to be the very first person notified of it."

She looked at him in that way she had which never quite struck him as straight and clear, yet which always struck him as kind and true. "Oh, if we come to London I should think you'd sufficiently hear of it."

Percy Beaumont felt it his duty also to embark, and this same rigour compelled him, one windless afternoon, in mid-Atlantic, to say to his friend that he suspected the Duchess's telegram to have been in part the result of something he himself had written her. "I wrote her—as I distinctly warned you I had promised in general to do—that you were extremely interested in a little American girl."

The young man, much upset by this avowal, indulged for some moments in the strong and simple language of resentment. But if I have described him as inclined to candour and to reason I can give no better proof of it than the fact of his being ready to face the truth by the end of half an hour. "You were quite right after all. I'm very much interested in her. Only, to be fair," he added, "you should have told my mother also that she's not—at all seriously—interested in poor me."

Mr. Beaumont gave the rein to mirth and mockery. "There's nothing so charming as modesty in a young man in the position of 'poor' you. That speech settles for me the question of what's the matter with you."

Lord Lambeth's handsome eyes turned rueful and queer. "Is anything so flagrantly the matter with me?"

"Everything, my dear boy," laughed his companion, passing a hand into his arm for a walk.

"Well, *she* isn't interested—she isn't!" the young man insisted.

"My poor friend," said Percy Beaumont rather gravely, "you're very far gone!"

IV

In point of fact, as the latter would have said, Mrs. Westgate disembarked by the next mid-May on the British coast. She was accompanied by her sister, but unattended by any other member of her family. To the lost comfort of a husband respectably to produce, as she phrased it, she was now habituated; she had made half a dozen journeys to Europe under this drawback of looking ill-temperedly separated and yet of being thanklessly enslaved, and she still decently accounted for her spurious singleness to wondering friends on this side of the Atlantic by formulating the grim truth—the only grimness indeed in all her view—that in America there is no leisure-class. The two ladies came up to London and alighted at Jones's Hotel, where Mrs. Westgate, who had made on former occasions the most agreeable impression at this establishment, received an obsequious greeting. Bessie Alden had felt much excited about coming to England; she had expected the "associations" would carry her away and counted on the joy of treating her eyes and her imagination to all the things she had read of in poets and historians. She was very fond of the poets and historians, of the picturesque, of the past, of associations, of relics and reverberations of greatness; so that on coming into the great English world, where strangeness and familiarity would go hand in hand, she was prepared for a swarm of fresh emotions. They began very promptly—these tender fluttering sensations; they began with the sight of the beautiful English landscape, whose dark richness was quickened and brightened by the season; with the carpeted fields and flowering hedge-rows, as she looked at them from the window of the train; with the spires of the rural churches peeping above the rook-haunted tree-tops; with the oak-studded, deer-peopled parks, the ancient homes, the cloudy light, the speech, the manners, all the significant differences. Mrs. Westgate's response was of course less quick and less extravagant, and she gave but a wandering attention to her sister's ejaculations and rhapsodies.

"You know my enjoyment of England's not so intellectual as Bessie's," she said to several of her friends in the course of her visit to this country. "And yet if it's not intellectual I can't say it's in the least sensual. I don't think I can quite say what it is, my enjoyment of England." When once it was settled that the two ladies should come abroad and should spend a few weeks in London and perhaps in other parts of the celebrated island on their way to the Continent, they of course exchanged a good many allusions to their English acquaintance.

"It will certainly be much nicer having friends there," was a remark that had one day dropped from Bessie while she sat on the sunny deck of the steamer, at her sister's feet, from under which spread conveniently a large soft rug.

"Whom do you mean by friends?" Mrs. Westgate had then invited the girl to say.

"All those English gentlemen you've known and entertained. Captain Littledale, for instance. And Lord Lambeth and Mr. Beaumont," the girl further mentioned.

"Do you expect them to give us a very grand reception?"

She reflected a moment; she was addicted, as we know, to fine reflexion. "Well—to be nice."

"My poor sweet child!" murmured her sister.

"What have I said that's so silly?" Bessie asked.

"You're a little too simple; just a little. It's very becoming, but it pleases people at your expense."

"I'm certainly too simple to understand you," said our young lady.

Mrs. Westgate had an ominous pause. "Shall I tell you a story?"

"If you'd be so good. That's what's frequently done to amuse simple people."

Mrs. Westgate consulted her memory while her companion sat at gaze of the shining sea. "Did you ever hear of the Duke of Green-Erin?"

"I think not," said Bessie.

"Well, it's no matter," her sister went on.

"It's a proof of my simplicity."

"My story's meant to illustrate that of some other people," said Mrs. Westgate. "The Duke of Green-Erin's what they call in England a great swell, and some five years ago he came to America. He spent most of his time in New York, and in New York he spent his days and his nights at the Butterworths'. You've heard at least of the Butterworths. *Bien.* They did everything in the world for him—the poor Butterworths—they turned themselves inside out. They gave him a dozen dinner-parties and balls, and were the means of his being invited to fifty more. At first he used to come into Mrs. Butterworth's box at the opera in a tweed travelling-suit, but some one stopped that. At any rate he had a beautiful time and they parted the best friends in the world. Two years elapse and the Butterworths come abroad and go to London. The first thing they see in all the papers—in England those things are in the most prominent place—is that the Duke of Green-Erin has arrived in town for the season. They wait a little, and then Mr. Butterworth—as polite as ever—goes and leaves a card. They wait a little more; the visit's not returned; they wait three weeks: *silence de mort*, the Duke gives no sign. The Butterworths see a lot of other people, put down the Duke of Green-Erin as a rude ungrateful man and forget all about him. One fine day they go to Ascot Races—where they meet him face to face. He stares a moment and then comes up to Mr. Butterworth, taking something from his pocket-book—something which proves to be a banknote. 'I'm glad to see you, Mr. Butterworth,' he says, 'so that I can pay you that ten pounds I lost to you in New York. I saw the other day you remembered our bet; here are the ten pounds, Mr. Butterworth. Good-bye, Mr. Butterworth.' And off he goes, and that's the last they see of the Duke of Green-Erin."

"Is that your story?" asked Bessie Alden.

"Don't tell me you don't think it interesting!" her sister replied.

"I don't think I believe it," said the girl.

"Ah, then," cried Mrs. Westgate, "mademoiselle isn't of such an unspotted *candeur*! Believe it or not as you like. There's at any rate no smoke without fire."

"Is that the way," asked Bessie after a moment, "that you expect your friends to treat you?"

"I defy them to treat me very ill, for the simple reason that I shall never give them the opportunity. With the best will in the world, in that case, they can't be very disobliging."

Our young lady for a time said nothing. "I don't see what makes you talk that way," she then resumed. "The English are a great people."

"Exactly; and that's just the way they've grown great—by dropping you when you've ceased to be useful. People say they aren't clever, but I find them prodigiously clever."

"You know you've liked them—all the Englishmen you've seen," Bessie brought up.

"They've liked *me*," her sister returned; "so I think I'd rather put it. And of course one likes that."

Bessie pursued for some moments her studies in sea-green. "Well," she said, "whether they like me or not, I mean to like them. And happily," she wound up, "Lord Lambeth doesn't owe me ten pounds."

During the first few days after their arrival at Jones's Hotel our charming Americans were much occupied with what they would have called looking about them. They found occasion to make numerous purchases, and their opportunities for inquiry and comment were only those supplied by the deferential London shopmen. Bessie Alden, even in driving from the station, felt to intensity the many-voiced appeal of the capital of the race from which she had sprung, and, at the risk of exhibiting her as a person of vulgar tastes, it must be recorded that for many days she desired no higher pleasure than to roll about the crowded streets in the public conveyances. They presented to her attentive eyes strange pictures and figures, and it's at least beneath the dignity of our historic muse to enumerate the trivial objects and incidents in which the imagination of this simple young lady from Boston lost itself. It may be freely mentioned, however, that whenever, after a round of visits in Bond Street and Regent Street, she was about to return with her sister to Jones's Hotel, she desired they should, at whatever cost to convenience, be driven home by way of Westminster Abbey. She had begun by asking if it wouldn't be possible to take the Tower *en route* to their lodgings; but it happened that at a more primitive stage of her culture Mrs. Westgate had paid a visit to this venerable relic, which she spoke of ever afterwards, vaguely, as a dreadful disappointment. She thus expressed the liveliest disapproval of any attempt to combine historical researches with the purchase of hair-brushes and notepaper. The most she would consent to do in the line of backward brooding was to spend half an hour at Madame Tussaud's, where she saw several dusty wax effigies of members of the Royal Family. It was made clear to Bessie that if she wished to go to the Tower she must get some one else to take her. Bessie expressed hereupon an earnest disposition to go alone; but in respect to this proposal as well Mrs. Westgate had the cold sense of complications.

"Remember," she said, "that you're not in your innocent little Boston. It's not a question of walking up and down Beacon Street." With which she went on to explain that there were two classes of American girls in Europe—those who walked about alone and those who didn't. "You happen to belong, my dear," she said to her sister, "to the class that doesn't."

"It's only," laughed Bessie, though all yearningly, "because you happen quite arbitrarily to place me." And she devoted much private meditation to this question of effecting a visit to the Tower of London.

Suddenly it seemed as if the problem might be solved; the two ladies at Jones's Hotel received a visit from Willie Woodley. So was familiarly designated a young American who had sailed from New York a few days after their own departure and who, enjoying some freedom of acquaintance with them in that city, had lost no time, on his arrival in London, in coming to pay them his respects. He had in fact gone to see them directly after going to see his tailor; than which there can be no greater exhibition of promptitude on the part of a young American just installed at the Charing Cross Hotel. He was a slight, mild youth, without high colour but with many elegant forms, famous for the authority with which he led the "German" in New York. He was indeed, by the young ladies who habitually figured in such evolutions, reckoned "the best dancer in the world"; it was in those terms he was always spoken of and his pleasant identity indicated. He was the most convenient gentle young man, for almost any casual light purpose, it was possible to meet; he was beautifully dressed—"in the English style"—and knew an immense deal about London. He had been at Newport during the previous summer, at the time of our young Englishmen's visit, and he took extreme pleasure in the society of Bessie Alden, whom he never addressed but as "Miss Bessie." She immediately arranged with him, in the presence of her sister, that he should guide her to the scene of Lady Jane Grey's execution.

"You may do as you please," said Mrs. Westgate. "Only—if you desire the information—it is not the custom here for young ladies to knock about London with wild young men."

"Miss Bessie has waltzed with me so often—not to call it so wildly," the young man returned, "that she can surely go out with me in a jog-trot cab."

"I consider public waltzing," said Mrs. Westgate, "the most innocent, because the most guarded and regulated, pleasure of our time."

"It's a jolly compliment to our time!" Mr. Woodley cried with a laugh of the most candid significance.

"I don't see why I should regard what's done here," Bessie pursued. "Why should I suffer the restrictions of a society of which I enjoy none of the privileges?"

"That's very good—very good," her friend applauded.

"Oh, go to the Tower and feel the axe if you like!" said Mrs. Westgate. "I consent to your going with Mr. Woodley; but I wouldn't let you go with an Englishman."

"Miss Bessie wouldn't care to go with an Englishman!" Mr. Woodley declared with an asperity doubtless not unnatural in a young man who, dressing in a manner that I have indicated and knowing a great deal, as I have said, about London, saw no reason for drawing these sharp distinctions. He agreed upon a day with Miss Bessie—a day of that same week; while an ingenious mind might perhaps have traced a connexion between the girl's reference to her lack of social privilege or festal initiation and a question she asked on the morrow as she sat with her sister at luncheon.

"Don't you mean to write to—to any one?"

"I wrote this morning to Captain Littledale," Mrs. Westgate replied.

"But Mr. Woodley believes Captain Littledale away in India."

"He said he thought he had heard so; he knows nothing about it."

For a moment Bessie said nothing more; then at last, "And don't you intend to write to—to Mr. Beaumont?" she inquired.

Her sister waited with a look at her. "You mean to Lord Lambeth."

"I said Mr. Beaumont because he was—at Newport—so good a friend of yours."

Mrs. Westgate prolonged the attitude of sisterly truth. "I don't really care two straws for Mr. Beaumont."

"You were certainly very nice to him."

"I'm very nice to every one," said Mrs. Westgate simply.

Nothing indeed could have been simpler save perhaps the way Bessie smiled back: "To every one but me."

Her sister continued to look at her. "Are you in love with Lord Lambeth?"

Our young woman stared a moment, and the question was too unattended with any train even to make her shy. "Not that I know of."

"Because if you are," Mrs. Westgate went on, "I shall certainly not send for him."

"That proves what I said," Bessie gaily insisted—"that you're not really nice to me."

"It would be a poor service, my dear child," said her sister.

"In what sense? There's nothing *against* Lord Lambeth that I know of."

Mrs. Westgate seemed to cover much country in a few moments. "You *are* in love with him then?"

Bessie stared again, but this time blushing a little. "Ah, if you'll not be serious we won't mention him again."

For some minutes accordingly Lord Lambeth was shrouded in silence, and it was Mrs. Westgate who, at the end of this period, removed the ban. "Of course I shall let him know we're here. I think he'd be hurt—justly enough—if we should go away without seeing him. It's fair to give him a chance to come and thank me for the kindness we showed him. But I don't want to seem eager."

"Neither do I," said Bessie very simply.

"Though I confess," her companion added, "that I'm curious to see how he'll behave."

"He behaved very well at Newport."

"Newport isn't London. At Newport he could do as he liked; but here it's another affair. He has to have an eye to consequences."

"If he had more freedom then at Newport," argued Bessie, "it's the more to his credit that he behaved well; and if he has to be so careful here it's possible he'll behave even better."

"Better, better?" echoed her sister a little impatiently. "My dear child, what do you mean by better and what's your point of view?"

Bessie wondered. "What do *you* mean by my point of view?"

"Don't you care for Lord Lambeth—a tiny speck?" Mrs. Westgate demanded.

This time Bessie Alden took it with still deeper reserve. She slowly got up from table, turning her face away. "You'll oblige me by not talking so."

Mrs. Westgate sat watching her for some moments as she moved slowly about the room and went and stood at the window. "I'll write to him this afternoon," she said at last.

"Do as you please!" Bessie answered; after which she turned round. "I'm not afraid to say I like Lord Lambeth. I like him very much."

Mrs. Westgate bethought herself. "He's not clever."

"Well, there have been clever people whom I've disliked," the girl said; "so I suppose I may like a stupid one. Besides, Lord Lambeth's no stupider than any one else."

"No stupider than he gives you warning of," her sister smiled.

"If I were in love with him as you said just now," Bessie returned, "it would be bad policy on your part to abuse him."

"My dear child, don't give me lessons in policy!" cried Mrs. Westgate. "The policy I mean to follow is very deep."

The girl began once more to walk about; then she stopped before her companion. "I've never heard in the course of five minutes so many hints and innuendoes. I wish you'd tell me in plain English what you mean."

"I mean you may be much annoyed."

"That's still only a hint," said Bessie.

Her sister just hesitated. "It will be said of you that you've come after him—that you followed him."

Bessie threw back her pretty head much as a startled hind, and a look flashed into her face that made Mrs. Westgate get up. "Who says such things as that?"

"People here."

"I don't believe it."

"You've a very convenient faculty of doubt. But my policy will be, as I say, very deep. I shall leave you to find out as many things as possible for yourself."

Bessie fixed her eyes on her sister, and Mrs. Westgate could have believed there were tears in them. "Do they talk that way here?"

"You'll see. I shall let you alone."

"Don't let me alone," said Bessie Alden. "Take me away."

"No; I want to see what you make of it," her sister continued.

"I don't understand."

"You'll understand after Lord Lambeth has come," said Mrs. Westgate with a persistence of private amusement.

The two ladies had arranged that on this afternoon Willie Woodley should go with them to Hyde Park, where Bessie expected it would prove a rich passage to have sat on a little green chair under the great trees and beside Rotten Row. The want of a suitable escort had hitherto hampered this adventure; but no escort, now, for such an expedition, could have been more suitable than their devoted young countryman, whose mission in life, it might almost be said, was to find chairs for ladies and who appeared on the stroke of half-past five adorned with every superficial grace that could qualify him for the scene.

"I've written to Lord Lambeth, my dear," Mrs. Westgate mentioned on coming into the room where Bessie, drawing on long grey gloves, had given their visitor the impression that she was particularly attuned. Bessie said nothing, but Willie Woodley exclaimed that his lordship was in town; he had seen his name in the *Morning Post*. "Do you read the *Morning Post*?" Mrs. Westgate thereupon asked.

"Oh yes; it's great fun." Mr. Woodley almost spoke as if the pleasure were attended with physical risk.

"I want so to see it," said Bessie, "there's so much about it in Thackeray."

"I'll send it to you every morning!" cried the young man with elation.

He found them what Bessie thought excellent places under the great trees and beside the famous avenue the humours of which had been made familiar to the girl's childhood by the pictures in *Punch*. The day was bright and warm and the crowd of riders and spectators, as well as the great procession of carriages, proportionately dense and many-coloured. The scene bore the stamp of the London social pressure at its highest, and it made our young woman think of more things than she could easily express to her companions. She sat silent, under her parasol, while her imagination, according to its wont, kept pace with the deep strong tide of the exhibition. Old impressions and preconceptions became living things before the show, and she found herself, amid the crowd of images, fitting a history to this person and a theory to that, and making a place for them all in her small private museum of types. But if she said little her sister on one side and Willie Woodley on the other delivered themselves in lively alternation.

"Look at that green dress with blue flounces. Quelle toilette!" said Mrs. Westgate.

"That's the Marquis of Blackborough," the young man was able to contribute—"the one in the queer white coat. I heard him speak the other night in the House of Lords; it was something about ramrods; he called them *wamwods*. He's an awful swell."

"Did you ever see anything like the way they're pinned back?" Mrs. Westgate resumed. "They never know where to stop."

"They do nothing but stop," said Willie Woodley. "It prevents them from walking. Here comes a great celebrity—Lady Beatrice Bellevue. She's awfully fast; see what little steps she takes."

"Well, my dear," Mrs. Westgate pursued to Bessie, "I hope you're getting some ideas for your couturière?"

"I'm getting plenty of ideas," said Bessie, "but I don't know that my couturière would particularly appreciate them."

Their companion presently perceived a mounted friend who drew up beside the barrier of the Row and beckoned to him. He went forward and the crowd of pedestrians closed about him, so that for some minutes he was hidden from sight. At last he reappeared, bringing a gentleman with him—a gentleman whom Bessie at first supposed to be his friend dismounted. But at a second glance she found herself looking at Lord Lambeth, who was shaking hands with her sister.

"I found him over there," said Willie Woodley, "and I told him you were here."

And then Lord Lambeth, raising his hat afresh, shook hands with Bessie—"Fancy your being here!" He was blushing and smiling; he looked very handsome and he had a note of splendour he had not had in America. The girl's free fancy, as we know, was just then in marked exercise; so that the tall young Englishman, as he stood there looking down at her, had the benefit of it. "He's handsomer and more splendid than anything I've ever seen," she said to herself. And then she remembered he was a Marquis and she thought he somehow looked a Marquis.

"Really, you know," he cried, "you ought to have let a fellow know you've come!"

"I wrote to you an hour ago," said Mrs. Westgate.

"Doesn't all the world know it?" smiled Bessie.

"I assure you I didn't know it!" he insisted. "Upon my honour I hadn't heard of it. Ask Woodley now; had I, Woodley?"

"Well, I think you're rather a humbug," this gentleman brought forth.

"You don't believe that—do you, Miss Alden?" asked his lordship. "You don't believe I'm rather a humbug, eh?"

"No," said Bessie after an instant, but choosing and conferring a grace on the literal—"I don't."

"You're too tall to stand up, Lord Lambeth," Mrs. Westgate pronounced. "You approach the normal only when you sit down. Be so good as to get a chair."

He found one and placed it sidewise, close to the two ladies. "If I hadn't met Woodley I should never have found you," he went on. "Should I, Woodley?"

"Well, I guess not," said the young American.

"Not even with my letter?" asked Mrs. Westgate.

"Ah, well, I haven't got your letter yet; I suppose I shall get it this evening. It was awfully kind of you to write."

"So I said to Bessie," the elder lady observed.

"*Did* she say so, Miss Alden?" Lord Lambeth a little pointlessly inquired. "I daresay you've been here a month."

"We've been here three," mocked Mrs. Westgate.

"*Have* you been here three months?" the young man asked again of Bessie.

"It seems a long time," Bessie answered.

He had but a brief wonder—he found something. "I say, after that you had better not call me a humbug! I've only been in town three weeks, but you must have been hiding away. I haven't seen you anywhere."

"Where should you have seen us—where should we have gone?" Mrs. Westgate fairly put to him.

It found Willie Woodley at least ready. "You should have gone to Hurlingham."

"No, let Lord Lambeth tell us," Mrs. Westgate insisted.

"There are plenty of places to go to," he said—"each one stupider than the other. I mean people's houses. They send you cards."

"No one has sent us a scrap of a card," Bessie laughed.

Mrs. Westgate attenuated. "We're very quiet. We're here as travellers."

"We've been to Madame Tussaud's," Bessie further mentioned.

"Oh I say!" cried Lord Lambeth.

"We thought we should find your image there," said Mrs. Westgate—"yours and Mr. Beaumont's."

264

"In the Chamber of Horrors?" laughed the young man.

"It did duty very well for a party," said Mrs. Westgate. "All the women were *décolletées*, and many of the figures looked as if they could almost speak."

"Upon my word," his lordship returned, "you see people at London parties who look a long way from that!"

"Do you think Mr. Woodley could find us Mr. Beaumont?" asked the elder of the ladies.

He stared and looked about. "I daresay he could. Percy sometimes comes here. Don't you think you could find him, Woodley? Make a dive or a dash for it."

"Thank you; I've had enough of violent movement," said Willie Woodley. "I'll wait till Mr. Beaumont comes to the surface."

"I'll bring him to see you," said Lord Lambeth. "Where are you staying?"

"You'll find the address in my letter—Jones's Hotel."

"Oh, one of those places just out of Piccadilly? Beastly hole, isn't it?" Lord Lambeth inquired.

"I believe it's the best hotel in London," said Mrs. Westgate.

"But they give you awful rubbish to eat, don't they?" his lordship went on.

Mrs. Westgate practised the same serenity. "Awful."

"I always feel so sorry for people who come up to town and go to live in those dens," continued the young man. "They eat nothing but filth."

"Oh I say!" cried Willie Woodley.

"Well, and how do you like London, Miss Alden?" Lord Lambeth asked, unperturbed by this ejaculation.

The girl was prompt. "I think it grand."

"My sister likes it, in spite of the 'filth'!" Mrs. Westgate recorded.

"I hope then you're going to stop a long time."

"As long as I can," Bessie replied.

"And where's wonderful Mr. Westgate?" asked Lord Lambeth of this gentleman's wife.

"He's where he always is—in that tiresome New York."

"He must have staying power," said the young man.

She appeared to consider. "Well, he stays ahead of every one else."

Lord Lambeth sat nearly an hour with his American friends; but it is not our purpose to relate their conversation in full. He addressed a great many remarks to the younger lady and finally turned toward her altogether, while Willie Woodley wasted a certain amount of effort to regale Mrs. Westgate. Bessie herself was sparing of effusion; she thought, on her guard, of what her sister had said to her at luncheon. Little by little, however, she interested herself again in her English friend very much as she had done at Newport; only it seemed to her he might here become more interesting. He would be an unconscious part of the antiquity, the impressiveness, the picturesqueness of England; of all of which things poor Bessie Alden, like most familiars of the overciphered *tabula rasa*, was terribly at the mercy.

"I've often wished I were back at Newport," the young man candidly stated. "Those days I spent at your sister's were awfully jolly."

"We enjoyed them very much; I hope your father's better."

"Oh dear yes. When I got to England the old humbug was out grouse-shooting. It was what you call in America a gigantic fraud. My mother had got nervous. My three weeks at Newport seemed a happy dream."

"America certainly is very different from England," said Bessie.

"I hope you like England better, eh?" he returned almost persuasively.

"No Englishman can ask that seriously of a person of another country."

266

He turned his cheerful brown eyes on her. "You mean it's a matter of course?"

"If I were English," said Bessie, "it would certainly seem to me a matter of course that every one should be a good patriot."

"Oh dear, yes; patriotism's everything." He appeared not quite to follow, but was clearly contented. "Now what are you going to do here?"

"On Thursday I'm going to the Tower."

"The Tower?"

"The Tower of London. Did you never hear of it?"

"Oh yes, I've been there," said Lord Lambeth. "I was taken there by my governess when I was six years old. It's a rum idea your going there."

"Do give me a few more rum ideas then. I want to see everything of that sort. I'm going to Hampton Court and to Windsor and to the Dulwich Gallery."

He seemed greatly amused. "I wonder you don't go to Rosherville Gardens."

Bessie yearned. "Are they interesting?"

"Oh wonderful!"

"Are they weirdly old? That's all I care for," she said.

"They're tremendously old; they're all falling to ruins."

The girl rose to it. "I think there's nothing so charming as an old ruinous garden. We must certainly go there."

Her friend broke out into mirth. "I say, Woodley, here's Miss Alden wants to go down to Rosherville Gardens! Hang it, they *are* 'weird'!"

Willie Woodley looked a little blank; he was caught in the fact of ignorance of an apparently conspicuous feature of London life. But in a moment he turned it off. "Very well," he said, "I'll write for a permit."

267

Lord Lambeth's exhilaration increased. "'Gad, I believe that, to get your money's worth over here, you Americans would go anywhere!"

"We wish to go to Parliament," said Bessie. "That's one of the first things."

"Ah, it would bore you to death!" he returned.

"We wish to hear you speak."

"I never speak—except to young ladies."

She looked at him from under the shade of her parasol. "You're very strange," she then quietly concluded. "I don't think I approve of you."

"Ah, now don't be severe, Miss Alden!" he cried with the note of sincerity. "Please don't be severe. I want you to like me—awfully."

"To like you awfully? You mustn't laugh at me then when I make mistakes. I regard it as my right—as a free-born American—to make as many mistakes as I choose."

"Upon my word I didn't laugh at you," the young man pleaded.

"And not only that," Bessie went on; "but I hold that all my mistakes should be set down to my credit. You must think the better of me for them."

"I can't think better of you than I do," he declared.

Again, shadily, she took him in. "You certainly speak very well to young ladies. But why don't you address the House?—isn't that what they call it?"

"Because I've nothing to say."

"Haven't you a great position?" she demanded.

He looked a moment at the back of his glove. "I'll set that down as one of your mistakes—to your credit." And as if he disliked talking about his position he changed the subject. "I wish you'd let me go with you to the Tower and to Hampton Court and to all those other places."

"We shall be most happy," said Bessie.

"And of course I shall be delighted to show you the Houses of Parliament—some day that suits you. There are a lot of things I want to do for you. I want you to have a good time. And I should like very much to present some of my friends to you if it wouldn't bore you. Then it would be awfully kind of you to come down to Branches."

"We're much obliged to you, Lord Lambeth," said Bessie. "And what may Branches be?"

"It's a house in the country. I think you might like it."

Willie Woodley and Mrs. Westgate were at this moment sitting in silence, and the young man's ear caught these last words of the other pair. "He's inviting Miss Bessie to one of his castles," he murmured to his companion.

Mrs. Westgate hereupon, foreseeing what she mentally called "complications," immediately got up; and the two ladies, taking leave of their English friend, returned, under conduct of their American, to Jones's Hotel.

V

Lord Lambeth came to see them on the morrow, bringing Percy Beaumont with him—the latter having at once declared his intention of neglecting none of the usual offices of civility. This declaration, however, on his kinsman's informing him of the advent of the two ladies, had been preceded by another exchange.

"Here they are then and you're in for it."

"And what am I in for?" the younger man had inquired.

"I'll let your mother give it a name. With all respect to whom," Percy had added, "I must decline on this occasion to do any more police duty. The Duchess must look after you herself."

"I'll give her a chance," the Duchess's son had returned a trifle grimly. "I shall make her go and see them."

269

"She won't do it, my boy."

"We'll see if she doesn't," said Lord Lambeth.

But if Mr. Beaumont took a subtle view of the arrival of the fair strangers at Jones's Hotel he was sufficiently capable of a still deeper refinement to offer them a smiling countenance. He fell into animated conversation—conversation animated at least on *her* side—with Mrs. Westgate, while his companion appealed more confusedly to the younger lady. Mrs. Westgate began confessing and protesting, declaring and discriminating.

"I must say London's a great deal brighter and prettier just now than it was when I was here last—in the month of November. There's evidently a great deal going on, and you seem to have a good many flowers. I've no doubt it's very charming for all you people and that you amuse yourselves immensely. It's very good of you to let Bessie and me come and sit and look at you. I suppose you'll think I'm very satirical, but I must confess that that's the feeling I have in London."

"I'm afraid I don't quite understand to what feeling you allude," said Percy Beaumont.

"The feeling that it's all very well for you English people. Everything's beautifully arranged for you."

"It seems to me it's very well arranged here for some Americans sometimes," Percy plucked up spirit to answer.

"For some of them, yes—if they like to be patronised. But I must say I don't like to be patronised. I may be very eccentric and undisciplined and unreasonable, but I confess I never was fond of patronage. I like to associate with people on the same terms as I do in my own country; that's a peculiar taste that I have. But here people seem to expect something else—really I can't make out quite what. I'm afraid you'll think I'm very ungrateful, for I certainly have received in one way and another a great deal of attention. The last time I was here a lady sent me a message that I was at liberty to come and pay her my respects."

"Dear me, I hope you didn't go," Mr. Beaumont cried.

"You're deliciously naïf, I must say that for you!" Mrs. Westgate promptly pursued. "It must be a great advantage to you here in London. I suppose that if I myself had a little more naïveté—of your blessed national lack of any approach to a sense for shades—I should enjoy it more. I should be content to sit on a chair in the Park and see the people pass, to be told that this is the Duchess of Suffolk and that the Lord Chamberlain, and that I must be thankful for the privilege of beholding them. I daresay it's very peevish and critical of me to ask for anything else. But I was always critical—it's the joy of my life—and I freely confess to the sin of being fastidious. I'm told there's some remarkably superior second-rate society provided here for strangers. *Merci*! I don't want any superior second-rate society. I want the society I've been accustomed to."

Percy mustered a rueful gaiety. "I hope you don't call Lambeth and me second-rate!"

"Oh I'm accustomed to you!" said Mrs. Westgate. "Do you know you English sometimes make the most wonderful speeches? The first time I came to London I went out to dine—as I told you, I've received a great deal of attention. After dinner, in the drawing-room, I had some conversation with an old lady—no, you mustn't look that way: I assure you I had! I forget what we talked about, but she presently said, in allusion to something we were discussing: 'Oh, you know, the aristocracy do so-and-so, but in one's own class of life it's very different.' In one's own class of life! What's a poor unprotected American woman to do in a country where she is liable to have that sort of thing said to her?"

"I should say she's not to mind, not a rap—though you seem to get hold of some very queer old ladies. I compliment you on your acquaintance!" Percy pursued. "If you're trying to bring me to admit that London's an odious place you'll not succeed. I'm extremely fond of it and think it the jolliest place in the world."

"Pour vous autres—I never said the contrary," Mrs. Westgate retorted—an expression made use of, this last, because both interlocutors had begun to

271

raise their voices. Mr. Beaumont naturally didn't like to hear the seat of his existence abused, and Mrs. Westgate, no less naturally, didn't like a stubborn debater.

"Hallo!" said Lord Lambeth; "what are they up to now?" And he came away from the window, where he had been standing with Bessie.

"I quite agree with a very clever countrywoman of mine," the elder lady continued with charming ardour even if with imperfect relevancy. She smiled at the two gentlemen for a moment with terrible brightness, as if to toss at their feet—upon their native heath—the gauntlet of defiance. "For me there are only two social positions worth speaking of—that of an American lady and that of the Emperor of Russia."

"And what do you do with the American gentlemen?" asked Lord Lambeth.

"She leaves them in America!" said his comrade.

On the departure of their visitors Bessie mentioned that Lord Lambeth would come the next day, to go with them to the Tower, and that he had kindly offered to bring his "trap" and drive them all through the city. Mrs. Westgate listened in silence to this news and for some time afterwards also said nothing. But at last, "If you hadn't requested me the other day not to speak of it," she began, "there's something I'd make bold to ask you." Bessie frowned a little; her dark blue eyes grew more dark than blue. But her sister went on. "As it is I'll take the risk. You're not in love with Lord Lambeth: I believe it perfectly. Very good. But is there by chance any danger of your becoming so? It's a very simple question—don't take offence. I've a particular reason," said Mrs. Westgate, "for wanting to know."

Bessie for some moments said nothing; she only looked displeased. "No; there's no danger," she at last answered with a certain dryness.

"Then I should like to frighten them!" cried her sister, clasping jewelled hands.

"To frighten whom?"

272

"All these people. Lord Lambeth's family and friends."

The girl wondered. "How should you frighten them?"

"It wouldn't be I—it would be you. It would frighten them to suppose you holding in thrall his lordship's young affections."

Our young lady, her clear eyes still overshadowed by her dark brows, continued to examine it. "Why should that frighten them?"

Mrs. Westgate winged her shaft with a smile before launching it. "Because they think you're not good enough. You're a charming girl, beautiful and amiable, intelligent and clever, and as *bien-élevée* as it is possible to be; but you're not a fit match for Lord Lambeth."

Bessie showed again a coldness. "Where do you get such extraordinary ideas? You've said some such odd things lately. My dear Kitty, where do you collect them?"

But Kitty, unabashed, held to her idea. "Yes, it would put them on pins and needles, and it wouldn't hurt you. Mr. Beaumont's already most uneasy. I could soon see that."

The girl turned it over. "Do you mean they spy on him, that they interfere with him?"

"I don't know what power they have to interfere, but I know that a British *materfamilias*—and when she's a Duchess into the bargain—is often a force to be reckoned with."

It has already been intimated that before certain appearances of strange or sinister cast our young woman was apt to shy off into scepticism. She abstained on the present occasion from expressing disbelief, for she wished not to irritate her sister. But she said to herself that Kitty had been misinformed—that this was a traveller's tale. Though she was a girl of quick imagination there could in the nature of things be no truth for her in the attribution to her of a vulgar identity. Only the form she gave her doubt was: "I must say that in that case I'm very sorry for Lord Lambeth."

Mrs. Westgate, more and more exhilarated by her own scheme, irradiated interest. "If I could only believe it was safe! But when you begin to pity him I, on my side, am afraid."

"Afraid of what?"

"Of your pitying him too much."

Bessie turned impatiently off—then at the end of a minute faced about. "What if I *should* pity him too much?"

Mrs. Westgate hereupon averted herself, but after a moment's reflexion met the case. "It would come, after all, to the same thing."

Lord Lambeth came the next day with his trap, when the two ladies, attended by Willie Woodley, placed themselves under his guidance and were conveyed eastward, through some of the most fascinating, as Bessie called them, even though the duskiest districts, to the great turreted donjon that overlooks the London shipping. They alighted together to enter the famous fortress, where they secured the services of a venerable beef-eater, who, ignoring the presence of other dependants on his leisure, made a fine exclusive party of them and marched them through courts and corridors, through armouries and prisons. He delivered his usual peripatetic discourse, and they stopped and stared and peeped and stooped according as he marshalled and directed them. Bessie appealed to this worthy—even on more heads than he seemed aware of; she overtaxed, in her earnestness, his learnt lesson and found the place, as she more than once mentioned to him, quite delirious. Lord Lambeth was in high good-humour; his delirium at least was gay and he betrayed afresh that aptitude for the simpler forms of ironic comment that the girl had noted in him. Willie Woodley kept looking at the ceilings and tapping the walls with the knuckle of a pearl-grey glove; and Mrs. Westgate, asking at frequent intervals to be allowed to sit down and wait till they came back, was as frequently informed that they would never do anything so weak. When it befell that Bessie's glowing appeals, chiefly on collateral points of English history, but left the warder gaping she resorted straight to Lord Lambeth. His lordship then pleaded gross incompetence, declaring he knew nothing about that sort of thing and greatly diverted, to all appearance, at being treated as an authority.

"You can't honestly expect people to know as awfully much as you," he said.

"I should expect you to know a great deal more," Bessie Alden returned.

"Well, women always know more than men about names and dates and historical characters," he said. "There was Lady Jane Grey we've just been hearing about, who went in for Latin and Greek and all the learning of her age."

"*You* have no right to be ignorant at all events," Bessie argued with all her freedom.

"Why haven't I as good a right as any one else?"

"Because you've lived in the midst of all these things."

"What things do you mean? Axes and blocks and thumbscrews?"

"All these historical things. You belong to an historical family."

"Bessie really harks back too much to the dead past—she makes too much of it," Mrs. Westgate opined, catching the sense of this colloquy.

"Yes, you hark back," the young man laughed, thankful for a formula. "You do make too much of the dead past."

He went with the ladies a couple of days later to Hampton Court, Willie Woodley being also of the party. The afternoon was charming, the famous horse-chestnuts blossomed to admiration, and Lord Lambeth, who found in Miss Alden the improving governess, he declared, of his later immaturity, as Mademoiselle Boquet, dragging him by the hand to view all lions, had been that of his earliest, pronounced the old red palace not half so beastly as he had supposed. Bessie herself rose to raptures; she went about murmuring and "raving." "It's too lovely; it's too enchanting; it's too exactly what it ought to be!"

At Hampton Court the tinkling flocks are not provided with an official bellwether, but are left to browse at discretion on the tough herbage of History. It happened in this manner that, in default of another informant, our young woman, who on doubtful questions was able to suggest a great many alternatives, found herself again apply for judicious support to Lord Lambeth. He, however, could but once more declare himself a broken reed and that his education, in such matters, had been sadly neglected.

"And I'm sorry it makes you so wretched," he further professed.

"You're so disappointing, you know," she returned; but more in pity—pity for herself—than in anger.

"Ah, now, don't say that! That's the worst thing you could possibly say."

"No"—she spoke with a sad lucidity—"it's not so bad as to say that I had expected nothing of you."

"I don't know"—and he seemed to rejoice in a chance to demur. "Give me a notion of the sort of thing you expected."

"Well, that you'd be more what I should like to be—what I should try to be—in your place."

"Ah, my place!" he groaned. "You're always talking about my place."

The girl gave him a look; he might have thought she coloured; and for a little she made no rejoinder. "Does it strike you that I'm always talking about your place?"

"I'm sure you do it a great honour," he said as if fearing he had sounded uncivil.

"I've often thought about it," she went on after a moment. "I've often thought of your future as an hereditary legislator. An hereditary legislator ought to know so many things, oughtn't he?"

"Not if he doesn't legislate."

"But you *will* legislate one of these days—you may have to at any time; it's absurd your saying you won't. You're very much looked up to here—I'm assured of that."

"I don't know that I ever noticed it."

276

"It's because you're used to it then. You ought to fill the place."

"How do you mean, fill it?" asked Lord Lambeth.

"You ought to be very clever and brilliant—to be 'up' in almost everything."

He turned on her his handsome young face of profane wonder. "Shall I tell you something? A young man in my position, as you call it—"

"I didn't invent the term," she interposed. "I've seen it in a great many books."

"Hang it, you're always at your books! A fellow in my position then does well enough at the worst—he muddles along whatever he does. That's about what I mean to say."

"Well, if your own people are content with you," Bessie laughed, "it's not for me to complain. But I shall always think that properly you should have a great mind—a great character."

"Ah, that's very theoretic!" the young man promptly brought out. "Depend upon it, that's a Yankee prejudice."

"Happy the country then," she as eagerly declared, "where people's prejudices make so for light."

He stopped short, with his slightly strained gaiety, as for the pleasantness of high argument. "What it comes to then is that we're all here a pack of fools and me the biggest of the lot?"

"I said nothing so rude of a great people—and a great person. But I must repeat that you personally are—in your representative capacity that's to be—disappointing."

"My dear Miss Alden," he simply cried at this, "I'm the best fellow in the world!"

"Ah, if it were not for that!" she beautifully smiled.

Mrs. Westgate had many more friends in London than she pretended, and before long had renewed acquaintance with most of them. Their hospitality was prompt, so that, one thing leading to another, she began, as the phrase is, to go out. Bessie Alden, in this way, saw a good deal of what she took great pleasure in calling to herself English society. She went to balls and danced, she went to dinners and talked, she went to concerts and listened—at concerts Bessie always listened—she went to exhibitions and wondered. Her enjoyment was keen and her curiosity insatiable, and, grateful in general for all her opportunities, she especially prized the privilege of meeting certain celebrated persons, authors and artists, philosophers and statesmen, of whose renown she had been a humble and distant beholder and who now, as part of the frequent furniture of London drawing-rooms, struck her as stars fallen from the firmament and become palpable—revealing also sometimes on contact qualities not to have been predicted of bodies sidereal. Bessie, who knew so many of her contemporaries by reputation, lost in this way certain fond illusions; but on the other hand she had innumerable satisfactions and enthusiasms, and she laid bare the wealth of her emotions to a dear friend of her own sex in Boston, with whom she was in voluminous correspondence. Some of her sentiments indeed she sought mildly to flash upon Lord Lambeth, who came almost every day to Jones's Hotel and whom Mrs. Westgate admitted to be really devoted. Captain Littledale, it appeared, had gone to India; and of several others of this lady's ex-pensioners—gentlemen who, as she said, had made, in New York, a club-house of her drawing-room—no tidings were to be obtained; but this particular friend of other days was certainly attentive enough to make up for the accidental absences, the short memories, the remarked lapses, of every one else. He drove the sisters in the Park, took them to visit private collections of pictures and, having a house of his own, invited them to luncheon, to tea, to dinner, to supper even after the arduous German opera. Mrs. Westgate, following the fashion of many of her countrywomen, caused herself and her companion to be presented at the English Court by her diplomatic representative—for it was in this manner that she alluded to the American Minister to England, inquiring what on earth he was put there for if not to make the proper arrangements for her reception at Court.

Lord Lambeth expressed a hatred of Courts, but he had social privileges or exercised some court function—these undiscriminated attributes, dim backgrounds where old gold seemed to shine through transparent conventions, were romantically rich to our young heroine—that involved his support of his sovereign on the day on which the two ladies at Jones's Hotel repaired to Buckingham Palace in a remarkable coach sent by his lordship to fetch them. He appeared in a gorgeous uniform, and Bessie Alden was particularly struck with his glory—especially when on her asking him, rather foolishly as she felt, if he were a loyal subject, he replied that he was a loyal subject to herself. This pronouncement was emphasised by his dancing with her at a royal ball to which the two ladies afterwards went, and was not impaired by the fact that she thought he danced very ill. He struck her as wonderfully kind; she asked herself with growing vivacity why he should be so kind. It was just his character—that seemed the natural reply. She had told her relative how much she liked him, and now that she liked him more she wondered at her excess. She liked him for his clear nature; to this question as well that seemed the natural answer. The truth was that when once the impressions of London life began to crowd thickly upon her she completely forgot her subtle sister's warning on the cynicism of public opinion. It had given her great pain at the moment; but there was no particular reason why she should remember it: it corresponded too little with any sensible reality. Besides which there was her habit, her beautiful system, of consenting to know nothing of human baseness or of the vulgar side. There were things, just as there were people, that were as nought from the moment one ignored them. She was accordingly not haunted with the sense of a low imputation. She wasn't in love with Lord Lambeth—she assured herself of that. It will immediately be observed that when such assurances become necessary the state of a young lady's affections is already ambiguous; and indeed the girl made no attempt to dissimulate (to her finer intelligence) that "appeal of type"—she had a ready name for it—to which her gallant hovering gentleman caused her wonderingly to respond. She was fully aware that she liked it, this so unalloyed image of the simple candid manly healthy English temperament. She spoke to herself of it as if she liked the man for it instead of her liking it for the man. She cherished the thought of his bravery, which she had never in the least seen tested, enjoyed a fond view in him of the free and instinctive range of the "gentlemanly" character, and was as familiar with his good looks as if she habitually handed him out his neckties. She was perfectly conscious, moreover, of privately

279

dilating on his more adventitious merits—of the effect on her imagination of the large opportunities of so splendid a person; opportunities she hardly knew for what, but, as she supposed, for doing great things, for setting an example, for exerting an influence, for conferring happiness, for encouraging the arts. She had an ideal of conduct for a young man who should find himself in this grand position, and she tried to adapt it to her friend's behaviour as you might attempt to fit a silhouette in cut paper over a shadow projected on a wall. Bessie Alden's silhouette, however, refused to coincide at all points with his lordship's figure; a want of harmony that she sometimes deplored beyond discretion. It was his own affair she at moments told herself—it wasn't *her* concern the least in the world. When he was absent it was of course less striking—then he might have seemed sufficiently to unite high responsibilities with high braveries. But when he sat there within sight, laughing and talking with his usual effect of natural salubrity and mental mediocrity, she took the measure of his shortcoming and felt acutely that if his position was, so to speak, heroic, there was little of that large line in the young man himself. Then her imagination wandered away from him—very far away; for it was an incontestable fact that at these moments he lagged ever so much behind it. He affected her as on occasion, dreadful to say, almost *actively* stupid. It may have been that while she so curiously inquired and so critically brooded *her* personal wit, her presence of mind, made no great show—though it is also possible that she sometimes positively charmed, or at least interested, her friend by this very betrayal of the frequent, the distant and unreported, excursion. So it would have hung together that a part of her unconscious appeal to him from the first had been in his feeling her judge and appraise him more freely and irresponsibly—more at her ease and her leisure, as it were—than several young ladies with whom he had passed for adventurously intimate. To be convinced of her "cleverness" and yet also to be aware of her appreciation—when the cleverness might have been after all but dangerous and complicating—all made, to Lord Lambeth's sense, for convenience and cheer. Hadn't he compassed the satisfaction, that high aim of young men greatly placed and greatly moneyed, of being liked for himself? It was true a cynical counsellor might have whispered to him: "Liked for yourself? Ah, not so very awfully *much*!" He had at any rate the constant hope of adding to that quantity.

It may not seem to fit in—but the truth was strange—that Bessie Alden, when he struck her as "deficient," found herself aspiring by that very reason to some finer way of liking him. This was fairly indeed on grounds of conscience—because she felt he had been thoroughly "nice" to her sister and so deemed it no more than fair that she should think as well of him as he thought of her. The effort in question was possibly sometimes not so successful as it might have been, the result being at moments an irritation, which, though consciously vague, was yet, with inconsequence, acute enough to express itself in hostile criticism of several British institutions. Bessie went to entertainments at which she met Lord Lambeth, but also to others at which he was neither actually nor imaginably present; and it was chiefly at these latter that she encountered those literary and artistic celebrities of whom mention has been made. After a while she reduced the matter to a principle. If he should appear anywhere she might take it for a flat sign that there would be neither poets nor philosophers; and as a result—for it was almost a direct result—she used to enumerate to the young man these objects of her admiration.

"You seem to be awfully fond of that sort of people," he said one day as if the idea had just occurred to him.

"They're the people in England I'm most curious to see," she promptly replied.

"I suppose that's because you've read so much," Lord Lambeth gallantly threw off.

"I've *not* read so much. It's because we think so much of them at home."

"Oh I see! In your so awfully clever Boston."

"Not only in our awfully clever Boston, but in our just commonly clever everywhere. We hold them in great honour," said Bessie. "It's they who go to the best dinner-parties."

"I daresay you're right. I can't say I know many of them."

"It's a pity you don't," she returned. "It would do you some good."

"I daresay it would," said the young man very humbly. "But I must say I don't like the looks of some of them."

"Neither do I—of some of them. But there are all kinds, and many of them are charming."

"I've talked with two or three of them," Lord Lambeth went on, "and I thought they had a kind of fawning manner."

"Why should they fawn?" Bessie demanded.

"I'm sure I don't know. Why indeed?"

"Perhaps you only thought so," she suggested.

"Well, of course," her companion allowed, "that's a kind of thing that can't be proved."

"In America they don't fawn," she went on.

"Don't they? Ah, well, then they must be better company."

She had a pause. "That's one of the few things I don't like about England—your keeping the distinguished people apart."

"How do you mean, apart?"

"Why, letting them come only to certain places. You never see them."

All his pleasant face wondered—he seemed to take it as another of her rather stiff riddles. "What people do you mean?"

"The eminent people; the authors and artists; the clever people."

"Oh there are other eminent people besides those!" said Lord Lambeth.

"Well, you certainly keep them apart," Bessie earnestly contended.

"And there are plenty of other clever people."

It was spoken with a fine simple faith, yet the tone of it made her laugh. "'Plenty'? How many?"

On another occasion—just after a dinner-party—she mentioned something else in England she didn't like.

"Oh I say!" he cried; "haven't you abused us enough?"

"I've never abused you at all," said Bessie; "but I don't like your 'precedence.'"

She was to feel relieved at his not taking it solemnly. "It isn't *my* precedence!"

"Yes, it's yours—just exactly yours; and I think it's odious," she insisted.

"I never saw such a young lady for discussing things! Has some one had the impudence to go before you?" Lord Lambeth asked.

"It's not the going before me I object to," said Bessie; "it's their pretending they've a right to do it—a right I should grovellingly recognise."

"I never saw such a person, either, for not 'recognising,' let alone for not 'grovelling.' Every one here has to grovel to somebody or to something—and no doubt it's all beastly. But one takes the thick with the thin, and it saves a lot of trouble."

"It *makes* a lot of trouble, by which I mean a lot of ugliness. It's horrid!" Bessie maintained.

"But how would you have the first people go?" the young man asked. "They can't go last, you know."

"Whom do you mean by the first people?"

"Ah, if you mean to question first principles!" said Lord Lambeth.

"If those are your first principles no wonder some of your arrangements are horrid!" she cried, with a charming but not wholly sincere ferocity. "I'm a silly chit, no doubt, so of course I go last; but imagine what Kitty must feel on being informed that she's not at liberty to budge till certain other ladies have passed out!"

"Oh I say, she's not 'informed'!" he protested. "No one would do such a thing as that."

"She's made to feel it—as if they were afraid she'd make a rush for the door. No, you've a lovely country"—she clung as for consistency to her discrimination—"but your precedence is horrid."

"I certainly shouldn't think your sister would like it," Lord Lambeth said, with even exaggerated gravity. But she couldn't induce him—amused as he almost always was at the effect of giving her, as he called it, her head—to join her in more formal reprobation of this repulsive custom, which he spoke of as a convenience she would destroy without offering a better in its place.

VI

Percy Beaumont had all this time been a very much less frequent visitor at Jones's Hotel than his former fellow traveller; he had in fact called but twice on the two American ladies. Lord Lambeth, who often saw him, reproached him with his neglect and declared that though Mrs. Westgate had said nothing about it he made no doubt she was secretly wounded by it. "She suffers too much to speak," said his comrade.

"That's all gammon," Percy returned; "there's a limit to what people can suffer!" And though sending no apologies to Jones's Hotel he undertook in a manner to explain his absence. "You're always there yourself, confound you, and that's reason enough for my not going."

"I don't see why. There's enough for both of us."

"Well, I don't care to be a witness of your reckless passion," said Percy Beaumont.

His friend turned on him a cold eye and for a moment said nothing, presently, however, speaking a little stiffly. "My passion doesn't make such a show as you might suppose, considering what a demonstrative beggar I am."

"I don't want to know anything about it—anything whatever," said Beaumont. "Your mother asks me every time she sees me whether I believe you're really lost—and Lady Pimlico does the same. I prefer to be able to answer that I'm in complete ignorance, that I never go there. I stay away for consistency's sake. As I said the other day, they must look after you themselves."

"Well, you're wonderfully considerate," the young man returned. "They never question *me*."

"They're afraid of you. They're afraid of annoying you and making you worse. So they go to work very cautiously, and, somewhere or other, they get their information. They know a great deal about you. They know you've been with those ladies to the dome of Saint Paul's and—where was the other place?—to the Thames Tunnel."

"If all their knowledge is as accurate as that it must be very valuable," said Lord Lambeth.

"Well, at any rate, they know you've been visiting the 'sights of the metropolis.' They think—very naturally, as it seems to me—that when you take to visiting the sights of the metropolis with a little nobody of an American girl something may be supposed to be 'up.'" The young man met this remark with scornful laughter, but his companion continued after a pause: "I told you just now that I cultivate my ignorance, but I find I can no longer stand my suspense. I confess I do want to know whether you propose to marry Miss Alden."

On this point Lord Lambeth gave his questioner no prompt satisfaction; he only mused—frowningly, portentously. "By Jove they go rather too far. They *shall* have cause to worry—I promise them."

Percy Beaumont, however, continued to aim at lucidity. "You don't, it's true, quite redeem your threats. You said the other day you'd make your mother call."

Lord Lambeth just hung fire. "Well, I asked her to."

"And she declined?"

"Yes, but she shall do it yet."

"Upon my word," said Percy, "if she gets much more scared I verily believe she will." His friend watched him on this, and he went on. "She'll go to the girl herself."

"How do you mean 'go' to her?"

"She'll try to get 'at' her—to square her. She won't care what she does."

Lord Lambeth turned away in silence; he took twenty steps and slowly returned. "She had better take care what she does. I've invited Mrs. Westgate and Miss Alden to Branches, and this evening I shall name a day."

"And shall you invite your mother and your sisters to meet them?"

Lord Lambeth indulged in one of his rare discriminations. "I shall give them the opportunity."

"That will touch the Duchess up," said Percy Beaumont. "I 'guess' she'll come."

"She may do as she pleases."

"Then do you really propose to marry the little sister?"

"I like the way you talk about it!" the young man cried. "She won't gobble me down. Don't be afraid."

"She won't leave you on your knees," Percy declared. "What the devil's the inducement?"

"You talk about proposing—wait till I *have* proposed," Lord Lambeth went on.

His friend looked at him harder. "That's right, my dear chap. Think of *all* the bearings."

"She's a charming girl," pursued his lordship.

"Of course she's a charming girl. I don't know a girl more charming—in a very quiet way. But there are other charming girls—charming in all sorts of ways—nearer home."

"I particularly like her spirit," said Bessie's admirer—almost as on a policy of aggravation.

"What's the peculiarity of her spirit?"

"She's not afraid, and she says things out and thinks herself as good as any one. She's the only girl I've ever seen," Lord Lambeth explained, "who hasn't seemed to me dying to marry me."

Mr. Beaumont considered it. "How do you know she isn't dying if you haven't felt her pulse? I mean if you haven't asked her?"

"I don't know how; but I know it."

"I'm sure she asked *me*—over there—questions enough about your property and your titles," Percy declared.

"She has done that to me too—again and again," his friend returned. "But she wants to know about everything."

"Everything? Ah, I'll warrant she wants to know. Depend upon it she's dying to marry you just as much, and just by the same law, as all the rest of them."

It appeared to give the young man, for a moment, something rather special to think of. "I shouldn't like her to refuse me—I shouldn't like that."

"If the thing would be so disagreeable then, both to you and to her, in heaven's name leave it alone." Such was the moral drawn by Mr. Beaumont; which left him practically the last word in the discussion.

Mrs. Westgate, on her side, had plenty to say to her sister about the rarity of the latter's visits and the non-appearance at their own door of the Duchess of Bayswater. She confessed, however, to taking more pleasure in this hush of symptoms than she could have taken in the most lavish attentions on the part of that great lady. "It's unmistakable," she said, "delightfully unmistakable; a most interesting sign that we've made them wretched. The day we dined with him I was really sorry for the poor boy." It will have been gathered that the entertainment offered by Lord Lambeth to his American friends had been graced by the presence of no near relation. He had invited several choice spirits to meet them, but the ladies of his immediate family were to Mrs. Westgate's sense—a sense perhaps morbidly acute—conspicuous by their hostile absence.

"I don't want to work you up any further," Bessie at last ventured to remark, "but I don't know why you should have so many theories about Lord Lambeth's poor mother. You know a great many young men in New York without knowing their mothers."

Mrs. Westgate rested deep eyes on her sister and then turned away. "My dear Bessie, you're superb!"

"One thing's certain"—the girl continued not to blench at her irony. "If I believed I were a cause of annoyance, however unwitting, to Lord Lambeth's family I should insist—"

"Insist on my leaving England?" Mrs. Westgate broke in.

"No, not that. I want to go to the National Gallery again; I want to see Stratford-on-Avon and Canterbury Cathedral. But I should insist on his ceasing relations with us."

"That would be very modest and very pretty of you—but you wouldn't do it at this point."

"Why do you say 'at this point'?" Bessie asked. "Have I ceased to be modest?"

"You care for him too much. A month ago, when you said you didn't, I believe it was quite true. But at present, my dear child," said Mrs. Westgate, "you wouldn't find it quite so simple a matter never to see Lord Lambeth again. I've watched it come on."

"You're mistaken," Bessie declared. "You don't understand."

"Ah, you poor proud thing, don't be perverse!" her companion returned.

The girl gave the matter, thus admonished, some visible thought. "I know him better certainly, if you mean that. And I like him very much. But I don't like him enough to make trouble for him with his family. However, I don't believe in that."

"I like the way you say 'however'!" Mrs. Westgate commented. "Do you pretend you wouldn't be glad to marry him?"

Again Bessie calmly considered. "It would take a great deal more than is at all imaginable to make me marry him."

Her relative showed an impatience. "And what's the great difficulty?"

"The great difficulty is that I shouldn't care to," said Bessie Alden.

The morning after Lord Lambeth had had with his own frankest critic that exchange of ideas which has just been narrated, the ladies at Jones's Hotel received from him a written invitation to pay their projected visit to Branches Castle on the following Tuesday. "I think I've made up a very pleasant party," his lordship went on. "Several people whom you know, and my mother and sisters, who have been accidentally prevented from making your acquaintance sooner." Bessie at this lost no time in calling her sister's attention to the injustice she had done the Duchess of Bayswater, whose hostility was now proved to be a vain illusion.

"Wait till you see if she comes," said Mrs. Westgate. "And if she's to meet us at her son's house the obligation's all the greater for her to call on us."

Bessie hadn't to wait long, for it appeared that her friend's parent now descried the direction in which, according to her companion's observation, courtesy pointed. On the morrow, early in the afternoon, two cards were brought to the apartment of the American ladies—one of them bearing the name of the Duchess of Bayswater and the other that of the Countess of Pimlico. Mrs. Westgate glanced at the clock. "It isn't yet four," she said; "they've come early; they want really to find us. We'll receive them." And she gave orders that her visitors should be admitted. A few moments later they were introduced and a solemn exchange of amenities took place. The

Duchess was a large lady with a fine fresh colour; the Countess of Pimlico was very pretty and elegant.

The Duchess looked about her as she sat down—looked not especially at Mrs. Westgate. "I daresay my son has told you that I've been wanting to come to see you," she dropped—and from no towering nor inconvenient height.

"You're very kind," said Mrs. Westgate vaguely—her conscience not allowing her to assent to this proposition, and indeed not permitting her to enunciate her own with any appreciable emphasis.

"He tells us you were so kind to him in America," said the Duchess.

"We're very glad," Mrs. Westgate replied, "to have been able to make him feel a little more—a little less—a little at home."

"I think he stayed at your house," the visitor more heavily breathed, but as an overture, across to Bessie Alden.

Mrs. Westgate intercepted the remark. "A very short time indeed."

"Oh!" said the Duchess; and she continued to address her interest to Bessie, who was engaged in conversation with her daughter.

"Do you like London?" Lady Pimlico had asked of Bessie, after looking at her a good deal—at her face and her hands, her dress and her hair.

The girl was prompt and clear. "Very much indeed."

"Do you like this hotel?"

"It's very comfortable."

"Do you like stopping at hotels?" Lady Pimlico asked after a pause.

"I'm very fond of travelling, and I suppose hotels are a necessary part of it. But they're not the part I'm fondest of," Bessie without difficulty admitted.

"Oh I hate travelling!" said Lord Lambeth's sister, who transferred her attention to Mrs. Westgate.

290

"My son tells me you're going to Branches," the Duchess presently resumed.

"Lord Lambeth has been so good as to ask us," said Mrs. Westgate, who felt herself now under the eyes of both visitors and who had her customary happy consciousness of a distinguished appearance. The only mitigation of her felicity on this point was that, having taken in every item of that of the Duchess, she said to herself: "She won't know how well I'm dressed!"

"He has been so good as to tell me he expects me, but I'm not quite sure of what I can do," the noble lady exhaled.

"He had offered us the p—the prospect of meeting you," Mrs. Westgate further contributed.

"I hate the country at this season," the Duchess went on.

Her hostess melted to sweetness. "I delight in it at all seasons. And I think it now above all pleasanter than London."

But the Duchess's eyes were absent again; she was looking very fixedly at Bessie. In a minute she slowly rose, passed across the room with a great rustle and an effect of momentous displacement, reached a chair that stood empty at the girl's right hand and silently seated herself. As she was a majestic voluminous woman this little transaction had inevitably an air of somewhat impressive intention. It diffused a certain awkwardness, which Lady Pimlico, as a sympathetic daughter, perhaps desired to rectify in turning to Mrs. Westgate. "I suppose you go out immensely."

"No, very little. We're strangers, and we didn't come for the local society."

"I see," said Lady Pimlico. "It's rather nice in town just now."

"I've known it of course duskier and dingier. But we only go to see a few people," Mrs. Westgate added—"old friends or persons we particularly like."

"Of course one can't like every one," Lady Pimlico conceded.

"It depends on one's society," Mrs. Westgate returned.

The Duchess meanwhile had addressed herself to Bessie. "My son tells me the young ladies in America are so clever."

"I'm glad they made so good an impression on him," our heroine smiled.

The Duchess took the case, clearly, as no matter for grimacing; there reigned in her large pink face a meridian calm. "He's very susceptible. He thinks every one clever—and sometimes they are."

"Sometimes," Bessie cheerfully assented.

The Duchess continued all serenely and publicly to appraise her. "Lambeth's very susceptible, but he's very volatile too."

"Volatile?" Bessie echoed.

"He's very inconstant. It won't do to depend on him."

"Ah," the girl returned, "I don't recognise that description. We've depended on him greatly, my sister and I, and have found him so faithful. He has never disappointed us."

"He'll disappoint you yet," said her Grace with a certain rich force.

Bessie gave a laugh of amusement as at such a contention from such a quarter. "I suppose it will depend on what we expect of him."

"The less you expect the better," said her massive monitress.

"Well, we expect nothing unreasonable."

The Duchess had a fine contemplative pause—evidently with more to say. She made, in the quantity, her next selection. "Lambeth says he has seen so much of you."

"He has been with us very often—he has been a ministering angel," Bessie hastened to put on record.

292

"I daresay you're used to that. I'm told there's a great deal of that in America."

"A great deal of angelic ministering?" the girl laughed again.

"Is that what you call it? I know you've different expressions."

"We certainly don't always understand each other," said Mrs. Westgate, the termination of whose interview with Lady Pimlico had allowed her to revert to their elder visitor.

"I'm speaking of the young men calling so much on the young ladies," the Duchess explained.

"But surely in England," Mrs. Westgate appealed, "the young ladies don't call on the young men?"

"Some of them do—almost!" Lady Pimlico declared. "When a young man's a great *parti*."

"Bessie, you must make a note of that," said Mrs. Westgate. "My sister"—she gave their friends the benefit of the knowledge—"is a model traveller. She writes down all the curious facts she hears in a little book she keeps for the purpose."

The Duchess took it, with a noble art of her own, as if she hadn't heard it; and while she was so occupied—for this involved a large deliberation—her daughter turned to Bessie. "My brother has told us of your being so clever."

"He should have said my sister," Bessie returned—"when she treats you to such flights as that."

"Shall you be long at Branches?" the Duchess abruptly asked of her.

Bessie was to have afterwards a vivid remembrance of wondering what her Grace (she was so glad Duchesses had that predicate) would mean by "long." But she might as well somehow have wondered what the occupants of the planet Mars would. "He has invited us for three days."

"I think I must really manage it," the Duchess declared—"and my daughter too."

"That will be charming!"

"Delightful!" cried Mrs. Westgate.

"I shall expect to see a deal of you," the Duchess continued. "When I go to Branches I monopolise my son's guests."

"They must give themselves up to you," said Mrs. Westgate all graciously.

"I quite yearn to see it—to see the Castle," Bessie went on to the larger lady. "I've never seen one—in England at least; and you know we've none in America."

"Ah, you're fond of castles?"—her Grace quite took it up.

"Of the idea of them—which is all I know—immensely." And the girl's pale light deepened for the assurance. "It has been the dream of my life to live in one."

The Duchess looked at her as if hardly knowing how to take such words, which, from the ducal point of view, had either to be very artless or very aggressive. "Well," she said, rising, "I'll show you Branches myself." And upon this the noble ladies took their departure.

"What did they mean by it?" Mrs. Westgate sought to know when they had gone.

"They meant to do the friendly thing," Bessie surmised, "because we're going to meet them."

"It's too late to do the friendly thing," Mrs. Westgate replied almost grimly. "They meant to overawe us by their fine manners and their grandeur; they meant to make you *lâcher prise*."

"*Lâcher prise*? What strange things you say!" the girl sighed as fairly for pain.

"They meant to snub us so that we shouldn't dare to go to Branches," Mrs. Westgate substituted with confidence.

"On the contrary," said Bessie, "the Duchess offered to show me the place herself."

"Yes, you may depend upon it she won't let you out of her sight. She'll show you the place from morning till night."

"You've a theory for everything," our young woman a little more helplessly allowed.

"And you apparently have none for anything."

"I saw no attempt to 'overawe' us," Bessie nevertheless persisted. "Their manners weren't fine."

"They were not even good!" Mrs. Westgate declared.

Her sister had a pause, but in a few moments claimed the possession of an excellent theory. "They just came to look at me!" she brought out as with much ingenuity. Mrs. Westgate did the idea justice; she greeted it with a smile and pronounced it a credit to a fresh young mind; while in reality she felt that the girl's scepticism, or her charity, or, as she had sometimes called it appropriately, her idealism, was proof against irony. Bessie, however, remained meditative all the rest of that day and well on into the morrow. She privately ached—almost as under a dishonour—with the aftersense of having been inspected in that particular way.

On the morrow before luncheon Mrs. Westgate, having occasion to go out for an hour, left her sister writing a letter. When she came back she met Lord Lambeth at the door of the hotel and in the act of leaving it. She thought he looked considerably embarrassed; he certainly, she said to herself, had no spring. "I'm sorry to have missed you. Won't you come back?" she asked.

"No—I can't. I've seen your sister. I can never come back." Then he looked at her a moment and took her hand. "Good-bye, Mrs. Westgate—

you've been very kind to me." And with what she thought a strange sad air on his handsome young face he turned away.

She went in only to find Bessie still writing her letter; find her, that is, seated at the table with the arrested pen in her hand. She put her question after a moment. "Lord Lambeth has been here?"

Then Bessie got up and showed her a pale serious face—bending it on her for some time, confessing silently and, a little, pleading. "I told him," the girl said at last, "that we couldn't go to Branches."

Mrs. Westgate gave a gasp of temporary disappointment. "He might have waited," she nevertheless smiled, "till one had seen the Castle." An hour afterwards she spoke again. "I do wish, you know, you might have accepted him."

"I couldn't," said Bessie, with the slowest gravest gentlest of headshakes.

"He's really such a dear," Mrs. Westgate pursued.

"I couldn't," Bessie repeated.

"If it's only," her sister added, "because those women will think they succeeded—that they paralysed us!"

Our young lady turned away, but presently added: "They were interesting. I should have liked to see them again."

"So should I!" cried Mrs. Westgate, with much point.

"And I should have liked to see the Castle," said Bessie. "But now we must leave England."

Her sister's eyes studied her. "You won't wait to go to the National Gallery?"

"Not now."

"Nor to Canterbury Cathedral?"

Bessie lost herself for a little in this. "We can stop there on our way to Paris," she then said.

Lord Lambeth didn't tell Percy Beaumont that the contingency he was not prepared at all to like had occurred; but that gentleman, on hearing that the two ladies had left London, wondered with some intensity what had happened; wondered, that is, till the Duchess of Bayswater came a little to his assistance. The two ladies went to Paris—when Mrs. Westgate beguiled the journey by repeating several times: "That's what I regret; they'll think they petrified us." But Bessie Alden, strange and charming girl, seemed to regret nothing.

THE PENSION BEAUREPAS

I

I was not rich—on the contrary; and I had been told the Pension Beaurepas was cheap. I had further been told that a boarding-house is a capital place for the study of human nature. I was inclined to a literary career and a friend had said to me: "If you mean to write you ought to go and live in a boarding-house: there's no other such way to pick up material." I had read something of this kind in a letter addressed by the celebrated Stendhal to his sister: "I have a passionate desire to know human nature, and a great mind to live in a boarding-house, where people can't conceal their real characters." I was an admirer of *La Chartreuse de Parme*, and easily believed one couldn't do better than follow in the footsteps of its author. I remembered, too, the magnificent boarding-house in Balzac's *Père Goriot*—the "pension bourgeoise des deux sexes et autres," kept by Madame Vauquer, née de Conflans. Magnificent, I mean, as a piece of portraiture; the establishment, as an establishment, was certainly sordid enough, and I hoped for better things from the Pension Beaurepas. This institution was one of the most esteemed in Geneva and, standing in a little garden of its own not far from the lake, had a very homely comfortable sociable aspect. The regular entrance was, as one might say, at the back, which looked upon the street, or rather upon a little *place* adorned, like every *place* in Geneva, great or small, with a generous cool fountain. That approach was not prepossessing, for on crossing the threshold you found yourself more or less in the kitchen—amid the "offices" and struck with their assault on your nostril. This, however, was no great matter, for at the Pension Beaurepas things conformed frankly to their nature and the whole mechanism lay bare. It was rather primitive, the mechanism, but it worked in a friendly homely regular way. Madame Beaurepas was an honest little old woman—she was far advanced in life and had been keeping a pension for more than forty years—whose only faults were that she was slightly deaf, that she was fond of a surreptitious pinch of snuff, and that, at the age of seventy-four, she wore stacks of flowers in her cap. There was a legend in the house that she wasn't so deaf as she pretended and that she feigned this infirmity in order to possess herself of the secrets of her lodgers. I never indeed subscribed to this theory, convinced as I became that Madame Beaurepas had outlived the period of indiscreet curiosity. She dealt with the present and the future in the steady light of a long experience; she had been having lodgers for nearly half a century and all her concern with them was that they should pay their bills, fold their napkins and make use of the doormat. She cared very little for their secrets. "J'en ai vus de toutes les couleurs," she said to me. She had quite ceased to trouble about individuals; she cared only for types and clear categories. Her large observation had made her acquainted with a number of these and her mind become a complete collection of "heads." She flattered herself that she knew at a glance where to pigeonhole a new-comer, and if she made mistakes her deportment never betrayed them. I felt that as regards particular persons—once they conformed to the few rules—she had neither likes nor dislikes; but she was capable of expressing esteem or contempt for a species. She had her own ways, I suppose, of manifesting her approval, but her manner of indicating the reverse was simple and unvarying. "Je trouve que c'est déplacé!"—this exhausted her view of the matter. If one of her inmates had put arsenic into the *pot-au-feu* I believe Madame Beaurepas would have been satisfied to remark that this receptacle was not the place for arsenic. She could have imagined it otherwise and suitably applied. The line of misconduct to which she most objected was an undue assumption of gentility; she had no patience with boarders who gave themselves airs. "When people come chez moi it isn't to cut a figure in the world; I've never so flattered myself," I remember hearing her say; "and when you pay seven francs a day, tout compris, it comprises everything but the right to look down on the others. Yet there are people who, the less they pay, take themselves the more au sérieux. My most difficult boarders have always been those who've fiercely bargained and had the cheapest rooms."

Madame Beaurepas had a niece, a young woman of some forty odd years; and the two ladies, with the assistance of a couple of thick-waisted red-armed peasant-women, kept the house going. If on your exits and entrances you peeped into the kitchen it made very little difference; as Célestine the cook shrouded herself in no mystery and announced the day's fare, amid her fumes, quite with the resonance of the priestess of the tripod foretelling the future. She was always at your service with a grateful grin: she blacked your boots; she trudged off to fetch a cab; she would have carried your baggage, if you had allowed her, on her broad little back. She was always tramping in and out between her kitchen and the fountain in the *place*, where it often seemed to me that a large part of the preparation for our meals went forward—the wringing-out of towels and table-cloths, the washing of potatoes and cabbages, the scouring of saucepans and cleansing of water-bottles. You enjoyed from the door-step a perpetual back-view of Célestine and of her large loose woollen ankles as she craned, from the waist, over into the fountain and dabbled in her various utensils. This sounds as if life proceeded but in a makeshift fashion at the Pension Beaurepas—as if we suffered from a sordid tone. But such was not at all the case. We were simply very bourgeois; we practised the good old Genevese principle of not sacrificing to appearances. Nothing can be better than that principle when the rich real underlies it. We had the rich real at the Pension Beaurepas: we had it in the shape of soft short beds equipped with fluffy *duvets*; of admirable coffee, served to us in the morning by Célestine in person as we lay recumbent on these downy couches; of copious wholesome succulent dinners, conformable to the best provincial traditions. For myself, I thought the Pension Beaurepas local colour, and this, with me, at that time, was a grand term. I was young and ingenuous and had just come from America. I wished to perfect myself in the French tongue and innocently believed it to flourish by Lake Leman. I used to go to lectures at the Academy, the nursing mother of the present University, and come home with a violent appetite. I always enjoyed my morning walk across the long bridge—there was only one just there in those days—which spans the deep blue out-gush of the lake, and up the dark steep streets of the old Calvinistic city. The garden faced this way, toward the lake and the old town, and gave properest access to the house. There was a high wall with a double gate in the middle and flanked by a couple of ancient massive posts; the big rusty grille bristled with old-fashioned iron-work. The garden was rather mouldy and weedy, tangled and untended; but it contained a small thin-flowing fountain, several green benches, a rickety little table of the same complexion, together with three orange-trees in tubs disposed as effectively as possible in front of the windows of the salon.

II

As commonly happens in boarding-houses the rustle of petticoats was at the Pension Beaurepas the most familiar form of the human tread. We enjoyed the usual allowance of economical widows and old maids and, to maintain the balance of the sexes, could boast but of a finished old Frenchman and an obscure young American. It hardly made the matter easier that the old Frenchman came from Lausanne. He was a native of that well-perched place, but had once spent six months in Paris, where he had tasted of the tree of knowledge; he had got beyond Lausanne, whose resources he pronounced inadequate. Lausanne, as he said, "*manquait d'agrêments.*" When obliged, for reasons he never specified, to bring his residence in Paris to a close, he had fallen back on Geneva; he had broken his fall at the Pension Beaurepas. Geneva was after all more like Paris, and at a Genevese boarding-house there was sure to be plenty of Americans who might be more or less counted on to add to the resemblance. M. Pigeonneau was a little lean man with a vast narrow nose, who sat a great deal in the garden and bent his eyes, with the aid of a large magnifying glass, on a volume from the *cabinet de lecture*.

One day a fortnight after my adoption of the retreat I describe I came back rather earlier than usual from my academic session; it wanted half an hour of the midday breakfast. I entered the salon with the design of possessing myself of the day's *Galignani* before one of the little English old maids should have removed it to her virginal bower—a privilege to which Madame Beaurepas frequently alluded as one of the attractions of the establishment. In the salon I found a new-comer, a tall gentleman in a high black hat, whom I immediately recognised as a compatriot. I had often seen him, or his equivalent, in the hotel-parlours of my native land. He apparently supposed himself to be at the present moment in an hotel-parlour; his hat was on his head or rather half off it—pushed back from his forehead and more suspended than poised. He stood before a table on which old newspapers were scattered; one of these he had taken up and, with his eye-glass on his nose, was holding out at arm's length. It was that honourable but extremely diminutive sheet the *Journal de Genève*, a newspaper then of about the size

301

of a pocket-handkerchief. As I drew near, looking for my *Galignani*, the tall gentleman gave me, over the top of his eyeglass, a sad and solemn stare. Presently, however, before I had time to lay my hand on the object of my search, he silently offered me the *Journal de Genève*.

"It appears," he said, "to be the paper of the country."

"Yes," I answered, "I believe it's the best."

He gazed at it again, still holding it at arm's-length as if it had been a looking-glass. "Well," he concluded, "I suppose it's natural a small country should have small papers. You could wrap this one up, mountains and all, in one of our dailies!"

I found my *Galignani* and went off with it into the garden, where I seated myself on a bench in the shade. Presently I saw the tall gentleman in the hat appear at one of the open windows of the salon and stand there with his hands in his pockets and his legs a little apart. He looked infinitely bored, and—I don't know why—I immediately felt sorry for him. He hadn't at all—as M. Pigeonneau, for instance, in his way, had it—the romantic note; he looked just a jaded, faded, absolutely voided man of business. But after a little he came into the garden and began to stroll about; and then his restless helpless carriage and the vague unacquainted manner in which his eyes wandered over the place seemed to make it proper that, as an older resident, I should offer him a certain hospitality. I addressed him some remark founded on our passage of a moment before, and he came and sat down beside me on my bench, clasping one of his long knees in his hands.

"When is it this big breakfast of theirs comes off?" he inquired. "That's what I call it—the little breakfast and the big breakfast. I never thought I should live to see the time when I'd want to eat two breakfasts. But a man's glad to do anything over here."

"For myself," I dropped, "I find plenty to do."

He turned his head and glanced at me with an effect of bottomless wonder and dry despair. "You're getting used to the life, are you?"

"I like the life very much," I laughed.

"How long have you tried it?"

"Do you mean this place?"

"Well, I mean anywhere. It seems to me pretty much the same all over."

"I've been in this house only a fortnight," I said.

"Well, what should you say, from what you've seen?" my companion asked.

"Oh you can see all there is at once. It's very simple."

"Sweet simplicity, eh? Well then I guess my two ladies will know right off what's the matter with it."

"Oh everything's very good," I hastened to explain. "And Madame Beaurepas is a charming old woman. And then it's very cheap."

"Cheap, is it?" my friend languidly echoed.

"Doesn't it strike you so?" I thought it possible he hadn't inquired the terms. But he appeared not to have heard me; he sat there, clasping his knee and absently blinking at the sunshine.

"Are you from the United States, sir?" he presently demanded, turning his head again.

"Well, I guess I am, sir," I felt it indicated to reply; and I mentioned the place of my nativity.

"I presumed you were American or English. I'm from the United States myself—from New York City. Many of our people here?" he went on.

"Not so many as I believe there have sometimes been. There are two or three ladies."

"Well," my interlocutor observed, "I'm very fond of ladies' society. I think when it's really nice there's nothing comes up to it. I've got two ladies here myself. I must make you acquainted with them." And then after I had rejoined that I should be delighted and had inquired of him if he had been long in Europe: "Well, it seems precious long, but my time's not up yet. We've been here nineteen weeks and a half."

"Are you travelling for pleasure?" I hazarded.

Once more he inclined his face to me—his face that was practically so odd a comment on my question, and I so felt his unspoken irony that I soon also turned and met his eyes. "No, sir. Not much, sir," he added after a considerable interval.

"Pardon me," I said; for his desolation had a little the effect of a rebuke.

He took no notice of my appeal; he simply continued to look at me. "I'm travelling," he said at last, "to please the doctors. They seemed to think *they'd* enjoy it."

"Ah, they sent you abroad for your health?"

"They sent me abroad because they were so plaguey muddled they didn't know what else to do."

"That's often the best thing," I ventured to remark.

"It was a confession of medical bankruptcy; they wanted to stop my run on them. They didn't know enough to cure me, as they had originally pretended they did, and that's the way they thought they'd get round it. I wanted to be cured—I didn't want to be transported. I hadn't done any harm." I could but assent to the general proposition of the inefficiency of doctors, and put to my companion that I hoped he hadn't been seriously ill. He only shook his foot at first, for some time, by way of answer; but at last, "I didn't get natural rest," he wearily observed.

"Ah, that's very annoying. I suppose you were overworked."

"I didn't have a natural appetite—nor even an unnatural, when they fixed up things for me. I took no interest in my food."

"Well, I guess you'll both eat and sleep here," I felt justified in remarking.

"I couldn't hold a pen," my neighbour went on. "I couldn't sit still. I couldn't walk from my house to the cars—and it's only a little way. I lost my interest in business."

"You needed a good holiday," I concluded.

"That's what the doctors said. It wasn't so very smart of them. I had been paying strict attention to business for twenty-three years."

"And in all that time you had never let up?" I cried in horror.

My companion waited a little. "I kind o' let up Sundays."

"Oh that's nothing—because our Sundays themselves never let up."

"I guess they do over here," said my friend.

"Yes, but you weren't over here."

"No, I wasn't over here. I shouldn't have been where I was three years ago if I had spent my time travelling round Europe. I was in a very advantageous position. I did a very large business. I was considerably interested in lumber." He paused, bending, though a little hopelessly, about to me again. "Have you any business interests yourself?" I answered that I had none, and he proceeded slowly, mildly and deliberately. "Well, sir, perhaps you're not aware that business in the United States is not what it was a short time since. Business interests are very insecure. There seems to be a general falling-off. Different parties offer different explanations of the fact, but so far as I'm aware none of their fine talk has set things going again." I ingeniously intimated that if business was dull the time was good for coming away; whereupon my compatriot threw back his head and stretched his legs a while. "Well, sir, that's one view of the matter certainly. There's something to be said for that. These things should be looked at all round. That's the ground my wife took. That's the ground," he added in a moment, "that a lady would naturally take." To which he added a laugh as ghostly as a dried flower.

"You think there's a flaw in the reasoning?" I asked.

"Well, sir, the ground I took was that the worse a man's business is the more it requires looking after. I shouldn't want to go out to recreation—not even to go to church—if my house was on fire. My firm's not doing the business it was; it's like a sick child—it requires nursing. What I wanted the doctors to do was to fix me up so that I could go on at home. I'd have taken anything they'd have given me, and as many times a day. I wanted to be right there; I had my reasons; I have them still. But I came off all the same," said my friend with a melancholy smile.

I was a great deal younger than he, but there was something so simple and communicative in his tone, so expressive of a desire to fraternise and so exempt from any theory of human differences, that I quite forgot his seniority and found myself offering him paternal advice. "Don't think about all that. Simply enjoy yourself, amuse yourself, get well. Travel about and see Europe. At the end of a year, by the time you're ready to go home, things will have improved over there, and you'll be quite well and happy."

He laid his hand on my knee; his wan kind eyes considered me, and I thought he was going to say "You're very young!" But he only brought out: "*You've* got used to Europe anyway!"

III

At breakfast I encountered his ladies—his wife and daughter. They were placed, however, at a distance from me, and it was not until the pensionnaires had dispersed and some of them, according to custom, had come out into the garden, that he had an opportunity of carrying out his offer.

"Will you allow me to introduce you to my daughter?" he said, moved apparently by a paternal inclination to provide this young lady with social diversion. She was standing with her mother in one of the paths, where she looked about with no great complacency, I inferred, at the homely characteristics of the place. Old M. Pigeonneau meanwhile hovered near, hesitating apparently between the desire to be urbane and the absence of a pretext. "Mrs. Ruck, Miss Sophy Ruck"—my friend led me up.

Mrs. Ruck was a ponderous light-coloured person with a smooth fair face, a somnolent eye and an arrangement of hair, with forehead-tendrils, water-waves and other complications, that reminded me of those framed "capillary" tributes to the dead which used long ago to hang over artless mantel-shelves between the pair of glass domes protecting wax flowers. Miss Sophy was a girl of one-and-twenty, tiny and pretty and lively, with no more maiden shyness than a feminine terrier in a tinkling collar. Both of these ladies were arrayed in black silk dresses, much ruffled and flounced, and if elegance were *all* a matter of trimming they would have been elegant.

"Do you think highly of this pension?" asked Mrs. Ruck after a few preliminaries.

"It's a little rough," I made answer, "but it seems to me comfortable."

"Does it take a high rank in Geneva?"

"I imagine it enjoys a very fair fame."

"I should never dream of comparing it to a New York boarding-house," Mrs. Ruck pursued.

"It's quite in a different style," her daughter observed. Miss Ruck had folded her arms; she held her elbows with a pair of small white hands and tapped the ground with a pretty little foot.

"We hardly expected to come to a pension," said Mrs. Ruck, who looked considerably over my head and seemed to confide the truth in question, as with an odd austerity or chastity, a marked remoteness, to the general air. "But we thought we'd try; we had heard so much about Swiss pensions. I was saying to Mr. Ruck that I wondered if this is a favourable specimen. I was afraid we might have made a mistake."

"Well, we know some people who have been here; they think everything of Madame Beaurepas," said Miss Sophy. "They say she's a real friend."

Mrs. Ruck, at this, drew down a little. "Mr. and Mrs. Parker—perhaps you've heard her speak of them."

"Madame Beaurepas has had a great many Americans; she's very fond of Americans," I replied.

"Well, I must say I should think she would be if she compares them with some others."

"Mother's death on comparing," remarked Miss Ruck.

"Of course I like to study things and to see for myself," the elder lady returned. "I never had a chance till now; I never knew my privileges. Give me an American!" And, recovering her distance again, she seemed to impose this tax on the universe.

"Well, I must say there are some things I like over here," said Miss Sophy with courage. And indeed I could see that she was a young woman of sharp affirmations.

Her father gave one of his ghostly grunts. "You like the stores—that's what you like most, I guess."

The young lady addressed herself to me without heeding this charge. "I suppose you feel quite at home here."

"Oh he likes it—he has got used to the life. He says you *can*!" Mr. Ruck proclaimed.

"I wish you'd teach Mr. Ruck then," said his wife. "It seems as if he couldn't get used to anything."

"I'm used to you, my dear," he retorted, but with his melancholy eyes on me.

"He's intensely restless," continued Mrs. Ruck. "That's what made me want to come to a pension. I thought he'd settle down more."

"Well, lovey," he sighed, "I've had hitherto mainly to settle up!"

In view of a possible clash between her parents I took refuge in conversation with Miss Ruck, who struck me as well out in the open—as leaning, subject to any swing, so to speak, on the easy gate of the house of life. I learned from her that with her companions, after a visit to the British islands, she had been spending a month in Paris and that she thought she should have died on quitting that city. "I hung out of the carriage, when we left the hotel—I assure you I did. And I guess mother did, too."

"Out of the other window, I hope," said I.

"Yes, one out of each window"—her promptitude was perfect. "Father had hard work, I can tell you. We hadn't half-finished—there were ever so many other places we wanted to go to."

"Your father insisted on coming away?"

"Yes—after we had been there about a month he claimed he had had enough. He's fearfully restless; he's very much out of health. Mother and I took the ground that if he was restless in Paris he needn't hope for peace anywhere. We don't mean to let up on him till he takes us back." There was an air of keen resolution in Miss Ruck's pretty face, of the lucid apprehension of desirable ends, which made me, as she pronounced these words, direct a glance of covert compassion toward her poor recalcitrant sire. He had walked away a little with his wife, and I saw only his back and his stooping patient-looking shoulders, whose air of acute resignation was thrown into relief by the cold serenity of his companion. "He'll have to take us back in September anyway," the girl pursued; "he'll have to take us back to get some things we've ordered."

I had an idea it was my duty to draw her out. "Have you ordered a great many things?"

"Well, I guess we've ordered *some*. Of course we wanted to take advantage of being in Paris—ladies always do. We've left the most important ones till we go back. Of course that's the principal interest for ladies. Mother said she'd feel so shabby if she just passed through. We've promised all the people to be right there in September, and I never broke a promise yet. So Mr. Ruck has got to make his plans accordingly."

"And what are his plans?" I continued, true to my high conception.

"I don't know; he doesn't seem able to make any. His great idea was to get to Geneva, but now that he has got here he doesn't seem to see the point. It's the effect of bad health. He used to be so bright and natural, but now he's quite subdued. It's about time he should improve, anyway. We went out last night to look at the jewellers' windows—in that street behind the hotel.

I had always heard of those jewellers' windows. We saw some lovely things, but it didn't seem to rouse father. He'll get tired of Geneva sooner than he did of Paris."

"Ah," said I, "there are finer things here than the jewellers' windows. We're very near some of the most beautiful scenery in Europe."

"I suppose you mean the mountains. Well, I guess we've seen plenty of mountains at home. We used to go to the mountains every summer. We're familiar enough with the mountains. Aren't we, mother?" my young woman demanded, appealing to Mrs. Ruck, who, with her husband, had drawn near again.

"Aren't we what?" inquired the elder lady.

"Aren't we familiar with the mountains?"

"Well, I hope so," said Mrs. Ruck.

Mr. Ruck, with his hands in his pockets, gave me a sociable wink. "There's nothing much you can *tell* them!"

The two ladies stood face to face a few moments, surveying each other's garments. Then the girl put her mother a question. "Don't you want to go out?"

"Well, I think we'd better. We've got to go up to that place."

"To what place?" asked Mr. Ruck.

"To that jeweller's—to that big one."

"They all seemed big enough—they were *too* big!" And he gave me another dry wink.

"That one where we saw the blue cross," said his daughter.

"Oh come, what do you want of that blue cross?" poor Mr. Ruck demanded.

"She wants to hang it on a black velvet ribbon and tie it round her neck," said his wife.

310

"A black velvet ribbon? Not much!" cried the young lady. "Do you suppose I'd wear that cross on a black velvet ribbon? On a nice little gold chain, if you please—a little narrow gold chain like an old-fashioned watch-chain. That's the proper thing for that blue cross. I know the sort of chain I mean; I'm going to look for one. When I want a thing," said Miss Ruck with decision, "I can generally find it."

"Look here, Sophy," her father urged, "you don't want that blue cross."

"I do want it—I happen to want it." And her light laugh, with which she glanced at me, was like the flutter of some gage of battle.

The grace of this demonstration, in itself marked, suggested that there were various relations in which one might stand to Miss Ruck; but I felt that the sharpest of the strain would come on the paternal. "Don't worry the poor child," said her mother.

She took it sharply up. "Come on, mother."

"We're going to look round a little," the elder lady explained to me by way of taking leave.

"I know what that means," their companion dropped as they moved away. He stood looking at them while he raised his hand to his head, behind, and rubbed it with a movement that displaced his hat. (I may remark in parenthesis that I never saw a hat more easily displaced than Mr. Ruck's.) I supposed him about to exhale some plaint, but I was mistaken. Mr. Ruck was unhappy, but he was a touching fatalist. "Well, they want to pick up something," he contented himself with recognising. "That's the principal interest for ladies."

IV

He distinguished me, as the French say; he honoured me with his esteem and, as the days elapsed, with no small share of his confidence. Sometimes he bored me a little, for the tone of his conversation was not cheerful, tending as it did almost exclusively to a melancholy dirge over the financial prostration of our common country. "No, sir, business in the United States is not what it once was," he found occasion to remark several times a day. "There's not the same spring—there's not the same hopeful feeling. You can see it in all departments." He used to sit by the hour in the little garden of the pension with a roll of American newspapers in his lap and his high hat pushed back, swinging one of his long legs and reading the *New York Herald*. He paid a daily visit to the American banker's on the other side of the Rhône and remained there a long time, turning over the old papers on the green velvet table in the centre of the Salon des Etrangers and fraternising with chance compatriots. But in spite of these diversions the time was heavy on his hands. I used at times to propose him a walk, but he had a mortal horror of any use of his legs other than endlessly dangling or crossing them, and regarded my direct employment of my own as a morbid form of activity. "You'll kill yourself if you don't look out," he said, "walking all over the country. I don't want to stump round that way—I ain't a postman!" Briefly speaking, Mr. Ruck had few resources. His wife and daughter, on the other hand, it was to be supposed, were possessed of a good many that couldn't be apparent to an unobtrusive young man. They also sat a great deal in the garden or in the salon, side by side, with folded hands, taking in, to vague ends, material objects, and were remarkably independent of most of the usual feminine aids to idleness—light literature, tapestry, the use of the piano. They lent themselves to complete displacement, however, much more than their companion, and I often met them, in the Rue du Rhône and on the quays, loitering in front of the jewellers' windows. They might have had a cavalier in the person of old M. Pigeonneau, who professed a high appreciation of their charms, but who, owing to the absence of a common idiom, was deprived, in the connexion, of the pleasures of intimacy. He knew no English, and Mrs. Ruck and her daughter had, as it seemed, an incurable mistrust of the beautiful tongue which, as the old man endeavoured to impress upon them, was pre-eminently the language of conversation.

"They have a tournure de princesse—a distinction suprême," he said to me. "One's surprised to find them in a little pension bourgeoise at seven francs a day."

312

"Oh they don't come for economy. They must be rich."

"They don't come for my beaux yeux—for mine," said M. Pigeonneau sadly. "Perhaps it's for yours, young man. Je vous recommande la maman!"

I considered the case. "They came on account of Mr. Ruck because at hotels he's so restless."

M. Pigeonneau gave me a knowing nod. "Of course he is, with such a wife as that!—a femme superbe. She's preserved in perfection—a miraculous fraîcheur. I like those large, fair, quiet women; they're often, dans l'intimité, the most agreeable. I'll warrant you that at heart Madame Roque is a finished coquette." And then as I demurred: "You suppose her cold? Ne vous y fiez pas!"

"It's a matter in which I've nothing at stake."

"You young Americans are droll," said M. Pigeonneau; "you never have anything at stake! But the little one, for example; I'll warrant you she's not cold. Toute menue as she is she's admirably made."

"She's very pretty."

"'She's very pretty'! Vous dites cela d'un ton! When you pay compliments to Mees Roque I hope that's not the way you do it."

"I don't pay compliments to Miss Ruck."

"Ah, decidedly," said M. Pigeonneau, "you young Americans are droll!"

I should have suspected that these two ladies wouldn't especially commend themselves to Madame Beaurepas; that as a maîtresse de salon, which she in some degree aspired to be, she would have found them wanting in a certain colloquial ease. But I should have gone quite wrong: Madame Beaurepas had no fault at all to find with her new pensionnaires. "I've no observation whatever to make about them," she said to me one evening. "I see nothing in those ladies at all déplacé. They don't complain of anything; they don't meddle; they take what's given them; they leave me tranquil. The Americans are often like that. Often, but not always," Madame Beaurepas pursued. "We're to have a specimen to-morrow of a very different sort."

"An American?" I was duly interested.

"Two Américaines—a mother and a daughter. There are Americans and Americans: when you're difficiles you're more so than any one, and when you've pretensions—ah, par exemple, it's serious. I foresee that with this little lady everything will be serious, beginning with her café au lait. She has been staying at the Pension Chamousset—my concurrente, you know, further up the street; but she's coming away because the coffee's bad. She holds to her coffee, it appears. I don't know what liquid Madame Chamousset may dispense under that name, but we'll do the best we can for her. Only I know she'll make me des histoires about something else. She'll demand a new lamp for the salon; vous allez voir cela. She wishes to pay but eleven francs a day for herself and her daughter, tout compris; and for their eleven francs they expect to be lodged like princesses. But she's very 'ladylike'—isn't that what you call it in English? Oh, pour cela, she's ladylike!"

I caught a glimpse on the morrow of the source of these portents, who had presented herself at our door as I came in from a walk. She had come in a cab, with her daughter and her luggage; and with an air of perfect softness and serenity she now disputed the fare as she stood on the steps and among her boxes. She addressed her cabman in a very English accent, but with extreme precision and correctness. "I wish to be perfectly reasonable, but don't wish to encourage you in exorbitant demands. With a franc and a half you're sufficiently paid. It's not the custom at Geneva to give a pourboire for so short a drive. I've made inquiries and find it's not the custom even in the best families. I'm a stranger, yes, but I always adopt the custom of the native families. I think it my duty to the natives."

"But I'm a native too, moi!" cried the cabman in high derision.

"You seem to me to speak with a German accent," continued the lady. "You're probably from Basel. A franc and a half are sufficient. I see you've left behind the little red bag I asked you to hold between your knees; you'll please to go back to the other house and get it. Very well, si vous me manquez I'll make a complaint of you to-morrow at the administration. Aurora, you'll find a pencil in the outer pocket of my embroidered satchel; please write down his number—87; do you see it distinctly?—in case we should forget it."

The young lady so addressed—a slight fair girl holding a large parcel of umbrellas—stood at hand while this allocution went forward, but apparently gave no heed to it. She stood looking about her in a listless manner—looking at the front of the house, at the corridor, at Célestine tucking back her apron in the doorway, at me as I passed in amid the disseminated luggage; her mother's parsimonious attitude seeming to produce in Miss Aurora neither sympathy nor embarrassment. At dinner the two ladies were placed on the same side of the table as myself and below Mrs. Ruck and her daughter—my own position being on the right of Mr. Ruck. I had therefore little observation of Mrs. Church—such I learned to be her name—but I occasionally heard her soft distinct voice.

"White wine, if you please; we prefer white wine. There's none on the table? Then you'll please get some and remember to place a bottle of it always here between my daughter and myself."

"That lady seems to know what she wants," said Mr. Ruck, "and she speaks so I can understand her. I can't understand every one over here. I'd like to make that lady's acquaintance. Perhaps she knows what *I* want, too: it seems so hard to find out! But I don't want any of their sour white wine; that's one of the things I don't want. I guess she'll be an addition to the pension."

Mr. Ruck made the acquaintance of Mrs. Church that evening in the parlour, being presented to her by his wife, who presumed on the rights conferred upon herself by the mutual proximity, at table, of the two ladies. I seemed to make out that in Mrs. Church's view Mrs. Ruck presumed too far. The fugitive from the Pension Chamousset, as M. Pigeonneau called her, was a little fresh plump comely woman, looking less than her age, with a round bright serious face. She was very simply and frugally dressed, not at all in the manner of Mr. Ruck's companions, and had an air of quiet distinction which was an excellent defensive weapon. She exhibited a polite disposition to listen to what Mr. Ruck might have to say, but her manner was equivalent to an intimation that what she valued least in boarding-house life was its social opportunities. She had placed herself near a lamp, after carefully screwing it and turning it up, and she had opened in her lap, with the assistance of a large embroidered marker, an octavo volume which I perceived to be in

German. To Mrs. Ruck and her daughter she was evidently a puzzle; they were mystified beyond appeal by her frugal attire and expensive culture. The two younger ladies, however, had begun to fraternise freely, and Miss Ruck presently went wandering out of the room with her arm round the waist of Miss Church. It was a warm evening; the long windows of the salon stood wide open to the garden, and, inspired by the balmy darkness, M. Pigeonneau and Mademoiselle Beaurepas, a most obliging little woman who lisped and always wore a huge cravat, declared they would organise a fête de nuit. They engaged in this enterprise, and the fête developed itself on the lines of half a dozen red paper lanterns hung about in the trees, and of several glasses of *sirop* carried on a tray by the stout-armed Célestine. As the occasion deepened to its climax I went out into the garden, where M. Pigeonneau was master of ceremonies.

"But where are those charming young ladies," he cried, "Mees Roque and the new-comer, l'aimable transfuge? Their absence has been remarked and they're wanting to the brilliancy of the scene. Voyez, I have selected a glass of syrup—a generous glass—for Mees Roque, and I advise you, my young friend, if you wish to make a good impression, to put aside one which you may offer to the other young lady. What's her name? Mees Cheurche? I see; it's a singular name. Ca veut dire 'église,' n'est-ce-pas? Voilà, a church where I'd willingly worship!"

Mr. Ruck presently came out of the salon, having concluded his interview with the elder of the pair. Through the open window I saw that accomplished woman seated under the lamp with her German octavo, while Mrs. Ruck, established empty-handed in an armchair near her, fairly glowered at her for fascination.

"Well, I told you she'd know what I want," he promptly observed to me. "She says I want to go right up to Appenzell, wherever that is; that I want to drink whey and live in a high latitude—what did she call it?—a high altitude. She seemed to think we ought to leave for Appenzell to-morrow; she'd got it all fixed. She says this ain't a high enough lat—a high enough altitude. And she says I mustn't go too high either; that would be just as bad; she seems to know just the right figure. She says she'll give me a list of the hotels where we must stop on the way to Appenzell. I asked her if she didn't want to go with us, but she says she'd rather sit still and read. I guess she's a big reader."

The daughter of this devotee now reappeared, in company with Miss Ruck, with whom she had been strolling through the outlying parts of the garden; and that young lady noted with interest the red paper lanterns. "Good gracious," she inquired, "are they trying to stick the flower-pots into the trees?"

"It's an illumination in honour of our arrival," her companion returned. "It's a triumph over Madame Chamousset."

"Meanwhile, at the Pension Chamousset," I ventured to suggest, "they've put out their lights—they're sitting in darkness and lamenting your departure."

She smiled at me—she was standing in the light that came from the house. M. Pigeonneau meanwhile, who had awaited his chance, advanced to Miss Ruck with his glass of syrup. "I've kept it for you, mademoiselle," he said; "I've jealously guarded it. It's very delicious!"

Miss Ruck looked at him and his syrup without making any motion to take the glass. "Well, I guess it's sour," she dropped with a small shake of her head.

M. Pigeonneau stood staring, his syrup in his hand; then he slowly turned away. He looked about at the rest of us as to appeal from Miss Ruck's insensibility, and went to deposit his rejected tribute on a bench. "Won't you give it to me?" asked Miss Church in faultless French. "J'adore le sirop, moi."

M. Pigeonneau came back with alacrity and presented the glass with a very low bow. "I adore good manners."

This incident caused me to look at Miss Church with quickened interest. She was not strikingly pretty, but in her charming irregular face was a light of ardour. Like her mother, though in a less degree, she was simply dressed.

"She wants to go to America, and her mother won't let her"—Miss Sophy explained to me her friend's situation.

"I'm very sorry—for America," I responsively laughed.

"Well, I don't want to say anything against your mother, but I think it's shameful," Miss Ruck pursued.

"Mamma has very good reasons. She'll tell you them all."

"Well, I'm sure I don't want to hear them," said Miss Ruck. "You've got a right to your own country; every one has a right to their own country."

"Mamma's not very patriotic," Aurora was at any rate not too spiritless to mention.

"Well, I call that dreadful," her companion declared. "I've heard there are some Americans like that, but I never believed it."

"Oh there are all sorts of Americans."

"Aurora's one of the right sort," cried Miss Ruck, ready, it seemed, for the closest comradeship.

"Are you very patriotic," I asked of the attractive exile.

Miss Ruck, however, promptly answered for her. "She's right down homesick—she's dying to go. If you were me," she went on to her friend, "I guess your mother would *have* to take me."

"Mamma's going to take me to Dresden."

"Well, I never heard of anything so cold-blooded!" said Miss Ruck. "It's like something in a weird story."

"I never heard Dresden was so awful a fate," I ventured to interpose.

Miss Ruck's eyes made light of me. "Well, I don't believe *you're* a good American," she smartly said, "and I never supposed you were. You'd better go right in there and talk to Mrs. Church."

"Dresden's really very nice, isn't it?" I asked of her companion.

"It isn't nice if you happen to prefer New York," Miss Ruck at once returned. "Miss Church prefers New York. Tell him you're dying to see New York; it will make him mad," she went on.

Henry James

"I've no desire to make him mad," Aurora smiled.

"It's only Miss Ruck who can do that," I hastened to state. "Have you been a long time in Europe?" I added.

"As long as I can remember."

"I call that wicked!" Miss Ruck declared.

"You might be in a worse place," I continued. "I find Europe very interesting."

Miss Ruck fairly snorted. "I was just *saying* that you wanted to pass for a European."

Well, I saw my way to admit it. "Yes, I want to pass for a Dalmatian."

Miss Ruck pounced straight. "Then you had better not come home. We know how to treat your sort."

"Were you born in these countries?" I asked of Aurora Church.

"Oh no—I came to Europe a small child. But I remember America a little, and it seems delightful."

"Wait till you see it again. It's just too lovely," said Miss Ruck.

"The grandest country in all the world," I added.

Miss Ruck began to toss her head. "Come away, my dear. If there's a creature I despise it's a man who tries to say funny things about his own country."

But Aurora lingered while she all appealingly put it to me. "Don't you think one can be tired of Europe?"

"Well—as one may be tired of life."

"Tired of the life?" cried Miss Ruck. "Father was tired of it after three weeks."

319

"I've been here sixteen years," her friend went on, looking at me as for some charming intelligence. "It used to be for my education. I don't know what it's for now."

"She's beautifully educated," Miss Ruck guaranteed. "She knows four languages."

"I'm not very sure I know English!"

"You should go to Boston!" said our companion. "They speak splendidly in Boston."

"C'est mon rêve," said Aurora, still looking at me. "Have you been all over Europe," I asked—"in all the different countries?"

She consulted her reminiscences. "Everywhere you can find a pension. Mamma's devoted to pensions. We've lived at one time or another in every pension in Europe—say at some five or six hundred."

"Well, I should think you had seen about enough!" Miss Ruck exhaled.

"It's a delightful way of seeing Europe"—our friend rose to a bright high irony. "You may imagine how it has attached me to the different countries. I have such charming souvenirs! There's a pension awaiting us now at Dresden—eight francs a day, without wine. That's so much beyond our mark that mamma means to make them give us wine. Mamma's a great authority on pensions; she's known, that way, all over Europe. Last winter we were in Italy, and she discovered one at Piacenza—four francs a day. We made economies."

"Your mother doesn't seem to mingle much," observed Miss Ruck, who had glanced through the window at Mrs. Church's concentration.

"No, she doesn't mingle, except in the native society. Though she lives in pensions she detests our vulgar life."

"'Vulgar'?" cried Miss Ruck. "Why then does she skimp so?" This young woman had clearly no other notion of vulgarity.

"Oh because we're so poor; it's the cheapest way to live. We've tried having a cook, but the cook always steals. Mamma used to set me to watch her; that's the way I passed my jeunesse—my belle jeunesse. We're frightfully poor," she went on with the same strange frankness—a curious mixture of girlish grace and conscious cynicism. "Nous n'avons pas le sou. That's one of the reasons we don't go back to America. Mamma says we could never afford to live there."

"Well, any one can see that you're an American girl," Miss Ruck remarked in a consolatory manner. "I can tell an American girl a mile off. You've got the natural American style."

"I'm afraid I haven't the natural American clothes," said Aurora in tribute to the other's splendour.

"Well, your dress was cut in France; any one can see that."

"Yes," our young lady laughed, "my dress was cut in France—at Avranches."

"Well, you've got a lovely figure anyway," pursued her companion.

"Ah," she said for the pleasantry of it, "at Avranches, too, my figure was admired." And she looked at me askance and with no clear poverty of intention. But I was an innocent youth and I only looked back at her and wondered. She was a great deal nicer than Miss Ruck, and yet Miss Ruck wouldn't have said that in that way. "I try to be the American girl," she continued; "I do my best, though mamma doesn't at all encourage it. I'm very patriotic. I try to strike for freedom, though mamma has brought me up à la française; that is as much as one can in pensions. For instance I've never been out of the house without mamma—oh never never! But sometimes I despair; American girls do come out so with things. I can't come out, I can't rush in, like that. I'm awfully pinched, I'm always afraid. But I do what I can, as you see. Excusez du peu!"

I thought this young lady of an inspiration at least as untrammelled as her unexpatriated sisters, and her despondency in the true note of much of their predominant prattle. At the same time she had by no means caught, as it seemed to me, what Miss Ruck called the natural American style. Whatever her style was, however, it had a fascination—I knew not what (as I called it) distinction, and yet I knew not what odd freedom.

The young ladies began to stroll about the garden again, and I enjoyed their society until M. Pigeonneau's conception of a "high time" began to languish.

<h2 style="text-align:center"><u>V</u></h2>

Mr. Ruck failed to take his departure for Appenzell on the morrow, in spite of the eagerness to see him off quaintly attributed by him to Mrs. Church. He continued on the contrary for many days after to hang about the garden, to wander up to the banker's and back again, to engage in desultory conversation with his fellow boarders, and to endeavour to assuage his constitutional restlessness by perusal of the American journals. But it was at least on the morrow that I had the honour of making Mrs. Church's acquaintance. She came into the salon after the midday breakfast, her German octavo under her arm, and appealed to me for assistance in selecting a quiet corner.

"Would you very kindly," she said, "move that large fauteuil a little more this way? Not the largest; the one with the little cushion. The fauteuils here are very insufficient; I must ask Madame Beaurepas for another. Thank you; a little more to the left, please; that will do. Are you particularly engaged?" she inquired after she had seated herself. "If not I should like briefly to converse with you. It's some time since I've met a young American of your—what shall I call it?—affiliations. I've learned your name from Madame Beaurepas; I must have known in other days some of your people. I ask myself what has become of all my friends. I used to have a charming little circle at home, but now I meet no one I either know or desire to know. Don't you think there's a great difference between the people one meets and the people one would like to meet? Fortunately, sometimes," my patroness graciously added, "there's no great difference. I suppose you're a specimen—and I take you for a good one," she imperturbably went on—"of modern young America. Tell me, then, what modern young America is thinking of in these strange days of ours. What are its feelings, its opinions, its aspirations? What is its *ideal*?" I had seated myself and she had pointed this interrogation with the gaze of her curiously bright and impersonal little eyes. I felt it embarrassing to be taken for a superior specimen of modern young America and to be expected to answer for looming millions. Observing my hesitation Mrs. Church clasped her hands on the open page of her book and gave a dismal, a desperate smile. "*Has* it an ideal?" she softly asked. "Well, we must talk of this," she proceeded without insisting. "Speak just now for yourself simply. Have you come to Europe to any intelligent conscious end?"

"No great end to boast of," I said. "But I seem to feel myself study a little."

"Ah, I'm glad to hear that. You're gathering up a little European culture; that's what we lack, you know, at home. No individual can do much, of course; but one mustn't be discouraged—every little so counts."

"I see that you at least are doing your part," I bravely answered, dropping my eyes on my companion's learned volume.

"Ah yes, I go as straight as possible to the sources. There's no one after all like the Germans. That is for digging up the facts and the evidence. For conclusions I frequently diverge. I form my opinions myself. I'm sorry to say, however," Mrs. Church continued, "that I don't do much to spread the light. I'm afraid I'm sadly selfish; I do little to irrigate the soil. I belong—I frankly confess it—to the class of impenitent absentees."

"I had the pleasure, last evening," I said, "of making the acquaintance of your daughter. She tells me you've been a long time in Europe."

She took it blandly. "Can one ever be *too* long? You see it's *our* world, that of us few real fugitives from the rule of the mob. We shall never go back to that."

"Your daughter nevertheless fancies she yearns!" I replied.

"Has she been taking you into her confidence? She's a more sensible young lady than she sometimes appears. I've taken great pains with her; she's really—I may be permitted to say it—superbly educated."

"She seemed to me to do you honour," I made answer. "And I hear she speaks fluently four languages."

"It's not only that," said Mrs. Church in the tone of one sated with fluencies and disillusioned of diplomas. "She has made what we call *de fortes études*—such as I suppose you're making now. She's familiar with the results of modern science; she keeps pace with the new historical school."

"Ah," said I, "she has gone much further than I!"

She seemed to look at me a moment as for the tip of the ear of irony. "You doubtless think I exaggerate, and you force me therefore to mention the fact that I speak of such matters with a certain intelligence."

"I should never dream of doubting it," I returned, "but your daughter nevertheless strongly holds that you ought to take her home." I might have feared that these words would practically represent treachery to the young lady, but I was reassured by seeing them produce in her mother's placid surface no symptom whatever of irritation.

"My daughter has her little theories," that lady observed; "she has, I may say, her small fond illusions and rebellions. And what wonder! What would youth be without its Sturm and Drang? Aurora says to herself—all at her ease—that she would be happier in their dreadful New York, in their dreary Boston, in their desperate Philadelphia, than in one of the charming old cities in which our lot is cast. But she knows not what she babbles of—that's all. We must allow our children their yearning to make mistakes, mustn't we? But we must keep the mistakes down to as few as possible."

Her soft sweet positiveness, beneath which I recognised all sorts of really hard rigours of resistance and aggression, somehow breathed a chill on me. "American cities," I none the less threw off, "are the paradise of the female young."

"Do you mean," she inquired, "that the generations reared in those places are angels?"

"Well," I said resolutely, "they're the nicest of all girls."

"This young lady—what's her odd name?—with whom my daughter has formed a somewhat precipitate acquaintance: is Miss Ruck an angel and one of the nicest of all? But I won't," she amusedly added, "force you to describe her as she deserves. It would be too cruel to make a single exception."

"Well," I at any rate pleaded, "in America they've the easiest lot and the best time. They've the most innocent liberty."

My companion laid her hand an instant on my arm. "My dear young friend, I know America, I know the conditions of life there down to the ground. There's perhaps no subject on which I've reflected more than on our national idiosyncrasies."

"To the effect, I see, of your holding them in horror," I said a little roughly.

Rude indeed as was my young presumption Mrs. Church had still her cultivated patience, even her pity, for it. "We're very crude," she blandly remarked, "and we're proportionately indigestible." And lest her own refined strictures should seem to savour of the vice she deprecated she went on to explain. "There are two classes of minds, you know—those that hold back and those that push forward. My daughter and I are not pushers; we move with the slow considerate steps to which a little dignity may still cling. We like the old trodden paths; we like the old old world."

"Ah," said I, "you know what you like. There's a great virtue in that."

"Yes, we like Europe; we prefer it. We like the opportunities of Europe; we like the *rest*. There's so much in that, you know. The world seems to me to be hurrying, pressing forward so fiercely, without knowing in the least where it's going. 'Whither?' I often ask in my little quiet way. But I've yet to learn that any one can tell me."

"You're a grand old conservative," I returned while I wondered whether I myself might have been able to meet her question.

Mrs. Church gave me a smile that was equivalent to a confession. "I wish to retain a wee bit—just a wee bit. Surely we've done so much we might rest a while; we might pause. That's all my feeling—just to stop a little, to wait, to take breath. I've seen so many changes. I want to draw in, to draw in—to hold back, to hold back."

"You shouldn't hold your daughter back!" I laughed as I got up. I rose not by way of closing our small discussion, for I felt my friend's exposition of her views to be by no means complete, but in order to offer a chair to Miss Aurora, who at this moment drew near. She thanked me and remained standing, but without at first, as I noticed, really facing her parent.

"You've been engaged with your new acquaintance, my dear?" this lady inquired.

"Yes, mamma," said the girl with a sort of prompt sweet dryness.

"Do you find her very edifying?"

Aurora had a silence; then she met her mother's eyes. "I don't know, mamma. She's very fresh."

I ventured a respectful laugh. "Your mother has another word for that. But I must not," I added, "be indigestibly raw."

"Ah, vous m'en voulez?" Mrs. Church serenely sighed. "And yet I can't pretend I said it in jest. I feel it too much. We've been having a little social discussion," she said to her daughter. "There's still so much to be said. And I wish," she continued, turning to me, "that I could give you our point of view. Don't you wish, Aurora, that we could give him our point of view?"

"Yes, mamma," said Aurora.

"We consider ourselves very fortunate in our point of view, don't we, dearest?" mamma demanded.

"Very fortunate indeed, mamma."

"You see we've acquired an insight into European life," the elder lady pursued. "We've our place at many a European fireside. We find so much to esteem—so much to enjoy. Don't we find delightful things, my daughter?"

"So very delightful, mamma," the girl went on with her colourless calm. I wondered at it; it offered so strange a contrast to the mocking freedom of her tone the night before; but while I wondered I desired to testify to the interest at least with which she inspired me.

"I don't know what impression you ladies may have found at European firesides," I again ventured, "but there can be very little doubt of the impression you must have made there."

Mrs. Church got in motion to acknowledge my compliment. "We've spent some charming hours. And that reminds me that we've just now such an occasion in prospect. We're to call upon some Genevese friends—the family of the Pasteur Galopin. They're to go with us to the old library at the Hôtel de Ville, where there are some very interesting documents of the period of the Reformation: we're promised a glimpse of some manuscripts of poor Servetus, the antagonist and victim, you know, of the dire Calvin. Here of course one can only speak of ce monsieur under one's breath, but some day when we're more private"—Mrs. Church looked round the room—"I'll give you my view of him. I think it has a force of its own. Aurora's familiar with it—aren't you, my daughter, familiar with my view of the evil genius of the Reformation?"

"Yes, mamma—*very*," said Aurora with docility—and also, as I thought, with subtlety—while the two ladies went to prepare for their visit to the Pasteur Galopin.

VI

"She has demanded a new lamp: I told you she would!" This communication was made me by Madame Beaurepas a couple of days later. "And she has asked for a new tapis de lit, and she has requested me to provide Célestine with a pair of light shoes. I remarked to her that, as a general thing, domestic drudges aren't shod with satin. That brave Célestine!"

"Mrs. Church may be exacting," I said, "but she's a clever little woman."

"A lady who pays but five francs and a half shouldn't be too clever. C'est déplacé. I don't like the type."

"What type then," I asked, "do you pronounce Mrs. Church's?"

"Mon Dieu," said Madame Beaurepas, "c'est une de ces mamans, comme vous en avez, qui promènent leur fille."

"She's trying to marry her daughter? I don't think she's of that sort."

But Madame Beaurepas shrewdly held to her idea. "She's trying it in her own way; she does it very quietly. She doesn't want an American; she wants a foreigner. And she wants a mari sérieux. But she's travelling over Europe in search of one. She would like a magistrate."

"A magistrate?"

"A gros bonnet of some kind; a professor or a deputy."

"I'm awfully sorry for the poor girl," I found myself moved to declare.

"You needn't pity her too much; she's a *fine mouche*—a sly thing."

"Ah, for that, no!" I protested. "She's no fool, but she's an honest creature."

My hostess gave an ancient grin. "She has hooked you, eh? But the mother won't have you."

I developed my idea without heeding this insinuation. "She's a charming girl, but she's a shrewd politician. It's a necessity of her case. She's less submissive to her mother than she has to pretend to be. That's in self-defence. It's to make her life possible."

"She wants to get away from her mother"—Madame Beaurepas so far confirmed me. "She wants to *courir les champs*."

"She wants to go to America, her native country."

"Precisely. And she'll certainly manage it."

"I hope so!" I laughed.

"Some fine morning—or evening—she'll go off with a young man; probably with a young American."

"Allons donc!" I cried with disgust.

"That will be quite America enough," pursued my cynical hostess. "I've kept a boarding-house for nearly half a century. I've seen that type."

"Have such things as that happened chez vous?" I asked.

"Everything has happened chez moi. But nothing has happened more than once. Therefore this won't happen here. It will be at the next place they go to, or the next. Besides, there's here no young American pour la partie—none except you, monsieur. You're susceptible but you're too reasonable."

"It's lucky for you I'm reasonable," I answered. "It's thanks to my cold blood you escape a scolding!"

One morning about this time, instead of coming back to breakfast at the pension after my lectures at the Academy, I went to partake of this meal with a fellow student at an ancient eating-house in the collegiate quarter. On separating from my friend I took my way along that charming public walk known in Geneva as the Treille, a shady terrace, of immense elevation, overhanging a stretch of the lower town. Here are spreading trees and well-worn benches, and over the tiles and chimneys of the *ville basse* a view of the snow-crested Alps. On the other side, as you turn your back to the view, the high level is overlooked by a row of tall sober-faced *hôtels*, the dwellings of the local aristocracy. I was fond of the place, resorting to it for stimulation of my sense of the social scene at large. Presently, as I lingered there on this occasion, I became aware of a gentleman seated not far from where I stood, his back to the Alpine chain, which this morning was all radiant, and a newspaper unfolded in his lap. He wasn't reading, however; he only stared before him in gloomy contemplation. I don't know whether I recognised first the newspaper or its detainer; one, in either case, would have helped me to identify the other. One was the *New York Herald*—the other of course was Mr. Ruck. As I drew nearer he moved his eyes from the stony succession, the grey old high-featured house-masks, on the other side of the terrace, and I knew by the expression of his face just how he had been feeling about these distinguished abodes. He had made up his mind that their proprietors were a "mean" narrow-minded unsociable company that plunged its knotted roots into a superfluous past. I endeavoured therefore, as I sat down beside him, to strike a pleasanter note.

"The Alps, from here, do make a wondrous show!"

"Yes, sir," said Mr. Ruck without a stir, "I've examined the Alps. Fine thing in its way, the view—fine thing. Beauties of nature—that sort of thing. We came up on purpose to look at it."

"Your ladies then have been with you?"

"Yes—I guess they're fooling round. They're awfully restless. They keep saying *I'm* restless, but I'm as quiet as a sleeping child to *them*. It takes," he added in a moment dryly, "the form of an interest in the stores."

"And are the stores what they're after now?"

"Yes—unless this is one of the days the stores don't keep. They regret them, but I wish there were more of them! They told me to sit here a while and they'd just have a look. I generally know what that means—it's *their* form of scenery. But that's the principal interest for ladies," he added, retracting his irony. "We thought we'd come up here and see the cathedral; Mrs. Church seemed to think it a dead loss we shouldn't see the cathedral, especially as we hadn't seen many yet. And I had to come up to the banker's anyway. Well, we certainly saw the cathedral. I don't know as we're any the better for it, and I don't know as I should know it again. But we saw it anyway, stone by stone—and heard about it century by century. I don't know as I should want to go there regularly, but I suppose it will give us in conversation a kind of hold on Mrs. Church, hey? I guess we want something of that kind. Well," Mr. Ruck continued, "I stepped in at the banker's to see if there wasn't something, and they handed me out an old *Herald*."

"Well, I hope the *Herald's* full of good news," I returned.

"Can't say it is. Damned bad news."

"Political," I inquired, "or commercial?"

"Oh hang politics! It's business, sir. There *ain't* any business. It's all gone to—" and Mr. Ruck became profane. "Nine failures in one day, and two of them in our locality. What do you say to that?"

330

"I greatly hope they haven't inconvenienced you," was all I could gratify him with.

"Well, I guess they haven't affected me quite desirably. So many houses on fire, that's all. If they happen to take place right where you live they don't increase the value of your own property. When mine catches I suppose they'll write and tell me—one of these days when they get round to me. I didn't get a blamed letter this morning; I suppose they think I'm having such a good time over here it's a pity to break in. If I could attend to business for about half an hour I'd find out something. But I can't, and it's no use talking. The state of my health was never so unsatisfactory as it was about five o'clock this morning."

"I'm very sorry to hear that," I said, "and I recommend you strongly not to think of business."

"I don't," Mr. Ruck replied. "You can't *make* me. I'm thinking of cathedrals. I'm thinking of the way they used to chain you up under them or burn you up in front of them—in those high old times. I'm thinking of the beauties of nature too," he went on, turning round on the bench and leaning his elbow on the parapet. "You can get killed over there I suppose also"— and he nodded at the shining crests. "I'm thinking of going over—because, whatever the danger, I seem more afraid not to. That's why I do most things. How do you get over?" he sighed.

"Over to Chamouni?"

"Over to those hills. Don't they run a train right up?"

"You can go to Chamouni," I said. "You can go to Grindelwald and Zermatt and fifty other places. You can't go by rail, but you can drive."

"All right, we'll drive—you can't tell the difference in these cars. Yes," Mr. Ruck proceeded, "Chamouni's one of the places we put down. I hope there are good stores in Chamouni." He spoke with a quickened ring and with an irony more pointed than commonly served him. It was as if he had been wrought upon, and yet his general submission to fate was still there. I judged he had simply taken, in the face of disaster, a sudden sublime resolution not to worry. He presently twisted himself about on his bench again and began to look out for his companions. "Well, they *are* taking a look," he resumed; "I guess they've struck something somewhere. And they've got a carriage waiting outside of that archway too. They seem to do a big business in archways here, don't they? They like to have a carriage to carry home the things—those ladies of mine. Then they're sure they've got 'em." The ladies, after this, to do them justice, were not very long in appearing. They came toward us from under the archway to which Mr. Ruck had somewhat invidiously alluded, slowly and with a jaded air. My companion watched them as they advanced. "They're right down tired. When they look like that it kind o' foots up."

"Well," said Mrs. Ruck, "I'm glad you've had some company." Her husband looked at her, in silence, through narrowed eyelids, and I suspected that her unusually gracious observation was prompted by the less innocent aftertaste of her own late pastime.

Her daughter glanced at me with the habit of straighter defiance. "It would have been more proper if *we* had had the company. Why didn't you come after us instead of sneaking there?" she asked of Mr. Ruck's companion.

"I was told by your father," I explained, "that you were engaged in sacred rites." If Miss Ruck was less conciliatory it would be scarcely, I felt sure, because she had been more frugal. It was rather because her conception of social intercourse appeared to consist of the imputation to as many persons as possible—that is to as many subject males—of some scandalous neglect of her charms and her claims. "Well, for a gentleman there's nothing so sacred as ladies' society," she replied in the manner of a person accustomed to giving neat retorts.

"I suppose you refer to the cathedral," said her mother. "Well, I must say we didn't go back there. I don't know what it may be for regular attendants, but it doesn't meet my idea of a really pleasant place of worship. Few of these old buildings do," Mrs. Ruck further mentioned.

"Well, we discovered a little lace-shop, where I guess I could regularly attend!" her daughter took occasion to announce without weak delay.

Mr. Ruck looked at his child; then he turned about again, leaning on the parapet and gazing away at the "hills."

"Well, the place was certainly not expensive," his wife said with her eyes also on the Alps.

"We're going up to Chamouni," he pursued. "You haven't any call for lace up there."

"Well, I'm glad to hear you've decided to go somewhere," Mrs. Ruck returned. "I don't want to be a fixture at an old pension."

"You can wear lace anywhere," her daughter reminded us, "if you put it on right. That's the great thing with lace. I don't think they know how to wear lace in Europe. I know how I mean to wear mine; but I mean to keep it till I get home."

Mr. Ruck transferred his melancholy gaze to her elaborately-appointed little person; there was a great deal of very new-looking detail in Miss Ruck's appearance. Then in a tone of voice quite out of consonance with his facial despondency, "Have you purchased a great deal?" he inquired.

"I've purchased enough for you to make a fuss about."

"He can't make a fuss about *that*," said Mrs. Ruck.

"Well, you'll see!"—the girl had unshaken confidence.

The subject of this serenity, however, went on in the same tone: "Have you got it in your pocket? Why don't you put it on—why don't you hang it round you?"

"I'll hang it round *you* if you don't look out!" cried Miss Ruck.

"Don't you want to show it off to this gentleman?" he sociably continued.

"Mercy, how you do carry on!" his wife sighed.

"Well, I want to be lively. There's every reason for it. We're going up to Chamouni."

"You're real restless—that's what's the matter with you." And Mrs. Ruck roused herself from her own repose.

"No, I ain't," said her husband. "I never felt so quiet. I feel as peaceful as a little child."

Mrs. Ruck, who had no play of mind, looked at her daughter and at me. "Well, I hope you'll improve," she stated with a certain flatness.

"Send in the bills," he went on, rising to match. "Don't let yourself suffer from want, Sophy. I don't care what you do now. We can't be more than gay, and we can't be worse than broke."

Sophy joined her mother with a little toss of her head, and we followed the ladies to the carriage, where the younger addressed her father. "In your place, Mr. Ruck, I wouldn't want to flaunt my meanness quite so much before strangers."

He appeared to feel the force of this rebuke, surely deserved by a man on whom the humiliation of seeing the main ornaments of his hearth betray the ascendency of that character had never yet been laid. He flushed and was silent; his companions got into their vehicle, the front seat of which was adorned with a large parcel. Mr. Ruck gave the parcel a poke with his umbrella and turned to me with a grimly penitent smile. "After all, for the ladies, that's the principal interest."

VII

Old M. Pigeonneau had more than once offered me the privilege of a walk in his company, but his invitation had hitherto, for one reason or another, always found me hampered. It befell, however, one afternoon that I saw him go forth for a vague airing with an unattended patience that attracted my sympathy. I hastily overtook him and passed my hand into his venerable arm, an overture that produced in the good old man so rejoicing a response that he at once proposed we should direct our steps to the English Garden: no scene less consecrated to social ease was worthy of our union. To the English

Garden accordingly we went; it lay beyond the bridge and beside the lake. It was always pretty and now was really recreative; a band played furiously in the centre and a number of discreet listeners sat under the small trees on benches and little chairs or strolled beside the blue water. We joined the strollers, we observed our companions and conversed on obvious topics. Some of these last, of course, were the pretty women who graced the prospect and who, in the light of M. Pigeonneau's comprehensive criticism, appeared surprisingly numerous. He seemed bent upon our making up our minds as to which might be prettiest, and this was an innocent game in which I consented to take a hand.

Suddenly my companion stopped, pressing my arm with the liveliest emotion. "La voilà, la voilà, the prettiest!" he quickly murmured; "coming toward us in a blue dress with the other." It was at the other I was looking, for the other, to my surprise, was our interesting fellow pensioner, the daughter of the most systematic of mothers. M. Pigeonneau meanwhile had redoubled his transports—he had recognised Miss Ruck. "Oh la belle rencontre, nos aimables convives—the prettiest girl in the world in effect!" And then after we had greeted and joined the young ladies, who, like ourselves, were walking arm in arm and enjoying the scene, he addressed himself to the special object of his admiration, Mees Roque. "I was citing you with enthusiasm to my young friend here even before I had recognised you, mademoiselle."

"I don't believe in French compliments," remarked Miss Sophy, who presented her back to the smiling old man.

"Are you and Miss Ruck walking alone?" I asked of her companion. "You had better accept M. Pigeonneau's gallant protection, to say nothing of mine."

Aurora Church had taken her hand from Miss Ruck's arm; she inclined her head to the side and shone at me while her open parasol revolved on her shoulder. "Which is most improper—to walk alone or to walk with gentlemen that one picks up? I want to do what's most improper."

"What perversity," I asked, "are you, with an ingenuity worthy of a better cause, trying to work out?"

"He thinks you can't understand him when he talks like that," said Miss Ruck. "But I *do* understand you," she flirted at me—"always!"

"So I've always ventured to hope, my dear Miss Ruck."

"Well, if I didn't it wouldn't be much loss!" cried this young lady.

"Allons, en marche!" trumpeted M. Pigeonneau, all gallant urbanity and undiscouraged by her impertinence. "Let us make together the tour of the garden." And he attached himself to Miss Ruck with a respectful elderly grace which treated her own lack even of the juvenile form of that attraction as some flower of alien modesty, and was ever sublimely conscious of a mission to place modesty at its ease. This ill-assorted couple walked in front, while Aurora Church and I strolled along together.

"I'm sure this is more improper," said my companion; "this is delightfully improper. I don't say that as a compliment to you," she added. "I'd say it to any clinging man, no matter how stupid."

"Oh I'm clinging enough," I answered; "but I'm as stupid as you could wish, and this doesn't seem to me wrong."

"Not for you, no; only for me. There's nothing that a man can do that's wrong, is there? *En morale*, you know, I mean. Ah, yes, he can kill and steal; but I think there's nothing else, is there?"

"Well, it's a nice question. One doesn't know how those things are taken till after one has done them. Then one's enlightened."

"And you mean you've never been enlightened? You make yourself out very good."

"That's better than making one's self out very bad, as you do."

"Ah," she explained, "you don't know the consequences of a false position."

I was amused at her great formula. "What do you mean by yours being one?"

"Oh I mean everything. For instance, I've to pretend to be a jeune fille. I'm not a jeune fille; no American girl's a jeune fille; an American girl's an intelligent responsible creature. I've to pretend to be idiotically innocent, but I'm not in the least innocent."

This, however, was easy to meet. "You don't in the least pretend to be innocent; you pretend to be—what shall I call it?—uncannily wise."

"That's no pretence. I *am* uncannily wise. You could call it nothing more true."

I went along with her a little, rather thrilled by this finer freedom. "You're essentially not an American girl."

She almost stopped, looking at me; there came a flush to her cheek. "Voilà!" she said. "There's my false position. I want to be an American girl, and I've been hideously deprived of that immense convenience, that beautiful resource."

"Do you want me to tell you?" I pursued with interest. "It would be utterly impossible to an American girl—I mean unperverted, and that's the whole point—to talk as you're talking to me now."

The expressive eagerness she showed for this was charming. "Please tell me then! How would she talk?"

"I can't tell you all the things she'd say, but I think I can tell you most of the things she wouldn't. She wouldn't reason out her conduct as you seem to me to do."

Aurora gave me the most flattering attention. "I see. She would be simpler. To do very simply things not at all simple—that's the American girl!"

I greatly enjoyed our intellectual relation. "I don't know whether you're a French girl, or what you are, but, you know, I find you witty."

"Ah, you mean I strike false notes!" she quite comically wailed. "See how my whole sense for such things has been ruined. False notes are just what I want to avoid. I wish you'd always tell me."

The conversational union between Miss Ruck and her neighbour, in front of us, had evidently not borne fruit. Miss Ruck suddenly turned round to us with a question. "Don't you want some ice-cream?"

"*She* doesn't strike false notes," I declared.

We had come into view of a manner of pavilion or large kiosk, which served as a café and at which the delicacies generally procurable at such an establishment were dispensed. Miss Ruck pointed to the little green tables and chairs set out on the gravel; M. Pigeonneau, fluttering with a sense of dissipation, seconded the proposal, and we presently sat down and gave our order to a nimble attendant. I managed again to place myself next Aurora; our companions were on the other side of the table.

My neighbour rejoiced to extravagance in our situation. "This is best of all—I never believed I should come to a café with two strange and possibly depraved men! Now you can't persuade me this isn't wrong."

"To make it wrong," I returned, "we ought to see your mother coming down that path."

"Ah, my mother makes everything wrong," she cried, attacking with a little spoon in the shape of a spade the apex of a pink ice. And then she returned to her idea of a moment before. "You must promise to tell me—to warn me in some way—whenever I strike a false note. You must give a little cough, like that—ahem!"

"You'll keep me very busy and people will think I'm in a consumption."

"Voyons," she continued, "why have you never talked to me more? Is that a false note? Why haven't you been 'attentive'? That's what American girls call it; that's what Miss Ruck calls it."

I assured myself that our companions were out of ear-shot and that Miss Ruck was much occupied with a large vanilla cream. "Because you're always interlaced with that young lady. There's no getting near you."

Aurora watched her friend while the latter devoted herself to her ice. "You wonder, no doubt, why I should care for her at all. So does mamma;

elle s'y perd. I don't like her particularly; je n'en suis pas folle. But she gives me information; she tells me about her—your—everything but *my*—extraordinary country. Mamma has always tried to prevent my knowing anything about it, and I'm all the more devoured with curiosity. And then Miss Ruck's so very fresh."

"I may not be so fresh as Miss Ruck," I said, "but in future, when you want information, I recommend you to come to me for it."

"Ah, but our friend offers to take me there; she invites me to go back with her, to stay with her. You couldn't do that, could you?" And my companion beautifully faced me on it. "Bon, a false note! I can see it by your face; you remind me of an outraged maître de piano."

"You overdo the character—the poor American girl," I said. "Are you going to stay with that delightful family?"

"I'll go and stay with any one who will take me or ask me. It's a real nostalgie. She says that in New York—in Thirty-Seventh Street near Fourth Avenue—I should have the most lovely time."

"I've no doubt you'd enjoy it."

"Absolute liberty to begin with."

"It seems to me you've a certain liberty here," I returned.

"Ah, *this*? Oh I shall pay for this. I shall be punished by mamma and lectured by Madame Galopin."

"The wife of the pasteur?"

"His digne épouse. Madame Galopin, for mamma, is the incarnation of European opinion. That's what vexes me with mamma, her thinking so much of people like Madame Galopin. Going to see Madame Galopin—mamma calls that being in European society. European society! I'm so sick of that expression; I've heard it since I was six years old. Who's Madame Galopin—who the devil thinks anything of her here? She's nobody; she's the dreariest of frumps; she's perfectly third-rate. If I like your America better than mamma I also know my Europe better."

"But your mother, certainly," I objected a trifle timidly—for my young lady was excited and had a charming little passion in her eye—"your mother has a great many social relations all over the continent."

"She thinks so, but half the people don't care for us. They're not so good as we and they know it—I'll do them that justice—so that they wonder why we should care for them. When we're polite to them they think the less of us; there are plenty of people like that. Mamma thinks so much of them simply because they're foreigners. If I could tell you all the ugly stupid tenth-rate people I've had to talk to for no better reason than that they were *de leur pays!*—Germans, French, Italians, Turks, everything. When I complain mamma always says that at any rate it's practice in the language. And she makes so much of the most impossible English too; I don't know what *that's* practice in."

Before I had time to suggest an hypothesis as regards this latter point I saw something that made me rise—I fear with an undissimulated start—from my chair. This was nothing less than the neat little figure of Mrs. Church—a perfect model of the femme comme il faut—approaching our table with an impatient step and followed most unexpectedly in her advance by the pre-eminent form of Mr. Ruck, whose high hat had never looked so high. She had evidently come in search of her daughter, and if she had commanded this gentleman's attendance it had been on no more intimate ground than that of his unenvied paternity to her guilty child's accomplice. My movement had given the alarm and my young friend and M. Pigeonneau got up; Miss Ruck alone didn't, in the local phrase, derange herself. Mrs. Church, beneath her modest little bonnet, looked thoroughly resolute though not at all agitated; she came straight to her daughter, who received her with a smile, and then she took the rest of us in very fixedly and tranquilly and without bowing. I must do both these ladies the justice that neither of them made the least little "scene."

"I've come for you, dearest," said the mother.

"Yes, dear mamma."

"Come for you—come for you," Mrs. Church repeated, looking down at the relics of our little feast, on which she seemed somehow to shed at once the lurid light of the disreputable. "I was obliged to appeal to Mr. Ruck's assistance. I was much perplexed. I thought a long time."

"Well, Mrs. Church, I was glad to see you perplexed once in your life!" cried Mr. Ruck with friendly jocosity. "But you came pretty straight for all that. I had hard work to keep up with you."

"We'll take a cab, Aurora," Mrs. Church went on without heeding this pleasantry—"a closed one; we'll enter it at once. Come, ma fille."

"Yes, dear mamma." The girl had flushed for humiliation, but she carried it bravely off; and her grimace as she looked round at us all and her eyes met mine didn't keep her, I thought, from being beautiful. "Good-bye. I've had a ripping time."

"We mustn't linger," said her mother; "it's five o'clock. We're to dine, you know, with Madame Galopin."

"I had quite forgotten," Aurora declared. "That will be even more charming."

"Do you want me to assist you to carry her back, ma'am?" asked Mr. Ruck.

Mrs. Church covered him for a little with her coldest contemplation. "Do you prefer then to leave your daughter to finish the evening with these gentlemen?"

Mr. Ruck pushed back his hat and scratched the top of his head. "Well, I don't know. How'd you like that, Sophy?"

"Well, I never!" gasped Sophy as Mrs. Church marched off with her daughter.

VIII

I had half-expected a person of so much decision, and above all of so much consistency, would make me feel the weight of her disapproval of my own share in that little act of revelry by the most raffish part of the lakeside. But she maintained her claim to being a highly reasonable woman—I couldn't but admire the justice of this pretension—by recognising my practical detachment. I had taken her daughter as I found her, which was, according to Mrs. Church's view, in a very equivocal position. The natural instinct of a young man in such a situation is not to protest but to profit; and it was clear to Mrs. Church that I had had nothing to do with Miss Aurora's appearing in public under the compromising countenance, as she regarded the matter, of Miss Ruck. Besides, she liked to converse, and she apparently did me the honour to consider that of all the inmates of the Pension Beaurepas I was the best prepared for that exercise. I found her in the salon a couple of evenings after the incident I have just narrated, and I approached her with a view to making my peace with her if this should prove necessary. But Mrs. Church was as gracious as I could have desired; she put her marker into her inveterate volume and folded her plump little hands on the cover. She made no specific allusion to the English Garden; she embarked rather on those general considerations in which her cultivated mind was so much at home.

"Always at your deep studies, Mrs. Church," I didn't hesitate freely to observe.

"Que voulez-vous, monsieur? To say studies is to say too much; one doesn't study in the parlour of a boarding-house of this character. But I do what I can; I've always done what I can. That's all I've ever claimed."

"No one can do more, and you appear to have done a great deal."

"Do you know my secret?" she asked with an air of brightening confidence. And this treasure hung there a little temptingly before she revealed it. "To care only for the *best*! To do the best, to know the best—to have, to desire, to recognise, only the best. That's what I've always done in my little quiet persistent way. I've gone through Europe on my devoted little errand, seeking, seeing, heeding, only the best. And it hasn't been for myself alone—it has been for my daughter. My daughter has had the best. We're not rich, but I can say that."

"She has had *you*, madam," I pronounced finely.

"Certainly, such as I am, I've been devoted. We've got something everywhere; a little here, a little there. That's the real secret—to get something everywhere; you always can if you *are* devoted. Sometimes it has been a little music, sometimes a little deeper insight into the history of art; sometimes into that of literature, politics, economics: every little counts, you know. Sometimes it has been just a glimpse, a view, a lovely landscape, a mere impression. We've always been on the look-out. Sometimes it has been a valued friendship, a delightful social tie."

"Here comes the 'European society,' the poor daughter's bugbear," I said to myself. "Certainly," I remarked aloud—I admit rather hypocritically—"if you've lived a great deal in pensions you must have got acquainted with lots of people."

Mrs. Church dropped her eyes an instant; taking it up, however, as one for whom discrimination was always at hand. "I think the European pension system in many respects remarkable and in some satisfactory. But of the friendships that we've formed few have been contracted in establishments of this stamp."

"I'm sorry to hear that!" I ruefully laughed.

"I don't say it for you, though I might say it for some others. We've been interested in European *homes*."

"Ah there you're beyond me!"

"Naturally"—she quietly assented. "We have the entrée of the old Genevese society. I like its tone. I prefer it to that of Mr. Ruck," added Mrs. Church calmly; "to that of Mrs. Ruck and Miss Ruck. To that of Miss Ruck in particular."

"Ah the poor Rucks *have* no tone," I pleaded. "That's just the point of them. Don't take them more seriously than they take themselves."

Well, she would see what she could do. But she bent grave eyes on me. "Are they really fair examples?"

"Examples of what?"

"Of our American tendencies."

"'Tendencies' is a big word, dear lady; tendencies are difficult to calculate." I used even a greater freedom. "And you shouldn't abuse those good Rucks, who have been so kind to your daughter. They've invited her to come and stay with them in Thirty-Seventh Street near Fourth Avenue."

"Aurora has told me. It might be very serious."

"It might be very droll," I said.

"To me," she declared, "it's all too terrible. I think we shall have to leave the Pension Beaurepas. I shall go back to Madame Chamousset."

"On account of the Rucks?" I asked.

"Pray why don't they go themselves? I've given them some excellent addresses—written down the very hours of the trains. They were going to Appenzell; I thought it was arranged."

"They talk of Chamouni now," I said; "but they're very helpless and undecided."

"I'll give them some Chamouni addresses. Mrs. Ruck will send for a *chaise à porteurs*; I'll give her the name of a man who lets them lower than you get them at the hotels. After that they *must* go."

She had thoroughly fixed it, as we said; but her large assumptions ruffled me. "I nevertheless doubt," I returned, "if Mr. Ruck will ever really be seen on the Mer de Glace—great as might be the effect there of that high hat. He's not like you; he doesn't value his European privileges. He takes no interest. He misses Wall Street all the time. As his wife says, he's deplorably restless, but I guess Chamouni won't quiet him. So you mustn't depend too much on the effect of your addresses."

"Is it, in its strange mixture of the barbaric and the effete, a frequent type?" asked Mrs. Church with all the force of her noble appetite for knowledge.

"I'm afraid so. Mr. Ruck's a broken-down man of business. He's broken-down in health and I think he must be broken-down in fortune. He has spent his whole life in buying and selling and watching prices, so that he knows how to do nothing else. His wife and daughter have spent their lives, not in selling, but in buying—with a considerable indifference to prices— and they on their side know how to do nothing else. To get something in a 'store' that they can put on their backs—that's their one idea; they haven't another in their heads. Of course they spend no end of money, and they do it with an implacable persistence, with a mixture of audacity and of cunning. They do it in his teeth and they do it behind his back; the mother protects the daughter, while the daughter eggs on the mother. Between them they're bleeding him to death."

"Ah what a picture!" my friend calmly sighed. "I'm afraid they're grossly illiterate."

"I share your fears. We make a great talk at home about education, but see how little that ideal has ever breathed on them. The vision of fine clothes rides them like a fury. They haven't an idea of any sort—not even a worse one—to compete with it. Poor Mr. Ruck, who's a mush of personal and private concession—I don't know what he may have been in the business world—strikes me as a really tragic figure. He's getting bad news every day from home; his affairs may be going to the dogs. He's unable, with his lost nerve, to apply himself; so he has to stand and watch his fortunes ebb. He has been used to doing things in a big way and he feels 'mean' if he makes a fuss about bills. So the ladies keep sending them in."

"But haven't they common sense? Don't they know they're marching to ruin?"

"They don't believe it. The duty of an American husband and father is to keep them going. If he asks them how, that's his own affair. So by way of not being mean, of being a good American husband and father, poor Ruck stands staring at bankruptcy."

Mrs. Church, with her cold competence, picked my story over. "Why, if Aurora were to go to stay with them she mightn't even have a good *nourriture*."

"I don't on the whole recommend," I smiled, "that your daughter should pay a visit to Thirty-Seventh Street."

She took it in—with its various bearings—and had after all, I think, to renounce the shrewd view of a contingency. "Why should I be subjected to such trials—so sadly éprouveé?" From the moment nothing at all was to be got from the Rucks—not even eventual gratuitous board—she washed her hands of them altogether. "Why should a daughter of mine like that dreadful girl?"

"*Does* she like her?"

She challenged me nobly. "Pray do you mean that Aurora's such a hypocrite?"

I saw no reason to hesitate. "A little, since you inquire. I think you've forced her to be."

"I?"—she was shocked. "I *never* force my daughter!"

"She's nevertheless in a false position," I returned. "She hungers and thirsts for her own great country; she wants to 'come out' in New York, which is certainly, socially speaking, the El Dorado of young ladies. She likes any one, for the moment, who will talk to her of that and serve as a connecting-link with the paradise she imagines there. Miss Ruck performs this agreeable office."

"Your idea is, then, that if she were to go with such a person to America she could drop her afterwards?"

I complimented Mrs. Church on her quickly-working mind, but I explained that I prescribed no such course. "I can't imagine her—when it should come to the point—embarking with the famille Roque. But I wish she might go nevertheless."

Mrs. Church shook her head lucidly—she found amusement in my inappropriate zeal. "I trust my poor child may never be guilty of so fatal a mistake. She's completely in error; she's wholly unadapted to the peculiar conditions of American life. It wouldn't please her. She wouldn't sympathise. My daughter's ideal's not the ideal of the class of young women to which Miss Ruck belongs. I fear they're very numerous; they pervade the place, they give the tone."

"It's you who are mistaken," I said. "There are plenty of Miss Rucks, and she has a terrible significance—though largely as the product of her weak-kneed sire and his 'absorption in business.' But there are other forms. Go home for six months and see."

"I've not, unfortunately, the means to make costly experiments. My daughter," Mrs. Church pursued, "has had great advantages—rare advantages—and I should be very sorry to believe that *au fond* she doesn't appreciate them. One thing's certain: I must remove her from this pernicious influence. We must part company with this deplorable family. If Mr. Ruck and his ladies can't be induced to proceed to Chamouni—a journey from which no traveller with the smallest self-respect can dispense himself—my daughter and I shall be obliged to retire from the field. We shall go to Dresden."

"To Dresden?" I submissively echoed.

"The capital of Saxony. I had arranged to go there for the autumn, but it will be simpler to go immediately. There are several works in the gallery with which Aurora has not, I think, sufficiently familiarised herself. It's especially strong in the seventeenth-century schools."

As my companion offered me this information I caught sight of Mr. Ruck, who lounged in with his hands in his pockets and his elbows making acute angles. He had his usual anomalous appearance of both seeking and avoiding society, and he wandered obliquely toward Mrs. Church, whose last words he had overheard. "The seventeenth-century schools," he said as if he were slowly weighing some very small object in a very large pair of scales. "Now do you suppose they *had* schools at that period?"

Mrs. Church rose with a good deal of majesty, making no answer to this incongruous jest. She clasped her large volume to her neat little bosom and looked at our luckless friend more in pity than in anger, though more in edification than in either. "I had a letter this morning from Chamouni."

"Well," he made answer, "I suppose you've got friends all round."

"I've friends at Chamouni, but they're called away. To their great regret." I had got up too; I listened to this statement and wondered. I'm almost ashamed to mention my wanton thought. I asked myself whether this mightn't be a mere extemporised and unestablished truth—a truth begotten of a deep desire; but the point has never been cleared. "They're giving up some charming rooms; perhaps you'd like them. I would suggest your telegraphing. The weather's glorious," continued Mrs. Church, "and the highest peaks are now perceived with extraordinary distinctness."

Mr. Ruck listened, as he always listened, respectfully. "Well," he said, "I don't know as I want to go up Mount Blank. That's the principal attraction, ain't it?"

"There are many others. I thought I would offer you an exceptional opportunity."

"Well," he returned, "I guess you know, and if I could *let* you fix me we'd probably have some big times. But I seem to strike opportunities—well, in excess of my powers. I don't seem able to respond."

"It only needs a little decision," remarked Mrs. Church with an air that was a perfect example of this virtue. "I wish you good-night, sir." And she moved noiselessly away.

Mr. Ruck, with his long legs apart, stood staring after her; then he transferred his perfectly quiet eyes to me. "Does she own a hotel over there? Has she got any stock in Mount Blank?" Indeed in view of the way he had answered her I thought the dear man—to whom I found myself becoming hourly more attached—had beautiful manners.

IX

The next day Madame Beaurepas held out to me with her own venerable fingers a missive which proved to be a telegram. After glancing at it I let her know that it appeared to call me away. My brother had arrived in England and he proposed I should meet him there; he had come on business and was to spend but three weeks in Europe. "But my house empties itself!" the old woman cried on this. "The famille Roque talks of leaving me and Madame Cheurche nous fait la révérence."

"Mrs. Church is going away?"

"She's packing her trunk; she's a very extraordinary person. Do you know what she asked me this morning? To invent some combination by which the famille Roque should take itself off. I assured her I was no such inventor. That poor famille Roque! 'Oblige me by getting rid of them,' said Madame Cheurche—quite as she would have asked Célestine to remove a strong cheese. She speaks as if the world were made for Madame Cheurche. I hinted that if she objected to the company there was a very simple remedy—and at present elle fait ses paquets."

"She really asked you to get the Rucks out of the house?"

"She asked me to tell them that their rooms had been let three months ago to another family. She has an aplomb!"

Mrs. Church's aplomb caused me considerable diversion; I'm not sure that it wasn't in some degree to laugh at my leisure that I went out into the garden that evening to smoke a cigar. The night was dark and not particularly balmy, and most of my fellow pensioners, after dinner, had remained indoors. A long straight walk conducted from the door of the house to the ancient grille I've described, and I stood here for some time looking through the iron bars at the silent empty street. The prospect was not enlivening and I presently turned away. At this moment I saw in the distance the door of the house open and throw a shaft of lamplight into the darkness. Into the lamplight stepped the figure of an apparently circumspect female, as they say in the old stories, who presently closed the door behind her. She disappeared in the dusk of the garden and I had seen her but an instant; yet I remained under the impression that Aurora Church, on the eve of departure, had come out to commune, like myself, with isolation.

I lingered near the gate, keeping the red tip of my cigar turned toward the house, and before long a slight but interesting figure emerged from among the shadows of the trees and encountered the rays of a lamp that stood just outside the gate. My fellow solitary was in fact Aurora Church, who acknowledged my presence with an impatience not wholly convincing.

"Ought I to retire—to return to the house?"

"If you ought," I replied, "I should be very sorry to tell you so."

"But we're all alone. There's no one else in the garden."

"It's not the first time, then, that I've been alone with a young lady. I'm not at all terrified."

"Ah, but I?" she wailed to extravagance. "I've *never* been alone—!" Quickly, however, she interrupted herself. "Bon, there's another false note!"

"Yes, I'm obliged to admit that one's very false."

She stood looking at me. "I'm going away to-morrow; after that there will be no one to tell me."

"That will matter little," I presently returned. "Telling you will do no good."

"Ah, why do you say that?" she all ruefully asked.

I said it partly because it was true, but I said it for other reasons, as well, which I found hard to define. Standing there bareheaded in the night air, in the vague light, this young lady took on an extreme interest, which was moreover not diminished by a suspicion on my own part that she had come into the garden knowing me to be there. I thought her charming, I thought her remarkable and felt very sorry for her; but as I looked at her the terms in which Madame Beaurepas had ventured to characterise her recurred to me with a certain force. I had professed a contempt for them at the time, but it now came into my head that perhaps this unfortunately situated, this insidiously mutinous young creature was in quest of an effective preserver. She was certainly not a girl to throw herself at a man's head, but it was possible that in her intense—her almost morbid—desire to render operative an ideal charged perhaps after all with as many fallacies as her mother affirmed, she might do something reckless and irregular—something in which a sympathetic compatriot, as yet unknown, would find his profit. The image, unshaped though it was, of this sympathetic compatriot filled me with a semblance of envy. For some moments I was silent, conscious of these things; after which I answered her question. "Because some things—some differences—are felt, not learned. To you liberty's not natural; you're like a person who has bought a repeating watch and is, in his satisfaction, constantly taking it out of his pocket to hear it sound. To a real American girl her liberty's a very vulgarly-ticking old clock."

"Ah, you mean then," said my young friend, "that my mother has ruined me?"

"Ruined you?"

"She has so perverted my mind that when I try to be natural I'm necessarily indecent."

I threw up hopeless arms. "That again's a false note!"

She turned away. "I think you're cruel."

"By no means," I declared; "because, for my own taste, I prefer you as—as—"

On my hesitating she turned back. "As what?"

"As you are!"

She looked at me a while again, and then she said in a little reasoning tone that reminded me of her mother's, only that it was conscious and studied, "I wasn't aware that I'm under any particular obligation to please you!" But she also gave a clear laugh, quite at variance with this stiffness. Suddenly I thought her adorable.

"Oh there's no obligation," I said, "but people sometimes have preferences. I'm very sorry you're going away."

"What does it matter to you? You are going yourself."

"As I'm going in a different direction, that makes all the greater separation."

She answered nothing; she stood looking through the bars of the tall gate at the empty dusky street. "This grille is like a cage," she said at last.

"Fortunately it's a cage that will open." And I laid my hand on the lock.

"Don't open it"; and she pressed the gate close. "If you should open it I'd go out. There you'd be, monsieur—for I should never return."

I treated it as wholly thrilling, and indeed I quite found it so. "Where should you go?"

"To America."

"Straight away?"

"Somehow or other. I'd go to the American consul. I'd beg him to give me money—to help me."

I received this assertion without a smile; I was not in a smiling humour. On the contrary I felt singularly excited and kept my hand on the lock of the gate. I believed, or I thought I believed, what my companion said, and I had—absurd as it may appear—an irritated vision of her throwing herself on consular tenderness. It struck me for a moment that to pass out of that gate with this yearning straining young creature would be to pass to some mysterious felicity. If I were only a hero of romance I would myself offer to take her to America.

In a moment more perhaps I should have persuaded myself that I was one, but at this juncture I heard a sound hostile to the romantic note. It was nothing less than the substantial tread of Célestine, the cook, who stood grinning at us as we turned about from our colloquy.

"I ask bien pardon," said Célestine. "The mother of mademoiselle desires that mademoiselle should come in immediately. M. le Pasteur Galopin has come to make his adieux to ces dames."

Aurora gave me but one glance, the memory of which I treasure. Then she surrendered to Célestine, with whom she returned to the house.

The next morning, on coming into the garden, I learned that Mrs. Church and her daughter had effectively quitted us. I was informed of this fact by old M. Pigeonneau, who sat there under a tree drinking his café-au-lait at a little green table.

"I've nothing to envy you," he said; "I had the last glimpse of that charming Mees Aurore."

"I had a very late glimpse," I answered, "and it was all I could possibly desire."

"I've always noticed," rejoined M. Pigeonneau, "that your desires are more under control than mine. Que voulez-vous? I'm of the old school. Je crois que cette race se perd. I regret the departure of that attractive young person; she has an enchanting smile. Ce sera une femme d'esprit. For the mother, I can console myself. I'm not sure *she* was a femme d'esprit, though she wished so prodigiously to pass for one. Round, rosy, potelée, she yet had not the temperament of her appearance; she was a femme austère—I made up my mind to that. I've often noticed that contradiction in American ladies. You see a plump little woman with a speaking eye and the contour and complexion of a ripe peach, and if you venture to conduct yourself in the smallest degree in accordance with these *indices*, you discover a species of Methodist—of what do you call it?—of Quakeress. On the other hand, you encounter a tall lean angular form without colour, without grace, all elbows and knees, and you find it's a nature of the tropics! The women of duty look like coquettes, and the others look like alpenstocks! However, we've still la belle Madame Roque—a real femme de Rubens, celle-là. It's very true that to talk to her one must know the Flemish tongue!"

I had determined in accordance with my brother's telegram to go away in the afternoon; so that, having various duties to perform, I left M. Pigeonneau to his ethnic studies. Among other things I went in the course of the morning to the banker's, to draw money for my journey, and there I found Mr. Ruck with a pile of crumpled letters in his lap, his chair tipped back and his eyes gloomily fixed on the fringe of the green plush table-cloth. I timidly expressed the hope that he had got better news from home; whereupon he gave me a look in which, considering his provocation, the habit of forlorn patience was conspicuous.

He took up his letters in his large hand and, crushing them together, held it out to me. "That stack of postal matter," he said, "is worth about five cents. But I guess," he added, rising, "that I know where I am by this time." When I had drawn my money I asked him to come and breakfast with me at the little brasserie, much favoured by students, to which I used to resort in the old town. "I couldn't eat, sir," he frankly pleaded, "I couldn't eat. Bad disappointments strike at the seat of the appetite. But I guess I'll go with you, so as not to be on show down there at the pension. The old woman down there accuses me of turning up my nose at her food. Well, I guess I shan't turn up my nose at anything now."

We went to the little brasserie, where poor Mr. Ruck made the lightest possible dejeuner. But if he ate very little he still moved his lean jaws—he mumbled over his spoilt repast of apprehended facts; strange tough financial fare into which I was unable to bite. I was very sorry for him, I wanted to ease him off; but the only thing I could do when we had breakfasted was to see him safely back to the Pension Beaurepas. We went across the Treille and down the Corraterie, out of which we turned into the Rue du Rhône. In this latter street, as all the world knows, prevail those shining shop-fronts of the watchmakers and jewellers for its long list of whom Geneva is famous. I had always admired these elegant exhibitions and never passed them without a lingering look. Even on this occasion, preoccupied as I was with my impending departure and with my companion's troubles, I attached my eyes to the precious tiers that flashed and twinkled behind the huge clear plates of glass. Thanks to this inveterate habit I recorded a fresh observation. In the largest and most irresistible of these repositories I distinguished two ladies, seated before the counter with an air of absorption which sufficiently proclaimed their identity. I hoped my companion wouldn't see them, but as we came abreast of the door, a little beyond, we found it open to the warm summer air. Mr. Ruck happened to glance in, and he immediately recognised his wife and daughter. He slowly stopped, his eyes fixed on them; I wondered what he would do. A salesman was in the act of holding up a bracelet before them on its velvet cushion and flashing it about in a winsome manner.

Mr. Ruck said nothing, but he presently went in; whereupon, feeling that I mustn't lose him, I did the same. "It will be an opportunity," I remarked as cheerfully as possible, "for me to bid good-bye to the ladies."

354

They turned round on the approach of their relative, opposing an indomitable front. "Well, you'd better get home to breakfast—that's what *you'd* better do," his wife at once remarked. Miss Sophy resisted in silence; she only took the bracelet from the attendant and gazed at it all fixedly. My friend seated himself on an empty stool and looked round the shop. "Well, we've been here before, and you ought to know it," Mrs. Ruck a trifle guiltily contended. "We were here the first day we came."

The younger lady held out to me the precious object in her hand. "Don't you think that's sweet?"

I looked at it a moment. "No, I think it's ugly."

She tossed her head as at a challenge to a romp. "Well, I don't believe you've any taste."

"Why, sir, it's just too lovely," said her mother.

"You'll see it some day *on* me, anyway," piped Miss Ruck.

"Not very much," said Mr. Ruck quietly.

"It will be his own fault, then," Miss Sophy returned.

"Well, if we're going up to Chamouni we want to get something here," said Mrs. Ruck. "We mayn't have another chance."

Her husband still turned his eyes over the shop, whistling half under his breath. "We ain't going up to Chamouni. We're going back to New York City straight."

"Well, I'm glad to hear that," she made answer. "Don't you suppose we want to take something home?"

"If we're going straight back I must have that bracelet," her daughter declared. "Only I don't want a velvet case; I want a satin case."

"I must bid you good-bye," I observed all irrelevantly to the ladies. "I'm leaving Geneva in an hour or two."

"Take a good look at that bracelet, so you'll know it when you see it," was hereupon Miss Sophy's form of farewell to me.

"She's bound to have something!" her mother almost proudly attested.

Mr. Ruck still vaguely examined the shop; he still just audibly whistled. "I'm afraid he's not at all well," I took occasion to intimate to his wife.

She twisted her head a little and glanced at him; she had a brief but pregnant pause. "Well, I must say I wish he'd improve!"

"A satin case, and a nice one!" cried Miss Ruck to the shopman.

I bade her other parent good-bye. "Don't wait for me," he said, sitting there on his stool and not meeting my eye. "I've got to see this thing through."

I went back to the Pension Beaurepas, and when an hour later I left it with my luggage these interesting friends had not returned.

A BUNDLE OF LETTERS

I. FROM MISS MIRANDA HOPE IN PARIS TO MRS. ABRAHAM C. HOPE AT BANGOR MAINE

September 5, 1879.

MY DEAR MOTHER,

I've kept you posted as far as Tuesday week last, and though my letter won't have reached you yet I'll begin another before my news accumulates too much. I'm glad you show my letters round in the family, for I like them all to know what I'm doing, and I can't write to every one, even if I do try to answer all reasonable expectations. There are a great many unreasonable ones, as I suppose you know—not yours, dear mother, for I'm bound to say that you never required of me more than was natural. You see you're reaping your reward: I write to you before I write to any one else.

There's one thing I hope—that you don't show any of my letters to William Platt. If he wants to see any of my letters he knows the right way to go to work. I wouldn't have him see one of these letters, written for circulation in the family, for anything in the world. If he wants one for himself he has got to write to me first. Let him write to me first and then I'll see about answering him. You can show him this if you like; but if you show him anything more I'll never write to you again.

I told you in my last about my farewell to England, my crossing the Channel and my first impressions of Paris. I've thought a great deal about that lovely England since I left it, and all the famous historic scenes I visited; but I've come to the conclusion that it's not a country in which I should care to reside. The position of woman doesn't seem to me at all satisfactory, and that's a point, you know, on which I feel very strongly. It seems to me that in England they play a very faded-out part, and those with whom I conversed had a kind of downtrodden tone, a spiritless and even benighted air, as if they were used to being snubbed and bullied *and as if they liked it*, which made me want to give them a good shaking. There are a great many people—and a great many things too—over here that I should like to get at for that purpose. I should like to shake the starch out of some of them and the dust out of the others. I know fifty girls in Bangor that come much more up to my notion of the stand a truly noble woman should take than those young ladies in England. But they had the sweetest way of speaking, as if it were a second nature, and the men are *remarkably handsome*. (You can show *that* to William Platt if you like.)

I gave you my first impressions of Paris, which quite came up to my expectations, much as I had heard and read about it. The objects of interest are extremely numerous, and the climate remarkably cheerful and sunny. I should say the position of woman here was considerably higher, though by no means up to the American standard. The manners of the people are in some respects extremely peculiar, and I feel at last that I'm indeed in *foreign parts*. It is, however, a truly elegant city (much more majestic than New York) and I've spent a great deal of time in visiting the various monuments and palaces. I won't give you an account of all my wanderings, though I've been most indefatigable; for I'm keeping, as I told you before, a most *exhaustive* journal, which I'll allow you the *privilege* of reading on my return to Bangor. I'm getting on remarkably well, and I must say I'm sometimes surprised at my universal good fortune. It only shows what a little Bangor energy and gumption will accomplish wherever applied. I've discovered none of those objections to a young lady travelling in Europe by herself of which we heard so much before I left, and I don't expect I ever shall, for I certainly don't mean to look for them. I know what I want and I always go straight for it.

I've received a great deal of politeness—some of it really most pressing, and have experienced no drawbacks whatever. I've made a great many pleasant acquaintances in travelling round—both ladies and gentlemen—and had a great many interesting and open-hearted, if quite informal, talks. I've collected a great many remarkable facts—I guess we don't know quite *everything* at Bangor—for which I refer you to my journal. I assure you my journal's going to be a splendid picture of an earnest young life. I do just exactly as I do in Bangor, and I find I do perfectly right. At any rate I don't care if I don't. I didn't come to Europe to lead a merely conventional society life: I could do that at Bangor. You know I never *would* do it at Bangor, so it isn't likely I'm going to worship false gods over here. So long as I accomplish what I desire and make my money hold out I shall regard the thing as a success. Sometimes I feel rather lonely, especially evenings; but I generally manage to interest myself in something or in some one. I mostly read up, evenings, on the objects of interest I've visited during the day, or put in time on my journal. Sometimes I go to the theatre or else play the piano in the public parlour. The public parlour at the hotel isn't much; but the piano's better than that fearful old thing at the Sebago House. Sometimes I go downstairs and talk to the lady who keeps the books—a real French lady, who's remarkably polite. She's very handsome, though in the peculiar French way, and always wears a black dress of the most beautiful fit. She speaks a little English; she tells me she had to learn it in order to converse with the Americans who come in such numbers to this hotel. She has given me lots of points on the position of woman in France, and seems to think that on the whole there's hope. But she has told me at the same time some things I shouldn't like to write to you—I'm hesitating even about putting them into my journal—especially if my letters are to be handed round in the family. I assure you they appear to talk about things here that we never think of mentioning at Bangor, even to ourselves or to our very closest; and it has struck me that people are closer—to each other—down in Maine than seems mostly to be expected here. This bright-minded lady appears at any rate to think she can tell me everything because I've told her I'm travelling for general culture. Well, I *do* want to know so much that it seems sometimes as if I wanted to know most everything; and yet I guess there are some things that don't count for improvement. But as a general thing everything's intensely interesting; I don't mean only everything this charming woman tells me, but everything I see and hear for myself. I guess I'll come out where I want.

I meet a great many Americans who, as a general thing, I must say, are not so polite to me as the people over here. The people over here—especially the gentlemen—are much more what I should call almost oppressively attentive. I don't know whether Americans are more truly sincere; I haven't yet made up my mind about that. The only drawback I experience is when

Americans sometimes express surprise that I should be travelling round alone; so you see it doesn't come from Europeans. I always have my answer ready: "For general culture, to acquire the languages and to see Europe for myself"; and that generally seems to calm them. Dear mother, my money holds out very well, and it is real interesting.

II. FROM THE SAME TO THE SAME

September 16.

Since I last wrote to you I've left that nice hotel and come to live in a French family—which, however, is nice too. This place is a kind of boarding-house that's at the same time a kind of school; only it's not like an American boarding-house, nor like an American school either. There are four or five people here that have come to learn the language—not to take lessons, but to have an opportunity for conversation. I was very glad to come to such a place, for I had begun to realise that I wasn't pressing onward quite as I had dreamed with the French. Wasn't I going to feel ashamed to have spent two months in Paris and not to have acquired more insight into the language? I had always heard so much of French conversation, and I found I wasn't having much more opportunity to practise it than if I had remained at Bangor. In fact I used to hear a great deal more at Bangor from those French-Canadians who came down to cut the ice than I saw I should ever hear at that nice hotel where was no struggle—*some* fond struggle being my real atmosphere. The lady who kept the books seemed to want so much to talk to me in English (for the sake of practice, too, I suppose)—she kind of yearned to struggle too: we don't yearn *only* down in Maine—that I couldn't bear to show her I didn't like it. The chambermaid was Irish and all the waiters German, so I never heard a word of French spoken. I suppose you might hear a great deal in the shops; but as I don't buy anything—I prefer to spend my money for purposes of culture—I don't have that advantage.

I've been thinking some of taking a teacher, but am well acquainted with the grammar already, and over here in Europe teachers don't seem to think it's *really* in their interest to let you press forward. The more you strike

360

out and realise your power the less they've got to teach you. I was a good deal troubled anyhow, for I felt as if I didn't want to go away without having at least got a general idea of French conversation. The theatre gives you a good deal of insight, and as I told you in my last I go a good deal to the brightest places of amusement. I find no difficulty whatever in going to such places alone, and am always treated with the politeness which, as I've mentioned—for I want you to feel happy about that—I encounter everywhere from the best people. I see plenty of other ladies alone (mostly French) and they generally seem to be enjoying themselves as much as I. Only on the stage every one talks so fast that I can scarcely make out what they say; and, besides, there are a great many vulgar expressions which it's unnecessary to learn. But it was this experience nevertheless that put me on the track. The very next day after I wrote to you last I went to the Palais Royal, which is one of the principal theatres in Paris. It's very small but very celebrated, and in my guide-book it's marked with *two stars*, which is a sign of importance attached only to *first-class* objects of interest. But after I had been there half an hour I found I couldn't understand a single word of the play, they gabbled it off so fast and made use of such peculiar expressions. I felt a good deal disappointed and checked—I saw I wasn't going to come out where I had dreamed. But while I was thinking it over—thinking what I *would* do—I heard two gentlemen talking behind me. It was between the acts, and I couldn't help listening to what they said. They were talking English, but I guess they were Americans.

"Well," said one of them, "it all depends on what you're after. I'm after French; that's what I'm after."

"Well," said the other, "I'm after Art."

"Well," said the first, "I'm after Art too; but I'm after French most."

Then, dear mother, I'm sorry to say the second one swore a little. He said, "Oh damn French!"

"No, I won't damn French," said his friend. "I'll acquire it—that's what I'll do with it. I'll go right into a family."

"What family'll you go into?"

361

"Into some nice French family. That's the only way to do—to go to some place where you can talk. If you're after Art you want to stick to the galleries; you want to go right through the Louvre, room by room; you want to take a room a day, or something of that sort. But if you want to acquire French the thing is to look out for some family that has got—and they mostly have—more of it than they've use for themselves. How *can* they have use for so much as they seem to *have* to have? They've got to work it off. Well, they work it off on *you*. There are lots of them that take you to board and teach you. My second cousin—that young lady I told you about—she got in with a crowd like that, and they posted her right up in three months. They just took her right in and let her have it—the full force. That's what they do to you; they set you right down and they talk *at* you. You've got to understand them or perish—so you strike out in self-defence; you can't help yourself. That family my cousin was with has moved away somewhere, or I should try and get in with them. They were real live people, that family; after she left my cousin corresponded with them in French. You've got to do *that* too, to make much real head. But I mean to find some other crowd, if it takes a lot of trouble!"

I listened to all this with great interest, and when he spoke about his cousin I was on the point of turning around to ask him the address of the family she was with; but the next moment he said they had moved away, so I sat still. The other gentleman, however, didn't seem to be affected in the same way as I was.

"Well," he said, "you may follow up that if you like; I mean to follow up the pictures. I don't believe there's ever going to be any considerable demand in the United States for French; but I can promise you that in about ten years there'll be a big demand for Art! And it won't be temporary either."

That remark may be very true, but I don't care anything about the demand; I want to know French for its own sake. "Art for art," they say; but I say French for French. I don't want to think I've been all this while without having gained an insight. . . . The very next day, I asked the lady who kept the books at the hotel whether she knew of any family that could take me to board and give me the benefit of their conversation. She instantly threw up her hands with little shrill cries—in their wonderful French way, you know—and told me that her dearest friend kept a regular place of that kind. If she had known I was looking out for such a place she would have told me before; she hadn't spoken of it herself because she didn't wish to injure the hotel by working me off on another house. She told me this was a charming family who had often received American ladies—and others, including three Tahitans—who wished to follow up the language, and she was sure I'd fall in love with them. So she gave me their address and offered to go with me to introduce me. But I was in such a hurry that I went off by myself and soon found them all right. They were sitting there as if they kind of expected me, and wouldn't scarcely let me come round again for my baggage. They seemed to have right there on hand, as those gentlemen of the theatre said, plenty of what I was after, and I now feel there'll be no trouble about *that*.

I came here to stay about three days ago, and by this time I've quite worked in. The price of board struck me as rather high, but I must remember what a chance to press onward it includes. I've a very pretty little room—without any carpet, but with seven mirrors, two clocks and five curtains. I was rather disappointed, however, after I arrived, to find that there are several other Americans here—all also bent on pressing onward. At least there are three American and two English pensioners, as they call them, as well as a German gentleman—and there seems nothing backward about *him*. I shouldn't wonder if we'd make a regular class, with "moving up" and moving down; anyhow I guess I won't be at the foot, but I've not yet time to judge. I try to talk with Madame de Maisonrouge all I can—she's the lady of the house, and the *real* family consists only of herself and her two daughters. They're bright enough to give points to our own brightest, and I guess we'll become quite intimate. I'll write you more about everything in my next. Tell William Platt I don't care a speck *what* he does.

III. FROM MISS VIOLET RAY IN PARIS TO MISS AGNES RICH IN NEW YORK

September 21.

We had hardly got here when father received a telegram saying he would have to come right back to New York. It was for something about his business—I don't know exactly what; you know I never understand those things and never want to. We had just got settled at the hotel, in some charming rooms, and mother and I, as you may imagine, were greatly annoyed. Father's extremely fussy, as you know, and his first idea, as soon as he found he should have to go back, was that we should go back with him. He declared he'd never leave us in Paris alone and that we must return and come out again. I don't know what he thought would happen to us; I suppose he thought we should be too extravagant. It's father's theory that we're always running-up bills, whereas a little observation would show him that we wear the same old *rags* FOR MONTHS. But father has no observation; he has nothing but blind theories. Mother and I, however, have fortunately a great deal of *practice*, and we succeeded in making him understand that we wouldn't budge from Paris and that we'd rather be chopped into small pieces than cross that squalid sea again. So at last he decided to go back alone and to leave us here for three months. Only, to show you how fussy he is, he refused to let us stay at the hotel and insisted that we should go into a *family*. I don't know what put such an idea into his head unless it was some advertisement that he saw in one of the American papers that are published here. Don't think you can escape from them anywhere.

There are families here who receive American and English people to live with them under the pretence of teaching them French. You may imagine what people they are—I mean the families themselves. But the Americans who choose this peculiar manner of seeing Paris must be actually just as bad. Mother and I were horrified—we declared that *main force* shouldn't remove us from the hotel. But father has a way of arriving at his ends which is more effective than violence. He worries and goes on; he "nags," as we used to say at school; and when mother and I are quite worn to the bone his triumph is assured. Mother's more quickly ground down than I, and she ends by siding with father; so that at last when they combine their forces against poor little me I've naturally to succumb. You should have heard the way father went on about this "family" plan; he talked to every one he saw about it; he used to go round to the banker's and talk to the people there—the people in the post-office; he used to try and exchange ideas about it with the waiters at the hotel. He said it would be more safe, more respectable, more economical; that I should pick up more French; that mother would learn how a French household's conducted; that he should feel more easy, and that we ourselves should enjoy it when we came to see. All this meant nothing, but that made no difference. It's positively cruel his harping on our pinching and saving when every one knows that business in America has completely recovered, that the prostration's all over and that *immense fortunes* are being made. We've been depriving ourselves of the commonest necessities for the last five years, and I supposed we came abroad to reap the benefits of it.

As for my French it's already much better than that of most of our helpless compatriots, who are all unblushingly destitute of the very rudiments. (I assure you I'm often surprised at my own fluency, and when I get a little more practice in the circumflex accents and the genders and the idioms I shall quite hold my own.) To make a long story short, however, father carried his point as usual; mother basely deserted me at the last moment, and after holding out alone for three days I told them to do with me what they would. Father lost three steamers in succession by remaining in Paris to argue with me. You know he's like the schoolmaster in Goldsmith's *Deserted Village*—"e'en though vanquished" he always argues still. He and mother went to look at some seventeen families—they had got the addresses somewhere—while I retired to my sofa and would have nothing to do with it. At last they made arrangements and I was transported, as in chains, to the establishment from which I now write you. I address you from the bosom of a Parisian ménage—from the depths of a second-rate boarding-house.

Father only left Paris after he had seen us what he calls comfortably settled here and had informed Madame de Maisonrouge—the mistress of the establishment, the head of the "family"—that he wished my French pronunciation especially attended to. The pronunciation, as it happens, is just what I'm most at home in; if he had said my genders or my subjunctives or my idioms there would have been some sense. But poor father has no native tact, and this deficiency has become flagrant since we've been in Europe. He'll be absent, however, for three months, and mother and I shall breathe more freely; the situation will be less tense. I must confess that we breathe more freely than I expected in this place, where we've been about a week. I was sure before we came that it would prove to be an establishment of the *lowest description*; but I must say that in this respect I'm agreeably disappointed. The French spirit is able to throw a sort of grace even over a swindle of this general order. Of course it's very disagreeable to live with strangers, but as, after all, if I weren't staying with Madame de Maisonrouge I shouldn't be *vautrée* in the Faubourg Saint-Germain, I don't know that from the point of view of exclusiveness I'm much the loser.

Our rooms are very prettily arranged and the table's remarkably good. Mamma thinks the whole thing—the place and the people, the manners and customs—very amusing; but mamma can be put off with any imposture. As for me, you know, all that I ask is to be let alone and not to have people's society *forced upon me*. I've never wanted for society of my own choosing, and, so long as I retain possession of my faculties, I don't suppose I ever shall. As I said, however, the place seems to scramble along, and I succeed in doing as I please, which, you know, is my most cherished pursuit. Madame de Maisonrouge has a great deal of tact—much more than poor floundering father. She's what they call here a *grande belle femme*, which means that she's high-shouldered and short-necked and literally hideous, but with a certain quantity of false type. She has a good many clothes, some rather bad; but a very good manner—only one, and worked to death, but intended to be of the best. Though she's a very good imitation of a *femme du monde* I never see her behind the dinner-table in the evening, never see her smile and bow and duck as the people come in, really glaring all the while at the dishes and the servants, without thinking of a *dame de comptoir* blooming in a corner of a shop or a restaurant. I'm sure that in spite of her *beau nom* she was once a paid book-keeper. I'm also sure that in spite of her smiles and the pretty things she says to every one, she hates us all and would like to murder us. She is a hard clever Frenchwoman who would like to amuse herself and enjoy her Paris, and she must be furious at having to pass her time grinning at specimens of the stupid races who mumble broken French at her. Some day she'll poison the soup or the *vin rouge*, but I hope that won't be until after mother and I shall have left her. She has two daughters who, except that one's decidedly pretty, are meagre imitations of herself.

The "family," for the rest, consists altogether of our beloved compatriots and of still more beloved Englanders. There's an Englander with his sister, and they seem rather decent. He's remarkably handsome, but excessively affected and patronising, especially to us Americans; and I hope to have a chance of biting his head off before long. The sister's very pretty and apparently very nice, but in costume Britannia incarnate. There's a very pleasant little Frenchman—when they're nice they're charming—and a German doctor, a big blond man who looks like a great white bull; and two Americans besides mother and me. One of them's a young man from Boston—an esthetic young man who talks about its being "a real Corot day," and a young woman—a girl, a female, I don't know what to call her—from Vermont or Minnesota or some such place. This young woman's the most extraordinary specimen of self-complacent provinciality that I've ever encountered; she's really too horrible and too humiliating. I've been three times to Clémentine about your underskirt, etc.

IV. FROM LOUIS LEVERETT IN PARIS TO HARVARD TREMONT IN BOSTON

September 25.

MY DEAR HARVARD,

I've carried out my plan, of which I gave you a hint in my last, and I only regret I shouldn't have done it before. It's human nature, after all, that's the most interesting thing in the world, and it only reveals itself to the truly earnest seeker. There's a want of earnestness in that life of hotels and railroad-trains which so many of our countrymen are content to lead in this strange rich elder world, and I was distressed to find how far I myself had been led along the dusty beaten track. I had, however, constantly wanted to turn aside into more unfrequented ways—to plunge beneath the surface and see what I should discover. But the opportunity had always been missing; somehow I seem never to meet those opportunities that we hear about and read about—the things that happen to people in novels and biographies. And yet I'm always on the watch to take advantage of any opening that may present itself;

I'm always looking out for experiences, for sensations—I might almost say for adventures.

The great thing is to *live*, you know—to feel, to be conscious of one's possibilities; not to pass through life mechanically and insensibly, even as a letter through the post-office. There are times, my dear Harvard, when I feel as if I were really capable of everything—*capable de tout*, as they say here—of the greatest excesses as well as the greatest heroism. Oh to be able to say that one has lived—*qu'on a vécu*, as they say here—that idea exercises an indefinable attraction for me. You'll perhaps reply that nothing's easier than to say it! Only the thing's to make people believe you—to make above all one's self. And then I don't want any second-hand spurious sensations; I want the knowledge that leaves a trace—that leaves strange scars and stains, ineffable reveries and aftertastes, behind it! But I'm afraid I shock you, perhaps even frighten you.

If you repeat my remarks to any of the West Cedar Street circle be sure you tone them down as your discretion will suggest. For yourself you'll know that I have always had an intense desire to see something of *real French life*. You're acquainted with my great sympathy with the French; with my natural tendency to enter into their so supremely fine exploitation of the whole personal consciousness. I sympathise with the artistic temperament; I remember you used sometimes to hint to me that you thought my own temperament *too* artistic. I don't consider that in Boston there's any real sympathy with the artistic temperament; we tend to make everything a matter of right and wrong. And in Boston one can't *live*—*on ne peut pas vivre*, as they say here. I don't mean one can't reside—for a great many people manage that; but one can't live esthetically—I almost venture to say one can't live sensuously. This is why I've always been so much drawn to the French, who are so esthetic, so sensuous, so *entirely* living. I'm so sorry dear Théophile Gautier has passed away; I should have liked so much to go and see him and tell him all I owe him. He was living when I was here before; but, you know, at that time I was travelling with the Johnsons, who are not esthetic and who used to make me feel rather ashamed of my love and my need of beauty. If I had gone to see the great apostle of that religion I should have had to go clandestinely—*en cachette,* as they say here; and that's not my nature; I like to do everything frankly, freely, *naïvement, au grand jour.* That's the great thing—to be free, to be frank, to be naïf. Doesn't Matthew Arnold say that somewhere—or is it Swinburne or Pater?

When I was with the Johnsons everything was superficial, and, as regards life, everything was brought down to the question of right and wrong. They were eternally didactic; art should never be didactic; and what's life but the finest of arts? Pater has said that so well somewhere. With the Johnsons I'm afraid I lost many opportunities; the whole outlook or at least the whole medium—of feeling, of appreciation—was grey and cottony, I might almost say woolly. Now, however, as I tell you, I've determined to take right hold for myself; to look right into European life and judge it without Johnsonian prejudices. I've taken up my residence in a French family, in a real Parisian house. You see I've the courage of my opinions; I don't shrink from carrying out my theory that the great thing is to *live.*

You know I've always been intensely interested in Balzac, who never shrank from the reality and whose almost *lurid* pictures of Parisian life have often haunted me in my wanderings through the old wicked-looking streets on the other side of the river. I'm only sorry that my new friends—my French family—don't live in the old city, *au cour de vieux Paris,* as they say here. They live only on the Boulevard Haussmann, which is a compromise, but in spite of this they have a great deal of the Balzac tone. Madame de Maisonrouge belongs to one of the oldest and proudest families in France, but has had reverses which have compelled her to open an establishment in which a limited number of travellers, who are weary of the beaten track, who shun the great caravanseries, who cherish the tradition of the old French sociability— she explains it herself, she expresses it so well—in short to open a "select" boarding-house. I don't see why I shouldn't after all use that expression, for it's the correlative of the term pension bourgeoise, employed by Balzac in *Le Père Goriot.* Do you remember the pension bourgeoise of Madame Vauquer née de Conflans? But this establishment isn't at all like that, and indeed isn't bourgeois at all; I don't quite know how the machinery of selection operates, but we unmistakably feel we're select. The Pension Vauquer was dark, brown, sordid, graisseuse; but this is in quite a different tone, with high clear lightly-draped windows and several rather good Louis Seize pieces—family heirlooms, Madame de Maisonrouge explains. She recalls to me Madame Hulot—do you remember "la belle Madame Hulot"?—in *Les Parents Pauvres*. She has a great charm—though a little artificial, a little jaded and faded, with a suggestion of hidden things in her life. But I've always been sensitive to the seduction of an ambiguous fatigue.

I'm rather disappointed, I confess, in the society I find here; it isn't so richly native, of so indigenous a note, as I could have desired. Indeed, to tell the truth, it's not native at all; though on the other hand it *is* furiously cosmopolite, and that speaks to me too at my hours. We're French *and* we're English; we're American *and* we're German; I believe too there are some Spaniards and some Hungarians expected. I'm much interested in the study of racial types; in comparing, contrasting, seizing the strong points, the weak points, in identifying, however muffled by social hypocrisy, the sharp keynote of each. It's interesting to shift one's point of view, to despoil one's self of one's idiotic prejudices, to enter into strange exotic ways of looking at life.

The American types don't, I much regret to say, make a strong or rich affirmation, and, excepting my own (and what *is* my own, dear Harvard, I ask you?), are wholly negative and feminine. We're *thin*—that I should have to say it! we're pale, we're poor, we're flat. There's something meagre about us; our line is wanting in roundness, our composition in richness. We lack temperament; we don't know how to live; *nous ne savons pas vivre*, as they say here. The American temperament is represented—putting myself aside, and I often think that my temperament isn't at all American—by a young girl and her mother and by another young girl without her mother, without either parent or any attendant or appendage whatever. These inevitable creatures are more or less in the picture; they have a certain interest, they have a certain stamp, but they're disappointing too: they don't go far; they don't keep all they promise; they don't satisfy the imagination. They are cold slim sexless; the physique's not generous, not abundant; it's only the drapery, the skirts and furbelows—that is, I mean in the young lady who has her mother—that are abundant. They're rather different—we *have* our little differences, thank

God: one of them all elegance, all "paid bills" and extra-fresh *gants de Suède*, from New York; the other a plain pure clear-eyed narrow-chested straight-stepping maiden from the heart of New England. And yet they're very much alike too—more alike than they would care to think themselves; for they face each other with scarcely disguised opposition and disavowal. They're both specimens of the practical positive passionless young thing as we let her loose on the world—and yet with a certain fineness and knowing, as you please, either too much or too little. With all of which, as I say, they have their spontaneity and even their oddity; though no more mystery, either of them, than the printed circular thrust into your hand on the street-corner.

The little New Yorker's sometimes very amusing; she asks me if every one in Boston talks like me—if every one's as "intellectual" as your poor correspondent. She's for ever throwing Boston up at me; I can't get rid of poor dear little Boston. The other one rubs it into me too, but in a different way; she seems to feel about it as a good Mahommedan feels toward Mecca, and regards it as a focus of light for the whole human race. Yes, poor little Boston, what nonsense is talked in thy name! But this New England maiden is in her way a rare white flower; she's travelling all over Europe alone—"to see it," she says, "for herself." For herself! What can that strangely serene self of hers do with such sights, such depths! She looks at everything, goes everywhere, passes her way with her clear quiet eyes wide open; skirting the edge of obscene abysses without suspecting them; pushing through brambles without tearing her robe; exciting, without knowing it, the most injurious suspicions; and always holding her course—without a stain, without a sense, without a fear, without a charm!

Then by way of contrast there's a lovely English girl with eyes as shy as violets and a voice as sweet!—the difference between the printed, the distributed, the gratuitous hand-bill and the shy scrap of a *billet-doux* dropped where you may pick it up. She has a sweet Gainsborough head and a great Gainsborough hat with a mighty plume in front of it that makes a shadow over her quiet English eyes. Then she has a sage-green robe, "mystic wonderful," all embroidered with subtle devices and flowers, with birds and beasts of tender tint; very straight and tight in front and adorned behind, along the spine, with large strange iridescent buttons. The revival of taste, of the sense of beauty, in England, interests me deeply; what is there in a simple row of spinal buttons to make one dream—to *donner à rêver*, as they say here? I believe a grand esthetic renascence to be at hand and that a great light will be kindled in England for all the world to see. There are spirits there I should like to commune with; I think they'd understand me.

This gracious English maiden, with her clinging robes, her amulets and girdles, with something quaint and angular in her step, her carriage, something medieval and Gothic in the details of her person and dress, this lovely Evelyn Vane (isn't it a beautiful name?) exhales association and implication. She's so much a woman—*elle est bien femme*, as they say here; simpler softer rounder richer than the easy products I spoke of just now. Not much talk—a great sweet silence. Then the violet eye—the very eye itself seems to blush; the great shadowy hat making the brow so quiet; the strange clinging clutched pictured raiment! As I say, it's a very gracious tender type. She has her brother with her, who's a beautiful fair-haired grey-eyed young Englishman. He's purely objective, but he too is very plastic.

V. FROM MIRANDA HOPE TO HER MOTHER

September 26.

You mustn't be frightened at not hearing from me oftener; it isn't because I'm in any trouble, but because I'm getting on so well. If I were in any trouble I don't think I'd write to you; I'd just keep quiet and see it through myself. But that's not the case at present; and if I don't write to you it's because I'm so deeply interested over here that I don't seem to find time. It was a real providence that brought me to this house, where, in spite of all obstacles, I *am* able to press onward. I wonder how I find time for all I do, but when I realise I've only got about a year left, all told, I feel as if I wouldn't sacrifice a single hour.

The obstacles I refer to are the disadvantages I have in acquiring the language, there being so many persons round me speaking English, and that, as you may say, in the very bosom of a regular French family. It seems as if you heard English everywhere; but I certainly didn't expect to find it in a place like this. I'm not discouraged, however, and I exercise all I can, even with the other English boarders. Then I've a lesson every day from Mademoiselle— the elder daughter of the lady of the house and the intellectual one; she has a wonderful fearless mind, almost like my friend at the hotel—and French give-and-take every evening in the salon, from eight to eleven, with Madame herself and some friends of hers who often come in. Her cousin, Mr. Verdier, a young French gentleman, is fortunately staying with her, and I make a point of talking with him as much as possible. I have *extra-private lessons* from him, and I often ramble round with him. Some night soon he's to accompany me to the comic opera. We've also a most interesting plan of visiting the galleries successively together and taking the schools in their order—for they mean by "the schools" here something quite different from what we do. Like most of the French Mr. Verdier converses with great fluency, and I feel I may really gain from him. He's remarkably handsome, in the French style, and extremely polite—making a great many speeches which I'm afraid it wouldn't always do to pin one's faith on. When I get down in Maine again I guess I'll tell you some of the things he has said to me. I think you'll consider them extremely curious—very beautiful *in their French way.*

The conversation in the parlour (from eight to eleven) ranges over many subjects—I sometimes feel as if it really avoided *none*; and I often wish you or some of the Bangor folks could be there to enjoy it. Even though you couldn't understand it I think you'd like to hear the way they go on; they seem to express so much. I sometimes think that at Bangor they don't express enough—except that it seems as if over there they've less *to* express. It seems as if at Bangor there were things that folks never *tried* to say; but I seem to have learned here from studying French that you've no idea what you *can* say before you try. At Bangor they kind of give it up beforehand; they don't make any effort. (I don't say this in the least for William Platt *in particular.*)

I'm sure I don't know what they'll think of me when I get back anyway. It seems as if over here I had learned to come out with everything. I suppose they'll think I'm not sincere; but isn't it more sincere to come right out with things than just to keep feeling of them in your mind—without giving any one the benefit? I've become very good friends with every one in the house—that is (you see I *am* sincere) with *almost* every one. It's the most interesting circle I ever was in. There's a girl here, an American, that I don't like so much as the rest; but that's only because she won't let me. I should like to like her, ever so much, because she's most lovely and most attractive; but she doesn't seem to want to know me or to take to me. She comes from New York and she's remarkably pretty, with beautiful eyes and the most delicate features; she's also splendidly stylish—in this respect would bear comparison with any one I've seen over here. But it seems as if she didn't want to recognise me or associate with me, as if she wanted to make a difference between us. It is like people they call "haughty" in books. I've never seen any one like that before—any one that wanted to make a difference; and at first I was right down interested, she seemed to me so like a proud young lady in a novel. I kept saying to myself all day "haughty, haughty," and I wished she'd keep on so. But she did keep on—she kept on too long; and then I began to feel it in a different way, to feel as if it kind of wronged me. I couldn't think what I've done, and I can't think yet. It's as if she had got some idea about me or had heard some one say something. If some girls should behave like that I wouldn't make any account of it; but this one's so refined, and looks as if she might be so fascinating if I once got to know her, that I think about it a good deal. I'm bound to find out what her reason is—for of course she has got some reason; I'm right down curious to know.

I went up to her to ask her the day before yesterday; I thought that the best way. I told her I wanted to know her better and would like to come and see her in her room—they tell me she has got a lovely one—and that if she had heard anything against me perhaps she'd tell me when I came. But she was more distant than ever and just turned it off; said she had never heard me mentioned and that her room was too small to receive visitors. I suppose she spoke the truth, but I'm sure she has some peculiar ground, all the same. She has got some idea; which I'll die if I don't find out soon—if I have to ask every one in the house. I never *could* be happy under an appearance of wrong. I wonder if she doesn't think me refined—or if she had ever heard anything against Bangor? I can't think it's that. Don't you remember when

374

Clara Barnard went to visit in New York, three years ago, how much attention she received? And you know Clara *is* Bangor, to the soles of her shoes. Ask William Platt—so long as he isn't native—if he doesn't consider Clara Barnard refined.

Apropos, as they say here, of refinement, there's another American in the house—a gentleman from Boston—who's just crammed with it. His name's Mr. Louis Leverett (such a beautiful name I think) and he's about thirty years old. He's rather small and he looks pretty sick; he suffers from some affection of the liver. But his conversation leads you right on—they *do* go so far over here: even our people seem to strain ahead in Europe, and perhaps when I get back it may strike you I've learned to keep up with them. I delight to listen to him anyhow—he has such beautiful ideas. I feel as if these moments were hardly right, not being in French; but fortunately he uses a great many French expressions. It's in a different style from the dazzle of Mr. Verdier—not so personal, but much more earnest: he says the only earnestness left in the world now is French. He's intensely fond of pictures and has given me a great many ideas about them that I'd never have gained without him; I shouldn't have known how to go to work to strike them. He thinks everything of pictures; he thinks we don't make near enough of them. They seem to make a good deal of them here, but I couldn't help telling him the other day that in Bangor I really don't think we do.

If I had any money to spend I'd buy some and take them back to hang right up. Mr. Leverett says it would do them good—not the pictures, but the Bangor folks (though sometimes he seems to want to hang *them* up too). He thinks everything of the French, anyhow, and says we don't make nearly enough of them. I couldn't help telling him the other day that they certainly make enough of *themselves*. But it's very interesting to hear him go on about the French, and it's so much gain to me, since it's about the same as what I came for. I talk to him as much as I dare about Boston, but I do feel as if this were right down wrong—a stolen pleasure.

I can get all the Boston culture I want when I go back, if I carry out my plan, my heart's secret, of going there to reside. I ought to direct all my efforts to European culture now, so as to keep Boston to finish off. But it seems as if I couldn't help taking a peep now and then in advance—with a real Bostonian. I don't know when I may meet one again; but if there are many others like Mr. Leverett there I shall be certain not to lack when I carry out my dream. He's just as full of culture as he can live. But it seems strange how many different sorts there are.

There are two of the English who I suppose are very cultivated too; but it doesn't seem as if I could enter into theirs so easily, though I try all I can. I do love their way of speaking, and sometimes I feel almost as if it would be right to give up going for French and just try to get the hang of English as these people have got it. It doesn't come out in the things they say so much, though these are often rather curious, but in the sweet way they say them and in their kind of making so much, such an easy lovely effect, of saying almost anything. It seems as if they must try a good deal to sound like that; but these English who are here don't seem to try at all, either to speak or do anything else. They're a young lady and her brother, who belong, I believe, to some noble family. I've had a good deal of intercourse with them, because I've felt more free to talk to them than to the Americans—on account of the language. They often don't understand mine, and then it's as if I had to learn theirs to explain.

I never supposed when I left Bangor that I was coming to Europe to improve in *our* old language—and yet I feel I can. If I do get where I *may* in it I guess you'll scarcely understand me when I get back, and I don't think you'll particularly see the point. I'd be a good deal criticised if I spoke like that at Bangor. However, I verily believe Bangor's the most critical place on earth; I've seen nothing like it over here. Well, tell them I'll give them about all they can do. But I was speaking about this English young lady and her brother; I wish I could put them before you. She's lovely just to see; she seems so modest and retiring. In spite of this, however, she dresses in a way that attracts great attention, as I couldn't help noticing when one day I went out to walk with her. She was ever so much more looked at than what I'd have thought she'd like; but she didn't seem to care, till at last I couldn't help calling attention to it. Mr. Leverett thinks everything of it; he calls it the "costume of the future." I'd call it rather the costume of the past—you know the English have such an attachment to the past. I said this the other day to Madame de Maisonrouge—that Miss Vane dressed in the costume of the past. De l'an passé, vous voulez dire? she asked in her gay French way. (You can get William Platt to translate this; he used to tell me he knows so much French.)

You know I told you, in writing some time ago, that I had tried to get some insight into the position of woman in England, and, being here with Miss Vane, it has seemed to me to be a good opportunity to get a little more. I've asked her a great deal about it, but she doesn't seem able to tell me much. The first time I asked her she said the position of a lady depended on the rank of her father, her eldest brother, her husband—all on somebody else; and they, as to their position, on something quite else (than themselves) as well. She told me her own position was very good because her father was some relation—I forget what—to a lord. She thinks everything of this; and that proves to me their standing can't be *really* good, because if it were it wouldn't be involved in that of your relations, even your nearest. I don't know much about lords, and it does try my patience—though she's just as sweet as she can live—to hear her talk as if it were a matter of course I should.

I feel as if it were right to ask her as often as I can if she doesn't consider every one equal; but she always says she doesn't, and she confesses that she doesn't think *she's* equal to Lady Something-or-Other, who's the wife of that relation of her father. I try and persuade her all I can that she *is*; but it seems as if she didn't want to be persuaded, and when I ask her if that superior being is of the same opinion—that Miss Vane isn't her equal—she looks so soft and pretty with her eyes and says "How can she not be?" When I tell her that this is right down bad for the other person it seems as if she wouldn't believe me, and the only answer she'll make is that the other person's "awfully nice." I don't believe she's nice at all; if she were nice she wouldn't have such ideas as that. I tell Miss Vane that at Bangor we think such ideas vulgar, but then she looks as though she had never heard of Bangor. I often want to shake her, though she *is* so sweet. If she isn't angry with the people who make her feel that way at least I'm angry *for* her. I'm angry with her brother too, for she's evidently very much afraid of him, and this gives me some further insight into the subject. She thinks everything of her brother; she thinks it natural she should be afraid of him not only physically—for that is natural, as he's enormously tall and strong, and has very big fists—but morally and intellectually. She seems unable, however, to take in any argument, and she makes me realise what I've often heard—that if you're timid nothing will reason you out of it.

Mr. Vane also, the brother, seems to have the same prejudices, and when I tell him, as I often think it right to do, that his sister's not his subordinate, even if she does think so, but his equal, and perhaps in some respects his superior, and that if my brother in Bangor were to treat me as he treats this charming but abject creature, who has not spirit enough to see the question in its true light, there would be an indignation-meeting of the citizens to protest against such an outrage to the sanctity of womanhood—when I tell him all this, at breakfast or dinner, he only bursts out laughing so loud that all the plates clatter on the table.

But at such a time as this there's always one person who seems interested in what I say—a German gentleman, a professor, who sits next to me at dinner and whom I must tell you more about another time. He's very learned, but wants to push further and further all the time; he appreciates a great many of my remarks, and after dinner, in the salon, he often comes to me to ask me questions about them. I have to think a little sometimes to know what I did say or what I do think. He takes you right up where you left off, and he's most as fond of discussing things as William Platt ever was. He's splendidly educated, in the German style, and he told me the other day that he was an "intellectual broom." Well, if he is he sweeps clean; I told him that. After he has been talking to me I feel as if I hadn't got a speck of dust left in my mind anywhere. It's a most delightful feeling. He says he's a remorseless observer, and though I don't know about remorse—for a bright mind isn't a crime, is it?—I'm sure there's plenty over here to observe. But I've told you enough for to-day. I don't know how much longer I shall stay here; I'm getting on now so fast that it has come to seem sometimes as if I shouldn't need all the time I've laid out. I suppose your cold weather has promptly begun, as usual; it sometimes makes me envy you. The fall weather here is very dull and damp, and I often suffer from the want of bracing.

VI. FROM MISS EVELYN VANE IN PARIS TO THE LADY AUGUSTA FLEMING AT BRIGHTON

PARIS, *September* 30.

DEAR LADY AUGUSTA,

I'm afraid I shall not be able to come to you on January 7th, as you kindly proposed at Homburg. I'm so very very sorry; it's an immense disappointment. But I've just heard that it has been settled that mamma and the children come abroad for a part of the winter, and mamma wishes me to go with them to Hyères, where Georgina has been ordered for her lungs. She has not been at all well these three months, and now that the damp weather has begun she's very poorly indeed; so that last week papa decided to have a consultation, and he and mamma went with her up to town and saw some three or four doctors. They all of them ordered the south of France, but they didn't agree about the place; so that mamma herself decided for Hyères, because it's the most economical. I believe it's very dull, but I hope it will do Georgina good. I'm afraid, however, that nothing will do her good until she consents to take more care of herself; I'm afraid she's very wild and wilful, and mamma tells me that all this month it has taken papa's positive orders to make her stop indoors. She's very cross (mamma writes me) about coming abroad, and doesn't seem at all to mind the expense papa has been put to—talks very ill-naturedly about her loss of the hunting and even perhaps of the early spring meetings. She expected to begin to hunt in December and wants to know whether anybody keeps hounds at Hyères. Fancy that rot when she's too ill to sit a horse or to go anywhere. But I daresay that when she gets there she'll be glad enough to keep quiet, as they say the heat's intense. It may cure Georgina, but I'm sure it will make the rest of us very ill.

Mamma, however, is only going to bring Mary and Gus and Fred and Adelaide abroad with her: the others will remain at Kingscote till February (about the 3rd) when they'll go to Eastbourne for a month with Miss Turnover, the new governess, who has proved such a very nice person. She's going to take Miss Travers, who has been with us so long, but is only qualified for the younger

379

children, to Hyères, and I believe some of the Kingscote servants. She has perfect confidence in Miss T.; it's only a pity the poor woman has such an odd name. Mamma thought of asking her if she would mind taking another when she came; but papa thought she might object. Lady Battledown makes all her governesses take the same name; she gives £5 more a year for the purpose. I forget what it is she calls them; I think it's Johnson (which to me always suggests a lady's maid). Governesses shouldn't have too pretty a name—they shouldn't have a nicer name than the family.

I suppose you heard from the Desmonds that I didn't go back to England with them. When it began to be talked about that Georgina should be taken abroad mamma wrote to me that I had better stop in Paris for a month with Harold, so that she could pick me up on their way to Hyères. It saves the expense of my journey to Kingscote and back, and gives me the opportunity to "finish" a little in French.

You know Harold came here six weeks ago to get up his French for those dreadful exams that he has to pass so soon. He came to live with some French people that take in young men (and others) for this purpose; it's a kind of coaching-place, only kept by women. Mamma had heard it was very nice, so she wrote to me that I was to come and stop here with Harold. The Desmonds brought me and made the arrangement or the bargain or whatever you call it. Poor Harold was naturally not at all pleased, but he has been very kind and has treated me like an angel. He's getting on beautifully with his French, for though I don't think the place is so good as papa supposed, yet Harold is so immensely clever that he can scarcely help learning. I'm afraid I learn much less, but fortunately I haven't to go up for anything—unless perhaps to mamma if she takes it into her head to examine me. But she'll have so much to think of with Georgina that I hope this won't occur to her. If it does I shall be, as Harold says, in a dreadful funk.

This isn't such a nice place for a girl as for a gentleman, and the Desmonds thought it *exceedingly odd* that mamma should wish me to come here. As Mrs. Desmond said, it's because she's so very unconventional. But you know Paris is so very amusing, and if only Harold remains good-natured about it

I shall be content to wait for the caravan—which is what he calls mamma and the children. The person who keeps the establishment, or whatever they call it, is rather odd and *exceedingly foreign*; but she's wonderfully civil and is perpetually sending to my door to see if I want anything. She's tremendously pretentious and of course isn't a lady. The servants are not at all like English ones and come bursting in, the footman—they've only one—and the maids alike, at all sorts of hours, in the *most sudden way*. Then when one rings it takes ages. Some of the food too is rather nasty. All of which is very uncomfortable, and I daresay will be worse at Hyères. There, however, fortunately, we shall have our own people.

There are some very odd Americans here who keep throwing Harold into fits of laughter. One's a dreadful little man whom indeed he also wants to kick and who's always sitting over the fire and talking about the colour of the sky. I don't believe he ever saw the sky except through the window-pane. The other day he took hold of my frock—that green one you thought so nice at Homburg—and told me that it reminded him of the texture of the Devonshire turf. And then he talked for half an hour about the Devonshire turf, which I thought such a very extraordinary subject. Harold firmly believes him mad. It's rather horrid to be living in this way with people one doesn't know—I mean doesn't know as one knows them in England.

The other Americans, beside the madman, are two girls about my own age, one of whom is rather nice. She has a mother; but the mother always sits in her bedroom, which seems so very odd. I should like mamma to ask them to Kingscote, but I'm afraid mamma wouldn't like the mother, who's awfully vulgar. The other girl is awfully vulgar herself—she's travelling about quite alone. I think she's a middle-class schoolmistress—sacked perhaps for some irregularity; but the other girl (I mean the nicer one, with the objectionable mother) tells me she's more respectable than she seems. She has, however, the most extraordinary opinions—wishes to do away with the aristocracy, thinks it wrong that Arthur should have Kingscote when papa dies, etc. I don't see what it signifies to her that poor Arthur should come into the property, which will be so delightful—except for papa dying. But Harold says she's mad too. He chaffs her tremendously about her radicalism, and he's so immensely clever that she can't answer him, though she has a supply of the most extraordinary big words.

There's also a Frenchman, a nephew or cousin or something of the person of the house, who's a horrid low cad; and a German professor or doctor who eats with his knife and is a great bore. I'm so very sorry about giving up my visit. I'm afraid you'll never ask me again.

VII. FROM LÉON VERDIER IN PARIS TO PROSPER GOBAIN AT LILLE

September 28.

MON GROS VIEUX,

It's a long time since I've given you of my news, and I don't know what puts it into my head to-night to recall myself to your affectionate memory. I suppose it is that when we're happy the mind reverts instinctively to those with whom formerly we shared our vicissitudes, and *je t'en ai trop dit dans le bon temps, cher vieux,* and you always listened to me too imperturbably, with your pipe in your mouth and your waistcoat unbuttoned, for me not to feel that I can count on your sympathy to-day. *Nous en sommes-nous flanqués, des confidences?*—in those happy days when my first thought in seeing an adventure *poindre à l'horizon* was of the pleasure I should have in relating it to the great Prosper. As I tell thee, I'm happy; decidedly *j'ai de la chance,* and from that avowal I trust thee to construct the rest. Shall I help thee a little? Take three adorable girls—three, my good Prosper, the mystic number, neither more nor less. Take them and place in the midst of them thy insatiable little Léon. Is the situation sufficiently indicated, or does the scene take more doing?

You expected perhaps I was going to tell thee I had made my fortune, or that the Uncle Blondeau had at last decided to recommit himself to the breast of nature after having constituted me his universal legatee. But I needn't remind you for how much women have always been in any happiness of him who thus overflows to you—for how much in any happiness and for how much more in any misery. But don't let me talk of misery now; time enough when it comes, when *ces demoiselles* shall have joined the serried ranks of their amiable predecessors. Ah, I comprehend your impatience. I must tell you of whom *ces demoiselles* consist.

You've heard me speak of my *cousine* de Maisonrouge, that *grande belle femme* who, after having married, *en secondes noces*—there had been, to tell the truth, some irregularity about her first union—a venerable relic of the old noblesse of Poitou, was left, by the death of her husband, complicated by the crash of expensive tastes against an income of 17,000 francs, on the pavement of Paris with two little demons of daughters to bring up in the path of virtue. She managed to bring them up; my little cousins are ferociously *sages*. If you ask me how she managed it I can't tell you; it's no business of mine, and *a fortiori* none of yours. She's now fifty years old—she confesses to thirty-eight—and her daughters, whom she has never been able to place, are respectively twenty-seven and twenty-three (they confess to twenty and to seventeen). Three years ago she had the thrice-blest idea of opening a well-upholstered and otherwise attractive *asile* for the blundering barbarians who come to Paris in the hope of picking up a few stray pearls from the *écrin* of Voltaire—or of Zola. The idea has brought her luck; the house does an excellent business. Until within a few months ago it was carried on by my cousins alone; but lately the need of a few extensions and improvements has caused itself to be felt. My cousin has undertaken them, regardless of expense; in other words she has asked me to come and stay with her—board and lodging gratis—and correct the conversational exercises of her *pensionnaire*-pupils. I'm the extension, my good Prosper; I'm the improvement. She has enlarged the *personnel*—I'm the enlargement. I form the exemplary sounds that the prettiest English lips are invited to imitate. The English lips are not all pretty, heaven knows, but enough of them are so to make it a good bargain for me.

Just now, as I told you, I'm in daily relation with three separate pairs. The owner of one of them has private lessons; she pays extra. My cousin doesn't give me a sou of the money, but I consider nevertheless that I'm not a loser by the arrangement. Also I'm well, very very well, with the proprietors of the two other pairs. One of these is a little Anglaise of twenty—a *figure de keepsake*; the most adorable miss you ever, or at least I ever, beheld. She's hung all over with beads and bracelets and amulets, she's embroidered all over like a sampler or a vestment; but her principal decoration consists of the softest and almost the hugest grey eyes in the world, which rest upon you with a profundity of confidence—a confidence I really feel some compunction in betraying. She has a tint as white as this sheet of paper, except just in the middle of each cheek, where it passes into the purest and most transparent, most liquid, carmine. Occasionally this rosy fluid overflows into the rest of her face—by which I mean that she blushes—as softly as the mark of your breath on the window-pane.

Like every Anglaise she's rather pinched and prim in public; but it's easy to see that when no one's looking *elle ne demande qu'à se laisser aller!* Whenever she wants it I'm always there, and I've given her to understand she can count upon me. I've reason to believe she appreciates the assurance, though I'm bound in honesty to confess that with her the situation's a little less advanced than with the others. *Que voulez-vous?* The English are heavy and the Anglaises move slowly, that's all. The movement, however, is perceptible, and once this fact's established I can let the soup simmer, I can give her time to arrive, for I'm beautifully occupied with her competitors. *They* don't keep me waiting, please believe.

These young ladies are Americans, and it belongs to that national character to move fast. "All right—go ahead!" (I'm learning a great deal of English, or rather a great deal of American.) They go ahead at a rate that sometimes makes it difficult for me to keep up. One of them's prettier than the other; but this latter—the one that takes the extra-private lessons— is really *une fille étonnante. Ah par exemple, elle brûle ses vaisseaux, celle-là!* She threw herself into my arms the very first day, and I almost owed her a grudge for having deprived me of that pleasure of gradation, of carrying the defences one by one, which is almost as great as that of entering the place. For would you believe that at the end of exactly twelve minutes she gave me a rendezvous? In the Galerie d'Apollon at the Louvre I admit; but that was respectable for a beginning, and since then we've had them by the dozen; I've ceased to keep the account. *Non, c'est une fille qui me dépasse.*

The other, the slighter but "smarter" little person—she has a mother somewhere out of sight, shut up in a closet or a trunk—is a good deal prettier, and perhaps on that account *elle y met plus de façons.* She doesn't knock about Paris with me by the hour; she contents herself with long interviews in the *petit salon*, with the blinds half-drawn, beginning at about three o'clock, when every one is *à la promenade.* She's admirable, *cette petite*, a little too immaterial, with the bones rather over-accentuated, yet of a detail, on the whole, most satisfactory. And you can say anything to her. She takes the trouble to appear not to understand, but her conduct, half an hour afterwards, reassures you completely—oh completely!

However, it's the big bouncer of the extra-private lessons who's the most remarkable. These private lessons, my good Prosper, are the most brilliant invention of the age, and a real stroke of genius on the part of Miss Miranda! They also take place in the *petit salon*, but with the doors tightly closed and with explicit directions to every one in the house that we are not to be disturbed. And we're not, *mon gros*, we're not! Not a sound, not a shadow, interrupts our felicity. My cousins are on the right track—such a house must make its fortune. Miss Miranda's too tall and too flat, with a certain want of coloration; she hasn't the transparent *rougeurs* of the little Anglaise. But she has wonderful far-gazing eyes, superb teeth, a nose modelled by a sculptor, and a way of holding up her head and looking every one in the face, which combines apparent innocence with complete assurance in a way I've never seen equalled. She's making the *tour du monde*, entirely alone, without even a soubrette to carry the ensign, for the purpose of seeing for herself, seeing *à quoi s'en tenir sur les hommes et les choses*—on *les hommes* particularly. *Dis donc, mon vieux*, it must be a *drôle de pays* over there, where such a view of the right thing for the aspiring young bourgeoises is taken. If we should turn the tables some day, thou and I, and go over and see it for ourselves? Why isn't it as well we should go and find them *chez elles*, as that they should come out here after us? *Dis donc, mon gros Prosper . . .* !

VIII. FROM DR. RUDOLPH STAUB IN PARIS TO DR. JULIUS HIRSCH AT GÖTTINGEN

My dear Brother in Science,

I resume my hasty notes, of which I sent you the first instalment some weeks ago. I mentioned that I intended to leave my hotel, not finding in it real matter. It was kept by a Pomeranian and the waiters without exception were from the Fatherland. I might as well have sat down with my note-book Unter den Linden, and I felt that, having come here for documentation, or to put my finger straight upon the social pulse, I should project myself as much as possible into the circumstances which are in part the consequence and in part the cause of its activities and intermittences. I saw there could be no well-grounded knowledge without this preliminary operation of my getting a near view, as slightly as possible modified by elements proceeding from a different combination of forces, of the spontaneous home-life of the nation.

I accordingly engaged a room in the house of a lady of pure French extraction and education, who supplements the shortcomings of an income insufficient to the ever-growing demands of the Parisian system of sense-gratification by providing food and lodging for a limited number of distinguished strangers. I should have preferred to have my room here only, and to take my meals in a brewery, of very good appearance, which I speedily discovered in the same street; but this arrangement, though very clearly set out by myself, was not acceptable to the mistress of the establishment—a woman with a mathematical head—and I have consoled myself for the extra expense by fixing my thoughts upon the great chance that conformity to the customs of the house gives me of studying the table-manners of my companions, and of observing the French nature at a peculiarly physiological moment, the moment when the satisfaction of the *taste*, which is the governing quality in its composition, produces a kind of exhalation, an intellectual transpiration, which, though light and perhaps invisible to a superficial spectator, is nevertheless appreciable by a properly adjusted instrument. I've adjusted my instrument very satisfactorily—I mean the one I carry in my good square German head—and I'm not afraid of losing a single drop of this valuable fluid as it condenses itself upon the plate of my observation. A prepared surface is what I need, and I've prepared my surface.

Unfortunately here also I find the individual native in the minority. There are only four French persons in the house—the individuals concerned in its management, three of whom are women, and one a man. Such a preponderance of the Weibliche is, however, in itself characteristic, as I needn't remind you what an abnormally-developed part this sex has played in French history. The remaining figure is ostensibly that of a biped, and apparently that of a man, but I hesitate to allow him the whole benefit of the higher classification. He strikes me as less human than simian, and whenever I hear him talk I seem to myself to have paused in the street to listen to the shrill clatter of a hand-organ, to which the gambols of a hairy *homunculus* form an accompaniment.

I mentioned to you before that my expectation of rough usage in consequence of my unattenuated, even if not frivolously aggressive, Teutonism was to prove completely unfounded. No one seems either unduly conscious or affectedly unperceiving of my so rich Berlin background; I'm treated on the contrary with the positive civility which is the portion of every traveller who pays the bill without scanning the items too narrowly. This, I confess, has been something of a surprise to me, and I've not yet made up my mind as to the fundamental cause of the anomaly. My determination to take up my abode in a French interior was largely dictated by the supposition that I should be substantially disagreeable to its inmates. I wished to catch in the fact the different forms taken by the irritation I should naturally produce; for it is under the influence of irritation that the French character most completely expresses itself. My presence, however, operates, as I say, less than could have been hoped as a stimulus, and in this respect I'm materially disappointed. They treat me as they treat every one else; whereas, in order to be treated differently, I was resigned in advance to being treated worse. A further proof, if any were needed, of that vast and, as it were, fluid *waste* (I have so often dwelt on to you) which attends the process of philosophic secretion. I've not, I repeat, fully explained to myself this logical contradiction; but this is the explanation to which I tend. The French are so exclusively occupied with the idea of themselves that in spite of the very definite image the German personality presented to them by the war of 1870 they have at present no distinct apprehension of its existence. They are not very sure that there *are*, concretely, any Germans; they have already forgotten the convincing proofs presented to them nine years ago. A German was something disagreeable and disconcerting, an irreducible mass, which they determined to keep out of their conception of things. I therefore hold we're wrong to govern ourselves upon the hypothesis of the *revanche*; the French nature is too shallow for that large and powerful plant to bloom in it.

The English-speaking specimens, too, I've not been willing to neglect the opportunity to examine; and among these I've paid special attention to the American varieties, of which I find here several singular examples. The two most remarkable are a young man who presents all the characteristics of a period of national decadence; reminding me strongly of some diminutive Hellenised Roman of the third century. He's an illustration of the period of culture in which the faculty of appreciation has obtained such a preponderance over that of production that the latter sinks into a kind of rank sterility, and the mental condition becomes analogous to that of a malarious bog. I hear from him of the existence of an immense number of Americans exactly resembling him, and that the city of Boston indeed is almost exclusively composed of them. (He communicated this fact very proudly, as if it were greatly to the credit of his native country; little perceiving the truly sinister impression it made on me.)

What strikes one in it is that it is a phenomenon to the best of my knowledge—and you know what my knowledge is—unprecedented and unique in the history of mankind; the arrival of a nation at an ultimate stage of evolution without having passed through the mediate one; the passage of the fruit, in other words, from crudity to rottenness, without the interposition of a period of useful (and ornamental) ripeness. With the Americans indeed the crudity and the rottenness are identical and simultaneous; it is impossible to say, as in the conversation of this deplorable young man, which is the one and which the other: they're inextricably confused. Homunculus for homunculus I prefer that of the Frenchman; he's at least more amusing.

It's interesting in this manner to perceive, so largely developed, the germs of extinction in the so-called powerful Anglo-Saxon family. I find them in almost as recognisable a form in a young woman from the State of Maine, in the province of New England, with whom I have had a good deal of conversation. She differs somewhat from the young man I just mentioned in that the state of affirmation, faculty of production and capacity for action are things, in her, less inanimate; she has more of the freshness and vigour that we suppose to belong to a young civilisation. But unfortunately she produces nothing but evil, and her tastes and habits are similarly those of a Roman lady of the lower Empire. She makes no secret of them and has in fact worked out a complete scheme of experimental adventure, that is of personal licence, which she is now engaged in carrying out. As the opportunities she finds in her own country fail to satisfy her she has come to Europe "to try," as she says, "for herself." It's the doctrine of universal "unprejudiced" experience professed with a cynicism that is really most extraordinary, and which, presenting itself in a young woman of considerable education, appears to me to be the judgement of a society.

Another observation which pushes me to the same induction—that of the premature vitiation of the American population—is the attitude of the Americans whom I have before me with regard to each other. I have before me a second flower of the same huge so-called democratic garden, who is less abnormally developed than the one I have just described, but who yet bears the stamp of this peculiar combination of the barbarous and, to apply to them one of their own favourite terms, the *ausgespielt*, the "played-out." These three little persons look with the greatest mistrust and aversion upon each other; and each has repeatedly taken me apart and assured me secretly, that he or she only is the real, the genuine, the typical American. A type that has lost itself before it has been fixed—what can you look for from this?

Add to this that there are two young Englanders in the house who hate all the Americans in a lump, making between them none of the distinctions and favourable comparisons which they insist upon, and for which, as involving the recognition of shades and a certain play of the critical sense, the still quite primitive insular understanding is wholly inapt, and you will, I think, hold me warranted in believing that, between precipitate decay and internecine enmities, the English-speaking family is destined to consume itself, and that with its decline the prospect of successfully-organised conquest and unarrested incalculable expansion, to which I alluded above, will brighten for the deep-lunged children of the Fatherland!

IX. MIRANDA HOPE TO HER MOTHER

October 22.

DEAR MOTHER,

I'm off in a day or two to visit some new country; I haven't yet decided which. I've satisfied myself with regard to France, and obtained a good knowledge of the language. I've enjoyed my visit to Madame de Maisonrouge deeply, and feel as if I were leaving a circle of real friends. Everything has gone on beautifully up to the end, and every one has been as kind and attentive as if I were their own sister, especially Mr. Verdier, the French gentleman, from whom I have gained more than I ever expected (in six weeks) and with whom I have promised to *correspond*. So you can imagine me dashing off the liveliest and yet the most elegant French letters; and if you don't believe in them I'll keep the rough drafts to show you when I go back.

The German gentleman is also more interesting the more you know him; it seems sometimes as if I could fairly drink in his ideas. I've found out why the young lady from New York doesn't like me! It's because I said one day at dinner that I *admired* to go to the Louvre. Well, when I first came it seemed as if I *did* admire everything! Tell William Platt his letter has come. I knew he'd have to write, and I was bound I'd make him! I haven't decided what country I'll visit next; it seems as if there were so many to choose from. But I must take care to pick out a good one and to meet plenty of fresh experiences. Dearest mother, my money holds out, and it is most interesting!

THE POINT OF VIEW

I. FROM MISS AURORA CHURCH AT SEA TO MISS WHITESIDE IN PARIS

September 1880.

. . . My dear child, the bromide of sodium (if that's what you call it) proved perfectly useless. I don't mean that it did me no good, but that I never had occasion to take the bottle out of my bag. It might have done wonders for me if I had needed it; but I didn't, simply because I've been a wonder myself. Will you believe that I've spent the whole voyage on deck, in the most animated conversation and exercise? Twelve times round the deck make a mile, I believe; and by this measurement I've been walking twenty miles a day. And down to every meal, if you please, where I've displayed the appetite of a fishwife. Of course the weather has been lovely; so there's no great merit. The wicked old Atlantic has been as blue as the sapphire in my only ring— rather a good one—and as smooth as the slippery floor of Madame Galopin's dining-room. We've been for the last three hours in sight of land, and are soon to enter the Bay of New York which is said to be exquisitely beautiful. But of course you recall it, though they say everything changes so fast over here. I find I don't remember anything, for my recollections of our voyage to Europe so many years ago are exceedingly dim; I've only a painful impression that mamma shut me up for an hour every day in the stateroom and made me learn by heart some religious poem. I was only five years old and I believe that as a child I was extremely timid; on the other hand mamma, as you know, had what she called a method with me. She has it to this day; only I've become indifferent; I've been so pinched and pushed—morally speaking, *bien entendu*. It's true, however, that there are children of five on the vessel to-day who have been extremely conspicuous—ranging all over the ship and always under one's feet. Of course they're little compatriots, which means that they're little barbarians. I don't mean to pronounce *all* our compatriots barbarous; they seem to improve somehow after their first communion. I don't know whether it's that ceremony that improves them, especially as so few of them go in for it; but the women are certainly nicer than the little girls; I mean of course in proportion, you know. You warned me not to generalise, and you see I've already begun, before we've arrived. But I suppose there's no harm in it so long as it's favourable.

Isn't it favourable when I say I've had the most lovely time? I've never had so much liberty in my life, and I've been out alone, as you may say, every day of the voyage. If it's a foretaste of what's to come I shall take very kindly to that. When I say I've been out alone I mean we've always been two. But we two were alone, so to speak, and it wasn't like always having mamma or Madame Galopin, or some lady in the pension or the temporary cook. Mamma has been very poorly; she's so very well on land that it's a wonder to see her at all taken down. She says, however, that it isn't the being at sea; it's on the contrary approaching the land. She's not in a hurry to arrive; she keeps well before her that great disillusions await us. I didn't know she *had* any illusions—she has too many opinions, I should think, for that: she discriminates, as she's always saying, from morning till night. Where would the poor illusions find room? She's meanwhile very serious; she sits for hours in perfect silence, her eyes fixed on the horizon. I heard her say yesterday to an English gentleman—a very odd Mr. Antrobus, the only person with whom she converses—that she was afraid she shouldn't like her native land, and that she shouldn't like not liking it. But this is a mistake; she'll like that immensely—I mean the not liking it. If it should prove at all agreeable she'll be furious, for that will go against her system. You know all about mamma's system; I've explained it so often. It goes against her system that we should come back at all; that was *my* system—I've had at last to invent one! She consented to come only because she saw that, having no *dot*, I should never marry in Europe; and I pretended to be immensely preoccupied with this idea in order to make her start. In reality *cela m'est parfaitement égal*. I'm only afraid I shall like it too much—I don't mean marriage, of course, but the sense of a native land. Say what you will, it's a charming thing to go out alone, and I've given notice that I mean to be always *en course*. When I tell mamma this she looks at me in the same silence; her eyes dilate and then she slowly closes them. It's as if the sea were affecting her a little, though it's so beautifully calm. I ask her if she'll try my bromide, which is there in my bag;

but she motions me off and I begin to walk again, tapping my little boot-soles on the smooth clean deck. This allusion to my boot-soles, by the way, isn't prompted by vanity; but it's a fact that at sea one's feet and one's shoes assume the most extraordinary importance, so that one should take the precaution to have nice ones. They're all you seem to see as the people walk about the deck; you get to know them intimately and to dislike some of them so much. I'm afraid you'll think that I've already broken loose; and for aught I know I'm writing as a demoiselle bien-élévee shouldn't write. I don't know whether it's the American air; if it is, all I can say is that the American air's very charming. It makes me impatient and restless, and I sit scribbling here because I'm so eager to arrive and the time passes better if I occupy myself.

I'm in the saloon, where we have our meals, and opposite me is a big round porthole, wide open to let in the smell of the land. Every now and then I rise a little and look through it to see if we're arriving. I mean in the Bay, you know, for we shall not come up to the city till dark. I don't want to lose the Bay; it appears it's so wonderful. I don't exactly understand what it contains except some beautiful islands; but I suppose you'll know all about that. It's easy to see that these are the last hours, for all the people about me are writing letters to put into the post as soon as we come up to the dock. I believe they're dreadful at the custom-house, and you'll remember how many new things you persuaded mamma that—with my preoccupation of marriage—I should take to this country, where even the prettiest girls are expected not to go unadorned. We ruined ourselves in Paris—that's partly accountable for mamma's solemnity—*mais au moins je serai belle*! Moreover I believe that mamma's prepared to say or to do anything that may be necessary for escaping from their odious duties; as she very justly remarks she can't afford to be ruined twice. I don't know how one approaches these terrible *douaniers*, but I mean to invent something very charming. I mean to say "Voyons, Messieurs, a young girl like me, brought up in the strictest foreign traditions, kept always in the background by a very superior mother—*la voilà*; you can see for yourself!—what is it possible that she should attempt to smuggle in? Nothing but a few simple relics of her convent!" I won't tell them my convent was called the Magasin du Bon Marché. Mamma began to scold me three days ago for insisting on so many trunks, and the truth is that between us we've not fewer than seven. For relics, that's a good many! We're all writing very long letters—or at least we're writing a great number. There's no news of the Bay as yet. Mr. Antrobus, mamma's friend, opposite to me, is beginning on his ninth. He's a Right Honourable and a Member of Parliament; he has written during the voyage about a hundred letters and seems greatly alarmed at the number of stamps he'll have to buy when he arrives. He's full of information, but he hasn't enough, for he asks as many questions as mamma when she goes to hire apartments. He's going to "look into" various things; he speaks as if they had a little hole for the purpose. He walks almost as much as I, and has enormous shoes. He asks questions even of me, and I tell him again and again that I know nothing about America. But it makes no difference; he always begins again, and indeed it's not strange he should find my ignorance incredible. "Now how would it be in one of your South-western States?"—that's his favourite way of opening conversation. Fancy me giving an account of one of "my" South-western States! I tell him he had better ask mamma—a little to tease that lady, who knows no more about such places than I. Mr. Antrobus is very big and black; he speaks with a sort of brogue; he has a wife and ten children; he doesn't say—apart from his talking—anything at all to me. But he has lots of letters to people là-bas—I forget that we're just arriving—and mamma, who takes an interest in him in spite of his views (which are dreadfully advanced, and not at all like mamma's own) has promised to give him the entrée to the best society. I don't know what she knows about the best society over here to-day, for we've not kept up our connexions at all, and no one will know—or, I am afraid, care—anything about us. She has an idea we shall be immensely recognised; but really, except the poor little Rucks, who are bankrupt and, I'm told, in no society at all, I don't know on whom we can count. C'est égal, mamma has an idea that, whether or no we appreciate America ourselves, we shall at least be universally appreciated. It's true we have begun to be, a little; you would see that from the way Mr. Cockerel and Mr. Louis Leverett are always inviting me to walk. Both of these gentlemen, who are Americans, have asked leave to call on me in New York, and I've said *Mon Dieu oui*, if it's the custom of the country. Of course I've not dared to tell this to mamma, who flatters herself that we've brought with us in our trunks a complete set of customs of our own and that we shall only have to shake them out a little and put them on when we arrive. If only the two gentlemen I just spoke of don't call at the same time I don't think I shall be too much frightened. If they do, on the other hand, I won't answer for it. They've a particular aversion to each other and are ready to fight about poor little me. I'm only the pretext, however; for, as Mr. Leverett says, it's really the opposition of temperaments. I hope they won't cut each other's throats, for I'm not crazy about either of them. They're very well for the deck of a ship, but I shouldn't care about them in a salon; they're not at all distinguished. They think they are, but they're not; at least Mr. Louis Leverett does; Mr. Cockerel doesn't appear to care so much. They're extremely different—with their opposed temperaments—and each very amusing for a while; but I should get dreadfully tired of passing my life with either. Neither has proposed that as yet; but it's evidently what they're coming to. It will be in a great measure to spite each other, for I think that au fond they don't quite believe in me. If they don't, it's the only point on which they agree. They hate each other awfully; they take such different views. That is Mr. Cockerel hates Mr. Leverett—he calls him a sickly little ass; he pronounces his opinions half affectation and the other half dyspepsia. Mr. Leverett speaks of Mr. Cockerel as a "strident savage," but he allows he finds him most diverting. He says there's nothing in which we can't find a certain entertainment if we only look at it in the right way, and that we have no business with either hating or loving: we ought only to strive to understand. He "claims"—he's always claiming—that to understand is to forgive. Which is very pretty, but I don't like the suppression of our affections, though I've no desire to fix mine upon Mr. Leverett. He's very artistic and talks like an article in some review. He has lived a great deal in Paris, and Mr. Cockerel, who doesn't believe in Paris, says it's what has made him such an idiot.

That's not complimentary to you, dear Louisa, and still less to your brilliant brother; for Mr. Cockerel explains that he means it (the bad effect of Paris) chiefly of men. In fact he means the bad effect of Europe altogether. This, however, is compromising to mamma; and I'm afraid there's no doubt that, from what I've told him, he thinks mamma also an idiot. (I'm not responsible, you know—I've always wanted to go home.) If mamma knew him, which she doesn't, for she always closes her eyes when I pass on his arm, she would think him disgusting. Mr. Leverett meanwhile assures me he's nothing to what we shall see yet. He's from Philadelphia (Mr. Cockerel); he insists that we shall go and see Philadelphia, but mamma says she saw it in 1855 and it was then *affreux*. Mr. Cockerel says that mamma's evidently not familiar with the rush of improvement in this country; he speaks of 1855 as if it were a hundred years ago. Mamma says she knows it goes only too fast, the rush—it goes so fast that it has time to do nothing well; and then Mr. Cockerel, who, to do him justice, is perfectly good-natured, remarks that she had better wait till she has been ashore and seen the improvements. Mamma retorts that she sees them from here, the awful things, and that they give her a sinking of the heart. (This little exchange of ideas is carried on through me; they've never spoken to each other.) Mr. Cockerel, as I say, is extremely good-natured, and he bears out what I've heard said about the men in America being very considerate of the women. They evidently listen to them a great deal; they don't contradict them, but it seems to me this is rather negative. There's very little gallantry in not contradicting one; and it strikes me that there are some things the men don't express. There are others on the ship whom I've noticed. It's as if they were all one's brothers or one's cousins. The extent to which one isn't in danger from them—my dear, my dear! But I promised you not to generalise, and perhaps there will be more expression when we arrive. Mr. Cockerel returns to America, after a general tour, with a renewed conviction that this is the only country. I left him on deck an hour ago looking at the coast-line with an opera-glass and saying it was the prettiest thing he had seen in all his travels. When I remarked that the coast seemed rather low he said it would be all the easier to get ashore. Mr. Leverett at any rate doesn't seem in a hurry to get ashore, he's sitting within sight of me in a corner of the saloon—writing letters, I suppose, but looking, from the way he bites his pen and rolls his eyes about, as if he were composing a sonnet and waiting for a rhyme. Perhaps the sonnet's addressed to me; but I forget that he suppresses the affections! The only person in whom mamma takes much interest is the great French critic, M. Lejaune, whom we have the honour to carry with us. We've read a few of his works, though mamma disapproves of his tendencies and thinks him a dreadful materialist. We've read them for the style; you know he's one of the new Academicians.

He's a Frenchman like any other, except that he's rather more quiet; he has a grey moustache and the ribbon of the Legion of Honour. He's the first French writer of distinction who has been to America since De Tocqueville; the French, in such matters, are not very enterprising. Also he has the air of wondering what he's doing *dans cette galère*. He has come with his beau-frère, who's an engineer and is looking after some mines, and he talks with scarcely any one else, as he speaks no English and appears to take for granted that no one speaks French. Mamma would be delighted to convince him of the contrary; she has never conversed with an Academician. She always makes a little vague inclination, with a smile, when he passes her, and he answers with a most respectful bow; but it goes no further, to mamma's disappointment. He's always with the beau-frère, a rather untidy fat bearded man—decorated too, always smoking and looking at the feet of the ladies, whom mamma (though she has very good feet) has not the courage to *aborder*. I believe M. Lejaune is going to write a book about America, and Mr. Leverett says it will be terrible. Mr. Leverett has made his acquaintance and says M. Lejaune will put him into his book; he says the movement of the French intellect is superb. As a general thing he doesn't care for Academicians, but M. Lejaune's an exception—he's so living, so remorseless, so personal.

I've asked Mr. Cockerel meanwhile what he thinks of M. Lejaune's plan of writing a book, and he answers that he doesn't see what it matters to him that a Frenchman the more should make the motions of a monkey—on that side poor Mr. Cockerel is *de cette force*. I asked him why he hadn't written a book about Europe, and he says that in the first place Europe isn't worth writing about, and that in the second if he said what he thought people would call it a joke. He says they're very superstitious about Europe over here; he wants people in America to behave as if Europe didn't exist. I told this to Mr. Leverett, and he answered that if Europe didn't exist America wouldn't, for Europe keeps us alive by buying our corn. He said also that the trouble with America in the future will be that she'll produce things in such enormous quantities that there won't be enough people in the rest of the world to buy them, and that we shall be left with our productions—most of them very hideous—on our hands. I asked him if he thought corn a hideous production, and he replied that there's nothing more unbeautiful than too

397

much food. I think that to feed the world too well, however, will be after all a *beau rôle*. Of course I don't understand these things, and I don't believe Mr. Leverett does; but Mr. Cockerel seems to know what he's talking about, and he describes America as complete in herself. I don't know exactly what he means, but he speaks as if human affairs had somehow moved over to this side of the world. It may be a very good place for them, and heaven knows I'm extremely tired of Europe, which mamma has always insisted so on my appreciating; but I don't think I like the idea of our being so completely cut off. Mr. Cockerel says it is not we that are cut off, but Europe, and he seems to think Europe has somehow deserved it. That may be; our life over there was sometimes extremely tiresome, though mamma says it's now that our real fatigues will begin. I like to abuse those dreadful old countries myself, but I'm not sure I'm pleased when others do the same. We had some rather pretty moments there after all, and at Piacenza we certainly lived for four francs a day. Mamma's already in a terrible state of mind about the expenses here; she's frightened by what people on the ship (the few she has spoken to) have told her. There's one comfort at any rate—we've spent so much money in coming that we shall have none left to get away. I'm scribbling along, as you see, to occupy me till we get news of the islands. Here comes Mr. Cockerel to bring it. Yes, they're in sight; he tells me they're lovelier than ever and that I must come right up right away. I suppose you'll think I'm already beginning to use the language of the country. It's certain that at the end of the month I shall speak nothing else. I've picked up every dialect, wherever we've travelled; you've heard my Platt-Deutsch and my Neapolitan. But, *voyons un peu* the Bay! I've just called to Mr. Leverett to remind him of the islands. "The islands—the islands? Ah my dear young lady, I've seen Capri, I've seen Ischia!" Well, so have I, but that doesn't prevent . . . (*A little later.*) I've seen the islands—they're rather queer.

II. MRS. CHURCH IN NEW YORK TO MADAME GALOPIN AT GENEVA

October 1880.

If I felt far way from you in the middle of that deplorable Atlantic, chère Madame, how do I feel now, in the heart of this extraordinary city? We've

398

arrived—we've arrived, dear friend; but I don't know whether to tell you that I consider that an advantage. If we had been given our choice of coming safely to land or going down to the bottom of the sea I should doubtless have chosen the former course; for I hold, with your noble husband and in opposition to the general tendency of modern thought, that our lives are not our own to dispose of, but a sacred trust from a higher power by whom we shall be held responsible. Nevertheless if I had foreseen more vividly some of the impressions that awaited me here I'm not sure that, for my daughter at least, I shouldn't have preferred on the spot to hand in our account. Should I not have been less (rather than more) guilty in presuming to dispose of *her* destiny than of my own? There's a nice point for dear M. Galopin to settle—one of those points I've heard him discuss in the pulpit with such elevation. We're safe, however, as I say; by which I mean we're physically safe. We've taken up the thread of our familiar pension-life, but under strikingly different conditions. We've found a refuge in a boarding-house which has been highly recommended to me and where the arrangements partake of the barbarous magnificence that in this country is the only alternative from primitive rudeness. The terms per week are as magnificent as all the rest. The landlady wears diamond ear-rings and the drawing-rooms are decorated with marble statues. I should indeed be sorry to let you know how I've allowed myself to be rançonnée; and I should be still more sorry that it should come to the ears of any of my good friends in Geneva, who know me less well than you and might judge me more harshly. There's no wine given for dinner, and I've vainly requested the person who conducts the establishment to garnish her table more liberally. She says I may have all the wine I want if I will order it at the merchant's and settle the matter with himself. But I've never, as you know, consented to regard our modest allowance of eau rougie as an extra; indeed, I remember that it's largely to your excellent advice that I've owed my habit of being firm on this point.

There are, however, greater difficulties than the question of what we shall drink for dinner, chère Madame. Still, I've never lost courage and I shall not lose it now. At the worst we can re-embark again and seek repose and refreshment on the shores of your beautiful lake. (There's absolutely no scenery here!) We shall not perhaps in that case have achieved what we desired, but we shall at least have made an honourable retreat. What we desire—I know it's just this that puzzles you, dear friend; I don't think you ever really comprehended my motives in taking this formidable step, though you were good enough, and your magnanimous husband was good enough, to press my hand at parting in a way that seemed to tell me you'd still be with me even were I wrong. To be very brief, I wished to put an end to the ceaseless reclamations of my daughter. Many Americans had assured her that she was wasting her belle jeunesse in those historic lands which it was her privilege to see so intimately, and this unfortunate conviction had taken possession of her. "Let me at least see for myself," she used to say; "if I should dislike it over there as much as you promise me, so much the better for you. In that case we'll come back and make a new arrangement at Stuttgart." The experiment's a terribly expensive one, but you know how my devotion never has shrunk from an ordeal. There's another point moreover which, from a mother to a mother, it would be affectation not to touch upon. I remember the just satisfaction with which you announced to me the fiançailles of your charming Cécile. You know with what earnest care my Aurora has been educated—how thoroughly she's acquainted with the principal results of modern research. We've always studied together, we've always enjoyed together. It will perhaps surprise you to hear that she makes these very advantages a reproach to me—represents them as an injury to herself. "In this country," she says, "the gentlemen have not those accomplishments; they care nothing for the results of modern research. Therefore it won't help a young person to be sought in marriage that she can give an account of the latest German presentation of Pessimism." That's possible, and I've never concealed from her that it wasn't for this country I had educated her. If she marries in the United States it's of course my intention that my son-in-law shall accompany us to Europe. But when she calls my attention more and more to these facts I feel that we're moving in a different world. This is more and more the country of the many; the few find less and less place for them; and the individual—well, the individual has quite ceased to be recognised. He's recognised as a voter, but he's not recognised as a gentleman—still less as a lady. My daughter and I of course can only pretend to constitute a *few*!

You know that I've never for a moment remitted my pretensions as an individual, though among the agitations of pension-life I've sometimes needed all my energy to uphold them. "Oh yes, I may be poor," I've had occasion to say, "I may be unprotected, I may be reserved, I may occupy a small apartment au quatrième and be unable to scatter unscrupulous bribes among the domestics; but at least I'm a *person* and have personal rights." In this country the people have rights, but the person has none. You'd have perceived that if you had come with me to make arrangements at this establishment. The very fine lady who condescends to preside over it kept me waiting twenty minutes, and then came sailing in without a word of apology. I had sat very silent, with my eyes on the clock; Aurora amused herself with a false admiration of the room, a wonderful drawing-room with magenta curtains, frescoed walls and photographs of the landlady's friends—as if one cares for her friends! When this exalted personage came in she simply remarked that she had just been trying on a dress—that it took so long to get a skirt to hang. "It seems to take very long indeed!" I answered; "but I hope the skirt's right at last. You might have sent for us to come up and look at it!" She evidently didn't understand, and when I asked her to show us her rooms she handed us over to a negro as dégingandé as herself. While we looked at them I heard her sit down to the piano in the drawing-room; she began to sing an air from a comic opera. I felt certain we had gone quite astray; I didn't know in what house we could be, and was only reassured by seeing a Bible in every room. When we came down our musical hostess expressed no hope the rooms had pleased us, she seemed grossly indifferent to our taking them. She wouldn't consent moreover to the least diminution and was inflexible, as I told you, on the article of our common beverage. When I pushed this point she was so good as to observe that she didn't keep a cabaret. One's not in the least considered; there's no respect for one's privacy, for one's preferences, for one's reserves. The familiarity's without limits, and I've already made a dozen acquaintances, of whom I know, and wish to know, nothing. Aurora tells me she's the "belle of the boarding-house." It appears that this is a great distinction.

It brings me back to my poor child and her prospects. She takes a very critical view of them herself—she tells me I've given her a false education and that no one will marry her to-day. No American will marry her because she's too much of a foreigner, and no foreigner will marry her because she's too much of an American. I remind her how scarcely a day passes that a foreigner, usually of distinction, doesn't—as perversely as you will indeed—select an American bride, and she answers me that in these cases the young lady isn't married for her fine eyes. Not always, I reply; and then she declares that she'll marry no foreigner who shall not be one of the first of the first. You'll say doubtless that she should content herself with advantages that haven't been deemed insufficient for Cécile; but I'll not repeat to you the remark she made when I once employed this argument. You'll doubtless be surprised to hear that I've ceased to argue; but it's time I should confess that I've at last agreed to let her act for herself. She's to live for three months à l'Américaine and I'm to be a mere passive spectator. You'll feel with me that this is a cruel position for a cœur de mère. I count the days till our three months are over, and I know you'll join with me in my prayers. Aurora walks the streets alone; she goes out in the tramway: a voiture de place costs five francs for the least little *course*. (I beseech you not to let it be known that I've sometimes had the weakness.) My daughter's frequently accompanied by a gentleman—by a dozen gentlemen; she remains out for hours and her conduct excites no surprise in this establishment. I know but too well the emotions it will excite in your quiet home. If you betray us, chère Madame, we're lost; and why, after all, should any one know of these things in Geneva? Aurora pretends she has been able to persuade herself that she doesn't care who knows them; but there's a strange expression in her face which proves that her conscience isn't at rest. I watch her, I let her go, but I sit with my hands clasped. There's a peculiar custom in this country—I shouldn't know how to express it in Genevese: it's called "being attentive," and young girls are the object of the futile process. It hasn't necessarily anything to do with projects of marriage—though it's the privilege only of the unmarried and though at the same time (fortunately, and this may surprise you) it has no relation to other projects. It's simply an invention by which young persons of the two sexes pass large parts of their time together with no questions asked. How shall I muster courage to tell you that Aurora now constitutes the main apparent recreation of several gentlemen? Though it has no relation to marriage the practice happily doesn't exclude it, and marriages have been known to take place in consequence (or in spite) of it. It's true that even in this country a young lady may marry but one husband at a time, whereas she may receive at once the attentions of several gentlemen, who are equally entitled "admirers." My daughter then has admirers to an indefinite number. You'll think I'm joking perhaps when I tell you that I'm unable to be exact—I who was formerly l'exactitude même.

Two of these gentlemen are to a certain extent old friends, having been passengers on the steamer which carried us so far from you. One of them, still young, is typical of the American character, but a respectable person and a lawyer considerably launched. Every one in this country follows a profession, but it must be admitted that the professions are more highly remunerated than chez vous. Mr. Cockerel, even while I write you, is in not undisputed, but temporarily triumphant, possession of my child. He called for her an hour ago in a "boghey"—a strange unsafe rickety vehicle, mounted on enormous wheels, which holds two persons very near together; and I watched her from the window take her place at his side. Then he whirled her away behind two little horses with terribly thin legs; the whole equipage—and most of all her being in it—was in the most questionable taste. But she'll return—return positively very much as she went. It's the same when she goes down to Mr. Louis Leverett, who has no vehicle and who merely comes and sits with her in the front salon. He has lived a great deal in Europe and is very fond of the arts, and though I'm not sure I agree with him in his views of the relation of art to life and life to art, and in his interpretation of some of the great works that Aurora and I have studied together, he seems to me a sufficiently serious and intelligent young man. I don't regard him as intrinsically dangerous, but on the other hand he offers absolutely no guarantees. I've no means whatever of ascertaining his pecuniary situation. There's a vagueness on these points which is extremely embarrassing, and it never occurs to young men to offer you a reference. In Geneva I shouldn't be at a loss; I should come to you, chère Madame, with my little inquiry, and what you shouldn't be able to tell me wouldn't be worth my knowing. But no one in New York can give me the smallest information about the état de fortune of Mr. Louis Leverett. It's true that he's a native of Boston, where most of his friends reside; I can't, however, go to the expense of a journey to Boston simply to learn perhaps that Mr. Leverett (the young Louis) has an income of five thousand francs. As I say indeed, he doesn't strike me as dangerous. When Aurora comes back to me after having passed an hour with him she says he has described to her his emotions on visiting the home of Shelley or discussed some of the differences between the Boston temperament and that of the Italians of the Renaissance. You'll not enter into these rapprochements, and I can't blame you. But you won't betray me, chère Madame?

III. FROM MISS STURDY AT NEWPORT TO MRS. DRAPER AT OUCHY

September 1880.

I promised to tell you how I like it, but the truth is I've gone to and fro so often that I've ceased to like and dislike. Nothing strikes me as unexpected; I expect everything in its order. Then too, you know, I'm not a critic; I've no talent for keen analysis, as the magazines say; I don't go into the reasons of things. It's true I've been for a longer time than usual on the wrong side of the water, and I admit that I feel a little out of training for American life. They're breaking me in very fast, however. I don't mean that they bully me—I absolutely decline to be bullied. I say what I think, because I believe I've on the whole the advantage of knowing what I think—when I think anything; which is half the battle. Sometimes indeed I think nothing at all. They don't like that over here; they like you to have impressions. That they like these impressions to be favourable appears to me perfectly natural; I don't make a crime to them of this; it seems to me on the contrary a very amiable point. When individuals betray it we call them sympathetic; I don't see why we shouldn't give nations the same benefit. But there are things I haven't the least desire to have an opinion about. The privilege of indifference is the dearest we possess, and I hold that intelligent people are known by the way they exercise it. Life is full of rubbish, and we have at least our share of it over here. When you wake up in the morning you find that during the night a cartload has been deposited in your front garden. I decline, however, to have any of it in my premises; there are thousands of things I want to know nothing about. I've outlived the necessity of being hypocritical; I've nothing to gain and everything to lose. When one's fifty years old—single stout and red in the face—one has outlived a good many necessities. They tell me over here that my increase of weight's extremely marked, and though they don't tell me I'm coarse I feel they think me so. There's very little coarseness here—not quite enough, I think—though there's plenty of vulgarity, which is a very different thing. On the whole the country becomes much more agreeable. It isn't that the people are charming, for that they always were (the best of them, I mean—it isn't true of the others), but that places and things as well recognise the possibility of pleasing. The houses are extremely good and look extraordinarily fresh and clean. Many European interiors seem in comparison musty and gritty. We have a great deal of taste; I shouldn't wonder if we should end by inventing something pretty; we only need a little time. Of course as yet it's all imitation, except, by the way, these delicious piazzas. I'm sitting on one now; I'm writing to you with my portfolio on my knees. This broad light *loggia* surrounds the house with a movement as free as the expanded wings of a bird, and the wandering airs come up from the deep sea, which murmurs on the rocks at the end of the lawn.

Newport's more charming even than you remember it; like everything else over here it has improved. It's very exquisite to-day; it's indeed, I think, in all the world the only exquisite watering-place, for I detest the whole genus. The crowd has left it now, which makes it all the better, though plenty of talkers remain in these large light luxurious houses which are planted with a kind of Dutch definiteness all over the green carpet of the cliff. This carpet's very neatly laid and wonderfully well swept, and the sea, just at hand, is capable of prodigies of blue. Here and there a pretty woman strolls over one of the lawns, which all touch each other, you know, without hedges or fences; the light looks intense as it plays on her brilliant dress; her large parasol shines like a silver dome. The long lines of the far shores are soft and pure, though they are places one hasn't the least desire to visit. Altogether the effect's very delicate, and anything that's delicate counts immensely over here; for delicacy, I think, is as rare as coarseness. I'm talking to you of the sea, however, without having told you a word of my voyage. It was very comfortable and amusing; I should like to take another next month. You know I'm almost offensively well at sea—I breast the weather and brave the storm. We had no storm fortunately, and I had brought with me a supply of light literature; so I passed nine days on deck in my sea-chair with my heels up—passed them reading Tauchnitz novels. There was a great lot of people, but no one in particular save some fifty American girls. You know all about the American girl, however, having been one yourself. They're on the whole very nice, but fifty's too many; there are always too many. There was an inquiring Briton, a radical M.P., by name Mr. Antrobus, who entertained me as much as any one else. He's an excellent man; I even asked him to come down here and spend a couple of days. He looked rather frightened till I told him he shouldn't be alone with me, that the house was my brother's and that I gave the invitation in his name. He came a week ago; he goes everywhere; we've heard of him in a dozen places. The English are strangely simple, or at least they seem so over here. Their old measurements and comparisons desert them; they don't know whether it's all a joke or whether it's too serious by half. We're quicker than they, though we talk so much more slowly. We think fast, and yet we talk as deliberately as if we were speaking a foreign language. They toss off their sentences with an air of easy familiarity with the tongue, and yet they misunderstand two-thirds of what people say to them. Perhaps after all it is only *our* thoughts they think slowly; they think their own often to a lively tune enough.

Mr. Antrobus arrived here in any case at eight o'clock in the morning; I don't know how he managed it; it appears to be his favourite hour; wherever we've heard of him he has come in with the dawn. In England he would arrive at 5.30 P.M. He asks innumerable questions, but they're easy to answer, for he has a sweet credulity. He made me rather ashamed; he's a better American than so many of us; he takes us more seriously than we take ourselves. He seems to think we've an oligarchy of wealth growing up which he advised me to be on my guard against. I don't know exactly what I can do, but I promised him to look out. He's fearfully energetic; the energy of the people here is nothing to that of the inquiring Briton. If we should devote half the zeal to building up our institutions that they devote to obtaining information about them we should have a very satisfactory country. Mr. Antrobus seemed to think very well of us—which surprised me on the whole, since, say what one will, it's far from being so agreeable as England. It's very horrid that this should be; and it's delightful, when one thinks of it, that some things in England are after all so hateful. At the same time Mr. Antrobus appeared to be a good deal preoccupied with our dangers. I don't understand quite what they are; they seem to me so few on a Newport piazza this bright still day. Yet alas what one sees on a Newport piazza isn't America; it's only the back of Europe. I don't mean to say I haven't noticed any dangers since my return; there are two or three that seem to me very serious, but they aren't those Mr. Antrobus apprehends. One, for instance, is that we shall cease to speak the English language, which I prefer so to any other. It's less and less spoken; American's crowding it out. All the children speak American, which as a child's language is dreadfully rough. It's exclusively in use in the schools; all the magazines and newspapers are in American. Of course a people of fifty millions who have invented a new civilisation have a right to a language of their own; that's what they tell me, and I can't quarrel with it. But I wish they had made it as pretty as the mother-tongue, from which, when all's said, it's more or less derived. We ought to have invented something as noble as our country. They tell me it's more expressive, and yet some admirable things have been said in the Queen's English. There can be no question of the Queen over here of course, and American no doubt is the music of the future. Poor dear future, how "expressive" you'll be! For women and children, as I say, it strikes one as very rough; and, moreover, they don't speak it well, their own though it be. My small nephews, when I first came home, hadn't gone back to school, and it distressed me to see that, though they're charming children, they had the vocal inflexions of little news-boys. My niece is sixteen years old; she has the sweetest nature possible; she's extremely well-bred and is dressed to perfection. She chatters from morning till night; but its helplessness breaks my heart. These little persons are in the opposite case from so many English girls who know how to speak but don't know how to talk. My niece knows how to talk but doesn't know how to speak.

If I allude to the young people, that's our other danger; the young people are eating us up—there's nothing in America but the young people. The country's made for the rising generation; life's arranged for them; they're the destruction of society. People talk of them, consider them, defer to them, bow down to them. They're always present, and whenever they're present nothing else of the smallest interest is. They're often very pretty, and physically are wonderfully looked after; they're scoured and brushed, they wear hygienic clothes, they go every week to the dentist's. But the little boys kick your shins and the little girls offer to slap your face. There's an immense literature entirely addressed to them in which the kicking of shins and the slapping of faces carries the day. As a woman of fifty I protest, I insist on being judged by my peers. It's too late, however, for several millions of little feet are actively engaged in stamping out conversation, and I don't see how they can long fail to keep it under. The future's theirs; adult forms will evidently be at an increasing discount. Longfellow wrote a charming little poem called "The Children's Hour," but he ought to have called it "The Children's Century." And by children I naturally don't mean simple infants; I mean everything of less than twenty. The social importance of the young American increases steadily up to that age and then suddenly stops. The little girls of course are more important than the lads, but the lads are very important too. I'm struck with the way they're known and talked about; they're small celebrities; they have reputations and pretensions; they're taken very seriously. As for the little girls, as I just said, they're ever so much too many. You'll say perhaps that my fifty years and my red face are jealous of them. I don't think so, because I don't suffer; my red face doesn't frighten people away, and I always find plenty of talkers. The young things themselves, I believe, like me very much, and I delight in the young things. They're often very pretty; not so pretty as people say in the magazines, but pretty enough. The magazines rather overdo that; they make a mistake. I've seen no great beauties, but the level of prettiness is high, and occasionally one sees a woman completely handsome. (As a general thing, a pretty person here means a person with a pretty face. The figure's rarely mentioned, though there are several good ones.) The level of prettiness is high, but the level of conversation is low; that's one of the signs of its being a young ladies' country. There are a good many things young ladies can't talk about, but think of all the things they can when they are as clever as most of these. Perhaps one ought to content one's self with that measure, but it's difficult if one has lived long by a larger one. This one's decidedly narrow—I stretch it sometimes till it cracks. Then it is they call me coarse, which I undoubtedly am, thank goodness.

What it comes to, obviously, is that people's talk is much less conveniently free than in Europe; I'm struck with that wherever I go. There are certain things that are never said at all, certain allusions that are never made. There are no light stories, no propos risqués. I don't know exactly what people find to bite into, for the supply of scandal's small and it's little more than twaddle at that. They don't seem, however, to lack topics. The little girls are always there; they keep the gates of conversation; very little passes that's not innocent. I find we do very well without wickedness, and for myself, as I take my ease, I don't miss my liberties. You remember what I thought of the tone of your table in Florence last year, and how surprised you were when I asked you why you allowed such things. You said they were like the courses of the seasons; one couldn't prevent them; also that to change the tone of your table you'd have to change so many other things. Of course in your house one never saw a little girl; I was the only spinster and no one was afraid of me. Likewise if talk's more innocent in this country manners are so to begin with. The liberty of the young people is the strongest proof of it. The little girls are let loose in the world, and the world gets more good of it than ces demoiselles get harm. In your world—pardon me, but you know what I mean—this wouldn't do at all. Your world's a sad affair—the young ladies would encounter all sorts of horrors. Over here, considering the way they knock about, they remain wonderfully simple, and the reason is that society protects them instead of setting them traps. There's almost no gallantry as you understand it; the flirtations are child's play. People have no time for making love; the men in particular are extremely busy. I'm told that sort of thing consumes hours; I've never had any time for it myself. If the leisure class should increase here considerably there may possibly be a change; but I doubt it, for the women seem to me in all essentials exceedingly reserved. Great superficial frankness, but an extreme dread of complications. The men strike me as very good fellows. I find them at bottom better than the women, who if not inveterately hard haven't at least the European, the (as I heard some one once call it) chemical softness. They're not so nice to the men as the men are to them; I mean of course in proportion, you know. But women aren't so nice as men "anyway," as they say here.

The men at any rate are professional, commercial; there are very few gentlemen pure and simple. This personage needs to be very well done, however, to be of great utility; and I suppose you won't pretend he's always well done in your countries. When he's not, the less of him the better. It's very much the same indeed with the system on which the female young are brought up. (You see I have to come back to the female young.) When it succeeds they're the most charming creatures possible; when it doesn't the failure's disastrous. If a girl's a very nice girl the American method brings her to great completeness—makes all her graces flower; but if she isn't nice it plays the devil with any possible compromise or *biais* in the interest of social convenience. In a word the American girl's rarely negative, and when she isn't a great success she's a great warning. In nineteen cases out of twenty, among the people who know how to live—I won't say what *their* proportion is—the results are highly satisfactory. The girls aren't shy, but I don't know why they should be, for there's really nothing here to be afraid of. Manners are very gentle, very humane; the democratic system deprives people of weapons that every one doesn't equally possess. No one's formidable; no one's on stilts; no one has great pretensions or any recognised right to be arrogant. I think there's not much wickedness, and there's certainly less human or social cruelty—less than in "good" (that is in more amusing) society. Every one can sit—no one's kept standing. One's much less liable to be snubbed, which you will say is a pity. I think it is—to a certain extent; but on the other hand folly's less fatuous in form than in your countries; and as people generally have fewer revenges to take there's less need of their being squashed in advance. The general good nature, the social equality, deprive them of triumphs on the one hand and of grievances on the other. There's extremely little impertinence, there's almost none. You'll say I'm describing a terrible world, a world without great figures or great social prizes. You've hit it, my dear—there are no great figures. (The great prize of course in Europe is the opportunity to *be* a great figure.) You'd miss these things a good deal—you who delight to recognise greatness; and my advice to you therefore is never to come back. You'd miss the small people even more than the great; every one's middle-sized, and you can never have that momentary sense of profiting by the elevation of your class which is so agreeable in Europe. I needn't add that you don't, either, languish with its depression. There are at all events no brilliant types—the most important people seem to lack dignity. They're very bourgeois; they make little jokes; on occasion they make puns; they've no form; they're too good-natured. The men have no style; the women, who are fidgety and talk too much, have it only in their tournures, where they have it superabundantly.

Well, I console myself—since consolation is needed—with the greater bonhomie. Have you ever arrived at an English country-house in the dusk of a winter's day? Have you ever made a call in London when you knew nobody but the hostess? People here are more expressive, more demonstrative; and it's a pleasure, when one comes back—if one happens, like me, to be no one in particular—to feel one's merely personal and unclassified value rise. They attend to you more; they have you on their mind; they talk to you; they listen to you. That is the men do; the women listen very little—not enough. They interrupt, they prattle, one feels their presence too much as importunate and untrained sound. I imagine this is partly because their wits are quick and they think of a good many things to say; not indeed that they always say such wonders! Perfect repose, after all, is not *all* self-control; it's also partly stupidity. American women, however, make too many vague exclamations— say too many indefinite things, have in short still a great deal of nature. The American order or climate or whatever gives them a nature they *can* let loose. Europe has to protect itself with more art. On the whole I find very little affectation, though we shall probably have more as we improve. As yet people haven't the assurance that carries those things off; they know too much about each other. The trouble is that over here we've all been brought up together. You'll think this a picture of a dreadfully insipid society; but I hasten to add that it's not all so tame as that. I've been speaking of the people that one meets socially, and these're the smallest part of American life. The others—those one meets on a basis of mere convenience—are much more exciting; they keep one's temper in healthy exercise. I mean the people in the shops and on the railroads; the servants, the hack-men, the labourers, the conductors; every one of whom you buy anything or have occasion to make an inquiry. With them you need all your best manners, for you must always have enough for two. If you think we're *too* democratic taste a little of American life in these

411

walks and you'll be reassured. This is the region of inequality, and you'll find plenty of people to make your curtsey to. You see it from below—the weight of inequality's on your own back. You asked me to tell you about prices. They're unspeakable.

IV. FROM THE RIGHT HON. EDWARD ANTROBUS, M.P., IN BOSTON TO THE HONOURABLE MRS. ANTROBUS

November 1880.

MY DEAR SUSAN,

I sent you a post-card on the 13th and a native newspaper yesterday; I really have had no time to write. I sent you the newspaper partly because it contained a report—extremely incorrect—of some remarks I made at the meeting of the Association of the Teachers of New England; partly because it's so curious that I thought it would interest you and the children. I cut out some portions I didn't think it well the children should go into—the passages remaining contain the most striking features. Please point out to the children the peculiar orthography, which probably will be adopted in England by the time they are grown up; the amusing oddities of expression and the like. Some of them are intentional; you'll have heard of the celebrated American humour—remind me, by the way, on my return to Thistleton, to give you a few of the examples of it that my own experience supplies. Certain other of the journalistic eccentricities I speak of are unconscious and are perhaps on that account the more diverting. Point out to the children the difference—in so far as you're sure that you yourself perceive it. You must excuse me if these lines are not very legible; I'm writing them by the light of a railway lamp which rattles above my left ear; it being only at odd moments that I can find time to extend my personal researches. You'll say this is a very odd moment indeed when I tell you I'm in bed in a sleeping-car. I occupy the upper berth (I will explain to you the arrangement when I return) while the lower forms the couch—the jolts are fearful—of an unknown female. You'll be very anxious for my explanation, but I assure you that the circumstance I mention is the custom of the country. I myself am assured that a lady may travel in this manner all over the Union (the Union of States) without a loss of consideration. In case of her occupying the upper berth I presume it would be different, but I must make inquiries on this point. Whether it be the fact that a mysterious being of another sex has retired to rest behind the same curtains, or whether it be the swing of the train, which rushes through the air with very much the same movement as the tail of a kite, the situation is at the best so anomalous that I'm unable to sleep. A ventilator's open just over my head, and a lively draught, mingled with a drizzle of cinders, pours in through this dubious advantage. (I will describe to you its mechanism on my return.) If I had occupied the lower berth I should have had a whole window to myself, and by drawing back the blind—a safe proceeding at the dead of night—I should have been able, by the light of an extraordinary brilliant moon, to see a little better what I write. The question occurs to me, however, would the lady below me in that case have ascended to the upper berth? (You know my old taste for hypothetic questions.) I incline to think (from what I have seen) that she would simply have requested me to evacuate my own couch. (The ladies in this country ask for anything they want.) In this case, I suppose, I should have had an extensive view of the country, which, from what I saw of it before I turned in (while the sharer of my privacy was going to bed) offered a rather ragged expanse dotted with little white wooden houses that resembled in the moonshine large pasteboard boxes. I've been unable to ascertain as precisely as I should wish by whom these modest residences are occupied; for they are too small to be the homes of country gentlemen, there's no peasantry here, and (in New England, for all the corn comes from the far West) there are no yeomen nor farmers. The information one receives in this country is apt to be rather conflicting, but I'm determined to sift the mystery to the bottom.

I've already noted down a multitude of facts bearing on the points that interest me most—the operation of the school-boards, the co-education of the sexes, the elevation of the tone of the lower classes, the participation of the latter in political life. Political life indeed is almost wholly confined to the lower middle class and the upper section of the lower class. In fact in some of the large towns the lowest order of all participates considerably—a very interesting phase, to which I shall give more attention. It's very gratifying to see the taste for public affairs pervading so many social strata, but the indifference of the gentry is a fact not to be lightly considered. It may be objected perhaps that there are no gentry; and it's very true that I've not yet encountered a character of the type of Lord Bottomley—a type which I'm free to confess I should be sorry to see disappear from our English system, if system it may be called where so much is the growth of blind and incoherent forces. It's nevertheless obvious that an idle and luxurious class exists in this country and that it's less exempt than in our own from the reproach of preferring inglorious ease to the furtherance of liberal ideas. It's rapidly increasing, and I'm not sure that the indefinite growth of the dilettante spirit, in connexion with large and lavishly-expended wealth, is an unmixed good even in a society in which freedom of development has obtained so many interesting triumphs. The fact that this body is not represented in the governing class is perhaps as much the result of the jealousy with which it is viewed by the more earnest workers as of its own (I dare not perhaps apply a harsher term than) levity. Such at least is the impression made on me in the Middle States and in New England; in the South-west, the North-west and the far West it will doubtless be liable to correction. These divisions are probably new to you; but they are the general denomination of large and flourishing communities, with which I hope to make myself at least superficially acquainted. The fatigue of traversing, as I habitually do, three or four hundred miles at a bound, is of course considerable; but there is usually much to feed the mind by the way. The conductors of the trains, with whom I freely converse, are often men of vigorous and original views and even of some social eminence. One of them a few days ago gave me a letter of introduction to his brother-in-law, who's president of a Western University. Don't have any fear therefore that I'm not in the best society!

The arrangements for travelling are as a general thing extremely ingenious, as you will probably have inferred from what I told you above; but it must at the same time be conceded that some of them are more ingenious than happy. Some of the facilities with regard to luggage, the transmission of parcels and the like are doubtless very useful when thoroughly mastered, but I've not yet succeeded in availing myself of them without disaster. There are on the other hand no cabs and no porters, and I've calculated that I've myself carried my *impedimenta*—which, you know, are somewhat numerous, and from which I can't bear to be separated—some seventy or eighty miles. I have sometimes thought it was a great mistake not to bring Plummeridge—he would have been useful on such occasions. On the other hand the startling question would have presented itself of who would have carried Plummeridge's portmanteau? He would have been useful indeed for brushing and packing my clothes and getting me my tub; I travel with a large tin one—there are none to be obtained at the inns—and the transport of this receptacle often presents the most insoluble difficulties. It is often too an object of considerable embarrassment in arriving at private houses, where the servants have less reserve of manner than in England; and to tell you the truth I'm by no means certain at the present moment that the tub has been placed in the train with me. "On board" the train is the consecrated phrase here; it's an allusion to the tossing and pitching of the concatenation of cars, so similar to that of a vessel in a storm. As I was about to inquire, however, Who would get Plummeridge *his* tub and attend to his little comforts? We couldn't very well make our appearance, on arriving for a visit, with *two* of the utensils I've named; even if as regards a single one I have had the courage, as I may say, of a lifelong habit. It would hardly be expected that we should both use the same; though there have been occasions in my travels as to which I see no way of blinking the fact that Plummeridge would have had to sit down to dinner with me. Such a contingency would completely have unnerved him, so that on the whole it was doubtless the wiser part to leave him respectfully touching his hat on the tender in the Mersey. No one touches his hat over here, and, deem this who will the sign of a more advanced social order, I confess that when I see poor Plummeridge again that familiar little gesture— familiar I mean only in the sense of one's immemorial acquaintance with it—will give me a measurable satisfaction. You'll see from what I tell you that democracy is not a mere word in this country, and I could give you many more instances of its universal reign. This, however, is what we come here to look at and, in so far as there appears proper occasion, to admire; though I'm by no means sure that we can hope to establish within an appreciable time a corresponding change in the somewhat rigid fabric of English manners. I'm not even inclined to believe such a change desirable; you know this is one of the points on which I don't as yet see my way to going so far as Lord B. I've always held that there's a certain social ideal of inequality as well as of equality, and if I've found the people of this country, as a general thing, quite equal to each other, I'm not quite ready to go so far as to say that, as a whole, they're equal to—pardon that dreadful blot! The movement of the train and the precarious nature of the light—it is close to my nose and most offensive—would, I flatter myself, long since have got the better of a less resolute diarist!

What I was distinctly *not* prepared for is the very considerable body of aristocratic feeling that lurks beneath this republican simplicity. I've on several occasions been made the confidant of these romantic but delusive vagaries, of which the stronghold appears to be the Empire City—a slang name for the rich and predominant, but unprecedentedly maladministered and disillusioned New York. I was assured in many quarters that this great desperate eternally-swindled city at least is ripe, everything else failing, for the monarchical experiment or revolution, and that if one of the Queen's sons would come over to sound the possibilities he would meet with the highest encouragement. This information was given me in strict confidence, with closed doors, as it were; it reminded me a good deal of the dreams of the old Jacobites when they whispered their messages to the king across the water. I doubt, however, whether these less excusable visionaries will be able to secure the services of a Pretender, for I fear that in such a case he would encounter a still more fatal Culloden. I have given a good deal of time, as I told you, to the educational system, and have visited no fewer than one hundred and forty-three schools and colleges. It's extraordinary the number of persons who are being educated in this country; and yet at the same time the tone of the people is less scholarly than one might expect. A lady a few days since described to me her daughter as being always "on the go," which I take to be a jocular way of saying that the young lady was very fond of paying visits. Another person, the wife of a United States Senator, informed me that if I should go to Washington in January I should be quite "in the swim." I don't regard myself as slow to grasp new meanings, however whimsical; but in this case the lady's explanation made her phrase rather more than less ambiguous. To say that I'm on the go describes very accurately my own situation. I went yesterday to the Poganuc High School, to hear fifty-seven boys and girls recite in unison a most remarkable ode to the American flag, and shortly afterward attended a ladies' luncheon at which some eighty or ninety of the sex were present. There was only one individual in trousers—his trousers, by the way, though he brought several pair, begin to testify to the fury of his movements! The men in America absent themselves systematically from this meal, at which ladies assemble in large numbers to discuss religious, political and social topics.

Immense female symposia at which every delicacy is provided are one of the most striking features of American life, and would seem to prove that our sex is scarcely so indispensable in the scheme of creation as it sometimes supposes. I've been admitted on the footing of an Englishman—"just to show you some of our bright women," the hostess yesterday remarked. ("Bright" here has the meaning of *intellectually remarkable*.) I noted indeed the frequency of the predominantly cerebral—as they call it here "brainy"—type. These rather oddly invidious banquets are organised according to age, for I've also been present as an inquiring stranger at several "girls' lunches," from which married ladies are rigidly excluded, but here the fair revellers were equally numerous and equally "bright." There's a good deal I should like to tell you about my study of the educational question, but my position's now somewhat cramped, and I must dismiss the subject briefly. My leading impression is that the children are better educated (in proportion of course) than the adults. The position of a child is on the whole one of great distinction. There's a popular ballad of which the refrain, if I'm not mistaken, is "Make me a child again just for to-night!" and which seems to express the sentiment of regret for lost privileges. At all events they are a powerful and independent class, and have organs, of immense circulation, in the press. They are often extremely "bright." I've talked with a great many teachers, most of them lady-teachers, as they are here called. The phrase doesn't mean teachers of ladies, as you might suppose, but applies to the sex of the instructress, who often has large classes of young men under her control. I was lately introduced to a young woman of twenty-three who occupies the chair of Moral Philosophy and Belles-Lettres in a Western University and who told me with the utmost frankness that she's "just adored" by the undergraduates. This young woman was the daughter of a petty trader in one of the South-western States and had studied at Amanda College in Missourah, an institution at which young people of the two sexes pursue their education together. She was very pretty and modest, and expressed a great desire to see something of English country life, in consequence of which I made her promise to come down to Thistleton in the event of her crossing the Atlantic. She's not the least like Gwendolen or Charlotte, and I'm not prepared to say how they would get on with her; the boys would probably do better. Still, I think her acquaintance would be of value to dear Miss Gulp, and the two might pass their time very pleasantly in the school-room. I grant you freely that those I have seen here are much less comfortable than the school-room at Thistleton. Has Charlotte, by the way, designed any more texts for the walls? I've been extremely interested in my visit to Philadelphia, where I saw several thousand little red houses with white steps, occupied by intelligent artisans and arranged (in streets) on the rectangular system. Improved cooking-stoves, rosewood pianos, gas and hot water, esthetic furniture and complete sets of the British Essayists. A tramway through every street; every block of exactly equal length; blocks and houses economically lettered and numbered. There's absolutely no loss of time and no need of looking for, or indeed *at,* anything. The mind always on one's object; it's very delightful.

V. FROM LOUIS LEVERETT IN BOSTON TO HARVARD TREMONT IN PARIS

November 1880.

The scales have turned, my sympathetic Harvard, and the beam that has lifted you up has dropped me again on this terribly hard spot. I'm extremely sorry to have missed you in London, but I received your little note and took due heed of your injunction to let you know how I got on. I don't get on at all, my dear Harvard—I'm consumed with the love of the further shore. I've been so long away that I've dropped out of my place in this little Boston world and the shallow tides of New England life have closed over it. I'm a stranger here and find it hard to believe I ever was a native. It's very hard, very cold, very vacant. I think of your warm rich Paris; I think of the Boulevard Saint-

Michel on the mild spring evenings; I see the little corner by the window (of the Café de la Jeunesse) where I used to sit: the doors are open, the soft deep breath of the great city comes in. The sense is of a supreme splendour and an incomparable arrangement, yet there's a kind of tone, of body, in the radiance; the mighty murmur of the ripest civilisation in the world comes in; the dear old *peuple de Paris*, the most interesting people in the world, pass by. I've a little book in my pocket; it's exquisitely printed, a modern Elzevir. It consists of a lyric cry from the heart of young France and is full of the sentiment of form. There's no form here, dear Harvard; I had no idea how little form there is. I don't know what I shall do; I feel so undraped, so uncurtained, so uncushioned; I feel as if I were sitting in the centre of a mighty "reflector." A terrible crude glare is over everything; the earth looks peeled and excoriated; the raw heavens seem to bleed with the quick hard light.

I've not got back my rooms in West Cedar Street; they're occupied by a mesmeric healer. I'm staying at an hotel and it's all very dreadful. Nothing for one's self, nothing for one's preferences and habits. No one to receive you when you arrive; you push in through a crowd, you edge up to a counter, you write your name in a horrible book where every one may come and stare at it and finger it. A man behind the counter stares at you in silence; his stare seems to say "What the devil do *you* want?" But after this stare he never looks at you again. He tosses down a key at you; he presses a bell; a savage Irishman arrives. "Take him away," he seems to say to the Irishman; but it's all done in silence; there's no answer to your own wild wail—"What's to be done with me, please?" "Wait and you'll see" the awful silence seems to say. There's a great crowd round you, but there's also a great stillness; every now and then you hear some one expectorate. There are a thousand people in this huge and hideous structure; they feed together in a big white-walled room. It's lighted by a thousand gas-jets and heated by cast-iron screens which vomit forth torrents of scorching air. The temperature's terrible; the atmosphere's more so; the furious light and heat seem to intensify the dreadful definiteness. When things are so ugly they shouldn't be so definite, and they're terribly ugly here. There's no mystery in the corners, there's no light and shade in the types. The people are haggard and joyless; they look as if they had no passions, no tastes, no senses. They sit feeding in silence under the dry hard

419

light; occasionally I hear the high firm note of a child. The servants are black and familiar; their faces shine as they shuffle about; there are blue tones in their dark masks. They've no manners; they address but don't answer you; they plant themselves at your elbow (it rubs their clothes as you eat) and watch you as if your proceedings were strange. They deluge you with iced water; it's the only thing they'll bring you; if you look round to summon them they've gone for more. If you read the newspaper—which I don't, gracious heaven, I can't!—they hang over your shoulder and peruse it also. I always fold it up and present it to them; the newspapers here are indeed for an African taste.

Then there are long corridors defended by gusts of hot air; down the middle swoops a pale little girl on parlour skates. "Get out of my way!" she shrieks as she passes; she has ribbons in her hair and frills on her dress; she makes the tour of the immense hotel. I think of Puck, who put a girdle round the earth in forty minutes, and wonder what *he* said as he flitted by. A black waiter marches past me bearing a tray that he thrusts into my spine as he goes. It's laden with large white jugs; they tinkle as he moves, and I recognise the unconsoling fluid. We're dying of iced water, of hot air, of flaring gas. I sit in my room thinking of these things—this room of mine which is a chamber of pain. The walls are white and bare, they shine in the rays of a horrible chandelier of imitation bronze which depends from the middle of the ceiling. It flings a patch of shadow on a small table covered with white marble, of which the genial surface supports at the present moment the sheet of paper I thus employ for you; and when I go to bed (I like to read in bed, Harvard) it becomes an object of mockery and torment. It dangles at inaccessible heights; it stares me in the face; it flings the light on the covers of my book but not upon the page—the little French Elzevir I love so well. I rise and put out the gas—when my room becomes even lighter than before. Then a crude illumination from the hall, from the neighbouring room, pours through the glass openings that surmount the two doors of my apartment. It covers my bed, where I toss and groan; it beats in through my closed lids; it's accompanied by the most vulgar, though the most human, sounds. I spring up to call for some help, some remedy; but there's no bell and I feel desolate and weak. There's only a strange orifice in the wall, through which the traveller in distress may transmit his appeal. I fill it with incoherent sounds, and sounds more incoherent yet come back to me. I gather at last their meaning; they appear to constitute an awful inquiry. A hollow impersonal voice wishes to know what I want, and the very question paralyses me. I want everything—yet I want nothing, nothing this hard impersonality can give! I want my little corner of Paris; I want the rich, the deep, the dark Old World; I want to be out of this horrible place. Yet I can't confide all this to that mechanical tube; it would be of no use; a barbarous laugh would come up from the office. Fancy appealing in these sacred, these intimate moments to an "office"; fancy calling out into indifferent space for a candle, for a curtain! I pay incalculable sums in this dreadful house, and yet haven't a creature to assist me. I fling myself back on my couch and for a long time afterwards the orifice in the wall emits strange murmurs and rumblings. It seems unsatisfied and indignant and is evidently scolding me for my vagueness. My vagueness indeed, dear Harvard! I loathe their horrible arrangements—isn't that definite enough?

You asked me to tell you whom I see and what I think of my friends. I haven't very many; I don't feel at all *en rapport*. The people are very good, very serious, very devoted to their work; but there's a terrible absence of variety of type. Every one's Mr. Jones, Mr. Brown, and every one looks like Mr. Jones and Mr. Brown. They're thin, they're diluted in the great tepid bath of Democracy! They lack completeness of identity; they're quite without modelling. No, they're not beautiful, my poor Harvard; it must be whispered that they're not beautiful. You may say that they're as beautiful as the French, as the Germans; but I can't agree with you there. The French, the Germans, have the greatest beauty of all, the beauty of their ugliness—the beauty of the strange, the grotesque. These people are not even ugly—they're only plain. Many of the girls are pretty, but to be only pretty is (to my sense) to be plain. Yet I've had some talk. I've seen a young woman. She was on the steamer, and I afterwards saw her in New York—a mere maiden thing, yet a peculiar type, a real personality: a great deal of modelling, a great deal of colour, and withal something elusive and ambiguous. She was not, however, of this country; she was a compound of far-off things. But she was looking for something here—like me. We found each other, and for a moment that was enough. I've lost her now; I'm sorry, because she liked to listen to me. She has passed away; I shall not see her again. She liked to listen to me; she almost understood.

VI. FROM M. GUSTAVE LEJAUNE OF THE FRENCH ACADEMY IN WASHINGTON TO M. ADOLPHE BOUCHE IN PARIS

December 1880.

I give you my little notes; you must make allowances for haste, for bad inns, for the perpetual scramble, for ill-humour. Everywhere the same impression—the platitude of unbalanced democracy intensified by the platitude of the spirit of commerce. Everything on an immense scale—everything illustrated by millions of examples. My brother-in-law is always busy; he has appointments, inspections, interviews, disputes. The people, it appears, are incredibly sharp in conversation, in argument; they wait for you in silence at the corner of the road and then suddenly discharge their revolver. If you fall they empty your pockets; the only chance is to shoot them first. With this no amenities, no preliminaries, no manners, no care for the appearance. I wander about while my brother's occupied; I lounge along the streets; I stop at the corners; I look into the shops; *je regarde passer les femmes.* It's an easy country to see; one sees everything there is; the civilisation's skin deep; you don't have to dig. This positive practical pushing bourgeoisie is always about its business; it lives in the street, in the hotel, in the train; one's always in a crowd—there are seventy-five people in the tramway. They sit in your lap; they stand on your toes; when they wish to pass they simply push you. Everything in silence; they know that silence is golden and they've the worship of gold. When the conductor wishes your fare he gives you a poke, very serious, without a word. As for the types—but there's only one, they're all variations of the same—the commis-voyageur *minus* the gaiety. The women are often pretty; you meet the young ones in the streets, in the trains, in search of a husband. They look at you frankly, coldly, judicially, to see if you'll serve; but they don't want what you might think (*du moines on me l'assure*); they only want the husband. A Frenchman may mistake; he needs to be sure he's right, and I always make sure. They begin at fifteen; the mother sends them out; it lasts all day (with an interval for dinner at a pastry-cook's); sometimes it goes on for ten years. If they haven't by that time found him they give it up; they make place for the *cadettes*, as the number of women is enormous. No salons, no society, no conversation; people don't receive at home; the young girls have to look for the husband where they can. It's no disgrace not to find him—several have never done so. They continue to go about unmarried—from the force of habit, from the love of movement, without hopes, without regrets. There's no imagination, no sensibility, no desire for the convent.

We've made several journeys—few of less than three hundred miles. Enormous trains, enormous *wagons*, with beds and lavatories, with negroes who brush you with a big broom, as if they were grooming a horse. A bounding movement, a roaring noise, a crowd of people who look horribly tired, a boy who passes up and down hurling pamphlets and sweetmeats into your face: that's an American journey. There are windows in the *wagons*—enormous like everything else; but there's nothing to see. The country's a void—no features, no objects, no details, nothing to show you that you're in one place more than another. *Aussi* you're not in one place, you're everywhere, anywhere; the train goes a hundred miles an hour. The cities are all the same; little houses ten feet high or else big ones two hundred; tramways, telegraph-poles, enormous signs, holes in the pavement, oceans of mud, commis-voyageurs, young ladies looking for the husband. On the other hand no beggars and no *cocottes*—none at least that you see. A colossal mediocrity, except (my brother-in-law tells me) in the machinery, which is magnificent. Naturally no architecture (they make houses of wood and of iron), no art, no literature, no theatre. I've opened some of the books—*ils ne se laissent pas lire*. No form, no matter, no style, no general ideas: they seem written for children and young ladies. The most successful (those that they praise most) are the facetious; they sell in thousands of editions. I've looked into some of the most *vantés*; but you need to be forewarned to know they're amusing; grins through a horse-collar, burlesques of the Bible, *des plaisanteries de croquemort*. They've a novelist with pretensions to literature who writes about the chase for the husband and the adventures of the rich Americans in our corrupt old Europe, where their primeval candour puts the Europeans to shame. *C'est proprement écrit*, but it's terribly pale. What isn't pale is the newspapers—enormous, like everything else (fifty columns of advertisements), and full of the *commérages* of a continent. And such a tone, *grand Dieu*! The amenities, the personalities,

423

the recriminations, are like so many *coups de revolver*. Headings six inches tall; correspondences from places one never heard of; telegrams from Europe about Sarah Bernhardt; little paragraphs about nothing at all—the *menu* of the neighbour's dinner; articles on the European situation *à pouffer de rire*; all the *tripotage* of local politics. The *reportage* is incredible; I'm chased up and down by the interviewers. The matrimonial infelicities of M. and Madame X. (they give the name) *tout au long*, with every detail—not in six lines, discreetly veiled, with an art of insinuation, as with us; but with all the facts (or the fictions), the letters, the dates, the places, the hours. I open a paper at hazard and find *au beau milieu*, apropos of nothing, the announcement: "Miss Susan Green has the longest nose in Western New York." Miss Susan Green (*je me renseigne*) is a celebrated authoress, and the Americans have the reputation of spoiling their women. They spoil them *à coups de poing*.

We've seen few interiors (no one speaks French); but if the newspapers give an idea of the domestic *mœurs*, the *mœurs* must be curious. The passport's abolished, but they've printed my *signalement* in these sheets—perhaps for the young ladies who look for the husband. We went one night to the theatre; the piece was French (they are the only ones) but the acting American—too American; we came out in the middle. The want of taste is incredible. An Englishman whom I met tells me that even the language corrupts itself from day to day; the Englishman ceases to understand. It encourages me to find I'm not the only one. There are things every day that one can't describe. Such is Washington, where we arrived this morning, coming from Philadelphia. My brother-in-law wishes to see the Bureau of Patents, and on our arrival he went to look at his machines while I walked about the streets and visited the Capitol! The human machine is what interests me most. I don't even care for the political—for that's what they call their Government here, "the machine." It operates very roughly, and some day evidently will explode. It is true that you'd never suspect they *have* a government; this is the principal seat, but, save for three or four big buildings, most of them *affreux*, it looks like a settlement of negroes. No movement, no officials, no authority, no embodiment of the State. Enormous streets, *comme toujours*, lined with little red houses where nothing ever passes but the tramway. The Capitol—a vast structure, false classic, white marble, iron and stucco, which has *assez grand air*—must be seen to be appreciated. The goddess of liberty on the top, dressed in a bear's skin; their liberty over here is the liberty of bears. You go into the Capitol as you would into a railway station; you walk about as you would in the Palais Royal. No functionaries, no door-keepers, no officers, no uniforms, no badges, no reservations, no authority—nothing but a crowd of shabby people circulating in a labyrinth of spittoons. We're too much governed perhaps in France; but at least we have a certain incarnation of the national conscience, of the national dignity. The dignity's absent here, and I'm told the public conscience is an abyss. *"L'état c'est moi"* even—I like that better than the spittoons. These implements are architectural, monumental; they're the only monuments. *En somme* the country's interesting, now that we too have the Republic; it is the biggest illustration, the biggest warning. It's the last word of democracy, and that word is—platitude. It's very big, very rich, and perfectly ugly. A Frenchman couldn't live here; for life with us, after all, at the worst, is a sort of appreciation. Here one has nothing to appreciate. As for the people, they're the English *minus* the conventions. You can fancy what remains. The women, *pourtant*, are sometimes rather well turned. There was one at Philadelphia—I made her acquaintance by accident—whom it's probable I shall see again. She's not looking for the husband; she has already got one. It was at the hotel; I think the husband doesn't matter. A Frenchman, as I've said, may mistake, and he needs to be sure he's right. *Aussi* I always make sure!

VII. FROM MARCELLUS COCKEREL IN WASHINGTON TO MRS. COOLER, NÉE COCKEREL, AT OAKLAND, CALIFORNIA

October 1880.

I ought to have written you long before this, for I've had your last excellent letter these four months in my hands. The first half of that time I was still in Europe, the last I've spent on my native soil. I think accordingly my silence is owing to the fact that over there I was too miserable to write and that here I've been too happy. I got back the 1st of September—you'll have seen it in the papers. Delightful country where one sees everything in the papers—

the big familiar vulgar good-natured delightful papers, none of which has any reputation to keep up for anything but getting the news! I really think that has had as much to do as anything else with my satisfaction at getting home—the difference in what they call the "tone of the press." In Europe it's too dreary—the sapience, the solemnity, the false respectability, the verbosity, the long disquisitions on superannuated subjects. Here the newspapers are like the railroad-trains which carry everything that comes to the station and have only the religion of punctuality. As a woman, however, you probably detest them; you think they're (the great word) vulgar. I admitted it just now, and I'm very happy to have an early opportunity to announce to you that that idea has quite ceased to have any terrors for me. There are some conceptions to which the female mind can never rise. Vulgarity's a stupid superficial question-begging accusation, which has become to-day the easiest refuge of mediocrity. Better than anything else it saves people the trouble of thinking, and anything which does that succeeds. You must know that in these last three years in Europe I've become terribly vulgar myself; that's one service my travels have rendered me. By three years in Europe I mean three years in foreign parts altogether, for I spent several months of that time in Japan, India and the rest of the East. Do you remember when you bade me good-bye in San Francisco the night before I embarked for Yokohama? You foretold that I'd take such a fancy to foreign life that America would never see me more, and that if you should wish to see me (an event you were good enough to regard as possible) you'd have to make a rendezvous in Paris or in Rome. I think we made one—which you never kept; but I shall never make another for those cities. It was in Paris, however, that I got your letter; I remember the moment as well as if it were (to my honour) much more recent. You must know that among many places I dislike Paris carries the palm. I'm bored to death there; it's the home of every humbug. The life is full of that false comfort which is worse than discomfort, and the small fat irritable people give me the shivers.

I had been making these reflexions even more devoutly than usual one very tiresome evening toward the beginning of last summer when, as I re-entered my hotel at ten o'clock, the little reptile of a portress handed me your gracious lines. I was in a villainous humour. I had been having an overdressed dinner in a stuffy restaurant and had gone from there to a suffocating theatre, where, by way of amusement, I saw a play in which blood and lies were the least of the horrors. The theatres over there are insupportable; the atmosphere's pestilential. People sit with their elbows in your sides; they squeeze past you every half hour. It was one of my bad moments—I have a great many in Europe. The conventional mechanical play, all in falsetto, which I seemed to have seen a thousand times; the horrible faces of the people, the pushing bullying *ouvreuse* with her false politeness and her real rapacity, drove me out of the place at the end of an hour; and as it was too early to go home, I sat down before a café on the Boulevard, where they served me a glass of sour watery beer. There on the Boulevard, in the summer night, life itself was even uglier than the play, and it wouldn't do for me to tell you what I saw. Besides, I was sick of the Boulevard, with its eternal grimace and the deadly sameness of the *article de Paris,* which pretends to be so various—the shop-windows a wilderness of rubbish and the passers-by a procession of manikins. Suddenly it came over me that I was supposed to be amusing myself—my face was a yard long—and that you probably at that moment were saying to your husband: "He stays away so long! What a good time he must be having!" The idea was the first thing that had made me smile for a month; I got up and walked home, reflecting as I went that I was "seeing Europe" and that after all one *must* see Europe. It was because I had been convinced of this that I had come out, and it's because the operation has been brought to a close that I've been so happy for the last eight weeks. I was very conscientious about it, and, though your letter that night made me abominably homesick, I held out to the end, knowing it to be once for all. I shan't trouble Europe again; I shall see America for the rest of my days. My long delay has had the advantage that now at least I can give you my impressions—I don't mean of Europe; impressions of Europe are easy to get—but of this country as it strikes the reinstated exile. Very likely you'll think them queer; but keep my letter and twenty years hence they'll be quite commonplace. They won't even be vulgar. It was very deliberate, my going round the world. I knew that one ought to see for one's self and that I should have eternity, so to speak, to rest. I travelled energetically; I went everywhere and saw everything; took as many letters as possible and made as many acquaintances. In short I held my nose to the grindstone and here I am back.

Well, the upshot of it all is that I've got rid of a superstition. We have so many that one the less—perhaps the biggest of all—makes a real difference in one's comfort. The one in question—of course you have it—is that there's no salvation but through Europe. Our salvation is here, if we have eyes to see it, and the salvation of Europe into the bargain; that is if Europe's to be saved, which I rather doubt. Of course you'll call me a bird of freedom, a vulgar patriot, a waver of the stars and stripes; but I'm in the delightful position of not minding in the least what any one calls me. I haven't a mission; I don't want to preach; I've simply arrived at a state of mind. I've got Europe off my back. You've no idea how it simplifies things and how jolly it makes me feel. Now I can live, now I can talk. If we wretched Americans could only say once for all "Oh Europe be hanged!" we should attend much better to our proper business. We've simply to mind that business and the rest will look after itself. You'll probably inquire what it is I like better over here, and I'll answer that it's simply—life. Disagreeables for disagreeables I prefer our own. The way I've been bored and bullied in foreign parts, and the way I've had to say I found it pleasant! For a good while this appeared to be a sort of congenital obligation, but one fine day it occurred to me that there was no obligation at all and that it would ease me immensely to admit to myself that (for me at least) all those things had no importance. I mean the things they rub into you over there; the tiresome international topics, the petty politics, the stupid social customs, the baby-house scenery. The vastness and freshness of this American world, the great scale and great pace of our development, the good sense and good nature of the people, console me for there being no cathedrals and no Titians. I hear nothing about Prince Bismarck and Gambetta, about the Emperor William and the Czar of Russia, about Lord Beaconsfield and the Prince of Wales. I used to get so tired of their Mumbo-Jumbo of a Bismarck, of his secrets and surprises, his mysterious intentions and oracular words. They revile us for our party politics; but what are all the European jealousies and rivalries, their armaments and their wars, their rapacities and their mutual lies, but the intensity of the spirit of party? What question, what interest, what idea, what need of mankind, is involved in any of these things? Their big pompous armies drawn up in great silly rows, their gold lace, their salaams, their hierarchies, seem a pastime for children: there's a sense of humour and of reality over here that laughs at all that.

428

Yes, we're nearer the reality, nearer what they'll all have to come to. The questions of the future are social questions, which the Bismarcks and Beaconsfields are very much afraid to see settled; and the sight of a row of supercilious potentates holding their peoples like their personal property and bristling all over, to make a mutual impression, with feathers and sabres, strikes us as a mixture of the grotesque and the abominable. What do we care for the mutual impressions of potentates who amuse themselves with sitting on people? Those things are their own affair, and they ought to be shut up in a dark room to have it out together. Once one feels, over here, that the great questions of the future are social questions, that a mighty tide is sweeping the world to democracy, and that this country is the biggest stage on which the drama can be enacted, the fashionable European topics seem petty and parochial. They talk about things that we've settled ages ago, and the solemnity with which they propound to you their little domestic embarrassments makes a heavy draft on one's good nature. In England they were talking about the Hares and Rabbits Bill, about the extension of the County Franchise, about the Dissenters' Burials, about the Deceased Wife's Sister, about the abolition of the House of Lords, about heaven knows what ridiculous little measure for the propping-up of their ridiculous little country. And they call *us* provincial! It's hard to sit and look respectable while people discuss the utility of the House of Lords and the beauty of a State Church, and it's only in a dowdy musty civilisation that you'll find them doing such things. The lightness and clearness of the social air—*that's* the great relief in these parts. The gentility of bishops, the propriety of parsons, even the impressiveness of a restored cathedral, give less of a charm to life than that. I used to be furious with the bishops and beadles, with the humbuggery of the whole affair, which every one was conscious of but which people agreed not to expose because they'd be compromised all round. The convenience of life in our conditions, the quick and simple arrangements, the absence of the spirit of routine, are a blessed change from the stupid stiffness with which I struggled for two long years. There were people with swords and cockades who used to order me about; for the simplest operation of life I had to kootoo to some bloated official. When it was a question of my doing a little differently from others the bloated official gasped as if I had given him a blow on the stomach; he needed to take a week to think of it.

On the other hand it's impossible to take an American by surprise; he's ashamed to confess he hasn't the wit to do a thing another man has had the wit to think of. Besides being as good as his neighbour he must therefore be as clever—which is an affliction only to people who are afraid he may be cleverer. If this general efficiency and spontaneity of the people—the union of the sense of freedom with the love of knowledge—isn't the very essence of a high civilisation I don't know what a high civilisation is. I felt this greater ease on my first railroad journey—felt the blessing of sitting in a train where I could move about, where I could stretch my legs and come and go, where I had a seat and a window to myself, where there were chairs and tables and food and drink. The villainous little boxes on the European trains, in which you're stuck down in a corner with doubled-up knees, opposite to a row of people, often most offensive types, who stare at you for ten hours on end—these were part of my two years' ordeal. The large free way of doing things here is everywhere a pleasure. In London, at my hotel, they used to come to me on Saturday to make me order my Sunday's dinner, and when I asked for a sheet of paper they put it into the bill. The meagreness, the stinginess, the perpetual expectation of a sixpence, used to exasperate me. Of course I saw a great many people who were pleasant; but as I'm writing to you and not to one of them I may say that they were dreadfully apt to be dull. The imagination among the people I see here is more flexible, and then they have the advantage of a larger horizon. It's not bounded on the north by the British aristocracy and on the south by the *scrutin de liste*. (I mix up the countries a little, but they're not worth the keeping apart.) The absence of little conventional measurements, of little cut-and-dried judgements, is an immense refreshment. We're more analytic, more discriminating, more familiar with realities. As for manners, there are bad manners everywhere, but an aristocracy is bad manners organised. (I don't mean that they mayn't be polite among themselves, but they're rude to every one else.) The sight of all these growing millions simply minding their business is impressive to me—more so than all the gilt buttons and padded chests of the Old World; and there's a certain powerful type of "practical" American (you'll find him chiefly in the West) who doesn't "blow" as I do (I'm not practical) but who quietly feels that he has the Future in his vitals—a type that strikes me more than any I met in your favourite countries.

430

Of course you'll come back to the cathedrals and Titians, but there's a thought that helps one to do without them—the thought that, though we've an immense deal of pie-eating plainness, we've little misery, little squalor, little degradation. There's no regular wife-beating class, and there are none of the stultified peasants of whom it takes so many to make a European noble. The people here are more conscious of things; they invent, they act, they answer for themselves; they're not (I speak of social matters) tied up by authority and precedent. We shall have all the Titians by and by, and we shall move over a few cathedrals. You had better stay here if you want to have the best. Of course I'm a roaring Yankee; but you'll call me that if I say the least, so I may as well take my ease and say the most. Washington's a most entertaining place; and here at least, at the seat of government, one isn't overgoverned. In fact there's no government at all to speak of; it seems too good to be true. The first day I was here I went to the Capitol, and it took me ever so long to figure to myself that I had as good a right there as any one else—that the whole magnificent pile (it *is* magnificent, by the way) was in fact my own. In Europe one doesn't rise to such conceptions, and my spirit had been broken in Europe. The doors were gaping wide—I walked all about; there were no door-keepers, no officers nor flunkeys, there wasn't even a policeman to be seen. It seemed strange not to see a uniform, if only as a patch of colour. But this isn't government by livery. The absence of these things is odd at first; you seem to miss something, to fancy the machine has stopped. It hasn't, though; it only works without fire and smoke. At the end of three days this simple negative impression, the fact that there are no soldiers nor spies, nothing but plain black coats, begins to affect the imagination, becomes vivid, majestic, symbolic. It ends by being more impressive than the biggest review I saw in Germany. Of course I'm a roaring Yankee; but one has to take a big brush to copy a big model. The future's here of course, but it isn't only that—the present's here as well. You'll complain that I don't give you any personal news, but I'm more modest for myself than for my country. I spent a month in New York and while there saw a good deal of a rather interesting girl who came over with me in the steamer and whom for a day or two I thought I should like to marry. But I shouldn't. She has been spoiled by Europe—and yet the prime stuff struck me as so right.

VIII. FROM MISS AURORA CHURCH IN NEW YORK TO MISS WHITESIDE IN PARIS

January 1881.

I told you (after we landed) about my agreement with mamma—that I was to have my liberty for three months and that if at the end of this time I shouldn't have made a good use of it I was to give it back to her. Well, the time's up to-day, and I'm very much afraid I haven't made a good use of it. In fact I haven't made any use of it at all—I haven't got married, for that's what mamma meant by our little bargain. She has been trying to marry me in Europe for years, without a *dot*, and as she has never (to the best of my knowledge) even come near it, she thought at last that if she were to leave it to me I might possibly do better. I couldn't certainly do worse. Well, my dear, I've done very badly—that is I haven't done at all. I haven't even tried. I had an idea that the *coup* in question came of itself over here; but it hasn't come to *me*. I won't say I'm disappointed, for I haven't on the whole seen any one I should like to marry. When you marry people in these parts they expect you to love them, and I haven't seen any one I should like to love. I don't know what the reason is, but they're none of them what I've thought of. It may be that I've thought of the impossible; and yet I've seen people in Europe whom I should have liked to marry. It's true they were almost always married to some one else. What I *am* disappointed in is simply having to give back my liberty. I don't wish particularly to be married, and I do wish to do as I like—as I've been doing for the last month. All the same I'm sorry for poor mamma, since nothing has happened that she wished to happen. To begin with, we're not appreciated, not even by the Rucks, who have disappeared in the strange way in which people over here seem to vanish from the world. We've made no sensation; my new dresses count for nothing (they all have better ones); our philological and historical studies don't show. We've been told we might do better in Boston; but on the other hand mamma hears that in Boston the people only marry their cousins. Then mamma's out of sorts because the country's exceedingly dear and we've spent all our money. Moreover, I've neither eloped, nor been insulted, nor been talked about, nor—so far as I know—deteriorated in manners or character; so that she's wrong in all her previsions. I think she would have rather liked me to be insulted. But I've been insulted as little as I've been adored. They don't adore you over here; they only make you think they're going to.

Do you remember the two gentlemen who were on the ship, and who, after we arrived, came to see me *à tour de rôle*? At first I never dreamed they were making love to me, though mamma was sure it must be that; then, as it went on a good while, I thought perhaps it *was* that—after which I ended by seeing it wasn't anything! It was simply conversation—and conversation a precocious child might have listened to at that. Mr. Leverett and Mr. Cockerel disappeared one fine day without the smallest pretension to having broken my heart, I'm sure—though it only depended on me to think they must have tried to. All the gentlemen are like that; you can't tell what they mean; the "passions" don't rage, the appearances don't matter—nobody believes them. Society seems oddly to consist of a sort of innocent jilting. I think on the whole I *am* a little disappointed—I don't mean about one's not marrying; I mean about the life generally. It looks so different at first that you expect it will be very exciting; and then you find that after all, when you've walked out for a week or two by yourself and driven out with a gentleman in a buggy, that's about all there is to it, as they say here. Mamma's very angry at not finding more to dislike; she admitted yesterday that, once one has got a little settled, the country hasn't even the merit of being hateful. This has evidently something to do with her suddenly proposing three days ago that we should "go West." Imagine my surprise at such an idea coming from mamma! The people in the pension—who, as usual, wish immensely to get rid of her— have talked to her about the West, and she has taken it up with a kind of desperation. You see we must do something; we can't simply remain here. We're rapidly being ruined and we're not—so to speak—getting married. Perhaps it will be easier in the West; at any rate it will be cheaper and the country will have the advantage of being more hateful. It's a question between that and returning to Europe, and for the moment mamma's balancing. I say nothing: I'm really indifferent; perhaps I shall marry a pioneer. I'm just thinking how I shall give back my liberty. It really won't be possible; I haven't got it any more; I've given it away to others. Mamma may get it back if she can from *them*! She comes in at this moment to announce that we must push further—she has decided for the West. Wonderful mamma! It appears that my real chance is for a pioneer—they've sometimes millions. But fancy us at Oshkosh!

About Author

Henry James OM (15 April 1843 – 28 February 1916) was an American-British author regarded as a key transitional figure between literary realism and literary modernism, and is considered by many to be among the greatest novelists in the English language. He was the son of Henry James Sr. and the brother of renowned philosopher and psychologist William James and diarist Alice James.

He is best known for a number of novels dealing with the social and marital interplay between émigré Americans, English people, and continental Europeans. Examples of such novels include The Portrait of a Lady, The Ambassadors, and The Wings of the Dove. His later works were increasingly experimental. In describing the internal states of mind and social dynamics of his characters, James often made use of a style in which ambiguous or contradictory motives and impressions were overlaid or juxtaposed in the discussion of a character's psyche. For their unique ambiguity, as well as for other aspects of their composition, his late works have been compared to impressionist painting.

His novella The Turn of the Screw has garnered a reputation as the most analysed and ambiguous ghost story in the English language and remains his most widely adapted work in other media. He also wrote a number of other highly regarded ghost stories and is considered one of the greatest masters of the field.

James published articles and books of criticism, travel, biography, autobiography, and plays. Born in the United States, James largely relocated to Europe as a young man and eventually settled in England, becoming a British subject in 1915, one year before his death. James was nominated for the Nobel Prize in Literature in 1911, 1912 and 1916.

Life

Early years, 1843–1883

James was born at 2 Washington Place in New York City on 15 April 1843. His parents were Mary Walsh and Henry James Sr. His father was intelligent and steadfastly congenial. He was a lecturer and philosopher who had inherited independent means from his father, an Albany banker and investor. Mary came from a wealthy family long settled in New York City. Her sister Katherine lived with her adult family for an extended period of time. Henry Jr. had three brothers, William, who was one year his senior, and younger brothers Wilkinson (Wilkie) and Robertson. His younger sister was Alice. Both of his parents were of Irish and Scottish descent.

The family first lived in Albany, at 70 N. Pearl St., and then moved to Fourteenth Street in New York City when James was still a young boy. His education was calculated by his father to expose him to many influences, primarily scientific and philosophical; it was described by Percy Lubbock, the editor of his selected letters, as "extraordinarily haphazard and promiscuous." James did not share the usual education in Latin and Greek classics. Between 1855 and 1860, the James' household traveled to London, Paris, Geneva, Boulogne-sur-Mer and Newport, Rhode Island, according to the father's current interests and publishing ventures, retreating to the United States when funds were low. Henry studied primarily with tutors and briefly attended schools while the family traveled in Europe. Their longest stays were in France, where Henry began to feel at home and became fluent in French. He was afflicted with a stutter, which seems to have manifested itself only when he spoke English; in French, he did not stutter.

In 1860 the family returned to Newport. There Henry became a friend of the painter John La Farge, who introduced him to French literature, and in particular, to Balzac. James later called Balzac his "greatest master," and said that he had learned more about the craft of fiction from him than from anyone else.

In the autumn of 1861 Henry received an injury, probably to his back, while fighting a fire. This injury, which resurfaced at times throughout his life, made him unfit for military service in the American Civil War.

In 1864 the James family moved to Boston, Massachusetts to be near William, who had enrolled first in the Lawrence Scientific School at Harvard and then in the medical school. In 1862 Henry attended Harvard Law School, but realised that he was not interested in studying law. He pursued his interest in literature and associated with authors and critics William Dean Howells and Charles Eliot Norton in Boston and Cambridge, formed lifelong friendships with Oliver Wendell Holmes Jr., the future Supreme Court Justice, and with James and Annie Fields, his first professional mentors.

His first published work was a review of a stage performance, "Miss Maggie Mitchell in Fanchon the Cricket," published in 1863. About a year later, A Tragedy of Error, his first short story, was published anonymously. James's first payment was for an appreciation of Sir Walter Scott's novels, written for the North American Review. He wrote fiction and non-fiction pieces for The Nation and Atlantic Monthly, where Fields was editor. In 1871 he published his first novel, Watch and Ward, in serial form in the Atlantic Monthly. The novel was later published in book form in 1878.

During a 14-month trip through Europe in 1869–70 he met Ruskin, Dickens, Matthew Arnold, William Morris, and George Eliot. Rome impressed him profoundly. "Here I am then in the Eternal City," he wrote to his brother William. "At last—for the first time—I live!" He attempted to support himself as a freelance writer in Rome, then secured a position as Paris correspondent for the New York Tribune, through the influence of its editor John Hay. When these efforts failed he returned to New York City. During 1874 and 1875 he published Transatlantic Sketches, A Passionate Pilgrim, and Roderick Hudson. During this early period in his career he was influenced by Nathaniel Hawthorne.

In 1869 he settled in London. There he established relationships with Macmillan and other publishers, who paid for serial installments that they would later publish in book form. The audience for these serialized novels was largely made up of middle-class women, and James struggled to fashion serious literary work within the strictures imposed by editors' and publishers' notions of what was suitable for young women to read. He lived in rented rooms but was able to join gentlemen's clubs that had libraries and where he could entertain male friends. He was introduced to English society by Henry Adams and Charles Milnes Gaskell, the latter introducing him to the Travellers' and the Reform Clubs.

In the fall of 1875 he moved to the Latin Quarter of Paris. Aside from two trips to America, he spent the next three decades—the rest of his life—in Europe. In Paris he met Zola, Alphonse Daudet, Maupassant, Turgenev, and others. He stayed in Paris only a year before moving to London.

In England he met the leading figures of politics and culture. He continued to be a prolific writer, producing The American (1877), The Europeans (1878), a revision of Watch and Ward (1878), French Poets and Novelists (1878), Hawthorne (1879), and several shorter works of fiction. In 1878 Daisy Miller established his fame on both sides of the Atlantic. It drew notice perhaps mostly because it depicted a woman whose behavior is outside the social norms of Europe. He also began his first masterpiece, The Portrait of a Lady, which would appear in 1881.

In 1877 he first visited Wenlock Abbey in Shropshire, home of his friend Charles Milnes Gaskell whom he had met through Henry Adams. He was much inspired by the darkly romantic Abbey and the surrounding countryside, which features in his essay Abbeys and Castles. In particular the gloomy monastic fishponds behind the Abbey are said to have inspired the lake in The Turn of the Screw.

While living in London, James continued to follow the careers of the "French realists", Émile Zola in particular. Their stylistic methods influenced his own work in the years to come. Hawthorne's influence on him faded during this period, replaced by George Eliot and Ivan Turgenev. 1879–1882 saw the publication of The Europeans, Washington Square, Confidence, and The Portrait of a Lady. He visited America in 1882–1883, then returned to London.

The period from 1881 to 1883 was marked by several losses. His mother died in 1881, followed by his father a few months later, and then by his brother Wilkie. Emerson, an old family friend, died in 1882. His friend Turgenev died in 1883.

Middle years, 1884–1897

In 1884 James made another visit to Paris. There he met again with Zola, Daudet, and Goncourt. He had been following the careers of the French "realist" or "naturalist" writers, and was increasingly influenced by them. In 1886, he published The Bostonians and The Princess Casamassima, both influenced by the French writers he'd studied assiduously. Critical reaction and sales were poor. He wrote to Howells that the books had hurt his career rather than helped because they had "reduced the desire, and demand, for my productions to zero". During this time he became friends with Robert Louis Stevenson, John Singer Sargent, Edmund Gosse, George du Maurier, Paul Bourget, and Constance Fenimore Woolson. His third novel from the 1880s was The Tragic Muse. Although he was following the precepts of Zola in his novels of the '80s, their tone and attitude are closer to the fiction of Alphonse Daudet. The lack of critical and financial success for his novels during this period led him to try writing for the theatre. (His dramatic works and his experiences with theatre are discussed below.)

In the last quarter of 1889, he started translating "for pure and copious lucre" Port Tarascon, the third volume of Alphonse Daudet adventures of Tartarin de Tarascon. Serialized in Harper's Monthly Magazine from June 1890, this translation praised as "clever" by The Spectator was published in January 1891 by Sampson Low, Marston, Searle & Rivington.

After the stage failure of Guy Domville in 1895, James was near despair and thoughts of death plagued him. The years spent on dramatic works were not entirely a loss. As he moved into the last phase of his career he found ways to adapt dramatic techniques into the novel form.

In the late 1880s and throughout the 1890s James made several trips through Europe. He spent a long stay in Italy in 1887. In that year the short novel The Aspern Papers and The Reverberator were published.

Late years, 1898–1916

In 1897–1898 he moved to Rye, Sussex, and wrote The Turn of the Screw. 1899–1900 saw the publication of The Awkward Age and The Sacred

441

Fount. During 1902–1904 he wrote The Ambassadors, The Wings of the Dove, and The Golden Bowl.

In 1904 he revisited America and lectured on Balzac. In 1906–1910 he published The American Scene and edited the "New York Edition", a 24-volume collection of his works. In 1910 his brother William died; Henry had just joined William from an unsuccessful search for relief in Europe on what then turned out to be his (Henry's) last visit to the United States (from summer 1910 to July 1911), and was near him, according to a letter he wrote, when he died.

In 1913 he wrote his autobiographies, A Small Boy and Others, and Notes of a Son and Brother. After the outbreak of the First World War in 1914 he did war work. In 1915 he became a British subject and was awarded the Order of Merit the following year. He died on 28 February 1916, in Chelsea, London. As he requested, his ashes were buried in Cambridge Cemetery in Massachusetts.

Biographers

James regularly rejected suggestions that he should marry, and after settling in London proclaimed himself "a bachelor". F. W. Dupee, in several volumes on the James family, originated the theory that he had been in love with his cousin Mary ("Minnie") Temple, but that a neurotic fear of sex kept him from admitting such affections: "James's invalidism ... was itself the symptom of some fear of or scruple against sexual love on his part." Dupee used an episode from James's memoir A Small Boy and Others, recounting a dream of a Napoleonic image in the Louvre, to exemplify James's romanticism about Europe, a Napoleonic fantasy into which he fled.

Dupee had not had access to the James family papers and worked principally from James's published memoir of his older brother, William, and the limited collection of letters edited by Percy Lubbock, heavily weighted toward James's last years. His account therefore moved directly from James's childhood, when he trailed after his older brother, to elderly invalidism. As more material became available to scholars, including the diaries of contemporaries and hundreds of affectionate and sometimes erotic letters written by James to younger men, the picture of neurotic celibacy gave way to a portrait of a closeted homosexual.

Between 1953 and 1972, Leon Edel authored a major five-volume biography of James, which accessed unpublished letters and documents after Edel gained the permission of James's family. Edel's portrayal of James included the suggestion he was celibate. It was a view first propounded by critic Saul Rosenzweig in 1943. In 1996 Sheldon M. Novick published Henry James: The Young Master, followed by Henry James: The Mature Master (2007). The first book "caused something of an uproar in Jamesian circles" as it challenged the previous received notion of celibacy, a once-familiar paradigm in biographies of homosexuals when direct evidence was non-existent. Novick also criticised Edel for following the discounted Freudian interpretation of homosexuality "as a kind of failure." The difference of opinion erupted in a series of exchanges between Edel and Novick which were published by the online magazine Slate, with the latter arguing that even the suggestion of celibacy went against James's own injunction "live!"—not "fantasize!"

A letter James wrote in old age to Hugh Walpole has been cited as an explicit statement of this. Walpole confessed to him of indulging in "high jinks", and James wrote a reply endorsing it: "We must know, as much as possible, in our beautiful art, yours & mine, what we are talking about — & the only way to know it is to have lived & loved & cursed & floundered & enjoyed & suffered — I don't think I regret a single 'excess' of my responsive youth".

The interpretation of James as living a less austere emotional life has been subsequently explored by other scholars. The often intense politics of Jamesian scholarship has also been the subject of studies. Author Colm Tóibín has said that Eve Kosofsky Sedgwick's Epistemology of the Closet made a landmark difference to Jamesian scholarship by arguing that he be read as a homosexual writer whose desire to keep his sexuality a secret shaped his layered style and dramatic artistry. According to Tóibín such a reading "removed James from the realm of dead white males who wrote about posh people. He became our contemporary."

James's letters to expatriate American sculptor Hendrik Christian Andersen have attracted particular attention. James met the 27-year-old Andersen in Rome in 1899, when James was 56, and wrote letters to Andersen that are intensely emotional: "I hold you, dearest boy, in my innermost love, & count on your feeling me—in every throb of your soul". In a letter of 6 May 1904, to his brother William, James referred to himself as "always your hopelessly celibate even though sexagenarian Henry". How accurate that description might have been is the subject of contention among James's biographers, but the letters to Andersen were occasionally quasi-erotic: "I put, my dear boy, my arm around you, & feel the pulsation, thereby, as it were, of our excellent future & your admirable endowment." To his homosexual friend Howard Sturgis, James could write: "I repeat, almost to indiscretion, that I could live with you. Meanwhile I can only try to live without you."

His numerous letters to the many young gay men among his close male friends are more forthcoming. In a letter to Howard Sturgis, following a long visit, James refers jocularly to their "happy little congress of two" and in letters to Hugh Walpole he pursues convoluted jokes and puns about their relationship, referring to himself as an elephant who "paws you oh so benevolently" and winds about Walpole his "well meaning old trunk". His letters to Walter Berry printed by the Black Sun Press have long been celebrated for their lightly veiled eroticism.

He corresponded in almost equally extravagant language with his many female friends, writing, for example, to fellow novelist Lucy Clifford: "Dearest Lucy! What shall I say? when I love you so very, very much, and see you nine times for once that I see Others! Therefore I think that—if you want it made clear to the meanest intelligence—I love you more than I love Others." To his New York friend Mary Cadwalader Jones: "Dearest Mary Cadwalader. I yearn over you, but I yearn in vain; & your long silence really breaks my heart, mystifies, depresses, almost alarms me, to the point even of making me wonder if poor unconscious & doting old Célimare [Jones's pet name for James] has 'done' anything, in some dark somnambulism of the spirit, which has ... given you a bad moment, or a wrong impression, or a 'colourable pretext' ... However these things may be, he loves you as tenderly as ever;

nothing, to the end of time, will ever detach him from you, & he remembers those Eleventh St. matutinal intimes hours, those telephonic matinées, as the most romantic of his life ..." His long friendship with American novelist Constance Fenimore Woolson, in whose house he lived for a number of weeks in Italy in 1887, and his shock and grief over her suicide in 1894, are discussed in detail in Edel's biography and play a central role in a study by Lyndall Gordon. (Edel conjectured that Woolson was in love with James and killed herself in part because of his coldness, but Woolson's biographers have objected to Edel's account.)

Works

Style and themes

James is one of the major figures of trans-Atlantic literature. His works frequently juxtapose characters from the Old World (Europe), embodying a feudal civilisation that is beautiful, often corrupt, and alluring, and from the New World (United States), where people are often brash, open, and assertive and embody the virtues—freedom and a more highly evolved moral character—of the new American society. James explores this clash of personalities and cultures, in stories of personal relationships in which power is exercised well or badly. His protagonists were often young American women facing oppression or abuse, and as his secretary Theodora Bosanquet remarked in her monograph Henry James at Work:

> When he walked out of the refuge of his study and into the world and looked around him, he saw a place of torment, where creatures of prey perpetually thrust their claws into the quivering flesh of doomed, defenseless children of light ... His novels are a repeated exposure of this wickedness, a reiterated and passionate plea for the fullest freedom of development, unimperiled by reckless and barbarous stupidity.

Critics have jokingly described three phases in the development of James's prose: "James I, James II, and The Old Pretender." He wrote short stories and plays. Finally, in his third and last period he returned to the long, serialised novel. Beginning in the second period, but most noticeably in the third, he increasingly abandoned direct statement in favour of frequent

445

double negatives, and complex descriptive imagery. Single paragraphs began to run for page after page, in which an initial noun would be succeeded by pronouns surrounded by clouds of adjectives and prepositional clauses, far from their original referents, and verbs would be deferred and then preceded by a series of adverbs. The overall effect could be a vivid evocation of a scene as perceived by a sensitive observer. It has been debated whether this change of style was engendered by James's shifting from writing to dictating to a typist, a change made during the composition of What Maisie Knew.

In its intense focus on the consciousness of his major characters, James's later work foreshadows extensive developments in 20th century fiction. Indeed, he might have influenced stream-of-consciousness writers such as Virginia Woolf, who not only read some of his novels but also wrote essays about them. Both contemporary and modern readers have found the late style difficult and unnecessary; his friend Edith Wharton, who admired him greatly, said that there were passages in his work that were all but incomprehensible. James was harshly portrayed by H. G. Wells as a hippopotamus laboriously attempting to pick up a pea that had got into a corner of its cage. The "late James" style was ably parodied by Max Beerbohm in "The Mote in the Middle Distance".

More important for his work overall may have been his position as an expatriate, and in other ways an outsider, living in Europe. While he came from middle-class and provincial beginnings (seen from the perspective of European polite society) he worked very hard to gain access to all levels of society, and the settings of his fiction range from working class to aristocratic, and often describe the efforts of middle-class Americans to make their way in European capitals. He confessed he got some of his best story ideas from gossip at the dinner table or at country house weekends. He worked for a living, however, and lacked the experiences of select schools, university, and army service, the common bonds of masculine society. He was furthermore a man whose tastes and interests were, according to the prevailing standards of Victorian era Anglo-American culture, rather feminine, and who was shadowed by the cloud of prejudice that then and later accompanied suspicions of his homosexuality. Edmund Wilson famously compared James's objectivity to Shakespeare's:

One would be in a position to appreciate James better if one compared him with the dramatists of the seventeenth century—Racine and Molière, whom he resembles in form as well as in point of view, and even Shakespeare, when allowances are made for the most extreme differences in subject and form. These poets are not, like Dickens and Hardy, writers of melodrama—either humorous or pessimistic, nor secretaries of society like Balzac, nor prophets like Tolstoy: they are occupied simply with the presentation of conflicts of moral character, which they do not concern themselves about softening or averting. They do not indict society for these situations: they regard them as universal and inevitable. They do not even blame God for allowing them: they accept them as the conditions of life.

It is also possible to see many of James's stories as psychological thought-experiments. In his preface to the New York edition of The American he describes the development of the story in his mind as exactly such: the "situation" of an American, "some robust but insidiously beguiled and betrayed, some cruelly wronged, compatriot..." with the focus of the story being on the response of this wronged man. The Portrait of a Lady may be an experiment to see what happens when an idealistic young woman suddenly becomes very rich. In many of his tales, characters seem to exemplify alternative futures and possibilities, as most markedly in "The Jolly Corner", in which the protagonist and a ghost-doppelganger live alternative American and European lives; and in others, like The Ambassadors, an older James seems fondly to regard his own younger self facing a crucial moment.

Major novels

The first period of James's fiction, usually considered to have culminated in The Portrait of a Lady, concentrated on the contrast between Europe and America. The style of these novels is generally straightforward and, though personally characteristic, well within the norms of 19th-century fiction. Roderick Hudson (1875) is a Künstlerroman that traces the development of the title character, an extremely talented sculptor. Although the book shows some signs of immaturity—this was James's first serious attempt at a full-length novel—it has attracted favourable comment due to the vivid realisation of the three major characters: Roderick Hudson, superbly gifted but unstable and unreliable; Rowland Mallet, Roderick's limited but much more mature friend and patron; and Christina Light, one of James's most enchanting and maddening femmes fatales. The pair of Hudson and Mallet has been seen as representing the two sides of James's own nature: the wildly imaginative artist and the brooding conscientious mentor.

In The Portrait of a Lady (1881) James concluded the first phase of his career with a novel that remains his most popular piece of long fiction. The story is of a spirited young American woman, Isabel Archer, who "affronts her destiny" and finds it overwhelming. She inherits a large amount of money and subsequently becomes the victim of Machiavellian scheming by two American expatriates. The narrative is set mainly in Europe, especially in England and Italy. Generally regarded as the masterpiece of his early phase, The Portrait of a Lady is described as a psychological novel, exploring the minds of his characters, and almost a work of social science, exploring the differences between Europeans and Americans, the old and the new worlds.

The second period of James's career, which extends from the publication of The Portrait of a Lady through the end of the nineteenth century, features less popular novels including The Princess Casamassima, published serially in The Atlantic Monthly in 1885–1886, and The Bostonians, published serially in The Century Magazine during the same period. This period also featured James's celebrated Gothic novella, The Turn of the Screw.

The third period of James's career reached its most significant achievement in three novels published just around the start of the 20th century: The Wings of the Dove (1902), The Ambassadors (1903), and The Golden Bowl (1904). Critic F. O. Matthiessen called this "trilogy" James's major phase, and these novels have certainly received intense critical study. It was the second-written of the books, The Wings of the Dove (1902) that was the first published because it attracted no serialization. This novel tells the story of Milly Theale, an American heiress stricken with a serious disease, and her impact on the people around her. Some of these people befriend Milly with honourable motives, while others are more self-interested. James stated in his autobiographical books that Milly was based on Minny Temple, his beloved cousin who died at an early age of tuberculosis. He said that he attempted in the novel to wrap her memory in the "beauty and dignity of art".

Shorter narratives

James was particularly interested in what he called the "beautiful and blest nouvelle", or the longer form of short narrative. Still, he produced a number of very short stories in which he achieved notable compression of sometimes complex subjects. The following narratives are representative of James's achievement in the shorter forms of fiction.

- "A Tragedy of Error" (1864), short story
- "The Story of a Year" (1865), short story
- A Passionate Pilgrim (1871), novella
- Madame de Mauves (1874), novella
- Daisy Miller (1878), novella
- The Aspern Papers (1888), novella
- The Lesson of the Master (1888), novella
- The Pupil (1891), short story
- "The Figure in the Carpet" (1896), short story
- The Beast in the Jungle (1903), novella
- An International Episode (1878)
- Picture and Text
- Four Meetings (1885)
- A London Life, and Other Tales (1889)
- The Spoils of Poynton (1896)

- Embarrassments (1896)

- The Two Magics: The Turn of the Screw, Covering End (1898)

- A Little Tour of France (1900)

- The Sacred Fount (1901)

- Views and Reviews (1908)

- The Wings of the Dove, Volume I (1902)

- The Wings of the Dove, Volume II (1909)

- The Finer Grain (1910)

- The Outcry (1911)

- Lady Barbarina: The Siege of London, An International Episode and Other Tales (1922)

- The Birthplace (1922)

Plays

At several points in his career James wrote plays, beginning with one-act plays written for periodicals in 1869 and 1871 and a dramatisation of his popular novella Daisy Miller in 1882. From 1890 to 1892, having received a bequest that freed him from magazine publication, he made a strenuous effort to succeed on the London stage, writing a half-dozen plays of which only one, a dramatisation of his novel The American, was produced. This play was performed for several years by a touring repertory company and had a respectable run in London, but did not earn very much money for James. His other plays written at this time were not produced.

In 1893, however, he responded to a request from actor-manager George Alexander for a serious play for the opening of his renovated St. James's Theatre, and wrote a long drama, Guy Domville, which Alexander produced. There was a noisy uproar on the opening night, 5 January 1895, with hissing from the gallery when James took his bow after the final curtain, and the author was upset. The play received moderately good reviews and had a modest run of four weeks before being taken off to make way for Oscar Wilde's The Importance of Being Earnest, which Alexander thought would have better prospects for the coming season.

After the stresses and disappointment of these efforts James insisted that he would write no more for the theatre, but within weeks had agreed to write a curtain-raiser for Ellen Terry. This became the one-act "Summersoft", which he later rewrote into a short story, "Covering End", and then expanded into a full-length play, The High Bid, which had a brief run in London in 1907, when James made another concerted effort to write for the stage. He wrote three new plays, two of which were in production when the death of Edward VII on 6 May 1910 plunged London into mourning and theatres closed. Discouraged by failing health and the stresses of theatrical work, James did not renew his efforts in the theatre, but recycled his plays as successful novels. The Outcry was a best-seller in the United States when it was published in 1911. During the years 1890–1893 when he was most engaged with the theatre, James wrote a good deal of theatrical criticism and assisted Elizabeth Robins and others in translating and producing Henrik Ibsen for the first time in London.

Leon Edel argued in his psychoanalytic biography that James was traumatised by the opening night uproar that greeted Guy Domville, and that it plunged him into a prolonged depression. The successful later novels, in Edel's view, were the result of a kind of self-analysis, expressed in fiction, which partly freed him from his fears. Other biographers and scholars have not accepted this account, however; the more common view being that of F.O. Matthiessen, who wrote: "Instead of being crushed by the collapse of his hopes [for the theatre]... he felt a resurgence of new energy."

Non-fiction

Beyond his fiction, James was one of the more important literary critics in the history of the novel. In his classic essay The Art of Fiction (1884), he argued against rigid prescriptions on the novelist's choice of subject and method of treatment. He maintained that the widest possible freedom in content and approach would help ensure narrative fiction's continued vitality.

451

James wrote many valuable critical articles on other novelists; typical is his book-length study of Nathaniel Hawthorne, which has been the subject of critical debate. Richard Brodhead has suggested that the study was emblematic of James's struggle with Hawthorne's influence, and constituted an effort to place the elder writer "at a disadvantage." Gordon Fraser, meanwhile, has suggested that the study was part of a more commercial effort by James to introduce himself to British readers as Hawthorne's natural successor.

When James assembled the New York Edition of his fiction in his final years, he wrote a series of prefaces that subjected his own work to searching, occasionally harsh criticism.

At 22 James wrote The Noble School of Fiction for The Nation's first issue in 1865. He would write, in all, over 200 essays and book, art, and theatre reviews for the magazine.

For most of his life James harboured ambitions for success as a playwright. He converted his novel The American into a play that enjoyed modest returns in the early 1890s. In all he wrote about a dozen plays, most of which went unproduced. His costume drama Guy Domville failed disastrously on its opening night in 1895. James then largely abandoned his efforts to conquer the stage and returned to his fiction. In his Notebooks he maintained that his theatrical experiment benefited his novels and tales by helping him dramatise his characters' thoughts and emotions. James produced a small but valuable amount of theatrical criticism, including perceptive appreciations of Henrik Ibsen.

With his wide-ranging artistic interests, James occasionally wrote on the visual arts. Perhaps his most valuable contribution was his favourable assessment of fellow expatriate John Singer Sargent, a painter whose critical status has improved markedly in recent decades. James also wrote sometimes charming, sometimes brooding articles about various places he visited and lived in. His most famous books of travel writing include Italian Hours (an example of the charming approach) and The American Scene (most definitely on the brooding side).

James was one of the great letter-writers of any era. More than ten thousand of his personal letters are extant, and over three thousand have been published in a large number of collections. A complete edition of James's letters began publication in 2006, edited by Pierre Walker and Greg Zacharias. As of 2014, eight volumes have been published, covering the period from 1855 to 1880. James's correspondents included celebrated contemporaries like Robert Louis Stevenson, Edith Wharton and Joseph Conrad, along with many others in his wide circle of friends and acquaintances. The letters range from the "mere twaddle of graciousness" to serious discussions of artistic, social and personal issues.

Very late in life James began a series of autobiographical works: A Small Boy and Others, Notes of a Son and Brother, and the unfinished The Middle Years. These books portray the development of a classic observer who was passionately interested in artistic creation but was somewhat reticent about participating fully in the life around him.

Reception

Criticism, biographies and fictional treatments

James's work has remained steadily popular with the limited audience of educated readers to whom he spoke during his lifetime, and has remained firmly in the canon, but, after his death, some American critics, such as Van Wyck Brooks, expressed hostility towards James for his long expatriation and eventual naturalisation as a British subject. Other critics such as E. M. Forster complained about what they saw as James's squeamishness in the treatment of sex and other possibly controversial material, or dismissed his late style as difficult and obscure, relying heavily on extremely long sentences and excessively latinate language. Similarly Oscar Wilde criticised him for writing "fiction as if it were a painful duty". Vernon Parrington, composing a canon of American literature, condemned James for having cut himself off from America. Jorge Luis Borges wrote about him, "Despite the scruples and delicate complexities of James, his work suffers from a major defect: the absence of life." And Virginia Woolf, writing to Lytton Strachey, asked, "Please tell me what you find in Henry James. ... we have his works here, and

I read, and I can't find anything but faintly tinged rose water, urbane and sleek, but vulgar and pale as Walter Lamb. Is there really any sense in it?" The novelist W. Somerset Maugham wrote, "He did not know the English as an Englishman instinctively knows them and so his English characters never to my mind quite ring true," and argued "The great novelists, even in seclusion, have lived life passionately. Henry James was content to observe it from a window." Maugham nevertheless wrote, "The fact remains that those last novels of his, notwithstanding their unreality, make all other novels, except the very best, unreadable." Colm Tóibín observed that James "never really wrote about the English very well. His English characters don't work for me."

Despite these criticisms, James is now valued for his psychological and moral realism, his masterful creation of character, his low-key but playful humour, and his assured command of the language. In his 1983 book, The Novels of Henry James, Edward Wagenknecht offers an assessment that echoes Theodora Bosanquet's:

"To be completely great," Henry James wrote in an early review, "a work of art must lift up the heart," and his own novels do this to an outstanding degree ... More than sixty years after his death, the great novelist who sometimes professed to have no opinions stands foursquare in the great Christian humanistic and democratic tradition. The men and women who, at the height of World War II, raided the secondhand shops for his out-of-print books knew what they were about. For no writer ever raised a braver banner to which all who love freedom might adhere.

William Dean Howells saw James as a representative of a new realist school of literary art which broke with the English romantic tradition epitomised by the works of Charles Dickens and William Makepeace Thackeray. Howells wrote that realism found "its chief exemplar in Mr. James... A novelist he is not, after the old fashion, or after any fashion but his own." F.R. Leavis championed Henry James as a novelist of "established pre-eminence" in The Great Tradition (1948), asserting that The Portrait of a Lady and The Bostonians were "the two most brilliant novels in the language." James is now prized as a master of point of view who moved literary fiction forward by insisting in showing, not telling, his stories to the reader. (Source: Wikipedia)

NOTABLE WORKS

NOVELS

Watch and Ward (1871)

Roderick Hudson (1875)

The American (1877)

The Europeans (1878)

Confidence (1879)

Washington Square (1880)

The Portrait of a Lady (1881)

The Bostonians (1886)

The Princess Casamassima (1886)

The Reverberator (1888)

The Tragic Muse (1890)

The Other House (1896)

The Spoils of Poynton (1897)

What Maisie Knew (1897)

The Awkward Age (1899)

The Sacred Fount (1901)

The Wings of the Dove (1902)

The Ambassadors (1903)

The Golden Bowl (1904)

The Whole Family (collaborative novel with eleven other authors, 1908)

The Outcry (1911)

The Ivory Tower (unfinished, published posthumously 1917)

The Sense of the Past (unfinished, published posthumously 1917)

SHORT STORIES AND NOVELLAS

A Tragedy of Error (1864)

The Story of a Year (1865)

A Landscape Painter (1866)

A Day of Days (1866)

My Friend Bingham (1867)

Poor Richard (1867)

The Story of a Masterpiece (1868)

A Most Extraordinary Case (1868)

A Problem (1868)

De Grey: A Romance (1868)

Osborne's Revenge (1868)

The Romance of Certain Old Clothes (1868)

A Light Man (1869)

Gabrielle de Bergerac (1869)

Travelling Companions (1870)

A Passionate Pilgrim (1871)

At Isella (1871)

Master Eustace (1871)

Guest's Confession (1872)

The Madonna of the Future (1873)

The Sweetheart of M. Briseux (1873)

The Last of the Valerii (1874)

Madame de Mauves (1874)

Adina (1874)

Professor Fargo (1874)

Eugene Pickering (1874)

Benvolio (1875)

Crawford's Consistency (1876)

The Ghostly Rental (1876)

Four Meetings (1877)

Rose-Agathe (1878, as Théodolinde)

Daisy Miller (1878)

Longstaff's Marriage (1878)

An International Episode (1878)

The Pension Beaurepas (1879)

A Diary of a Man of Fifty (1879)

A Bundle of Letters (1879)

The Point of View (1882)

The Siege of London (1883)

Impressions of a Cousin (1883)

Lady Barberina (1884)

Pandora (1884)

The Author of Beltraffio (1884)

Georgina's Reasons (1884)

A New England Winter (1884)

The Path of Duty (1884)

Mrs. Temperly (1887)

Louisa Pallant (1888)

The Aspern Papers (1888)

The Liar (1888)

The Modern Warning (1888, originally published as The Two Countries)

A London Life (1888)

The Patagonia (1888)

The Lesson of the Master (1888)

The Solution (1888)

The Pupil (1891)

Brooksmith (1891)

The Marriages (1891)

The Chaperon (1891)

Sir Edmund Orme (1891)

Nona Vincent (1892)

The Real Thing (1892)

The Private Life (1892)

Lord Beaupré (1892)

The Visits (1892)

Sir Dominick Ferrand (1892)

Greville Fane (1892)

Collaboration (1892)

Owen Wingrave (1892)

The Wheel of Time (1892)

The Middle Years (1893)

The Death of the Lion (1894)

The Coxon Fund (1894)

The Next Time (1895)

Glasses (1896)

The Altar of the Dead (1895)

The Figure in the Carpet (1896)

The Way It Came (1896, also published as The Friends of the Friends)

The Turn of the Screw (1898)

Covering End (1898)

In the Cage (1898)

John Delavoy (1898)

The Given Case (1898)

Europe (1899)

The Great Condition (1899)

The Real Right Thing (1899)

Paste (1899)

The Great Good Place (1900)

Maud-Evelyn (1900)

Miss Gunton of Poughkeepsie (1900)

The Tree of Knowledge (1900)

The Abasement of the Northmores (1900)

The Third Person (1900)

The Special Type (1900)

The Tone of Time (1900)

Broken Wings (1900)

The Two Faces (1900)

Mrs. Medwin (1901)

The Beldonald Holbein (1901)

The Story in It (1902)

Flickerbridge (1902)

The Birthplace (1903)

The Beast in the Jungle (1903)

The Papers (1903)

Fordham Castle (1904)

Julia Bride (1908)

The Jolly Corner (1908)

The Velvet Glove (1909)

Mora Montravers (1909)

Crapy Cornelia (1909)

The Bench of Desolation (1909)

A Round of Visits (1910)

OTHER

Transatlantic Sketches (1875)

French Poets and Novelists (1878)

Hawthorne (1879)

Portraits of Places (1883)

A Little Tour in France (1884)

Partial Portraits (1888)

Essays in London and Elsewhere (1893)

Picture and Text (1893)

Terminations (1893)

Theatricals (1894)

Theatricals: Second Series (1895)

Guy Domville (1895)

The Soft Side (1900)

William Wetmore Story and His Friends (1903)

The Better Sort (1903)

English Hours (1905)

The Question of our Speech; The Lesson of Balzac. Two Lectures (1905)

The American Scene (1907)

Views and Reviews (1908)

Italian Hours (1909)

A Small Boy and Others (1913)

Notes on Novelists (1914)

Notes of a Son and Brother (1914)

Within the Rim (1918)

Travelling Companions (1919)

Notebooks (various, published posthumously)

The Middle Years (unfinished, published posthumously 1917)

A Most Unholy Trade (1925, published posthumously)

The Art of the Novel : Critical Prefaces (1934)

CPSIA information can be obtained
at www.ICGtesting.com
Printed in the USA
LVHW042122191020
669187LV00016B/89